Twist & Turn

Christa Simpson

The Twisted Trilogy
Book 2

CHRISTA SIMPSON, CANADA

Twist & Turn

Christa Simpson

Copyright © 2013 Christa Simpson
Revised Text Copyright © 2014 Christa Simpson

PRINT EDITION
ISBN: 978-0-9919070-5-2

Front Cover Design by Kellie Dennis of Book Cover By Design
http://www.bookcoverbydesign.co.uk

ACKNOWLEDGEMENTS

A special thanks goes out to the following lovely ladies:

Alexis Saviuk Rodewald
Cassandra Janey
Danielle Taylor
Gabbie Suarez Duran
Jennifer Grimm
Tiffany Tillman

And to all of my friends, fans and family who have helped me along the way. Thank you so much! Without you The Twisted Trilogy wouldn't be what it is today!

~ Christa Simpson

PROLOGUE

Six years earlier.

Tessa Clarke wiped the wetness from her eyes as she sobbed uncontrollably. She was shrouded in misery, but certain she was doing the right thing.

"She's *my* daughter. He's not taking her from me," she cried, as she sped away from her home with no intention of turning back.

Tessa squinted through the dirty windshield with blurry, enraged eyes and a heavy foot. She dangerously weaved through cars on the highway until she reached her exit. Relief overcame her, when she finally passed the City's boundary and dirt began to plume behind her on the freshly gravelled country road.

She looked in her rear-view mirror and then flashed a glance over her shoulder into the back seat. "I finally did it, baby. I did it for us," she said, a soft smile creeping onto her downturned lips.

A sudden flash of red light blinded her as she jerked her head forward and blinked her tired, burning eyes to focus on the oncoming headlights. A truck was crossing over a narrow bridge before her and it was coming at her head on. The driver eased his truck to the dirt shoulder and relief swamped her again, until the truck abruptly swerved out of control in her direction.

Unprepared, Tessa slammed on her brakes. But it was too late. She raised an arm to cover her eyes to hide from the imminent crash, as her car skidded through the gravel and collided with the truck at full speed.

Tessa's head violently cracked off the windshield, instantly spilling blood down her face. Her speeding car spun out of control and hit the bridge barricade. Momentum drove the car forward over the bridge as it begged to climb over the edge.

Sparks flew from the bumper as it screeched deafeningly along the metal barrier, waking Tessa from her nightmarish slumber. The friction was loud, but no sound could compare to the shrieking baby girl in the back seat of her car.

With blood obstructing what little vision she had left, Tessa reached for one last chance at their survival. She gripped the steering wheel and tugged on it, in an attempt to negotiate the curve at the base of the bridge, to no avail.

The car crashed into a concrete support beam and forcefully delivered Tessa's body through the windshield. She sailed through the air until her battered body crashed into a nearby tree and fell to its final resting place.

The little girl was secured in her car seat, locked inside the twisted heap of metal. She screamed in horror as the blood poured from her mother's cracked skull. A destroyed cell phone rang in the distance, as a man dragged himself out of the demolished truck.

The man limped quickly to Tessa's car and yanked on the crushed backdoor, but it wouldn't budge. The child continued to scream, her shrieks swallowing the only oxygen around him.

A strange noise escaped from the hood of the car only moments before flames burst from it. Adrenaline pumped through the man's veins as he crawled onto the trunk and shattered the cracked window with his elbow. He climbed into the now-flaming car, maneuvered around the crushed metal and pulled the screaming baby out of the jammed car seat.

"I'm so sorry," he blurted, his heart aching painfully for the child's loss.

Dark red blood ran down his arm and dripped all over the child as he reached her out of the broken window and then carried her to safety. He awkwardly yanked off his jacket and wrapped it around the baby, his eyes only momentarily resting on her small bleeding limb, as she choked on her desperate sob for comfort.

The man gently placed the baby in the dewy grass

against a nearby tree and scrambled away to examine her mother's mangled body. The man checked for Tessa's pulse, but found nothing.

A sudden flash of headlights in the distance told the man help was on its way. The oncoming car slowed as it approached the flaming scene. After waving the car over, the man turned around to check on the baby and was startled to find a beautiful young girl with long, straight, golden brown hair and pale skin tending to it in the impossible darkness.

"Help!" he hollered.

His eyes frantically searched the area for her parents. She couldn't have been a year over six. But when he looked back to the baby, the young girl was gone.

A fit young man hustled toward the scene of the accident, as his wife hurried to the screaming baby.

"Did you see that little girl?" the injured man hollered hysterically.

The young man stopped before him and looked back to his wife, worry written harshly across his brow. "I didn't see anyone, except for you."

CHAPTER ONE

The Present.

It was official. Edwin Santora and Abigail Jenkins were no more. I've even been a good girl lately, avoiding Edwin whenever possible. But I tell you, it's been tough.

Edwin Santora possessed the bod of a God and the charm of a prince. His playful charisma and sexy sarcasm made it incredibly difficult for me not to be attracted to him in a very bad way.

At least enough time had passed since our break-up that I could stand to be in the same room with him again. And yet, continuing to live with Edwin had its setbacks. He often strolled around the house like he owned the place. *Okay, so we own it fifty fifty, not the point.*

Was it really necessary for him to act like man candy, flaunting his chiseled abs and flexing his godly arms in front of me? Then he had to go and sweat over the flaming BBQ in preparation of a friendly home cooked meal. After a long day at work, how could I say no to that? *It was delish by the way.*

After I loaded the dishwasher, I clambered to the living room where Edwin was relaxing. Lying casually on the sofa, his muscles still looked incredibly defined, to the point where I could have just stood there and stared at him all night. Instead, I picked up his shirt off the otherwise empty chair and tossed it at him. He caught in one swift motion and then rested it on the arm of the couch.

Can't you take a hint? Put on the damn shirt!

"Thanks," he said, his aqua eyes glimmering at me.

Sigh. As if his flexing muscles weren't enough to get my attention, he had to turn those gorgeous eyes loose on me.

"We still on for tonight?" I plopped on the chair across from him and tried to remind myself why I had called it off between us in the first place. The chair was comfy, but it was only a temporary seat. Edwin was parked in my spot and he knew it.

"You know it," he replied, smiling. He looked rather comfy with his heavily muscled body stretched out on my couch, and he didn't make a move as the show started.

I dramatically cocked my head, to display how awkward it was for me to watch the TV from where I was sitting, but I realized then that Edwin wasn't going to shove over without a fight. Ignoring the delightful way he filled the sofa, I walked to the end of it and sat right on his feet. He groaned, but reluctantly moved his bare toes out of my way.

That had gone a lot easier than I thought it would. A winning smile spread across my face. We were finally getting the hang of being friendly roommates, *without benefits*, and it was incredibly therapeutic for me.

With my soft, brown hair draped straight down my back, I stretched my arms for the ceiling and moaned softly. "Oh, my aching neck. Can you believe it's still sore from my hip-hop class yesterday?" I groaned, not really expecting a reply.

Edwin pressed both of his bare feet onto the area rug and slid up next to me. "I can massage it for you," he said, his voice a deep seductive growl.

My achy-breaky muscles made it an easy decision. The TV was flashing commercials anyway, so I turned sideways and let him ease my tension with his magical fingers.

He swept my hair from the nape of my neck and brushed his fingers across my suddenly sensitized skin. I shivered with awareness as his fingers spread out over my shoulders and closed around them. His skillful hands massaged my tight muscles and whispered across my skin in such an erotic way.

I closed my eyes and enjoyed the instant relief, verbalizing my approval with a guttural moan. *It felt nice to be touched by him. So why did it feel so naughty?*

"Does that feel good?" Edwin smirked. He already knew the answer.

"Mmm, very."

When his fingers loosened, I wanted to cry out for him to keep going. Harder. Deeper.

"Why don't you lay on the floor so I can do a better job?" he suggested.

I knew it was a bad idea, but I couldn't resist the allure of Edwin's massage. I scurried to the floor, laid on my stomach, and then tucked my eyes into my folded arms, eager for more.

Edwin dropped to his knees and crawled over me, until his heavy muscles were resting on my thighs. "You getting shy on me all of a sudden?" he asked, as his hands slid under my shirt and whispered all the way up to my shoulders.

His hands explored all over my bare skin, overloading my sensory system with a guilty treat. I couldn't help but be turned on by his touch, whispers of pleasure escaping my lips as he caressed my lower back and wrapped his hands around my sides. His fingers tickled up the curve of my spine, gently teasing my sensitive skin, until he refocused a little higher.

"This is in the way," he explained, as he slipped his fingers beneath my bra strap. "Do you mind?" he asked, as he pulled my shirt over my head.

"No," I whimpered softly, hoping he didn't know the effect he was having on me.

Edwin unfastened my bra and slowly drew the straps over my shoulders, exposing my entire back and leaving but a small piece of fabric between my bare skin and the floor. He mounted my hips and touched me again, working his way from my shoulders downward. His fingers tickled down my sides, arousing the soft flesh only inches from my nearly naked breasts.

He gently tucked my hair behind my ear and brushed it all over my right shoulder, before deepening his massage. Suddenly the muscle pain was gone, but a new ache was spreading through me. Instead of stopping him, like I should have, I let out another moan, a little more provocative than the last.

Edwin's touch only grew more aggressive. He was intentionally tantalizing me. "How's that?"

"It's a little too hard," I groaned, craving his gentle touch.

"You used to like it hard," he said, his voice low and smooth. Then, without pressing his erotic suggestion, he lightened the pressure.

Unable to produce a constructive sentence, I ignored his point and enjoyed his gentle fingers. I had an incredible urge to flip over and pull him onto me, taking what I knew could be mine. *Whoa, what?* My own thoughts startled me, breaking through the thick fog hanging heavy over my brain.

It was now apparent to me that Edwin was trying to seduce me. And though my body ached with desire, I couldn't give in to him. We had made such progress over the past few months and it would be too painful to turn back that clock. I took a long deep breath to douse the flames licking across my body, hoping it'd be enough.

It wasn't.

I felt Edwin's warm body hovering close to mine, his steady breath warming the back of my neck. Every hair on my body stood on end, every nerve sensually aware of his closeness. I wanted to stop him, knowing how dangerous these intimate moments could be, but when his lips touched my bare shoulder, I couldn't breathe let alone speak.

A knock sounded at our unlocked door, like a warning sent from the heavens. The door clunked shut before I could react to the fact that the intruders had let themselves in.

Edwin jumped up and I wriggled my shirt on, leaving my bra loosely draped around my stomach. Peering over the couch, I saw my best friend Aliah standing there with her man. She looked as gorgeous as usual, with her long, dark hair tied up in a high pony. Her shocked expression told its own story.

"Uh, sorry. Did we walk in on something we shouldn't have?" she asked, a naughty smirk working her glossy lips.

Hunter was equally as surprised, mouth still gaping, his bold brown eyes zeroing right in on my waist, until Aliah elbowed him in his firm middle.

"What?" he chirped, his smirk firmly in place.

"Edwin was just giving me a massage," I said hastily. I draped one arm across my chest, the other over my stomach, hoping to hide the bra and the crisp peak of my bare nipples in my fitted t-shirt.

Aliah nodded her head mockingly and smiled, knowing me all too well.

Skipping the awkward niceties, Edwin rounded the couch and called out to Hunter, "Do you want a beer?"

"Yeah. Coors Light if you've got it," Hunter answered, following Edwin to the kitchen.

I flopped back onto the couch with a sigh, then refastened my bra.

Aliah kicked off her shoes and joined me within seconds. She narrowed her pale green eyes and locked them on mine. "What in the world were you doing?"

"I don't know. Gah! I didn't mean to," I replied, pressing my palm to my forehead.

"You did it?" Her melodramatic expression was priceless.

"We didn't have sex, if that's what you're implying. But I'm afraid it was about to turn more R-rated just as you showed up." I scrunched my eyes shut, acknowledging my error of judgment.

Aliah only shook her head smirking.

The guys were getting loud in the kitchen, which suggested to me that Hunter was giving Edwin his props and Edwin was berating him for tarnishing his efforts.

I needed to cool my jets. "Can I get you something to drink?"

"Definitely," Aliah replied.

We both moseyed to the large open kitchen and Aliah took a seat on a bar stool next to Hunter. I reached the fridge, without making eye contact with Edwin, but I could feel his gaze slipping over me. Ignoring that, I poured myself a tall glass of wine, and downed half of it before pouring the next glass.

Within minutes, the wine had my cheeks rosy with colour, and they stayed that way for the next hour. Lucky for me, Hunter and Aliah had plenty to say, to keep me from my own tiresome thoughts.

"Well... it's getting late," Hunter finally said, reaching his hand out to Aliah. "I think I'm ready to call it a night."

Aliah nodded her head and took his hand. She stood from her seat, then flashed me a sarcastic glance over her shoulder. "You two be good," she insisted, with pale probing eyes.

Keep my hands off of Edwin? I think I can do that.

Mere seconds later, Edwin closed the front door behind them, leaving us very alone in our front foyer. He spun around to face me. "So. Where were we?" He raised his eyebrows suggestively, a smug grin on his deviously sexy lips.

"Nice try, Slick Rick."

"What? Your neck is feeling better now?" He took a step closer to me, trying to feel me out.

"Yup. It's suddenly feeling all good." It wasn't a total lie. My neck was most definitely feeling better than before, but the soreness could have been hiding beneath the sexual charge arching through the air between us.

I took a step back from him, clinging to the safe distance between us, the only thing keeping Edwin's devouring hands from my needy body. I had bruised my self-control once tonight and I would not be so careless again.

Edwin took a step closer to me. "It's okay to fulfill your needs, you know. No one here is going to judge you, except for you."

I stumbled backward and fell onto the open bottom stair.

Edwin smiled at my clumsiness, but continued prowling toward me, like a creature of the night. "Would it kill you to give in to me every once in a while?"

"It might."

He laughed, but it was not a laughing matter.

Settling back against the stairs, I regained my self-control. The air was so much more breathable at that level. "You're just horny. Why don't you get a girlfriend if you want sex so bad?" I hated those words and regretted them in an instant.

It was no secret that neither Edwin nor I had dated since we had broken up. I also knew though, if Edwin wanted a girlfriend, he would have one. He had an endless number of options when it came to available women throwing themselves at him and yet he remained very single.

"I'm not looking for a girlfriend, Abs. But you do realize you don't exactly need a girlfriend to have sex," he advised, as though he were trying to educate me on the subject.

I cringed at the thought of him bringing some dirty skank home from the bar. He noticed my expression and seemed to take pleasure in my anguish. While I didn't want that mental picture tucked away in my mind, I also knew that having sex with Edwin was out of the question. We had been there before, and it had been amazing, but look where that got me.

Edwin acknowledged the wounded look displayed on my face, making me wish I didn't read like such an open book. That glimmer of our time together dredged up some gut-wrenching guilt from our break-up, as other more painful memories spilled into the present. In a sick way, I liked to remember it all. It reminded me that I was still alive. My twin sister, Jenny, wasn't so fortunate.

As the depression began to sink in, I got to my feet. "I think I'd better call it a night too."

The vibrant electricity between us was still magnetic, drawing out all of those bad feelings and replacing them with something else entirely. I knew if I didn't move fast, our bodies would be compelled to be together and the glimmer of my sister's tragic death from eighteen years earlier would be just that, a thing of the past.

Edwin tilted his head sideways and stared over at me with those gorgeous glimmering eyes. "Aww," he pleaded, in his last attempt to get some.

"You'll get over it," I told him sternly, though it was doubtful. I started up the stairs to put some much needed distance between us.

"Sweet dreams, Abs." Edwin's voice reached me, smooth as velvet. "You know, I wouldn't be too mad if I were in them." He chuckled. "If you're feeling what I'm feeling, and I have a feeling you are, you won't be able to keep me out of 'em."

My breath hitched as I tried to push that truth out of my head, and there was no hiding that Edwin's confidence, balancing on the brink of arrogance, was exactly what attracted me to him the most. I stopped one step from the top, knowing there were enough stairs between us for me to retort safely. "Keep dreaming, Eddie. My mind is free and clear, thank you very much."

"Night Abs," he said again, not buying it for a minute.

That sexy smile stuck me right in the gut, and an excruciating jolt struck my heart at once. I had to retreat to my bedroom and fast. "Night," I replied, breathless.

With a swift turn, I leapt up the last stair and trudged down the hall to my room. I quickly slipped into my pj's, turned out the light and shuffled toward my bed in the darkness. After diving under the sheets, I drew the covers to my chin, hoping to shake the adrenaline running rampant through my body long enough to ease the raw emotional reminder that my twin sister had died and I had lived.

I closed my eyes, hoping for some solitude, but I was a mess. Instead of giving in to the heavy weight of depression bearing down on me, I remembered how it felt to have Edwin's warm breath on my neck and his soft lips on my shoulder. I shook the thought from my head, but not before I shivered with a delicious awareness.

I had moved on and, though I wasn't out actively searching for a suitable replacement, I knew it was only a matter of time before I would be ready to throw myself back out into the sea of men. I had to be. I needed a man to make the family I so desperately desired, and not just any man would do.

The fact that I wanted to have a baby of my own had not changed. It would never change. The fact that Edwin wasn't ready to start a family still irked me as much as the night he shared that fact; the night I ended our relationship.

I forced my eyes open and experienced some relief. It was just a kiss. Nothing more. It wasn't even on the lips.

With a long, hushed sigh, I squeezed my eyes shut and was surprised to find that my mind had unexpectedly cleared. I rode the wave of unoccupied restfulness and sank into a deep, dream-filled sleep.

CHAPTER TWO

A few uneventful weeks had passed and my expectations were growing as cool as the late summer nights. It was a lonely, misty Monday morning and I was running a little later than usual. With only five minutes to spare, I blasted through the vestibule and clambered into the lobby of the law office I worked at.

Reality slammed me flat in the face when I noticed a client lingering by the empty reception desk. The man was facing away from me and yet he still managed to exude such confidence. The way his short, dark blonde hair was spiked in a sophisticated disarray was incredibly attractive. Then there was the way he stood with his hands casually tucked in the pockets of his expensive, black suit.

I knew I had to approach him.

"Hi. Can I help you with something?" I blurted, looking forward to setting eyes on that face of his, hopeful that it would be as intriguing as the rest of the package.

He spun around to face me and attacked me with his gorgeous features. I could not believe my eyeballs. His eyebrows hung low over his squinted sunset-shaped eyes. If eyes could smile, then his were beaming at me. Excitement flooded my chest with the instant realization that Taylor, the receptionist, was nowhere to be found.

When he caught my captivated stare, he glanced down momentarily, then wrinkled his sexy forehead, raising his eyebrows and giving me a better look into those gorgeous crystal eyes. *Oh. My. God. If possible, this man just got cuter.*

I could have torn that face out of the nearest heartthrob magazine, just like I would've liked to tear that sexy suit off of him to see what sleek muscle he had hiding beneath it.

I fluttered my eyelashes, as he extended out his hand. I gently gripped it for a shake. When he smiled, our hands latched together and my knees grew weak. Then he drew my hand to his perfect pink lips and time seemed to stand still. He smoothly kissed the back of my hand and lowered it, my fingers lingering in his firm, masculine grip.

Old fashioned. I like that. "Can I help you?" I breathed.

Oh shit! I just said that!

His gaze slipped casually down my body and, before I could tear my own eyes away, he struck me again with the most breathtaking blue eyes. When my lips parted, air slipped through them, as his mouth curled into a smile as glorious as the rest of him.

"You already have. Cameron Clarke. Pleased to meet you." He released my hand, but never removed that smile from his face and it was making it difficult for me to breathe. Think. Speak. There was no other way to put it: he was smooth and I was dazzled.

Finding my voice, I blurted, "Do you greet all the ladies like this?" *Why couldn't I just shut up already?*

His smile was so genuine my heart melted, but he didn't answer me. I tried to penetrate his charming gaze with my pining smile and ravenous green eyes, but felt delightfully pinned beneath his stare.

"Abigail. Abigail Jenkins," I told him with a sudden starkness.

His smiled grew wider. "My pleasure, Mrs. Jenkins."

"*Miss* Jenkins," I corrected instantly, then realized how dumb I must have sounded. *Abby. Damn it! I should have said call me Abby.*

"Good to know, *Miss* Jenkins."

I shouldn't have watched his mouth. My heart fluttered, as though his smooth velvet voice had just delivered an incredibly sexy promise. My embarrassment was palpable, but worth each rosy cheek.

I had wished for this man in my dreams and here he was sweeping me off my feet and charming me with his confidence. I was the one who captivated men with a glance. I was the one who was always in the power seat. And yet this time, I was the one frozen in place, enchanted, and reacting mindlessly to his witty lure.

"I have a meeting with Owen Wallace," he said, but then he went and wrinkled his forehead again.

Swoon!

He flashed me a selfless smile and, in the blink of an eye, I managed to break the spell and snap out of my foolish fascination with him. It was a good thing too, because Taylor was approaching her desk, giving me a quick reminder that I was now late for work.

"I'll let him know you're here," I said softly, my eyelashes fluttering with an unintentional grace.

"Thank you, Abigail."

A rush of excitement ran through me when I heard him say my name. He swiftly took a seat and I scurried for Owen's office, before Taylor could grasp the reason for my elation.

I glanced over my shoulder to steal a second look at him, confirming that my imagination hadn't been playing tricks on me. Sure enough, he was still there. Watching me. Sexy as ever. I smiled coyly and quickly turned the corner, a fresh blush warming my cheeks.

Embarrassed? Yes. But mostly just disappointed that I wasn't able to get another good look at him.

I slammed my back against the wall, closed my eyes with a giddy smile on my face and took long practiced breaths. *What is wrong with me? He's probably married. Look at him. He's definitely married. A man like that doesn't sit on the market for long.*

I tried to focus on the task at hand; that is, getting air into my empty lungs. Nothing could trump the importance of that, right? Wrong. The knowledge that someone was watching me swiftly took precedence. I slowly opened my heavy lids.

Owen Wallace, my boss, was standing right next to me. The hall suddenly felt like a stifling subway. "Everything okay, Abby?" he asked, truly concerned, but not having a clue.

I was sure the smile plastered on my face was enough to

prove that everything was just fine but, in case he truly needed confirmation, I told him. "Everything is just fine. Thank you for asking," I said softly, so no one else could hear. "Oh, yes, and a Mr. Cameron Clarke is here to see you." I finished that sentence with such a serene calm that even I couldn't believe it came from my lips.

Owen nodded, but hesitated, curiosity wrinkling his brow as he walked away.

With the last of my breath pressing out of my lungs, I dashed to my desk in a tizzy, locked my purse in a drawer and pressed the power button on my computer. Owen's calendar couldn't load fast enough.

My desktop slowly loaded and I anxiously opened the calendar as soon as the mouse would let me. There it was, Cameron Clarke, but there was no explanation to tell me why. Owen's practice was primarily Plaintiff litigation, specializing in personal injury cases, but it wasn't unheard of for him to take on a Defence for a high profile client. I prayed that Mr. Clarke was not a professional criminal.

The more I thought about the visit, the more suspicious I grew about it. Why hadn't Owen brought it up to me and why isn't there a brief explanation on the calendar? I had to know, and I had to know now.

I checked my emails, impatiently waiting for Owen to shut the boardroom door. Instead, to my surprise, I heard him pass right by the usual conference room and invite Cameron into his office. Owen rarely took clients in his office and, according to the schedule, the boardroom was available.

Unable to contain my curiosity for another second, I hopped to my feet and casually strolled past Owen's glazed glass door to Taylor's desk. She was on her phone, but it didn't sound like she would be too long. I stood there tapping my toe, until she finally put down the receiver.

A smile grew on her soft, round face. Knowing something was up, she blew her long bangs out of her eyes and looked up at me, with a quizzical look on her face "What is it?"

Damn it. Am I that transparent? I worried my bottom lip between my teeth. "Who is that guy meeting with Owen right now?"

"Oh! He's a hottie tottie, eh? He's an old friend of Owen. I guess they went to law school together. I hear he's meeting with him about the position we posted."

"You have got to be kidding me," I said, trying to hide my excitement.

"No kidding. I think Owen wants to offer him the job, but he doesn't know if it'll work out. I guess he's not from around here. But wouldn't it be nice to look at that every day?"

I nodded. *Yes. It. Would.*

"I can't believe Owen didn't talk to you about it." She continued to babble, as I sank into my own internal astonishment.

Why hadn't Owen told me? He usually told me everything. And why hadn't I recognized the obvious? Cameron was a lawyer. A damn fine lawyer. "Okay, Taylor, thanks!" I said.

She smiled, recognizing that she was blathering on. "No prob."

I smiled back and set off for Aliah's desk, to tell her about *Mr. Clarke.* I had to interrupt her to deliver the news. It was the price you pay for working so close to your best friend. I summed it up for her in as few words as possible and she shook her head clearly irritated with my giddiness.

"You horny beotch," she snapped.

"Shush, someone will hear you!"

"Who cares?"

"I do. I don't want Eddie to hear."

While Edwin and I were strictly friends, I still cared about his feelings and didn't want to see him hurt. His office was only a few paces away from her desk and, though Aliah didn't share the same concern, I wanted to keep our conversation private.

"Looking forward to meeting the stud then," Aliah said, a huge grin covering her face. "When are you two getting married?"

"Hah! First I have to find out if he's single."

She was still smiling grandly when she flashed me her ring finger. "Was he wearing a ring? That's usually a good indication."

I shook my head with disappointment. "My mind was a little distracted when I met him. I didn't think to check."

"You know where to find me if you need any help," she offered with a confident wink.

Yeah, right. I remember how she helped with Spencer and Dr. Dex months ago. "I can handle this one myself."

There was no further discussion about Cameron Clarke, and days had come and gone. Had Owen decided he wasn't the right man for the job? Taylor was so sure he was the one. So was I. Despite my curiosity, it would have to wait for another day. Today I was booked.

I drove down the long stretch of highway, toward the City of Toronto, to attend a law society program. Owen insisted that I go in person, though I begged to attend the webcast to save the cost of travel. He maintained that it was good for me to get out of the office from time to time and network with others in the same boat as me. I disagreed, but he was the boss.

I gave myself two hours to get there and had rehashed over Cameron's spectacular introduction the entire time. As I recalled his lips brushing over the back of my hand, I arrived at my destination with only ten minutes until the program started.

With my purse in hand, and a leather portfolio under my arm, I strode toward the brick building. I rushed the stairs and stopped in the lobby, totally forgetting where I was supposed to be. I pulled my phone from my bag and scanned through my emails for the room number.

The door of the classroom was open. I stepped inside and walked up the long, wide staircase, avoiding the first few rows of seats. After passing another couple of desks, I took my place next to two women who were clearly friends.

I reached for an agenda sitting in front of the empty seat next to me and was stunned when it was suddenly yanked from my hand.

"That's mine," the girl next to me snapped, scowling.

It was clearly not, but after the long drive up I wasn't up for the argument. "Oh! Sorry. Do you think you could pass an extra one down to me?" A stack of agendas were unmistakably within her reach and I had asked as nicely as possible.

Her friend went to reach for one and was bumped by the mean girl. "Sorry. There are none. Guess you'll have to go sit somewhere else," she snarled.

Bitch! Being that I was in a surprisingly good mood, I snatched up my things and gave a disgusted glance at the rude girl, as I rounded up to the next row. I imagined bumping my bag off the back of her head as I passed, and that helped me keep my cool.

I took another seat that was all on its own. I didn't care for the drama.

Another girl, who had to be fresh out of college, saw me sitting alone and picked up her things to join me. "Don't take it personally. Those girls don't like themselves." She flashed me a friendly smile. "I'm Brooke. Mind if I sit with you?"

"Please," I replied. "I'm Abigail." I shook her dainty hand and that was that.

A law society member welcomed us all and introduced the first presenter, getting right into the program. I sat through an *interesting* morning of presentations and, after an hour of listening to a law professional blather on about the technological advances for a civil litigation practice, I was in desperate need of a coffee. *I don't even drink coffee.*

The coffee break was fun. The bitchy girls flashed me dirty looks the entire time, while Brooke told me how she weaseled her way into the program by scamming another girl out of the opportunity.

Brooke kept me mostly entertained for the afternoon,

but it still felt like I was in high school all over again. When the question and answer period was coming to a close, I finally felt a sense of relief rush over me.

"Hey. Do you want to grab a bite to eat?" Brooke whispered, while the others intently listened to the Q and A.

"I'm actually just going to grab something quick on my way home. It was so nice meeting you though. Here's my card. If you ever need anything, drop me an email," I said. It had been a long, trying day and I was not looking forward to the extended drive home.

Brooke scribbled her number and email address onto a piece of paper and ripped it from her pad. "Here. That's my info. Are you on Twitter?" she asked.

I nodded, smiling.

"I'll look you up then. Great meeting you, Abigail. Talk to you later."

"Okay." I collected my notebook and tucked my phone in my purse. I cut the bitches off, as I headed for the door, and was soon caught in a human traffic jam.

Legal professionals of all ages poured from the neighbouring rooms as steadily as those coming from ours. I slowly pressed on, though most others weren't moving much at all. Slowed up by random groups of people socializing, I stared up at the ceiling, calling for some voiceless assistance.

To my astonishment, I finally caught a clearing. With my eyes on the doors, I hustled right for them, my heels clacking beneath my feet. As I reached my hand out to press the metal bar on the door, my hand landed on top of a warm masculine hand.

"Oh my gosh! I'm so sorry," I said, completely embarrassed. I retrieved my hand, like I had been scalded. My anxious green eyes fluttered up to the suited man, with strong, sleek hands. *Hot damn!*

"Miss Jenkins. What a pleasant surprise," he said, nearly knocking me off my feet.

"Mr. Clarke," I replied, without thinking.

"Please, call me Cam. After you." He held the door open

and I gratefully walked through, as did the two bitches. I paused momentarily, but when he didn't resurface from the crowd, I slowly, disappointedly, started down the stairs for my car.

My ears were on fire, as I listened for any sign that he had materialized behind me.

"Mr. Clarke, how are you?" the main bitch voiced, stepping in front of him.

"I'm very well, thank you, Shawna," he replied, skimming past her.

"Do you have plans for this evening?" her friend asked him, keeping up with his quickened pace.

They were a few long strides behind me, but I could hear the pleading in her voice. I should have known he got that all the time.

"I have plans. Now, if you'll excuse me. Abigail," he called and jogged up beside me.

I gasped for air and turned to smile at him. When he smiled back, my heart clenched and my throat turned to sandpaper.

"I almost lost you there," he said, smiling. "Are you in the City for long?"

The bitches didn't take the hint. They jealously scowled at me and then scurried up next to Cameron.

"You know Mr. Clarke?" the nicer girl asked me, interrupting as pleasantly as she could muster.

"Yes, Cam and I have met." I flashed a glance at Cameron and, when I caught his honest smile, I melted into a puddle at his feet.

"Whatever," Shawna muttered. Her features twisted in fury, her face reflecting nothing but pure hatred toward me, she spun around and stomped off. Her friend scurried after her.

"Thanks," I said appreciatively, flashing another glance at his incredibly handsome face. Today he was less than clean shaven, but his stubble made him look even sexier than before.

"For what?" Adorable wrinkles lined his forehead and

he delivered that irresistible smile like a gift.

It made me fumble through my thoughts, in hopes of finding something else to say that could get him to do that again. "Never mind," I answered, totally forgetting my point.

He smiled again. "They've got nothing on you."

As my heart did a flip, white doves flew around me in perfect harmony, and the wind seemed to blow my hair like a supermodel walking the catwalk. Okay, so maybe it was squawking seagulls and a vicious polluted breeze, but it felt like so much more when he spoke to me.

That's when my new friend Brooke walked up, dropping me back into reality. "Oh, Abigail. I thought you said were in a hurry," she said, effectively ruining my chances with Cameron.

"I am." *Damn it! Why did I say that?*

"Then I guess dinner is out of the question," Cameron said. "I don't mean to keep you."

Yes. Please keep me! Oh, how I wished he could read my mind.

Brooke waved erratically and proceeded to lollygag to her car.

To my surprise, Cameron remained by my side. "Unless you have time for a coffee," he added softly.

Brooke, being only a few nosy paces away, heard him and turned back to catch my answer.

I sighed with disappointment. "I really should get going. I have a long drive ahead of me."

He glanced ahead at Brooke, recognizing my predicament, and smiled back at me. "It was nice seeing you again. Another time?" he asked, taking my hand.

His eyes locked on mine as the pad of his thumb brushed over my knuckles, only inches from where he had once planted his lips. His crystal eyes sparkled like a glorious ocean view.

I chewed on my bottom lip as a delicious shimmer of awareness skipped up my spine. "I'd like that."

"Goodbye, Abigail." His squinted eyes continued to

dazzle me.

I didn't know how he did it, but I was mesmerized. "Bye," I said, as he released my hand. With a hopeless smile, I turned away and moped back to my car.

Deciding I needed one last glimpse of that dreamy charmer, I peeked over my shoulder. And there he was, watching me again. He smiled and lifted his hand for a faint wave. I waved back and continued toward my car.

I slipped into the driver's seat and poured my head into my hands. *Am I just going to let this second wave pass me by? How many more chances can a girl get?* My thoughts were getting more and more critical.

That's it! Who cares what Brooke thinks, we're doin' this damn thing.

With new resolve, I opened my car door, leapt out of my seat and ferociously stomped back in Cameron's direction. I was determined not to let this opportunity pass.

"There he is," I whispered to myself.

He was unlocking his shiny, expensive car when a brand-spanking new Toyota pulled up alongside him.

"Cameron!" a woman hollered. Her dark tinted window eased open further, exposing the beautiful brunette inside.

"Ashley," he said, clearly shocked. Cameron stepped closer to her window, glamouring her with that gorgeous smile. "What brings you here?"

I slumped behind a car hoping he hadn't seen me. *What was I thinking? Duh! Of course he has a girlfriend. I mean look at him.* I peeked at him again and his smile was unchanged. He leaned against her door, attentively gazing at the brunette beauty.

I ducked behind the car again, when I realized the bitches were watching me. They pointed and giggled, as if I didn't already feel like a total ass. I slumped my shoulders and slunk back to my car, taking my walk of shame. I sulked all the way home.

CHAPTER THREE

After suffering through my hopeless embarrassment the entire next day, I decided I would come right out with Owen to see what had happened with Cameron Clarke. *Okay, so he has a girlfriend. As if I thought it would work out between us anyway.*

Cameron Clarke was obviously an experienced, powerful professional. He was also sexy as hell and, regardless of our relationship, or lack of one, I needed to know what I was missing out on. He had asked me out on a date after all.

That is what it would have been, right? Yes. And he had a girlfriend. Their relationship was obviously not exclusive. A man like that probably liked to keep his options open. That wouldn't have worked for me anyway.

Ready to confront Owen, I cleared my desk for the night and headed off toward his office. I knocked lightly on his open door. "Owen. Do you have a minute?"

"Of course. Please. Pull up a seat." He gestured toward the padded leather chair.

I rolled it closer to his desk before sitting down. "There's something I wanted to ask you."

"Before we get into that, I wanted to let you know that I've hired a new lawyer on staff," he blurted.

My face froze in an icy state of shock. My stomach twisted into a knot. "About that. What I wanted to ask you..."

"His name is Cameron Clarke. But I suppose you've already met." His smirk told me he had already put two and two together.

Ugh! That's not embarrassing.

"Anyway," he continued. "He starts in a couple of days. We just have to get the spare office set up for him. Would you mind giving me a hand with that tomorrow?"

"I can do that."

"So, what is it you wanted to ask me about?"

My mind ran a blank, as I tried to cover up my embarrassment. "It was nothing. Tell me more about our new lawyer," I said, seeming a little too interested.

Owen smirked again, but went on. "He specializes in civil litigation. He's got loads of experience. Don't worry, he'll fit in here perfectly."

It was not exactly what I was hoping to hear, but it was a start and so I nodded my head to acknowledge it. "What brings him *here*?" I pressed, probing for more info.

"We really need the help. You know that. And he could use the change of pace. He's worked some pretty high profile cases in Toronto and he sort of buried himself in work. I guess he's moving back here to lighten the workload and focus on his family life."

Great. He's a good guy with a loving family. How have I read this all wrong? "Good to know," I said, somberly.

Owen stood from his desk and pressed his hands on the top. "He's a real nice guy. I think you'll get along well."

I raised from my seat and rolled it back into place. "Okay. Thanks for letting me know. If there's anything more I can do to help..."

"I'm sure he'll catch on real fast, but I was hoping you could help him find his way." Owen walked me to the door. "Cameron is very independent, but he's not afraid to ask for help if he needs it either. I think if you offered him your support, he'd be appreciative."

That made me smile. "Thanks for the advice, Owen. So, what do I owe you?" I teased.

"Get out of here," he said, grinning like a fool.

Cameron Clarke was in my dreams, day and night, as I anticipated his first day on the job. When that day finally came, I drove to the office extra early. Edwin seemed to notice the slight variation in my morning routine, but there was no way he could've known why.

Cameron's office was just around the corner from my desk, and I knew that I would be bumping into him on a regular basis. I was looking forward to it.

Promptly at eight thirty, Cameron arrived. I overheard Owen welcoming him and making it known that I would prove to be very useful to him. *I can think of a few other things he could use me for.*

As I anticipated our proper introduction my palms began to sweat and I forced the huge smile from my face. Daydreams floated dangerously in my head and, while I managed to force away the naughty Cameron thoughts, it only prompted images of *my* first day on the job.

It had been five years now. I started working for the firm on a part-time basis while I was still in college. Owen was just an articling student then, but he had always treated me like his equal. When a civil litigation practice opened up for Owen to command, he stepped up to the plate and joined the firm as an associate. That's when Owen hired me on as his full-time assistant.

Now, Owen was a well-established lawyer who had the record to prove it. Rumour has it, he's up for promotion.

Ten long minutes passed before I finally heard Owen and Cameron in the hallway nearby. I had supressed my nerves and hid my exhilaration by delving into a file that desperately needed my attention. I was working away diligently when the two men finally appeared in my open doorway.

I glanced over my shoulder and there they stood, waiting patiently for me to acknowledge their presence.

"You can finish what you were doing. Don't let us interrupt you," Owen insisted.

"No, it's alright." *I had been waiting for what seemed like forever for this very moment.*

"Abigail Jenkins, I'd like you to meet Cameron Clarke," Owen said. It was so formal, even though Owen knew this introduction wasn't our first official meeting.

"It's very nice to meet you, Miss Jenkins," Cameron said, smiling warmly. With a wink of those sunset eyes, he stepped inside my cozy cubby and reached out his hand.

"No need for that Cam. We're all on a first name basis here," Owen said.

Oh, but I liked the way he said it. He'd be repeating my name in my dreams all day. I stood to my feet, heart fluttering in my chest, in anticipation of his reception.

Cameron gripped onto my hand and gave it a firm shake. It was very professional, and very disappointing.

"Very nice meeting you," I said, while warmth crept up the back of my neck.

Cameron wrinkled his forehead in that all too adorable way and flashed me his glorious smile. His hand lingered in mine a little too long, though he released it before Owen seemed to notice.

"Now that we have the introductions out of the way, it's time for you to get to work," Owen said. "We've collected some files for you to familiarize yourself with. All of my resources are at your fingertips. If you have any questions, I'm sure Abby can help you. As you know, I have an open door policy if you need anything from me."

"I'll be sure to use the resources liberally," Cameron replied, pinning me with his crystal stare.

Swoon!

"Shall we get to it then?" Owen asked.

Yes! Let's please!

Cameron nodded. "I look forward to working with you, Abigail," he said, before following Owen back to his office.

I clenched my teeth together, in a ridiculously large smile, to withhold the squeal working its way past my throat. Then, unable to help myself, I peeked around the corner to watch Cameron's retreat. *Nice ass.*

I wasn't expecting him to steal a slanted glance over his shoulder, but he did. *Shit!* I ducked back into my room and squeezed my eyes shut with embarrassment. *Oh, but it was worth it.*

My heart still raced, my mouth long gone dry, and an

uncontrolled smile crept onto my face. After a few laboured breaths, I scurried to the lunch room to get a drink, but I couldn't free myself from my youthful elation.

CHAPTER FOUR

It was the last day of summer, a sweltering sunny day, and even with the air conditioner running full blast it couldn't seem to keep up. If that wasn't bad enough, ever since Cameron had greeted me with that scorching hot 'good morning', I couldn't seem to cool down.

After grabbing a quick lunch, I slumped into my chair and clicked on my small personal fan. I desperately needed to cool off, so I turned it on high and sat in front of it with my eyes pressed shut, waiting for the cool relief.

Despite the fact that I was wearing a soft flowing skirt, I had still started to perspire. My fragrant lotion immersed my workspace, and I breathed deeply to enjoy the flowery garden bouquet. The fan wafted the feminine fragrance around my room, just as my handsome new co-worker rounded the corner.

He paused outside my door, closed his eyes and visibly inhaled my scent. When he reopened his eyes, he snared my gaze, which left me unprepared for his seductive crooked smile.

Breathless, I held his stare, captivated by his handsome face and charming allure. With a nod of his head, he took a few steps toward the main office, but abruptly stopped.

Curiosity killing me, I rolled my chair backwards to steal a look at what had happened. Peering around the corner, I could see Edwin with his arms folded tightly over his firm muscled chest. His eyebrows formed a pretentious line, warning the intruder to back down, but Cameron stood his ground.

Neither of them flinched, too engrossed in their own masculine pride to notice me spectating. Then Cameron simply straightened himself up, patted Edwin on the back and, without a word, walked past him. His lingering smile had never left his lips.

I rolled back to my desk and tried to look busy, sensing Edwin's approach. He slowly paced to my doorway and cleared his throat when he reached it.

I wiped my face clear of emotion and smiled a friendly smile. "Oh! Hey, Eddie."

"Is everything alright?" he scorned.

What did I do? A fake wonder possessed my face. "What do you mean? Everything's good."

"Is there something going on here that I don't know about?"

In other words, what the hell did I think I was doing encouraging such behaviour in a man other than himself. "Eddie, you're overreacting over nothing."

He didn't seem convinced.

"Besides, it's not your concern," I insisted delicately. But I knew there were no words that would stop Edwin from having *the talk* with Cameron; the same talk he had with all of my ex-boyfriends. I smiled softly, keeping my calm, and the worry started to fade from his face.

"You know I'm just looking out. You tell me if you ever need me to take care of him, or anyone else," he said, completely serious.

"You know I will," I said, though I had no intention of taking him up on that anytime soon.

Suddenly, a spike of testosterone flooded the air and I knew that Cameron was passing through the hall. Edwin turned quiet as he bore his eyes through Cameron's skull, communicating his hatred with a crisp silence. I knew that this was not the end of it and I hoped that I wasn't around when their little talk finally went down.

A few days later, when I least expected it, yes at the breakfast table, Edwin returned to the Cameron subject.

"What is it with this new guy anyway?" he asked.

I stuffed a spoonful of cereal in my mouth and crunched

it slowly, delaying my response.

"Are you attracted to him? He's obviously fascinated with you," he snapped.

I took another bite of my cereal and proceeded to nod agreeably. *No comment.* I doubted talking would help the situation. It never did with Edwin. So I continued to eat my breakfast without answering.

Over the course of the next few weeks, I sensed Edwin gradually pulling away from me. We spent less and less time together and when we did spend time together he wasn't very playful with me. We had become very distant, until one day the flirting between us ceased altogether.

I had fallen for Cameron and he knew it.

It was officially autumn, Owen was up for promotion and Cameron was single. At least that's what I was told. Cameron never really opened up to anyone at the office and Owen had remained pretty tight-lipped about his personal life. That was about to change.

I stared out the boardroom window, my eyes drawn to the bright green leaves that were starting to turn colours.

"Beautiful isn't it?" Edwin asked, catching me off guard.

I watched him closely as he scanned over the view, blocking the only exit in the room. "Very."

He walked up to the boardroom table and pulled out the seat across from me. "Mind if I sit?"

I lifted my hand to welcome him. Who was I to tell him what he could and couldn't do? He anxiously tapped his fingers on the table.

"What is it, Eddie?" I asked, genuinely curious to know what was troubling him.

"Nothing." He stopped his deceiving fingers and an awkward silence hung in the air between us.

I slowly nodded my head and decided not to dwell on it. "Everyone's talking about Owen's promotion, eh?"

Edwin nodded his head, obviously thankful for the

distraction. "That would be a dream come true for me. I wonder what the likelihood of getting a promotion is now that Owen's moving up the ladder."

His aqua eyes met mine, but instead of absorbing his usual confident intensity, I only sensed his hideous self-doubt. I extended my cold hand in the friendliest of gestures and rested it on his. His hand was large and warm, but he trembled awkwardly from my touch.

I held my chin high, as if I hadn't felt a seriously painful stab of disappointment at that. "Owen has earned it. But I'm sure if you put in your time, you'll get what you deserve too, Eddie. These things take time."

He pulled his hand out from under mine and tucked it under the table. "Yeah, but I'm sure you don't really care about my position anyway; especially now that your little boyfriend's already made senior associate."

I narrowed my eyes at him and he looked away, out the window or out of this world, I couldn't tell. He was so distant. "Please leave Cameron out of this. You know he did his time at another firm." I growled out of frustration. "This hardly has anything to do with him, and I see no point in arguing with you about it."

I paused to catch my breath, but I just grew angrier. "And quit calling him my boyfriend! He hasn't even asked me on a date."

His eyes darted back into this world and swallowed mine whole. My heart rammed up my throat and blocked my wind pipe. "That's only because he's a pussy. Don't waste your time on him."

I swallowed the dry lump from my throat. "Whatever, Eddie. We're not talking about this." I dropped my chin and, when I flashed my eyes to the floor, I realized that Taylor was standing in the doorway, patiently waiting for one of us to end the conversation.

I stood from my chair, eager to finish with him. "I wasn't going to warn you, but maybe I'd better. You're right. I do like him. And I'm going to need a date for Owen's promotion party," I said, not caring what Taylor thought about it. "I might even get up the nerve to ask him out."

Edwin stood from his chair, sending it slamming backwards. "Asking him out or trying him on?" he growled, much too loud for the office.

"That's really none of your business, now is it?"

He pressed his hands into the table top and I worried that it might be crushed beneath his weight. He lowered his head and, despite the mean intensity storming in his eyes, I started to sense his misery. My heart swelled, but I knew what he was doing and I couldn't let him manipulate me like that.

I rounded the table and stopped a short distance away from him, my chin held high, as Taylor quietly snuck back to her desk. "Please, Eddie. I don't want to fight. Can't we be civil?"

He squeezed his eyes shut, then lightened his pressure on the table. "You're right. This has gotten out of hand. Maybe we just need to set some boundaries. You know, so there's no confusion when we're out together."

I nodded, as his eyes met mine again, and the anger seemed to have faded away.

He turned his bulky shoulders to face me, his eyes begging for my forgiveness. "Will you share a cab with me then, for Owen's party? I know *I* plan to take full advantage of the open bar."

I hesitated, unsure whether it was the best idea.

Edwin thought the worst. "That is if your date won't be picking you up," he jabbed.

I pressed my lips into a sour smile. "The cab sounds good, Eddie, but that's as far as it goes. We can ride there together, but after that you're a free man."

A smile crept over his mouth, lighting up his miserable face. "I'm already a free man, baby."

I slapped him on the shoulder and for a minute I started to believe that everything was going to be okay.

"Seriously though, I won't be doing anything more to hold you back," he said. "That night we'll go to the party together, but we're going single. I'm saying you can do whatever or *whoever* you want, without feeling guilty. I'm done shooting daggers at every guy that hits on you."

I smiled softly. "Whoever?"

He stepped closer to me, hiking my heartbeat and the temperature in my cheeks. He raised his sharp eyebrows, with a much too serious look painted on his face. "Don't get me wrong. I still love you, Abs," he whispered, in a low, deep voice.

I closed my eyes to mask my feelings. "Don't say that. You really can't say that anymore," I breathed. My eyes fell to the floor.

"Fine. Have it your way. I won't say it. But you can't stop me from feeling it," he answered, as he brushed past me and exited the room.

Regardless of what Edwin said, it didn't change that our relationship was over. I had given him the chance to be with me, but that included having babies. Soon. He refused. The end.

He was just trying to hinder me from having a guilt-free good time at Owen's party. Instead of letting that sadden me, like I would have in the past, it made me outright mad. That anger invigorated me and fueled my resolve to finally jump back into the dating scene.

I'm ready now. I think. No, I am.

CHAPTER FIVE

The clock read five fifteen and yet I had no intention of heading home in the foreseeable future. The mound of files that needed my attention were piled ridiculously high, and my obsession for clearing them off my desk as complete was even worse.

Aliah swung around my door for a visit, with her exercise bag in hand. "Care to join me for a cycling class?"

I spun my chair around to face her and smiled. "I told Owen I would stay late to catch up on some of this work."

"Enough about work already." Aliah plunked her bag on top of the heaped files and poked her head a little closer. "Have you finally grown a pair and asked Cam to take you to Owen's party?"

"No," I replied sheepishly. "I thought I told you. I'm going with Eddie."

A wicked grin formed on her mouth and a cackle escaped from her throat. "You lie."

My face remained serious and I shook my head no. "We're catching a cab together. After that, I'm free to do as I please."

"Mmm, hmm. You do realize he'll do anything to sabotage your chances with Cam, right?"

"What's he gonna do?"

"Who knows? But we're gonna find out soon. The party's only two nights away. It's coming so fast, eh?"

I stared off into space. "I know." How was I going to find the right moment to ask Cameron out? I was running out of time.

"Well, I have to get going. But I expect you to call me tonight, woman. Ask the man out already. And if you won't do that, at least make sure he's going."

"Yeah, it sounds easy enough. But Owen never leaves us

alone for more than five seconds."

Aliah picked up her heavy bag and strapped it over her shoulder. "If you want it to happen, make it happen. Laters." She walked away and left me to reflect on her words.

She was right.

Readying myself to meet with Owen and Cam, I took a deep breath and checked my reflection in my blackened monitor. *I'm gonna do it!* I picked up my pad of paper, slapped it on top of my rule book, and lugged it to the boardroom. I knocked lightly on the closed door, startling both Owen and Cam, before I let myself in and closed the door behind me.

Cam's eyes lingered on me a little too long. It warmed my blood and kicked my heart into high gear. Trying to avoid his seemingly casual glances, I plugged away in preparation for the Monday trial, but it didn't stop my heart from fluttering every time I caught his eye.

After a good hour of solid progress, Owen ordered a pizza. It arrived within the hour.

I swallowed my last bite, smudged my fingers onto a napkin and checked my phone for the time. "Oh, shit! Please tell me it's not eight o'clock already."

"Owen pulled up the sleeve of his jacket to look at his watch. Nope, it's seven fifty five. Why?"

My lips pressed into a worried line. "I was supposed to go out with my sister tonight. Aubrey was going to pick me up at eight."

Cam smiled, warmly. "Looks like you're going to be late."

I slammed my rule book shut and locked my pen into the coil of my notepad. "Aubrey's had this night planned for weeks and she wouldn't take no for an answer." I feverishly dialed her cell number, hoping to catch her before she got to my place.

She answered on the first ring. "Hey. Where are you?"

"Uhh. I might still be at work," I said, testing her mood.

"I figured. I'm already on my way."

"No, wait! Aub!" She ended the call, not leaving me a

chance to even apologize. I slipped my phone back into my zippered pocket and blew out a long breath.

Cam and Owen were both chuckling, as though I had told a modestly funny joke.

I glared at each of them down the long boardroom table. "You think it's funny now? Just wait till she gets here. She may look small and sweet, but she packs a big punch. I am so dead."

I hustled back to my desk, scrambled around to collect my things and then shuffled back into the boardroom, nudging the door shut behind me with my foot. Before it latched, it swung back open and bumped me in the back.

"What the hell?" I muttered, under my breath.

I spun around, stunned by the intrusion. Aubrey was there. But she wasn't alone. The beautiful brunette woman from my nightmares, all of which involved Cam, was standing right next to her. She was still holding the door that had recently rammed into my back. I was mad, but the beautiful brunette was furious.

"Oh, isn't this just cozy," she mocked. "I've been waiting in the lobby out there for like ever, and you're all in here just chatting each other up over pizza?"

Did she just growl at Cameron? I swear she just growled.

I didn't even have to beg for Aubrey's forgiveness, because this girl had stolen the limelight and turned all of the attention on Cam. I actually felt sorry for him. It's no wonder they broke up.

Cameron's face showed his regret, but he remained cool, as he checked his wristwatch. "Shit! I didn't even know you were waiting. I told you to call me when you got here," he said.

The brunette, fuming hotter than ever, mounted her hands on her slim hips. "I did! Like six times!" she hollered. "But you didn't pick up and you weren't in your office. Your damn phone was though!"

Aubrey remained silent, but turned her wide green eyes on me, as Owen stood to greet the bitchy brunette.

"Ashley, always a pleasure," Owen said to her, reaching

out for a hug.

They shared a brief squeeze. "Owen," she said, turning much sweeter. Then she turned back on Cameron and scowled at me. "Are you guys going to wrap this up now, or do I have to do it for you?"

What an evil bitch! I couldn't believe that Cameron would allow this girl to push him around like that. She must have been the girlfriend from hell.

When I glanced over to the guys, to my surprise, they were laughing. Ashley wasn't very amused. She folded her arms over her padded chest, outraged. From the look of her slutty attire and excess of exposed skin, it was clear that she was ready for a night out too. *Well damn.*

"Ashley, I'd like you to meet Abigail," Cam said firmly.

How awkward! Hi Ashley, I'm the girl trying to pick up your boyfriend. I thought you were on a break. "Nice to meet you," I said.

She snorted. "I wish I could say the same to you."

Ashley was certainly a spicy young lady. She was rail thin, but I still wouldn't want to get in her way. I had the distinct feeling that she would step all over me if given the chance.

"Cut it out, Ash," Cam ordered, and Ashley seemed to listen.

Okay, so maybe he doesn't just take her shit.

"Are you coming, Abby?" Aubrey said sweetly, anxiously tucking her honey blonde hair behind her ear.

I was relieved to find that the evilness had not rubbed off on her. Aubrey could only imagine being so devious and never in a million years could she have put on such a persistently wicked performance.

"Give me a minute?" I asked, as I tidied my things.

Aubrey nodded while Owen waved a hand at me. "Go on. I don't want to wreck your whole night. Go. Have a good time."

Cam had started to clean up his things too, while Ashley fumed across the table.

Aubrey meekly stepped closer to me. "If you're too busy,

I don't mind. Ashley was saying that the two of us could go out instead, since Cam bailed on her. No offence," she said to Cam.

I flashed a glance at Ashley. She nodded grumpily. Cameron was watching me intently.

I nodded at Aubrey and locked my eyes on hers to show my apology. "I'll make it up to you. I promise."

Ashley rolled her eyes and I couldn't help but notice how the chocolate brown colour seemed to turn black every time she set her eyes on me. "I'm sure you will," she sneered. Then she stealthily slithered up next to Aubrey, grabbed her arm and swiftly yanked her out of the room. "Come on," she ordered. "We are so out of here."

And just like that, Ashley stormed off with my poor sweet sister in tote.

Cameron stood to his feet and lifted both of his hands in defeat. "What about me?" he hollered after her, but it was too late. The ladies were already in the parking lot and he wasn't making any effort to chase them down.

Curiosity prickled my skin delightfully. "What about you?"

He sighed, lightheartedly. "My car's in the shop. She was my ride."

Owen stood next to his chair and scooped up one of the many files from the table. "No worries. I'll give you a ride."

"Nah, that's out of your way. I'll call a cab."

The fact that Cameron had a girlfriend in the picture made me sit tight-lipped. He deserved better than Ashley, but that was his problem.

"Abby lives out that way. I'm sure she could give you a ride," Owen said, looking to me.

So much for that. With all eyes on me, I awkwardly cleared my throat. "That's fine with me. Where do you live?"

His dazzling smile knocked me into a state of awe and, when he squinted those sparkling eyes, I nearly squealed with excitement. "Downtown, on Humber Street."

My breathing accelerated and my heart picked up

another beat, as I tried to regain my composure. "I go right by there on my way home anyway. I can take you."

When he wrinkled his forehead and looked up at me, my mouth went dry in anticipation of his words. "I don't want to impose on you."

Oh, baby, you can impose on me anytime. Oh. Wait! No! He's taken. And by the Devil herself at that.

"I don't mind at all. It's not like I have anywhere to be now that your girlfriend stole my sister away."

"Hah!" Owen sputtered, slapping his hand on the table.

"Uh, that's not my girlfriend," Cameron said, then joined in with Owen's laughter.

Confused and embarrassed I stood from my seat. "Ha, ha. Big joke. So, who is she then?" I asked.

"Ashley's my sister," Cameron said, his eyes smiling.

My heart did a back flip and went right into jumping jacks. I had to turn away to hide my excitement. Granted, the bitch was bound to be a nightmare to deal with; but he was so worth it.

"Okay, well if you'll excuse me a minute," I said, needing a minute to pull myself together. "I'll be right back."

"I'll be waiting," Cameron replied smoothly.

I bit my lip and scooted out the door, in need of a serious breather. I walked up the dimly lit hall, my smile ear to ear. After a few ridiculous tuck jumps, to release my pent up energy, I checked myself in the washroom mirror and slipped back into the hall. *Phew!* I was lucky no one had caught my teenage antics.

I hurried back down the hall and stopped just outside the boardroom. It sounded like Owen and Cameron were having a private conversation. You could say I was eavesdropping, but they knew I wouldn't be long and I didn't want to interrupt.

"Cam, you really need to stop it. Out of all of the women in this City, why her?"

"It is what it is," Cam replied.

What the hell is that supposed to mean?

Owen sounded angered. "Don't mess this up for me,

buddy."

"This has nothing to do with you, as far as I am concerned."

I had missed too much of their conversation. I had no idea what they were talking about. Instead of being a scummy spy, I walked right in on them, acting blissfully unaware. Sure enough, they both went silent immediately.

Great! It was definitely me they were talking about. I kept my mouth shut, since I sucked at lying. They knew I had heard something, but how much? Clearly not enough.

Cameron just smiled, and it sent a hoard of butterflies fluttering through my chest. "Are we ready to call it a night?" he asked.

"A few more minutes?" Owen begged.

Oh, I had definitely missed something. Just moments ago, Owen was ushering me off and now, all of a sudden, he so urgently needed us to hang around?

"We ready to go?" Cam asked me again, giving Owen the cold shoulder. "I mean, I am."

I smiled at his enthusiasm and then glanced at Owen. "Do you want me to clear the file out of here before I go?"

Owen sighed, recognizing his defeat. "No, I'll be working on this some more. You can leave it."

"Okay," I said smiling. "Have a good night, Owen." I draped my sweater over my arm, picked up my handbag and headed for the exit.

"Don't work too hard, buddy," Cameron said, as he patted Owen on the shoulder.

I slowed up in the lobby to check my reflection and then continued outside. I stepped off the curb, into the parking lot, and Cameron was suddenly a few strides behind me.

In an instant, I worried about how my butt looked, since he was most likely staring at it. I suddenly forgot how to walk and stumbled in my stilettos, only steps from my car. I turned back to see if Cameron noticed. He did, but he only smiled; that glorious, gut-wrenching smile.

I got into my car, embarrassed, and tore off the tall shoes instantly.

Cameron let himself into the passenger seat, as I cranked the volume of my music down low. He looked so gorgeous, and the shadows only intensified his amazing features. When his door closed, I became electrified and it felt like fireworks had been set off in the car.

As if he didn't notice my fascination with him, he casually gazed at me, with those beautiful blue eyes. A burning sensation spread across my cheeks. *Is it just me or is it hot in here?* I reached into the back seat for a pair of sensible flats and quickly slipped them on.

The music was low, but my heart was singing at the top of its lungs, as I put the car in reverse. Comforted by the silence, I drove down the surprisingly traffic-free streets. I knew I should spark a conversation, but I wondered if any words would even come out of my mouth if I tried. I took a deep breath and hoped he didn't notice how flustered I was.

"So, where do you live exactly?" I asked. It was the only practical thing that came to mind.

He directed me to Humber Street, though I already knew where it was. I had grew up in the City and could have named every street in it if I wanted to.

With every turn, I could feel Cameron's steady gaze on my face. Even though I had nothing to say, I couldn't help it anymore, I had to turn and look at him.

Bad idea. He was smiling at me, his eyes dark and dangerous. He was so damn mysterious and it was so damn sexy. As I smiled back, I could feel my cheeks getting warm again. I wished he would just say something to save me from the embarrassment.

"Are you finding your way around the office okay," I muttered, grasping at straws.

"It's alright. Everyone's been real nice to me. I'm happy to be working with Owen. He's a good guy."

"Did you guys know each other before?"

"I figured Owen told you. We went to the same law school. He graduated a few years before me, but we hung with the same crowd. We were pretty good friends; mind you it's been a few years now."

"Another ass kiss," I mumbled, hoping my tease would lighten the tension-filled car.

"Excuse me?" he said, stunned.

I smiled and glanced at him. "You heard me."

"You're one to talk," he insinuated, mischievously. "Owen tells me you've been a loyal assistant to him since day one, but I've found some inconsistencies in his stories."

My mouth dropped open and I turned to face him. "What's that supposed to mean?"

Cameron's face turned serious. "I didn't mean to offend you. It's just that Owen has a lot of great things to say about you."

I smiled, easing his worry. "I can't help it if I'm that good."

He chuckled, his blue eyes blazing. "You must be. I'll have to test that theory myself some time."

I raised my eyebrows, intrigued by his outspoken promise. *Was Mr. Clarke flirting with me?* "I don't know what you're implying, but I'll get it out of you another time." I smirked. *Oh yes, there would be another time.*

His house must have been getting close, as he squinted through the dark tinted windows. "That's mine; the small brick one," he said, pointing a masculine finger.

I wanted to gawk, but it was dark and I really couldn't see much of anything.

Cameron turned to me, as I pulled into his driveway. "I really appreciate the ride, Abigail." After he stepped out of the car, he leaned down and peered back inside, an adorable smile soft on his lips. "Looks like I owe you one now."

My heart skittered across my chest. "I'll remember that," I said, smiling.

With a raise of his brow, he closed the door and set off for his front door. My heart beat steadily from my chest as I watched his sexy swagger, my headlights the only thing keeping him from total blackness. Once he reached his doorstep, he dug into his pant pockets, but came up empty. He checked his designer jacket next, but again, nothing.

Cameron turned back to me with concern etched on his face and smoothed down his pink silk tie. When he finally moseyed back toward the car, I couldn't keep the smirk off my face as I put my window down.

"I don't have any keys," he said, looking apologetic. "They're on my other key chain and I'm sure the dealership is closed for the night."

"You haven't hidden a key anywhere in the yard?" *Not that I'm complaining.*

"I've been meaning to copy the key since I moved in, but I've just never gotten around to it," he said, wrinkling his forehead.

Oh, he looked so cute when he did that. I wanted to touch him, to smooth out those wrinkles with my thumbs and kiss those indentations with my lips. "Is there anyone else with a key?"

He tilted his head, clearly embarrassed now. "Ashley's got the only other copy."

"Hmm, so what do you want to do now?" My voice was pleasant but my thoughts were selfish, dark and devilish. *I'd love to take him back to my lair for a night or two.*

"I'd better call Ashley. Gah!" he moaned. "She's not going to be be happy with me."

I waved him into the car. "Why don't you get in? There's no need for your neighbours to hear her screaming at you," I teased.

He chuckled, as he pulled his cell from his pocket. He dialed her number and it was ringing before he returned to the passenger seat.

"Hello?" Ashley snapped.

I could hear her irritation through the phone, and there was music thundering loudly in the background.

"Ashley?" Cameron hollered.

"Yah! Who did you think would answer my phone?" she growled, as the deafening music subsided.

Cameron looked at me apologetically. "Hey. I hate to bother you, but do you think you could stop by my place to let me in sometime soon? I'm locked out and you have the only spare key."

"Are you kidding me? I'm out of town already. Me and Aubrey are like half way to Toronto. Isn't there someone else you can call?"

"I wish there were, but you're it. There's no one else."

His words rang in my ears like wedding bells and I couldn't wipe the joy from my face. I turned away and peered out my window, so he couldn't see my elation.

"Great, there goes *my* night," Ashley hollered.

"So, will you come then?" he asked anxiously.

I too wondered if she'd leave him high and dry.

"Ugh," Ashley crabbed. "I guess I don't have much of a choice, now do I?" After some mumbling I couldn't make out, she whined again. "Just so you know, it's going to be like an hour before I can get to you. I have to stop and get gas and I just passed an off ramp."

"Okay. Call me when you get in the City and I'll meet you here."

"Fine," she snapped, ending the call.

"Thank you," he said, his voice trailing off as he stared at his dead phone. Cameron's face showed that he was unimpressed, as he glanced over at me curiously. "You wouldn't want to spend another hour with me, would you? You're probably sick of me about now."

I tilted my head in disbelief. "Hardly, Cameron. Do you really think I would make you sit out here alone all night?" *Looking as fine as you are.* "I'm sure we can find something to do."

He smiled at me, acknowledging my kindness, not knowing the naughty ideas rolling around in my head. "I know a nice park we can drive up to and go for a walk by the water," he suggested.

"Sounds good to me. Show me the way," I said, sounding way less ecstatic than I was feeling inside. I was convinced that he didn't have a clue how I felt about him.

Minutes later, we arrived at the park. It was a gorgeous autumn night, but it was a bit chilly, so I pulled on my light cardigan before locking my doors. Cameron rounded the front of the car and met up with me before we set off.

We walked at each other's sides, close, but not too close. I couldn't help but notice other random couples strewn around the park past dark. Conversation seemed to flow easier now and I found that the more Cameron offered up about himself, the more there was to like.

When we reached the water's edge, we followed the brick pathway, staring out over the river and appreciating the beautiful autumn landscape. A soft breeze wafted his cologne my way, and it was so difficult to not inhale him the way I wanted to. Despite the light breeze, his gorgeous blonde hair stayed perfectly iced in place. It was perfect. He was perfect.

"What a beautiful night," Cameron said, his gaze meeting mine.

Lost in his sparkling eyes, my lips parted, but I was speechless, breathless. I could only smile, before turning my eyes to my feet.

"It's a good thing my daughter isn't with me," he added casually.

WHAT? I was totally not expecting to get the baby bomb dropped on me like that. I didn't even know what to say. *Why am I only finding this out now? Moreover, is he single or isn't he?*

At that very moment, I was so glad that my eyes were locked on the ground, so he couldn't decipher my uneasiness. I wasn't looking forward to hearing about how great his baby momma was, or maybe how often his ex-wife delivered their child for a visit. But I needed to know. I needed some finality.

I cleared my throat, but kept my eyes pinned to the ground. "You have your daughter on weekends?"

"No. I actually have her full-time," he said, willing me to look up at him. "Is that a problem?"

Why would it be a problem? This isn't a date. I lifted my lashes. "Of course not. How old is she?" I asked softly, honestly curious.

"Six, but she thinks she's ten." His smirk was adorable.

"I knew I was going to be without a vehicle for a couple of days, so we decided she'd stay with my parents for the night. God, I miss her."

I couldn't escape my smile, as my heart melted. *What a sweetheart! Why did he have to be so darn cute?*

"Do you have any kids?" he asked, wrinkling his brow.

I exhaled anxiously. "No. Unfortunately," I said, telling a little too much about my thoughts on the subject.

He nodded his head, his lips forming a tight line, still sexy as hell. "Being a single parent is a full-time job. It's hard to admit that you need a break sometimes. You want to be able to do it all, you know? It's funny though, whenever I do get a night off, I just spend the whole time worrying about her and wondering what she's doing."

"That's sweet."

His lips curled into a smile. "My parents tell me to get a life, but that's proving to be difficult. They'll be happy to hear I'm out with a woman."

My heart was swelling to an immeasurable size. *What a sweet, sweet, SINGLE man. What's more, he obviously loves kids.* "We're *out* right now?" I teased, loving the sound of it.

He grinned and glanced out over the water. "You know what I mean. I'm not sitting at home alone and I'm not working."

"Right," I replied, smiling from ear to ear.

We continued to walk farther, our bodies drawing closer, our conversation waning. I wanted to kiss him.

Cameron cleared his throat and distanced himself from me, then sighed and glanced up at the night sky. "I suppose I should've asked this sooner, since I've been getting mixed signals from the office gossip about you." For the first time, he sounded nervous.

When he hesitated, and glanced down at his feet, I interrupted his inner battle. "What do you want to know?" I asked, equally as nervous.

His eyes flashed up and caught mine like a snare. "Whether or not you're available." Such a dry statement, but it held such promise. "You know, to see *other* men."

"Men other than...?" I could barely choke out the sentence, wishing he would just ask me out already.

"Edwin."

There it was; Edwin making himself a nuisance long after we agreed to split.

"What's the going consensus?" I had to admit, I was a little curious.

Cameron's lips curved into a mischievous smile. "All the ladies seem to think you're available. A certain someone seems to think you're off limits though. Oh, and Owen's pretty touchy about it too. What's that all about?" he asked.

Shock overwhelmed all of my features. "With Owen? Your guess is as good as mine."

His smile turned wicked. "I think I know that one, but what about Edwin?" He raised his brow and wrinkled that forehead of his, making it difficult for me to think clearly.

"What about him?" I asked.

"Is there something there, or am I just seeing things?"

I took a deep breath. *I can't believe we're discussing this right now.* "We're housemates, nothing more. Yes, we've dated, but it's over between us and he knows it. He can be insanely jealous. And he doesn't think we separated for the right reasons."

"And why is that exactly?" Cameron pried.

"I can assure you, we're apart for all the right reasons. I'm moving on with my life but, as you can imagine, he's making it as difficult as possible for me to do that."

"I see."

I was unable to read his dark, brooding expression. *Did I blow it? Oh well, what's new?* "So yes, I'm single. And it's going to take someone pretty amazing to change that."

"Is that so?" That sexy smile returned to his lips and the pounding in my chest became deafening to my ears.

I smiled and nodded, then continued down the moonlit path, unsure how he was handling all of my baggage. He didn't bring up the baby momma thing and I sure as hell wasn't going to tonight either.

He is single. He has a daughter, who he loves very much

and lives with all the time. Nothing I couldn't deal with. But could *he* deal with the Edwin thing? A girl could only dream.

When he stopped at a park bench, I took a seat next to him. He stretched his arm out behind me, making me want to snuggle up closer to him, but I didn't have the balls. He was so attentive and sexy, impossible to resist; especially when he was still wearing that designer suit and pink silk tie.

Cameron exuded such confidence. The way his crystal eyes sparkled by the light of the large, round moon, made it very difficult for me to follow our mindless conversation. I watched his juicy lower lip as he spoke and, whenever he smiled, it made me squirm with excitement. As the night went on, it was getting harder for me to mask it.

He rested his hand on my knee. "We should probably head back. What do you say?"

My skin became electrified beneath his fingers and stayed charged after they slipped away. "Mmm, hmm," I agreed, though I had lost all sense of time.

He stood up next to the bench and held out his elbow to me.

What a gentleman.

I gladly reached for his arm and snuggled up close to him. He was warm and thoughtful and charming.

We walked most the way back like that, incredibly close, silent, simply enjoying a peaceful walk together. He smelled so good and I inwardly appreciated it, knowing our night would be coming to an end very soon.

I could see my car not far off in the parking lot, but before we left the waterfront, he stopped and leaned against the black metal railing. I let his elbow go, to grab the railing too, but I didn't distance myself at all.

"I thought I owed you before. Now I owe you big," he admitted, a sexy smile taking over his lips.

I chewed my own lip and smiled. "I'm sure we can work something out."

"I don't know. I'll be kissing the floor you walk on to

make up for this one," he joked.

I'd much prefer a different kind of kiss. "You don't owe me anything. I had a good time tonight. You can tell your mother that." I smirked momentarily, but only until Cameron stole my breath.

He straightened up and locked his sparkling gaze on mine. "It was good; wasn't it?" he asked, totally serious now.

His eyes left mine and slipped down my body, as he slowly, but deliberately, slid his hand on top of mine. Thrilling tingles coursed through my veins as his thumb took motion and softly brushed over my knuckles. His eyes exposed his indecision; though I was happy he made any move at all.

When he smiled at me again, I held my breath. His internal conflict had been resolved. My heart fluttered and I gasped for air, as his other hand carefully rested on my hip and gently guided me closer to him, until my body molded to his.

I studied his glorious face up close, swimming in his charm, as we gazed into each other's eyes. Wanting to make the next move was one thing, but I found myself unable to do it, too scared to muddle the magical moment.

Cameron smiled at me again and then slowly angled his head. When he dipped his chin, his eyes fell closed, and I knew he was coming in for a kiss. As he eased closer, time stood still. My heart thumped erratically in my chest, my lips parted, and I closed my eyes waiting for the glorious moment when our lips would touch.

His hand gripped me tighter, holding me flush against him. Peering out of half-closed lids, I watched his tongue dart out of his mouth to wet his plump lower lip. I swallowed hard and my lips parted again, urging him to do it. Our breath intermingled, our lips magnetic, and just as they were about to touch, his phone rang.

He jolted backwards, like I was suddenly on fire. My heart was, but he stood there frozen in place like an ice sculpture. Then a deep sigh pressed from his chest, as he dug his hand into his pocket.

"Saved by the bell," he said, retrieving his phone.

I could taste his sweet breath on my lips. I could feel his body against me, hard and lean. I could smell the essence of Cameron around me, but it was quickly dissolving as he stepped a few more paces away.

"Dammit, Ashley!" he snapped.

"Oh, really? Damn you, Cam. Where the hell are you? Get your ass over here like yesterday," she shouted through the phone.

Cameron nodded toward the car and started heading that way. I followed him quickly. So much for that magical moment. Now it would be known as the first kiss that never happened.

"Yes, yes. We'll be there in a few." He ended the call and got into the car as I turned over the ignition.

The dreamy mood that had once filled the night, had now felt like a distant hope fading from my memory. I sped off to his house and, after his apology, we didn't exchange another word. The air was thick with tension and I didn't know how to get past it. The night was old.

When we got to his house, I saw my sister's car parked alongside the curb. She was sitting on Cameron's front porch with Ashley, whose arms started flailing as soon as I pulled up.

He looked at me one last time and smiled, instantly reigniting my lust for him. "Thank you, again. For everything." He pressed his right hand on the dash and started to lean toward me.

Again, Ashley put a wrench in my luck. She opened the passenger door and yanked him backward by the back of his expensive jacket.

"Ashley! Enough already," he snapped, adjusting his wrinkled collar.

"What the hell took you so long?" she shouted at me, and then slammed the door in my face.

Cameron shook his head and mouthed 'I'm sorry', through the window, as Ashley grabbed onto him and dragged him to his front door. He lifted a hand to wave goodbye and disappeared inside his house with my sister and the devil herself.

CHAPTER SIX

Dark, gloomy storm clouds hovered over the office for the better part of my Friday morning, suiting my rotten mood perfectly. The morning was uneventful enough, though I was totally miserable. Cameron was acting as professional as ever, as though last night hadn't even happened. I began to wonder myself if I had dreamed up the entire atmosphere or if it had actually existed.

Leave it up to Taylor to stop me right outside of his door, just before lunch. I felt terribly uncomfortable standing there, totally visible from where Cameron was seated, but he didn't even seem to notice me.

"Hey, Abigail. Are you excited about the party tomorrow?" Taylor asked, a big smile giving away her excitement.

"Sure," I moaned.

"Oh, come on. It's your chance to drink until your heart's content and be all wild and unruly." She was acting all giddy, like a nosy, bothersome mother.

I'll be unruly alright, but my heart will never be content. I blew every chance of asking Cameron out last night. What a disaster. Now I'm stuck alone. Well not entirely alone. Edwin has every intention of delivering me to the party. After that, then I can sulk like the lonely lady that I am.

"Don't pout, dear, it's not very becoming of you," Taylor said. "If past events ring true to the last promotion party, then we're in for some fun. The Partners will make their grand exit after speeches wrap up and then the real party will begin. We'll have a blast. I just know it."

I still didn't speak. My mind stirred, as I stared outright at Cameron through his doorway.

"Oh, dear. I see," she said. "Don't you worry your little heart. It'll all work out in the end, hun. It always does."

"Mmm, hmm." *Not for me it doesn't.*

"You'll see. It'll be a night to remember. I promise you that," she insisted.

I had yet to be convinced, but I peeled my eyes from Cameron and smiled at Taylor. "Thanks, Taylor. I'm sure you're right. But you know, if you want a man to call you, I'd say the first step would be to give him your number."

She patted me on the back smiling, then we went our separate ways.

Cameron pulled his nose from his computer just in time to catch a glimpse of me walking away.

I heard his deep sigh, as I rounded the corner toward my desk. Unable to sit still, I continued straight past my hole in the wall and rushed to the copier, worrying myself with unexplainable questions, like: *Why was Cameron avoiding me?* I shook my head, to escape my overactive thoughts, and reached for some papers.

When I spun around to return to my desk, I slammed right into him. Cameron's body was the only thing keeping my papers from dropping to the floor between us. My breath was trapped in my lungs and I thought I might suffocate before taking my next one. As I tugged my arms up to my chest, to collect my paper and protect my personal space, one of my hands incidentally brushed across his and rested against his sleek core.

His reaction was horrific. *Take 'er easy. It was an accident.*

The gesture was unintentional, but he acted as though I had done something terribly wrong. Discovering his severe discomfort with me touching him was depressing. I wanted to cry, but the knowledge of how I affected him, good or bad, gave me an incredible sense of empowerment.

What did I do? Do I have cooties? He didn't seem to mind last night. I chuckled inside at the thought, and I couldn't help but smile as I collected my papers and walked off. "Sorry," I said, flashing a glance back at him.

He was a lost cause, and it wasn't long before I resumed sulking at my desk.

At the flash of twelve, I leapt from my seat and hurried to our office kitchen for my lunch date with Aliah. After a few people grabbed their things from the fridge, we were alone at last.

"What's your take on Cameron lately?" I asked her.

Aliah took a bite out of her small red apple. "What do you mean lately?"

I leaned across the table and rested my chin on my clasped hands. "I mean since last night. I accidentally touched his hand today and he nearly had a bird. What's his problem?"

"Would you like me to shed some light on that point for you? It's so obvious to me," Aliah replied.

"Um, yes," I said dramatically.

She leaned forward, her chin close to the table. "Did you ever consider that he's trying to keep your relationship strictly professional? He's fighting to control his manly urges. At least that's what I think." She smirked, but I didn't return the sentiment.

"I don't really see it that way."

"Abby, I know Owen doesn't want to lose you as an assistant. He's probably warned him to back off."

"Huh. I guess I never thought of that. I just thought maybe he didn't like women." I giggled, not noticing Cameron's entrance.

He disappeared behind the fridge door and I flashed an anxious glance from the door to Aliah. I'd recognize that ass anywhere. He retrieved his lunch and clutched it in one hand.

Why did he have to look so damn good? He wore his navy blue tie loosened at the neck and his jacket was unbuttoned. Instead of retreating to his office, as I prayed that he would, he pulled up a chair next to Aliah, uninvited.

"Ladies," he said, smooth and sexy, as he rummaged through his lunch.

"Hey," I replied, soft and anxious.

Aliah turned to face him. "If you'll just excuse me, I'll be back in a couple of minutes." She leaned over the table toward me and smiled. "I've suddenly got the urge to use the ladies room." She flashed a sneaky glance at Cameron, then headed for the door. She winked back at me, before she left the room.

I rolled my eyes, then realized that Cameron was gazing at me intently. *Aliah!*

"You know she's exactly right," Cameron said, once we were alone. He leaned toward me and looked me right in the eyes, as if I needed a reminder of how fascinating he was.

"Pardon me?" I said, hoping he'd planned on clarifying.

"I'm sorry. I thought you knew. I was standing in the doorway when you were talking about Owen just a minute ago. Aliah saw me standing there. I just assumed she told you."

"Well, she didn't. So, what do you mean exactly?" I probed, while twirling my hair around my finger. It seemed to distract him.

"What I'm saying is that Owen's no fool. It's true, I've been warned. But I can assure you, I like women. In fact, it's evident to me that I have a thing for you."

I batted my lashes as subtly as possible. "I don't get it." Among all the news he delivered, there was a hint of serious flirtation that had me begging for more. He was seducing me with his words now, but why the sudden change?

He smiled wickedly. "Enough about Owen, let's talk about you."

Who was talking about Owen? Just then, Aliah pranced back to her seat.

"Hey, guys. What did I miss?"

Cameron turned his head and dazzled her with a smile. "Abigail was just promising me that she would be my date for tomorrow night." He turned to me, holding his raised brows like he was expectant of an answer. "Pick you up at six?"

Before I could process, Aliah stuck her nose in my business. "That's not going to work for her. She's hitching a ride with me and Edwin to the dinner party."

"Aliah!"

"What? He already made the arrangements. The cab's booked to take us straight to the venue. You know that. None of us are driving there," she told him.

"Care to join us?" I asked, hoping the Edwin thing didn't offend him so much that he was put off of me entirely.

His eyes smoldered at me. "That's not really my style anyway; that is for a first date."

I swallowed the lump from the back of my throat and grew a pair. I fluttered my eyelashes softly. "Take it or leave it," I breathed.

He cocked a brow, intrigued. "I'll take what I can get. A dance?"

I smiled uncontrolledly, but replied smoothly. "Of course."

His blue eyes twinkled and targeted mine. "I'd still like to call it a date, if that's good with you."

I nodded, in an attempt to mask my giddiness, but my cheeks had already flared rosy colours. Aliah rolled her eyes, aghast by my unforgiving attraction to him.

Cameron stood from the table and flashed me a smile. "Well, ladies, I hate to eat and run but I have a million things to do. So, I will see you there?" he inquired, waiting for an answer.

"She'll be there with bells on," Aliah chimed, smirking.

Still not satisfied, he dropped his hand on mine. "Do you think I could I get your number?"

Aliah threw a pen and paper in front of me. It seemed to materialize out of nowhere. I smiled up at him, then scribbled my number on the pad of paper. I ripped it off and he took it from my willing fingers.

He spun around with dignified grace and returned to the doorway, where he put his hand on the frame and paused. He looked back at me and smiled, without saying a word, as his glorious face swarmed me with desire.

Once he was gone Aliah hopped to her feet and dropped both her hands flat on the table. "What was that?" she gasped, exaggeratedly.

I grinned to myself, my body flooded with endorphins.

"He is so intense. I had no idea! Tell me everything," she demanded.

I flashed my eyes to the door. "Shhh!" I demanded. But he was gone. I motioned for her to sit down, still concerned that another man could be drifting nearby to listen in. When she finally sat, I gave her a play-by-play, being sure to not skip one batted eyelash.

"How do you always manage to pick up the fine ones?" she complained.

I rolled my eyes. "You hardly have trouble in that department. You're dating a totally ripped fireman."

She flashed a thoughtful glance in the air. "Oh, that's right, I am." Her grin covered her face, then was replaced with a frown. "But while we're on that topic, you are not going to believe this. You know how I thought Hunter would come to the party with me tomorrow? Now he tells me Maddison already invited him and he agreed to go with her."

I gasped and my mouth fell open unattractively. "He didn't."

"He did! And apparently our relationship doesn't veto their plans. He says he's only looking out, since she's got his baby on board and all. Pregnant bitch. I swear she's still trying to move in on my man."

I laughed, knowing that all that drama was going to make for an entertaining night. And I was happy, knowing that there wasn't a whole lot of time to worry about what I was going to wear for my hot date.

CHAPTER SEVEN

It was the night of the big bash and Owen was the man of honour. Edwin was on my case all day, making sure I hadn't changed my mind about our travel arrangements. As I tossed another load of laundry into the washing machine, Edwin joined me there. Our laundry room was efficient, but it was small.

"Did you hear Owen has a date for tonight?" he asked, filling the small room with his broad shoulders and thick arms.

"No, who?" I asked.

"It's a surprise. Do you think it's a man or woman?" Edwin raised his eyebrows deviously.

"Edwin! You're bad. Sure, he dresses well and has a certain air about him, but I really don't think he's gay."

"Maybe I would be more convinced if I saw the man show an ounce of interest in a woman. Has he ever hit on you?"

"No," I said, scowling. "He's not like that."

Edwin leaned against the door frame, obstructing my only exit. The temperature in the room spiked beyond comfortable. "There you have it. He's not like that," he repeated, sarcastically. "He doesn't like women. What man in their right mind wouldn't find you attractive? A gay man," he answered. "Cameron better watch out."

Ignoring Edwin's jab at Cameron, I smirked knowing that even Edwin had to admit how gorgeous he was. "It's not hard to see why a man might not flirt with me." I turned the knob to the delicate cycle. "Owen's a respectful co-worker."

Edwin dropped his hand to his side. "Yeah, unlike some men."

I returned the jug of fabric softener to the shelf and gave Edwin an evil eye. "Don't go there."

He raised his hands in surrender. "Hey, don't look at me. I can't avoid all of the rumours around the office."

I blasted past Edwin, pushing him backwards into the hallway. "I'm done with this conversation, Eddie. I'm too busy right now."

"Really? Don't tell me you're getting ready for tonight already, because you have hours."

"Busy!" I hollered, before rushing to the front door and slamming it shut behind me.

Now that I had a date, I knew I had to pay my sister Aubrey a visit. Her closet was like the most amazing shopping mall. So, when she suggested I come to her place so she could make me fabulous, I couldn't resist. She always had the cutest outfits and I wanted to dress to impress.

Excited about my date with Cameron, I skipped to my car like a carefree little girl. I made the quick drive to Aubrey's condo and pulled into her lot. When I zoomed toward the building, I cut off another driver, stealing the last visitor parking space. *You snooze, you lose beotch!*

The driver waved erratically at me, and hollered through the window, though I couldn't hear a word of it as I snickered to myself. Ignoring that, I rushed to the building's entrance and quickly buzzed Aubrey's apartment before the lady could catch up with me.

Aubrey let me right in the main door and I quickly shuffled up the stairs to her floor. On the way, I thought about what tonight might bring. Despite the wild stories from the past, I was not a part of them. I usually steered clear of the drama those nights created. Tonight though, I would stir things up for a change.

I knocked at Aubrey's door and she instantly greeted me with a big smile. "Hey, sis, come on in. This is so exciting. I'm so excited for you."

Her high-energy made me giggle. "You're funny," I replied, though I was just as thrilled.

Aubrey hurried for her bedroom door, then glanced back to make sure I was following. "I picked out some outfits that I thought you might like. Oh, and you have got to see these shoes I picked up the other day. They're so hot."

I followed her into her bedroom, where she already had three different outfits strewn across her bed. Of course she had accessorized the looks and damn was she good! "Oh my gosh. Are these the shoes?"

She picked them up to display them on her hand. "Hot, right?"

I pulled them from her hands and compared them to the outfits, hoping I could make them work. "I love them, and they would be real cute with this dress."

"You're going to look amazeballs tonight," she said, smiling. "But I still can't believe you're dating Ashley's brother."

"Please don't call him that."

"Fine. Cameron," she exaggerated, teasing me. She giggled momentarily, then delivered her warning. "You'd better take good care of these shoes. I haven't even had a chance to wear them out yet."

"I'll guard them with my life," I teased, hugging them to my chest.

Aubrey couldn't stop smiling. I dropped the shoes on the bed and attacked her with a big squeeze.

"Oh, Aub, you're the best!"

She squeezed me back and pulled me off her smiling. "Come on now, this is me were talking, would I leave you hanging like that?" She flipped her silky blonde hair off her shoulder. "You should probably start getting ready. I can help you with your hair."

I stripped down and slipped on the sophisticated cream-coloured tank dress with stylish boning in it. The thick fabric hugged my curves and was exactly what I was looking for.

Aubrey squinted at me with envy. "Damn you. I love this dress, but it looks better on you."

"Oh, please. You know you looked hot in it."

Smiling, she zipped up the back of the dress for me and then picked up the matching accessories.

I put on the earrings and stared at myself in her mirror.

"Oh, I like it."

"I knew you probably wouldn't want too much bling. The shoes are the show stoppers for sure."

I put the shoes on and flashed her a confident smile, then admired myself in the long mirror. The shoes were gorgeous. I felt so sexy. Excitement started to overwhelm me, making my chest feel full and heavy, but hopeful. "This is perfect."

Man did I feel hot, and it had nothing to do with the exceptionally warm weather. I stepped outside my house and hurried toward Aliah and Edwin, who were impatiently waiting for me.

Aliah was tapping her pointy-toed shoe. "What took you so long?"

Edwin lowered his aviator glasses and gazed at me over the top of them. "I can see what," he said. His eyes slipped down my body and landed on my legs, staying focused there. "Damn!"

"I'll take that as a compliment," I said smiling, hopeful that Cameron would show the same interest.

Edwin helped me in and out of the cab. What was with him all of a sudden? He was very attentive too. Too attentive. Then he turned his gaze from me to Aliah, as we approached the entrance to the venue.

"Hey ladies, what do you say?" he asked, extending us each an elbow.

I figured I could've made it to the table without falling on my face but, just in case, I decided it wouldn't kill me to appease him.

"Oh, what the hell," Aliah said, taking his other arm.

My naughty side liked the idea of getting heads turning early in the night, being bold like that, but the last thing I wanted to do was make Cameron jealous. Our date wasn't official until the reception after dinner, and I didn't want to blow it before then.

My nerves caught my every breath, as I walked into the room on Edwin's arm, cool and confident. Wearing Aubrey's sexy dress and those tall skinny heels, I felt amazing, but my nerves had my tummy doing flip-flops.

Cameron's eyes quickly rose to me, as we entered the dining room. He didn't seem to notice Edwin at all, his sparkling eyes as wide as his grin. Pinned under his gaze, I tightened my grip on Edwin's arm, spellbound by the rush of realization that Cameron wouldn't be sharing his attention with anyone else tonight.

Hunter too was awestruck, when he caught us walking in the room. Aliah stole his attention from Maddie instantly, and it was apparent Aliah just loved that.

Being the last to arrive, there was no choice when it came to seat selection. Edwin led us to the end of the row, and everyone's eyes were locked on us. Three vacant seats were lined up on one side of the long rectangular table. Edwin inconveniently took the seat next to Aliah, so I had to sit at the end. It had to be the farthest seat from Cameron in the place.

Maddie and Hunter sat across from me, so I wasn't totally stranded. It looked like pregnancy was treating her well. Her cheeks were flushed with a healthy radiance and her dark hair glowed with a natural shine. She was surprisingly quiet though.

I sipped on a glass of wine and, before long, food started to line the table. When Edwin wasn't intentionally blocking my view with his imposing shoulders, I caught Cameron's heated glance a couple of times. I returned with a bashful smile each time. The man had such an effect on me.

After dessert, Cameron pushed out his chair and leaned back casually. I decided it was the perfect time to approach him. Edwin gave me a look of disapproval as I lifted my glass of wine from the table and stood from my seat. I ignored him. I had to do what was best for me.

With long, careful strides, I passed all of my coworkers and pulled out the recently vacated seat next to Cameron. When I sat down, I crossed my legs toward him. "We still on for tonight?"

He smirked and cocked his brow. "Unless something happened between yesterday and today that made you change your mind."

"Um...," I paused, teasing. "Nope, nothing I can think of." I rested my wine glass on the table and anxiously brushed my fingers up and down the smooth stem.

Cameron's eyes locked on my fingers, freezing them in place. "Then I'm all yours."

I chewed on my lower lip, while the young lady whose seat I was occupying approached us.

"Mr. Clarke, you're wanted in the reception hall," she said.

"Thank you. Please tell them I'll be right there," he replied, with a soft friendly smile.

Her face lit up, as if he had just complimented her, then she spun around and scurried off to deliver his message.

When Cameron turned that smile on me, it was far from friendly. It issued a warning of what was to come later. My heart thundered heavy in my chest, as he took my hand and kissed it.

"If you'll excuse me," he said, rising from the table. His eyes captured mine and he didn't break his glance until he reached the other end of the table, near my empty seat. He exchanged looks with Edwin as he passed, then stepped outside of the private dinner room.

My heart fluttered in my chest, and I tried to be disappointed. Instead an ecstatic grin was playing on my lips. I sighed aloud and slouched back in my seat, anticipating the rest of our evening together.

Across the table from me, Jacob Miller got up from his seat and left the room with a few others. His wife, Lacy, smiled softly at me, impatiently waiting for her husband to disappear. She finally leaned toward me, her long golden hair falling onto the table, as a thoughtful expression covered her beautiful porcelain face.

"You and Cameron?" she asked, catching me off guard.

"I beg your pardon?"

She leaned in closer. "You and Cameron. You're seeing each other? Jacob didn't tell me that there were any new office romances." She flashed a glance down the long table at Edwin, who was now deep in conversation with Hunter.

"Actually, tonight will be our first date," I explained.

She flashed me her most pleasant smile. "Good for you, Abby. I'm glad to hear you're finding your way. And I must say, you look absolutely beautiful tonight."

"Thank you." My cheeks warmed, so I took a sip of wine, hoping to hide that fact.

"Edwin doesn't look too happy about your date selection, but I think Cameron seems like a fine young man."

I smiled and nodded.

Lacy flashed another harmless glance at Edwin. "Maybe you should get back to him. I think I'm making him anxious," she whispered, smiling.

I stood from my chair and fixed my dress, then retrieved what was left of my glass of wine. "I think you're right," I replied. "It was so nice talking with you, Lacy. Enjoy your night."

She smiled warmly. "Always a pleasure. Good luck with your date."

"Thank you," I mouthed over my shoulder, as I walked away.

Lacy headed for the exit, followed by Maddie. By the time I reached my seat, Edwin and Hunter were the only people left at the table.

"You think maybe we should go see if they're ready for us? The reception is supposed to start in a few minutes," I said.

"Sweet. Let's get this party started," Hunter replied.

Edwin didn't share the same enthusiasm, but followed after me just the same. I headed toward the foyer, where Aliah and Maddie were sharing a surprisingly pleasant word. I checked my reflection in the glass window before proceeding closer to the reception hall.

"Are you ready for this?" Aliah asked, ignorant of Edwin staring her down.

"I think I've waited long enough for this night," I said, not sugar coating things for anyone.

When I noticed the elaborate decorations, I forgot about everything else. The tables were decorated with charming extravagance. No penny was spared for this formal event. As I took it all in, a petite party planner urgently ushered us to the seating chart. *A seating chart?*

I ducked away from Edwin and whispered to Aliah. "So much for that date. Did you know there was a seating plan?"

"Don't worry, it's in the bag," Aliah said, smirking. "I already checked it. Sorry about Cameron's luck, but I'm your date for the night. The chart doesn't lie." She snickered.

My disappointment settled in, as we met up with the party planner. "Abigail Jenkins," I said.

The woman brought her hand to her chin for a moment and appeared deep in thought. "Oh yes, you're at the table with Owen Wallace," she said, running her finger under my name. "Table number twenty one, right in the front there."

I tried to check the list, but only caught one name before she stole the flashlight from the dark page.

Edwin interrupted the woman. "Could you please check to see if Edwin Santora is at that table?" he asked, waiting patiently for confirmation.

"Ah, yes. Here you are, Mr. Santora. I'm afraid you're seated at table number one. It's right along the front as well. You'll be sitting with Jacob Miller's company."

"Lucky me," he said unhappily, slipping away without making a scene.

I turned to Aliah and shrugged my shoulders, as a pair of ushers approached me. Was it wrong that I was relieved that Edwin would be sitting elsewhere? Now I just had to find Cameron.

One of the ushers extended an elbow to each of Aliah and I. We agreeably took his long slim arms and strode alongside him, as he guided us to our table. Owen had just taken his seat, but was the first to stand to pull out my chair.

"Thanks, Owen. Congrats!" I gave him an awkward one-armed hug before taking my seat next to him.

The tall, thin usher pulled out Aliah's chair for her. "Allow me," he said.

"Thank you," she replied, flirtatiously. She lingered by his side flashing him a deviously sexy eye before taking her seat.

I shook my head in disbelief, my lips parted in a half smile, though I wondered how anything surprised me with her anymore. Hunter didn't seem to notice.

Owen nudged me with his elbow, smiling. "It looks like you're stuck sitting next to me tonight."

I smiled and teased him. "I guess it could be worse." Then I glanced at the snobby woman at his side. She was waiting for her formal introduction to the table rather impatiently. She cleared her throat to steal away Owen's attention.

"Oh, yes. How rude of me. This is my friend, Ashley Clarke," he said, tearing his gaze from Ashley long enough to flash a glance at Aliah. "She's my partner in crime for the evening."

Aliah nodded and smiled. "How are you?"

"Good, thanks," Ashley replied kindly.

"You've already met Hunter and Maddison," he continued.

She nodded agreeably, then Owen rested his hand on my shoulder.

"I'm sure you remember my assistant, Abigail," he said.

"Yeah, we've met," she snapped.

Owen seemed surprised by her rudeness. Funny, because it came as no surprise to me.

I fluttered my eyelashes, hoping it would piss her off. "Good to see you, Ashley," I said, lying through my teeth.

She was the only reason I didn't seal the deal with Cameron in the first place. And, speak of the devil. Before another word could be exchanged, the two empty seats across the table were filled with Cameron and some random temp girl, their fists full of drinks from the bar.

Cameron reached a drink out to Owen and Ashley, then took his seat across from me without batting an eye. He accepted his drink from the girl next to him and took a healthy swig of it. *What the hell?*

It was bad enough I had to sit across from him. To see this girl mooning over my new man, it really pressed my buttons. It was ridiculous that I had to sit this close and yet so far from my handsome date. It didn't seem fair.

Cameron, stealing my narrowed eyes, put down his drink in between us and then stared intently at me as our date began. My lips parted softly, so I could breathe, every breath fluttering through my chest as my blood rushed through every limb of my body with a purpose.

A voice boomed over the speakers. "If everyone could please have a seat. We're going to start the ceremony in just a moment."

I stole my eyes from Cameron's mesmeric gaze, when I felt someone else's eyes on me. I glanced over my shoulder casually, hoping to nix that eerie feeling. Sure enough, Edwin was watching me. His eyes were like icy daggers, warning me to stop at once. *Fat chance.*

Maddie seemed to notice and made a point of announcing it to our table. "I'm surprised you weren't put at Edwin's table, eh?" She was obviously ignorant to the date situation, but how could she have known?

Aliah glared at Maddie, displaying her anger and saving me the trouble. She had more reason to be upset with her than I did anyway. To my relief, Cameron only seemed amused by the whole interaction. With a casual glance across the table, I caught his smouldering eyes focused on me. He wasn't leaving anything off the table, including his attraction, and I loved it.

When I mindlessly wet my lips, it only seemed to intrigue him more. *God, I want to touch him. Even just to hold his hand. But to feel his mouth on mine would be magical.*

Ashley finally noticed our enchantment and slapped

Cameron's leg under the table. "Stop doing that," she snapped under her breath, careful to keep Owen from hearing.

Cameron ignored her warning and flashed me a wickedly sexy smile, as he leaned back casually in his chair. His smile softened, but his gorgeous lips continued to silently call my name. My mouth suddenly became very dry. I reached for the empty sparkling glass in front of me.

"Let me get that for you," Owen said, picking up the pitcher filled with ice water.

Aliah stood up and placed her hand over my glass. "Oh, no you don't!"

Owen carefully returned the glass pitcher to the middle of the table, as Aliah filled my wine glass to the brim.

"I'm getting my date drunk tonight," she teased, her grin stretching across her face. "No water for her."

Cameron shot Aliah a jealous glare and it made my heart skip a beat. Hunter broke out laughing and Maddie only smiled. *What has gotten into her?* She was awfully quiet. I only hoped everything was okay with the baby.

It was time for the reception to begin and all of the attention was on Owen. He was pulled from his seat and casually stood next to my chair, being congratulated by the late arrivers.

"Jaxon, take a seat," Joshua Bailey boomed over the speakers.

Justice Jaxon, a popular judge in the City, cocked a brow at the ingenious Bailey who was standing at the front of the room behind the microphone. Justice Jaxon patted Owen on the shoulder, bid him congratulations and moseyed back to his seat.

"I've always wanted to say that," Bailey added, getting the whole crowd to chuckle. "Welcome all and thank you for coming. It looks like it's up to me to give the opening statement. You would think they'd give me a night off," he teased.

There were more chuckles around the room.

Bailey gave the party a list of reasons why Owen was

best suited for the promotion. I myself had agreed just yesterday that I would say a little something, and that was only because Owen begged me to. *Why did I agree to that? I absolutely hate public speaking.*

As Bailey continued on, like he always did, I ticked off nearly every sentence I had so carefully prepared for my speech. *Now what the hell was I going to say?*

"Now I would ask Abigail Jenkins and Cameron Clarke to come on up and say a few words," Bailey announced.

Shit! Everyone started clapping and I squinted at Cameron, shocked yet relieved to hear that we were both going up together. We hadn't collaborated our speeches and suddenly I was petrified to say what little was left of mine. He, on the other hand, was a pro in a courtroom and so anything next to his speech would be mediocre at best.

He walked around the table nonchalantly and, when he got to my chair, he asked me to bring my drink. It was still rather full, and apart from not wanting to spill it all over, I needed a drink to get through this. I took two unattractive gulps before standing at his side. His understanding smile cut off my air supply and worried me even more.

Cameron held out his elbow and graciously escorted me to the stand. *Mmm, he smells so good.*

After we approached the podium, Cameron shook Bailey's hand and then rested his hand on the small of my back. My senses spiked on fire from the small gesture, making my arms cover in tiny mountains and my throat to burn in flames.

Cameron brought his lips to my ear, all eyes on me in front of the microphone. I thought I might faint. "Ladies first," he whispered.

I checked his eyes for inspiration. I found some, but not the kind needed to plough through a speech. Regardless, I smiled and nodded and opened my mouth. My voice sounded more than a little shaky at first. Then, with Cameron at my side, I found my ability to speak.

"Owen has worked really hard to get where he is, and it has been my pleasure to come along for the ride. It couldn't have happened to a better person," I said, with nothing more left on my crinkled paper.

Before I could spit out an awkward congratulations, Cameron stepped in and started speaking, making us sound like a cohesive unit. I looked to Cameron appreciatively and tried to take a step aside, but he pulled me back with his hand firmly gripped on my hip and included me in his deliverance.

"Doesn't Abigail look lovely tonight?" he announced.

Hoots and hollers poured from my friends and colleagues, only embarrassing me more, but my cheeks were already warm from the stress of it all. He delivered the rest of his speech smoothly, like a pro. He had the crowd laughing and hanging on his every word.

"I couldn't be luckier to work with such great people," Cameron announced, eyeing me like a piece of delicious meat. "Oh and Owen's great too."

I blushed again, but I doubt anyone but Cameron noticed, as they all laughed hysterically. *Now he's a comedian too? What can't this man do?*

Cameron told a brief story about Owen in University and everyone seemed to be devouring it. "Congratulations, Owen, from both of us," he said, his hand skimming sensually up my back.

I like the sound of that. I couldn't even wash the honest smile and breathless joy from my face.

Cameron raised his glass toward Owen and looked to me, then his eyes flashed over the crowd, as he waited for me to raise my glass.

"I would like to propose a toast, if everyone would please raise their glasses," he said, and paused for the crowd to follow. "To Owen: We wish you the brightest future filled with success and promises of a long and prosperous career."

The company cheered and glasses clinked all around the room. Cameron turned to me and smiled. "Cheers," he said, in a low sexy voice.

"Cheers," I said, gazing dreamily at him.

We clinked our wine glasses together before taking a sip, our eyes glued on each other. He was so steady and so confident, our lingering stare heated with a newfound connection.

"How do you do that?" I asked, still awestruck with his performance.

"Do what?" he replied, smoothly. He casually took my free hand in his and linked our fingers together, in front of the entire crowd.

I nearly lost my train of thought as he drew his thumb over my knuckles and slowly led me to my seat. "That whole witty charm thing. It's ridiculous," I said, smiling. *And utterly sexy.* I decidedly left that part out, knowing we still had an audience.

He laughed. "Oh, come on now, they loved it."

"No, it was great," I admitted. Sharing a moment, lost in time, his smiling eyes pierced my heart and swept me off my feet. I wanted nothing more than to kiss those smiling lips and lose myself in those dreamy eyes.

CHAPTER EIGHT

After the ceremonious introduction of Owen as Partner, the company applauded him and a few unruly drunks cheered as he shook hands with his new Partners. Cameron, sitting in Owen's seat, released my hand long enough to clap in congratulations, then swiftly seized it again. Owen quickly said his thank yous and wished everyone a fun and safe evening.

Aliah was rocking in her seat, eager to get to the partying, and I couldn't wait to leave myself in Cameron's capable hands. As the lights dimmed and the bar reopened, Aliah snatched my clasped hand from Cameron's grip. "What do you say we hit the ladies room?" she asked.

We were half way to the door before I could even gather my voice. I glanced at Cameron over my shoulder, a dainty shrug delivering my silent apology. Cameron flashed me a smile from across the room and it still appealed to me, even with his sister shrieking in his ear.

The line-up of thirsty professionals crowded the bar in a matter of seconds. Aliah had me by the hand and pulled me through the group of people already streaming from the bar. There was a line up for the facilities too, but Aliah didn't care. She happily took her place at the end of the line.

"Did I miss something here?" Aliah screeched. "Owen has a date and it's Cameron's sister?"

"They're likely just friends," I stated.

"I know who won't be friends with her any time soon. You."

"Tell me about it."

"Cameron certainly wasn't shy about you though. Man did that bug her." Aliah smiled wickedly.

"She's made it obvious on more than one occasion that she doesn't like me very much. She's the one I was telling you about. The one who ruined my night with Cameron."

"No shit! That explains a lot."

We finally made it inside the washroom, but stood motionless outside the first stall. The sounds of violent vomiting echoed through the room, followed by a swish of the toilet. It seemed awfully early for that, our party having just started. Something was definitely wrong.

"Everything okay in there?" Aliah called.

"I'm not well at all," the woman moaned.

"Maddison?" I said, shocked.

"Who do you think?" she snapped. "It must be morning sickness or something. I have to go home," she cried.

Aliah flashed me a devilish smile, making me wonder if she had something to do with it.

"Do you want us to call you a cab?" I asked, concerned.

Aliah started feverishly calling a cab company, like it was her life line.

"Could you, please? And can you tell Hunter too? I don't want to puke in front of him." She barely got the words out, before she filled the toilet again.

I suddenly lost the urge to pee and left the room to catch some fresh air. Moments later Maddie and Aliah joined me in the hall. Though Maddie was still looking a little green, Aliah glowed brighter than ever.

I stole a glance out the front doors where a cab had just pulled up. I hurried forward, racing to stop the cab before it left. "Come on," I said.

The cabbie took one look at Maddison and shook his head disapprovingly. She got in the car and Aliah politely closed the door behind her.

"Don't worry, she's just prego," Aliah called to the driver, through the open passenger window.

Maddie scowled at Aliah as the cab pulled away.

Aliah couldn't restrain herself. "Woo hoo!" she hollered, so loud it echoed into the night as the daylight faded.

"Whoa, what's that all about?" I asked, giggling.

Aliah's smile could've been seen from a mile away. "Hunter is all mine now!"

"Ah. I see." I ushered Aliah on, to get away from the stinky smokers who were hovering near the exit. "Let's get back in there."

"Right, I almost forgot, you have a studly man waiting for you."

I smiled and chewed on my bottom lip, remembering just how studly Cameron looked tonight. Aliah hooked onto my arm and dragged me inside. The DJ was already mixing some upbeat music and people had already made their way to the dance floor.

"Let's get our drink on! This is our night," Aliah shouted.

We headed to the bar and she instantly flagged down a handsome bartender, who wearing a crisp white shirt and silky black vest. Others had been anxiously awaiting their turn and weren't very pleased with the order of service.

"Just another advantage of looking hot," Aliah hollered to me.

I slapped her hand in a ridiculously immature high five.

Cameron caught the exchange, after shoving his way closer to me. "So, how does that work exactly?" he growled, close to my ear.

I turned and smiled at him, without speaking, and hooked my arms over his shoulders, letting my body language answer his question. *Mmm, and he was all mine.*

The bartender handed Aliah our drinks and I had to detach myself from Cameron to take mine from her. We squeezed free of the crowd in search of a clearing on the floor.

Before making it very far, we ran into Hunter, his black hair spiked up every which way. "Hey, Abigail. Nice speech," he hollered. "You guys must've practiced that one."

I glanced up at Cameron and his eyes smiled back, a shockwave of temptation slamming me right between the thighs. "Thanks, Hunter," I said, totally distracted.

"Have you met Hunter before?" Aliah asked Cameron, as he shook his head no. "This is Hunter Wight, my man!"

Cameron looked to me confused. "If he's *her* man, then

why was he sitting with Maddison?" he asked softly in my ear.

"Long story, buddy," Hunter replied, patting him on the back. "Abby can tell you that one another night when you have some time to spare." Hunter began to glance anxiously around the room. "Has anyone seen Maddie? She took off during the speeches and I haven't seen her since."

Aliah latched on to Hunter's side and wrapped her arms around his neck, dangling her drink behind his back. "Don't worry about Maddison, baby. She's fine."

"Just a little morning sickness," I added. "We sent her home in a cab."

Cameron's eyes opened wide and his eyebrows raised in surprise. He likely didn't even know Maddie was pregnant, since she had decidedly kept it quiet and was barely showing. Now he knew.

"I should go check on her," Hunter suggested.

"No!" Aliah cried out, then said more softly, "She said you shouldn't worry about her and that you should stay and have a good time with me."

A smile quickly formed on Hunter's mouth. "She said that, did she?"

"Oh, you shut up. Let's hit the dance floor," she hollered. She tugged him away and it was apparent he was staying whether he liked it or not.

Cameron took my hand in his and locked his sparkling eyes on me before slowly leading me to the packed dance floor. My heart thudded hard against my rib cage and a smile was plastered on my face for the rest of the evening.

We danced with the other partygoers and, as the night went on, Cameron and I became more and more flirtatious. He wouldn't let go of me and I didn't want him to. The more Aliah drank, the more she threw herself at Hunter. They were all over each other too.

Suddenly, the song changed and Aliah dropped Hunter to run to me. "Oh my God! I love this song," she screeched. She grabbed my hands and reached them for the sky. Then she leaned forward and shook her chest at me.

Cameron let me loose and I danced like no one was watching. But he was. And yet I felt so free, as Aliah and I pranced around like drunken lesbian lovers. I slid down to the floor and back up, erotically brushing myself against Aliah.

"Woo!" Aliah yelped.

Cameron's eyes never left my hips, a serious stare locked on his face. He slipped closer to us, staking his claim, so no other man would dare make a move on me. It wouldn't have mattered. I was as good as his.

The song ended and I realized I was out of a drink. I raised my glass in the air, to show Aliah the emptiness and to see if she wanted another. She shook her head no.

I wrapped an arm over Cameron's shoulder, plastering my body to his. "I'm going to go get another drink," I said provocatively. "Want to come with?"

He raised his eyebrows, and the way he wrinkled his forehead was so damn attractive that I couldn't take no for an answer. With a wicked smile, I grabbed him by the tie and playfully pulled it over my shoulder, dragging him behind me.

"You're outta control," he hollered, with a sexy grin slanted on his lips.

I spun around and pulled him up against me, releasing his tie, and looking him right in the eye. "But in a good kind of way right?"

His lips parted as he tilted his head to show me just how good. He lowered his mouth to mine, throwing caution to the wind, as he pressed the most heartfelt kiss against my lips. My eyes fell shut, as his lips captured mine, again and again, every nerve in my body standing on end like it had been electrocuted.

When he deepened the kiss, his warm tongue teased over my teeth like he was tasting a sample and his lips were as soft, sweet and delicious as they looked. I could kiss him all night.

After another soft brush over my lips, Cameron lifted his mouth from mine. "I've been waiting a long time for that," he said, in a low, velvet voice.

Some rough housing hooligans bumped me out of his arms, before I had the chance to respond. Cameron was shoved onto a pile of angered people who were all knocked to the floor. I stumbled against some others as another woman tripped and splashed her purple drink all over my creamy white dress.

My mouth dropped open in horror and my hands rose up to block the others from clobbering me. The crowd separated me farther from Cameron and closer to the woman with the dangerously empty cup. When she noticed the damage, her eyes popped wide open.

"Oh my gosh! I am so sorry," she squealed.

I didn't want to look down, but I could feel the wetness touching my skin. A quick glance exposed a terrible purple stain soaked into my sister's otherwise perfect dress. "My sister is going to kill me," I moaned. The dress looked hideous.

The woman paused a moment. "Abigail?"

I hesitated, then squinted up at her. The room was dark and my feet were unsteady. Perhaps I'd had one too many beverages already.

She smiled a familiar smile. "It's me! Come on now it hasn't been that long."

I squinted at her harder. "Jessica? It's been years."

"Yeah, but I see nothing's changed. Edwin's still getting in fights over you," she said, all smiles.

"What are you talking about?" I asked, confused.

She pointed a dainty finger. "Edwin just about took that guy's head off when he suggested that you were getting a little hot and heavy with blondie over there. If it weren't for Edwin, you wouldn't be wearing my drink right now."

I was unimpressed with Edwin's act of jealousy. "I think you've got it all wrong. I'm not with Eddie anymore."

Now she was the one marked with confusion. "Oh, so you don't live with him then?"

I sighed, not wanting to get into it; especially now that Cameron was making his way back to my side.

"Are you okay?" he asked, running his hand down my back and resting it on my hip.

I shook my head no, despite the spark of exhilaration running up my spine prompted by his touch. "Look at me. I'm a mess. I'm going to try and clean up a bit."

He kissed me on my flushed cheek. "You still look breathtaking to me," he whispered, close to my ear.

I couldn't help but smile, even considering the circumstances. Cameron could make anything seem trivial.

"I'm going to go now," I said, but didn't want to leave.

He winked at me. "I'll be here."

Jessica followed me to the exit. "I'll help you. It's the least I can do." She walked with me to the ladies room and we didn't exchange another word until we got inside.

"So, are you going to explain to me the whole living arrangements thing?" she asked, not wasting any time.

I squinted at her, a little angered by her selfishness. If it weren't for her clumsiness, I would be in Cameron's arms right now. "Why are you so concerned? Yeah, we live together, but that's as far as it goes. Eddie is single, as far as I know."

Jessica's smile grew five times larger, and I finally realized what was going on. "So, you wouldn't mind if I..."

"Absolutely. By all means. You don't need my permission," I said, cutting her off.

She sighed with relief. "Okay. Thanks. I just didn't want to step on anyone's toes."

Sudden realization stunned me. "No! The shoes!" I lifted one foot at a time to carefully inspect Aubrey's shoes. Somehow I managed to keep them spotless throughout the whole incident. "That was a close call. They're my sister's."

Jessica nodded. "Sorry about the dress."

"Yeah, that's Aubrey's too." I sighed. "So, how have you been? You kind of dropped off the map after high school. I haven't seen you around in a while."

"Good," Jessica replied. "Just came along with a friend to this party. I had no idea I'd catch up with all you guys here. We should get coffee some time," she offered.

"Absolutely," I replied, though I remembered our imperfect friendship and was undecided whether I was truly interested.

She typed my number into her cell phone, while I dabbed the last of the colour out of the dress. Despite my best efforts, there was a light stain that remained as a permanent reminder of Edwin's jealousy.

"Don't worry about it, Abby. No one will even notice," Jessica suggested.

That was an outright lie. The dress was ruined. I nodded and followed her out of the room.

"Is blondie, the guy you're here with, your new man? He's gorgeous."

I smiled in agreement. "Yeah, but he's not exactly my man just yet. This is sort of our first date."

"You could have fooled me," Jessica said, as we walked back toward the reception hall together.

When we returned, it felt like everyone was gawking at me. I worried that I looked horrendous in my stained dress, but when I glanced down at myself I was satisfied that my discoloured dress looked just fine in the dark.

Owen came toward us and slipped an arm over my shoulder. I laughed. He was drunk.

"Owen, don't you know you're supposed to be out of here by now," I teased. "The Partners always sneak off after speeches, so they can keep out of trouble."

"Yeah, keep out of trouble with their wives," he snapped loudly. "Not to worry, I'll be leaving shortly. I know my place," he said, smiling. "Thank you for coming. It means a lot." His face was right up in mine.

I flipped his arm off my shoulder. "You've had too much to drink, Owen. Get out of here," I said, laughing.

He nodded at Jessica and stumbled off. Jessica didn't even acknowledge him, lost in her own little world. She was obviously looking for someone in the thinning crowd. I knew exactly who she was looking for. It kind of bothered me, though I knew it shouldn't have.

My eyes wandered the room, casually looking for

Cameron. I found him near the bar and he seemed to be having a heated argument with his sister. It was actually pretty amusing to watch. It more looked like Ashley was arguing fiercely with him, but he wasn't really paying her any attention.

He caught my eye and raised his hand in acknowledgement. He started to make a yapping motion with his hand, mocking Ashley, and it made me laugh. I couldn't stop smiling at him and when Ashley discovered the distraction, she pulled him away for his undivided attention.

Would we ever get a chance to just be together? Everyone was making it so difficult. I redirected my eyes back to Jessica and by the look on her face I could tell she had spotted Edwin.

"Hey Jess, so did you move back home? I heard you were living in Toronto," I said.

"Actually, I was living in Toronto for a while, but I just wasn't cut out for the big City life, you know?" Jessica said. "I'm staying with my parents now, while I look for a place of my own. Who knew you had to leave this place to realize what it's worth?"

Having lived in the City of Rose Arbour my entire life, I really wouldn't know.

"Ladies!" Edwin hollered in his drunken stupor, traversing our stalemate conversation.

I looked around to see who was watching. Everyone was. "Shouldn't you be watching yourself, Eddie? You say you want to make Partner someday."

He playfully slapped his hand to the side of my cheek and held it there. "So concerned, Abby." His aqua eyes were all wishy-washy. "You really think I stand a chance now that they've got your boyfriend?"

Jealousy. Envy. Anger. And there was nothing I could say to make him feel better right now. What he said was true. Cameron was an excellent lawyer and he had a lot more experience than Edwin. Edwin would have to get in line.

At the risk of hurt feelings – mine - I decided to do one good deed for the night. "Hey, TJ!" I called. "You're not doing a very good job of keeping this unruly guy under control," I teased, squeezing onto Edwin's hulking arm.

A smile cracked on TJ's handsome face. "I can only do so much, girl," he replied, pulling up to Edwin's side.

"Did you guys see Jessica's here?" I asked, as I pushed her in front of me.

She immediately locked eyes on Edwin and her soft smile turned seductive. "Hey. Long-time no see," she said, lifting her chest in case the guys had missed her luscious endowment.

Edwin nearly knocked her over with a hug and her face told me that she enjoyed it. "Let's get you another drink," Edwin said, taking my bait. He lifted his beer bottle and stared at it for a second, then downed the last few gulps. "Let's do shots! Come on, Abs."

Dammit, Edwin. Just go with Jessica already!

"No, I probably shouldn't," I said. *I really shouldn't.* I didn't want to make myself sick and ruin what was left of my date.

"Oh, come on," TJ taunted.

"You're doing one," Edwin ordered. He took my hand and dragged me to the bar.

I figured it was harmless enough and maybe it would get him off my back. "Fine, but let's do it now before I change my mind."

"Yes!" Edwin hollered, like he had just won the lottery.

Jessica flashed me an unimpressed smile, as he ordered a round of tequila shots. It was clear she wanted Edwin to herself.

You want him? He's yours.

I crowded right up at the bar next to Edwin and watched the bartender pour the tequila down the long line of glasses. Hunter and Aliah scooted up next to me and were the first to drink their shots. Edwin looked to me, waiting for my move.

"You first," I said.

Without warning, he clasped onto my wrist, wet it with his long, warm tongue and shook some salt on it. He licked me again, more dramatically this time, then downed the shot, skipping the lemon. Everyone at the bar, except for Jessica, was laughing hysterically. I was standing there in shock.

"Now you," he insisted, as he rolled up his sleeves and extended out his naked arm.

"I don't think so," I said, laughing as I shoved his arm away.

Everyone else grabbed their shots and clinked their glasses together, splashing liquor everywhere, before swallowing them in unison.

Edwin looked at me with disgust, in a way that he had only once ever looked at me before. How can he be that upset about one shot? I shivered with dread as he held his icy stare, his eyes drilling through me and penetrating my heart.

When Cameron's arm came around my waist, I realized the evil eye wasn't meant for me at all.

"There's a better way," Cameron said smoothly, his lips close to my ear. He took my other wrist in his warm masculine hand, licked and salted it and then handed me the tequila.

Cameron sucked from my lemon slice and nudged me to lick the salt. I did, then downed the shot as quickly as I could. I slammed the glass on the bar and made a sour face from the flavour, as Cameron pulled me against him and sealed his lips to mine.

His kiss was slow and erotic, and his tongue tasted like warm, juicy lemons. He slowly tormented my mouth with unrestrained desire, his body long, hard and sleek. Unwilling to grasp reality and unable to stop, I wrapped my arms around his neck and drew my fingers through his short spiky hair. He held my weakened body against his, strong, lean and steady.

Hunter laughed and Aliah clapped. Even Jessica enjoyed the entertainment.

Cameron drew his lips away from mine. "And that, my friends, is how it's done," he said, his eyes capturing mine.

I panted for air, breathless from his devouring kiss. I wanted more. Needed more.

Edwin was unimpressed and motioned for two more shots from the bartender. He hauled Jessica into his arms, leaned her back, licked her neck and salted her to taste. No doubt, he was trying to show up Cameron. He gave Jessica his lemon and she sucked on it, delighted, as he licked the salt from her neck. Edwin drank his tequila, then shoved his tongue down her throat.

Cameron nodded his head at Edwin, acknowledging his concept.

The bartender pushed the next shot in my direction. Cameron watched me put my hand up and shake my head no. It would be the death of me.

Edwin reached for it and slid the shot down the bar for Jessica, before curling his arm around her. I could see that Jessica might just get what she wanted tonight. He motioned for the bartender to pour him another shot. Instead of a shot glass, a glass of clear liquid with ice slid his way.

"What's this? I ordered tequila!" he argued.

"You've had enough tonight," the bartender insisted.

"You're cutting me off? This is fucking ridiculous!" Edwin started to stomp around, his eyes scattering across the floor. He looked like he was ready to cause trouble.

"Come on Edwin, it's not worth it," Jessica suggested, flashing an icy stare at me.

"Fine. We'll go somewhere else. This party sucks anyways," he replied.

Aliah squeezed me into her arm, drunker than ever. "Abby! How's my best friend ever?" she hollered, not even noticing Edwin's fit.

"Drink much?" I teased.

"Yeah! Let's dance." She headed for the dance floor and pulled me behind her. Hunter followed us and Cameron wasn't far behind him.

When we reached an opening I stopped for a second and glanced back to the guys. Behind them in the distance I saw Edwin glaring at me, with Jessica wrapped around his waist. After stealing my eye, Edwin dropped a kiss on her, then they snuck off through the emergency exit.

Though I was mad at his childish behaviour, I refused to let him ruin my night. I focused in on the handsome blonde before me and he pulled me into his arms.

"Finally. I get you all to myself," Cameron said.

We danced and danced, until the crowd started to dwindle. Everyone formed a large circle on the floor and random guys took turns being goofs in the middle to get the ladies attention. Cameron was smiling and I couldn't stop laughing. We were all having such a great time.

By two thirty in the morning, nearly all of us had decided it was home time. Having had way too many cocktails to drive, I was happy to stumble to a cab. Though Cameron had driven himself, he too had too much to drink. We headed for the door and outside for some fresh air.

It was a beautiful starlit night. I inhaled a deep breath of the fresh cool air. I wasn't ready for the night to be over and I didn't want our date to end.

"You aren't driving home," I stated. It wasn't a question.

"I know," he replied, tugging me against him. "I'm going home with you."

I raised my eyebrows. *Okay.* "Is that so?"

He planted a soft kiss on my lips that I felt right down to my toes. "I'm just playing. This is a first date. Do I look like that kind of guy to you?"

After I mopped myself up off the ground, from laughing hysterically, I joined the rest of the group waiting at the curb.

Everyone was chatting about all the fun that they had and, as the first cab pulled up, I watched them all rush to it. It was a van, but it didn't take long for it to load up. Another cab slowly pulled up behind it. I stumbled in my heels and Cameron caught me before I fell.

I smiled up at him. "Are you coming?"

Smiling, he led me to the faded yellow car, as Hunter and Aliah ran from the building holding hands. She didn't see me and headed straight for the van.

"Wait for us!" Aliah hollered.

TJ caught Hunter's attention first. "Hunter, why don't you come with us? We're heading out your way," he shouted from the van.

Aliah had been attached to Hunter all night and I knew she wasn't going to let him leave her without a fight. "Do you have room for one more?" she asked, flashing Hunter a suggestive glance.

"Yeah, we can make two fit. But wouldn't it make more sense for you to go with Abby? Your house is way out of our way," TJ said.

Aliah's eyes dropped down the sidewalk and landed on me. "Are you okay?" she mouthed.

I nodded and smiled wide, my sophistication clearly altered by the alcohol in my system. "You go have fun. I'll talk to you in the morning," I insisted.

That was all Hunter needed to hear. "No, TJ. She's coming with me." He lifted Aliah into his arms and took the last seat in the van, propping her on his lap. She was elated.

The door closed and she waved back at me as they sped off. Only Cameron and I were left standing there. *Alone at last.*

CHAPTER NINE

The van drove off into the star-filled night, leaving Cameron and I gazing into each other's eyes.

He took both of my hands and linked them with his. "It looks like it's just you and me."

Butterflies danced in my belly. "Guess so," I answered, suddenly feeling shy and anxious.

He opened the cab door for me. My dress was short enough that I had to be careful not to give him a good peek at my panties. I sat down with my legs together and swung them into the car like a lady. He smiled at my efforts, but it didn't look as though he was expecting a show. I was amazed how composed he was, a complete gentleman, even after all he had to drink.

"So this is what I have to do to get you alone?" he said quietly, as he slid next to me on the seat.

He reached his arm around me and I nestled against him, fitting snuggly under his arm. It felt so nice.

"Where did you say you lived? I'd like him to drop you off first," he said, then directed the cabby downtown.

"No, no. We can drop you off first. Your house is on the way."

He tilted my chin, until our eyes met. "I don't want to leave you alone," he said, seemingly tormented. After a pause, he brushed my lips with another amazing kiss.

After redirecting the cab driver to Cameron's house, I nestled back into my place under his arm. When the cab came to a full stop on the side of the road, Cameron sighed, torn with a decision.

"Would you like to come in for a coffee?" he asked.

"I really shouldn't. It's pretty late," I said, wishing I didn't have to be so damn sensible.

"You have plans for the morning?" He was disappointed.

"No," I replied, smiling like a fool in love.

Not detaching from our cozy position, he whispered in my ear. "I'm going to ask you something and I'll understand if you say no." He hesitated for a second, then continued. "I would really love it if you would spend the night with me."

My eyes darted around the cab. "Uh... I..." I couldn't form a useful sentence. *Hell yeah!*

Cameron cut me off with a long cool finger to my well-kissed lips. "No expectations, of course. Just a warm body to lie next to," he said softly, sensing my distress. His eyes were completely serious and swelled with sweet desperation.

I wanted to say yes, but I had to say no. *I really want to jump his bones, but on a first date? I'm just not that kind of girl. I have rules.* I swallowed the lump from my throat and searched for the words to explain it to him.

Beating me to the chase, he continued. "In fact, my daughter's home and I have a strict rule about sexual intimacy before being in a serious relationship."

"Oh!" I replied, shocked by the sudden confession. I hoped my disappointment wasn't so transparent. "I have a three date rule anyway and this is hardly even a first date," I blurted, without thinking. "I'm sorry." I plastered my cold hands to my hot forehead.

He ignored my drunken comment. "Stay with me."

My tipsy mind was playing tricks on me and I couldn't think clearly being put on the spot like that. What man really wants to just cuddle? Cameron's eyes were even more persuasive than his words and they made my decision easy. I smiled warmly at him and let out a sigh.

Cameron smiled back, complete with unwavering patience and stunning sex appeal. The influence his confident smile had over my intoxicated body was even more convincing.

The cabby grew more impatient by the second. "Are you getting out here or what, lady?"

"Excuse me?" Cameron said firmly to the cab driver, leaning toward him in silent threat. He was brooding, draped in heavy shadows, and it looked like he might rip the cab driver's head off if he made any sudden moves. Dangerous. Protective. It was hot.

"I'm sorry," the driver insisted, his back pressed against the dash. "I have a family at home. This is my last call of the night; and it has been a long night."

I got out of the car as quickly as I could. "Thank you for the ride. Sorry for the trouble," I said, as I rummaged through my purse for some cash.

Cameron joined me on the side of the road and rested his hand on mine. Apparently he had already paid the driver and, by the look of astonishment on the family man's face, he had left a generous tip.

"Thank you," I said to Cameron, as the car pulled away.

"You never told me your decision," he teased, as we stood in the street under a dim lamp.

"What do *you* think?" I asked, stepping up onto the curb.

He sighed and stepped past me, his shiny black shoes sinking into the blue weed-free lawn. "I just hope it's not because you felt bad for that guy," he said. He looked me in the eye, then smiled and glanced down at the grass.

I stepped closer to him, clutched onto his jacket and glanced up through dark lashes. "Sure, I felt bad for the guy," I whispered, pausing. "But I'm only here for you."

Cameron carefully ran his fingers through my hair. So dreamy. He tucked his hand behind my neck and dropped a tender kiss on my lips. So romantic.

The experience was magical. Our emotions wrapped us in a warm barrier from the cold night. I hooked my arms around him and settled under his jacket. His back was firm beneath my fingers, his chest solid beneath my cheek.

He drew my lips back to his and, now that he was free of competition, all aggression had left him. His tongue gently explored my mouth and his hands tickled over my exposed back. After indulging in his dreamy kisses, I retrieved my arms from around him and wet my grinning lips, waiting for him to invite me inside.

He brushed his thumb across my sensitive lip, sending

shivers to my core. Then he took my hand and led me up his paved drive toward his subtle but cozy little brick bungalow. The closer we got to his front door, the more anxious I became. As I climbed the last stair on his small cement porch, I buckled at the knees.

Cameron collected me into his arms before I landed on my ass. "What is it?" he asked, concerned.

"I'm nervous," I whispered. *And drunk.*

His cool fingers brushed my warm cheek. "There's no need to be, Abby," he said, mere inches from my lips.

"But your daughter," I whispered.

"Don't worry. She's probably asleep." He clasped my hand firmly in his, each of our fingers intertwined, then he opened the sturdy red door very quietly.

I took a deep breath and my mobility returned to me, as he guided me slowly into his darkened home. I stumbled over a rug in my sexy shoes and bumped into his back. He spun around, tugged me into his arms and delivered another breathtaking kiss before exposing his amusement.

Then, he wrinkled his sexy forehead. "I should probably warn you. My babysitter, well it's Ashley. My mom had to call it an early night. Needless to say, she won't be too impressed that I've brought you home with me."

I gulped down my fear, preparing myself for the storm. "Anything else I should know?"

He smiled back. "I wish there weren't, but it seems that Pheobe is still awake. She doesn't like when I go out and she has a hard time sleeping when I leave. I thought she would've passed out by now."

I nodded with understanding, while my anxiety shot through the roof. Focusing on his lips didn't make relaxing any easier.

"It makes it difficult for me to have much of a social life, but she's more important to me than that. I may have to lie down with her for a bit to get her to fall asleep," he explained.

Swoon. He is so damn cute. "Of course," I replied softly. After slipping off my shoes, I tip-toed after him through the narrow doorway that led to his cozy living room.

There we found Ashley sitting on the sofa watching a children's movie. His daughter, Pheobe, was lying on her lap. Ashley exhaled with exhaustion, still wearing her dress from earlier in the night.

"I'm sorry Cam, but she just would not go to sleep," she said, before realizing he had company. "This is her third movie!"

A precious little girl was resting there quietly, not taking her sleepy eyes off the television. She was so adorable. Cameron looked at me and smiled, gauging my reaction to seeing his child.

He stepped closer to Ashley and kept his voice soft. "Thanks for watching her. I think I can take it from here."

"You know I'm here for you," she said, as she shimmied out from under Pheobe. It wasn't until she rounded the sofa that she realized I was in the room. She immediately showed herself to the door, anger coursing through her thin frame.

"I'm going now, but you'll have some explaining to do in the morning. I can't believe you brought her home with you after our talk," she snapped, glaring at me through evil eyes. She picked up her purse and searched for her keys. "At least he picked an attractive whore," she mumbled, in an attempt to offend me.

I took it as a compliment.

Cameron's exasperation was obvious. With his anger mounting, he followed Ashley to the door. "Come on, Ash. Give me a break." He turned back to me, with concern-filled eyes. "I apologize for my sister. Please excuse me for a minute."

He stopped at the front door before following Ashley outside. "You can't seriously be mad at me," Cameron said, loud enough that I heard him. "It's been over six years now. I'll have to get on with my life some time, you know."

In the next instant the door closed and the house was silent, except for the quiet hum of the television. I stood awkwardly next to the sofa and glanced at Pheobe, who had been lying there so quietly it was as though she wasn't even in the room.

I tip-toed around the sofa and peeked at the cutie curled up on the couch. She was obviously overtired and I figured it wouldn't hurt if I lent a helping hand.

"Hello there. I'm Abigail. But you can call me Abby. I'm a friend of your dad. We work together."

She answered with a smile. It was encouraging.

"I just wanted to make sure he got home okay. I hope you don't mind," I said softly. I sat beside her and smiled.

She flashed me her sleepy blue eyes, then widened them a little farther to examine me. "I'm Pheobe," she said, in an adorable little voice. "Your dress is pretty."

"Thank you. You're very sweet." *My gosh, I absolutely love kids and this one is a total sweetheart.* I patted the couch beside me. "Why don't you come lie next to me? It's really late. You should try to get some sleep," I said.

She sat up beside me, knocking her blanket to the floor. "But I'm hungry," she explained.

My tummy growled, not having eaten a morsel myself in hours. "Do you know where we can find a snack?" I asked.

She nodded eagerly and hopped up. "Come on," she whispered, like it was our little secret. I trailed behind her, until she needed my help to open the neatly organized pantry. She grabbed out two chocolate chip granola bars and handed one to me.

"Wow, thank you," I said, taking it from her precious little hand. "Where will I find the cups?"

She instantly pointed to an upper cabinet out of her reach. I pulled out two cups and filled them half full with water from the fridge dispenser, then placed one in front of her. She had already swallowed half of her snack before I sat down beside her. She *must* have been hungry.

"Look at your beautiful hair. You know people pay big bucks to get their hair to look just like yours," I told her.

She giggled with glee as I finished my snack. I was a little concerned that Cameron still hadn't come back inside, by the time we were finished eating, but watching Pheobe mindlessly twirl her hair around her little finger told me my job wasn't done just yet.

"Maybe we should move this party to your bedroom. What do you think?" I asked.

Pheobe nodded her head and hopped to her feet. She wrapped her little hand around my fingers and pulled me down the hall. "This way!" The old wood floors creaked beneath our feet in the otherwise quiet house.

She carefully clicked on her night light and crawled into her four poster bed fit for a princess. I pulled her covers up to her chin and sat down next to her. She rested her head on my lap and smiled at me unconditionally. She was so sweet and innocent, the exact opposite of the thoughts that had been twirling in my head about what I wanted to do with her father.

I couldn't keep the smile from my lips if I wanted to. "Daddy's home, you know. It's okay for you to go to sleep now," I reassured her. I stroked her soft hair and hummed a tune, my motherly instincts kicking in.

She closed her eyes in an instant, let out a yawn and quickly sank into a deep sleep.

"Goodnight, Pheobe," I whispered, but I don't even think she heard me. She was out like a light.

I heard the front door open and I hoped it wouldn't wake her. I continued to pet her hair and appreciate her sweetness, as the door latched shut.

Faintly, I heard creaky footsteps approaching the living room, then nothing. A moment later, I turned toward the door and there he was, watching me adore his daughter and her peaceful slumber.

The concern showing in Cameron's expression startled me. Perhaps I had crossed the line. Maybe I had overstepped some invisible boundary. Was I wrong to introduce myself to his daughter? I was too scared to leave the bedside and unsure how to explain myself, so I just continued to mindlessly brush Pheobe's hair with my fingers, my eyes locked on her soft, milky white skin.

Cameron crossed the room and settled into a white slip-covered comfy chair. I glanced up at him, hoping to figure out what he was thinking, but unable to read into his dark brooding stare. His intense eyes were bolted to mine, until he finally shifted them to the floor.

His quiet chuckle tickled my ears. "You're even more amazing than I thought," he whispered. "If that is at all possible."

His words filled my heart with love and made me feel pretty damn special. My cheeks flushed with heat, but I felt safe that the heavily shadowed room gave me good cover. I stared at Pheobe for another minute, too afraid to budge for fear of waking the sleeping beauty, and all the while wondering how she could be so accepting of me.

Cameron had said he was raising her himself, but I hadn't gotten any juicy details about her mother. I had no doubt that she would despise me for this.

When I gazed up this time, I noticed Cameron was resting his eyes. Knowing it would be my only escape, I gently lowered Pheobe's head onto her fluffy pink pillow. She shifted a little, but didn't wake up, and Cameron didn't move a muscle.

Relieved, I lifted my body from her bed and did a wobbly tip-toe out of the room. I scampered down the hall in search of my purse, but it wasn't in the front room. I hated the thought of hunting through his house to search for it, but I wasn't left with much of a choice. After scouring the living room, I slipped into the kitchen only to find my bag sitting on the table.

I snatched it up and quickly made my way for the front door. The hardwood floors released a sharp creak and I froze in panic. First, I worried that I might awaken Pheobe. Then, I decided waking Cameron would be worse yet. I took a deep breath and snuck through the last doorway to fetch my shoes.

Startled again, my hand flung up to my chest and I gasped for a breath, stolen by the man standing before me. He too was stunned, but stood there very still, wearing squinted sleepy eyes that tugged on every one of my heart strings.

"Where do you think you're going?" His voice was as deep and dark as the unlit room.

CHAPTER TEN

The small foyer was dark, the only light a small white glimmer shining in from the hallway. Cameron stood before me, sleepy and disoriented, but very aware of my intentions.

"Were you going somewhere?" he asked, more softly now.

I gently cleared my throat. "Well, I just thought..."

"Well, you thought wrong," he interjected, the depth returning to his voice. He held out his hand and stared at me through tired affectionate eyes. "Please don't go."

How could I now? Especially when I already agreed to spend the night. "Okay." I couldn't help it, even going against all of the internal alarms telling me not to. If I didn't know any better, I'd say I was having real feelings for this man, and I had just made a failed attempt at avoiding that fact.

I absorbed his blue bedroom eyes and I knew I had made the right decision. He took my hand and he pulled me into another room.

'No expectations', rang in my ears, as butterflies filled my otherwise hollow lungs. *Why wasn't he looking for anything more from me?*

Cameron ignored the light switch and turned on the bedside lamp. "Let's find you something a little more comfortable to sleep in, yes?" He released my hand and attentively searched his wardrobe for something suitable. He pulled out a soft white undershirt and smiled. "I'm sorry, but this is all I have."

"It's okay," I said, letting him draw me into his arms.

Wrapped around my slim waist, he nuzzled his nose against my neck. His soft tongue bit into my flesh and his warm breath tantalized my sensitive skin, as his fingers skipped along my bare back. "I hate for you to take your dress off because you look absolutely stunning in it."

Taking advantage of my liquid courage, I turned away from him, closed my eyes and arched my neck for him to have another taste. "Then I guess you'll have to take it off for me."

"Mmm." His voice rumbled in his chest like a wild animal. "I can definitely do that," he growled. He slowly and gently brushed my hair from the back of my neck and took the bait, fastening his lips to my exposed flesh. When he unzipped my tightly fitted dress, he slowly ran his fingers down my delicate skin, trailing it with soft wet kisses.

His touch made me want to rip his suit off and have my way with him right there, but he had rules and so did I. *So why was he tempting me like this and why was he torturing himself like that?* Unable to conjure up anything, being governed by his masculine allure, I closed my eyes and tilted my head back, leaving my neck exposed for more kisses.

With one final touch of his lips, much too soft, he stepped away from me. "I'll give you some privacy."

Not at all what I was expecting, but what did I expect? My bare skin tingled, begging for his return, but after a few quick strides he disappeared into his ensuite bathroom. The door closed firmly behind him.

I feverishly wiggled out of my dress, until it dropped to the floor. I scooped it up with one hand and shuffled across the room to toss it over the traditional armchair next to his bed. I hurriedly slipped on the t-shirt and leapt onto his oversized bed.

Cameron's shirt was so soft and it smelled like him. I lifted it to my nose and inhaled, then realized how psycho stalker-girl I was being. I dropped the shirt to my chest, feeling terribly embarrassed by my lack of control, and slipped underneath the covers.

His bed had unusually fluffy pillows like a posh hotel and it smelled as tempting as his cologne. I fussed with my hair and body position in an attempt to look hot, while I waited for him to return, but I only felt goofy. I was drunk.

Cameron knocked on the door twice before letting himself in. "Are you decent?" he asked, as he re-entered the room. He had removed his suit and was wearing nothing but boxers and a fitted white undershirt. But it was see-through. God, was it ever see-through.

He retrieved a hanger from his closet and walked to where I tossed my dress. I couldn't stop my eyes from zoning in on his chiseled abs, his thick legs and his fit body. He picked up my dress and slung it neatly on the hanger, before hanging it on the back of his door. His ass was just as amazing, two adorable mounds, hard as rocks and smooth like steel.

He cracked the bedroom door open, just enough to let a slit of light in from the hall, but I doubted Pheobe would be waking up for many hours. Unable to control myself, I continued to devour him with my eyes.

Cameron turned toward me and pulled his shirt over his head. I thought I was prepared to take in all that masculine glory, but when his back flexed as he flung the shirt into his basket, I gasped in amazement.

This man was the entire package. I could now add perfectly sculpted to his list of appealing qualities. He had distinct lines tracing every delicious muscle on his body. I knew he *looked* good, but I was sure he'd *feel* even better. I glanced up at his face with panic-filled eyes. *How would I ever control my urges around him?*

"Do I disappoint you?" he asked.

How could this incredibly gorgeous man be self-conscious at all? I bit my lip to reign in my attraction. "Quite the opposite," I answered, clearly troubled. "You come out looking like that and expect me to keep my hands off of you?"

"I apologize for the predicament you find yourself in," he said, wearing a dangerous smile.

I pulled back the covers, flashed him my naked legs and silently offered for him to slip into his bed next to me.

Instead, he stood very still and studied my body.

"Today would be nice, Cameron," I said, dropping the blanket dramatically.

"Oh, yeah?" He leapt on top of me and playfully pinned me to the bed. We tousled around and I couldn't stop giggling, despite my attempts to be quiet. His hands explored my thighs, as his lips connected again with my bare skin.

While staring at his dark-wood ceiling, my hand clasping his head, his words rang again in my ears. *'No expectations.'*

'I have a strict rule about sexual intimacy before being in a serious relationship.'

He instantly sensed my change in character and gently lowered me flat on my back. I looked up into his gorgeous blue eyes and lost myself in them. Yes, I had definitely fallen, but I would not speak a word of it.

"Thank you for staying." Cameron's low, smooth voice whispered over my body like his touch.

I smiled compassionately. "I'm glad I did."

After brushing the hair from my eyes, he rolled next to me and rested on his elbow, his bicep bulging delightfully, his right hand still cupping my cheek. "You have to tell me: how did you get Pheobe to go to bed so quickly?"

I shrugged my shoulders and smiled. "I guess that's our little secret."

"Seriously, I just can't believe it. You must be really special," he said.

My heart swelled in my chest. "I may have let her have a bedtime snack. I hope you don't mind. That's not to mention that the poor, sweet girl was already half asleep."

Cameron looked unconvinced. "Maybe it's because I like you so much," he offered. "I told Pheobe about you, you know. I thought she might like to meet you."

I didn't know whether I should be distressed or ecstatic. Either way, I was certainly confused. Had he deliberately left me alone with his daughter as a test? My eyes had glazed over, as I organized my tangled thoughts. Cameron pressed a kiss to my temple, bringing me back under his mystical spell.

'No expectations', rang in my ears again.

"Abigail."

I instantly snapped out of my drunken stupor and focused on him.

"There's something I've been meaning to tell you. I've been waiting for the right moment, but there never seems to be a right time, and I've never had to do this before."

I was terrified to hear what that might be.

He paused, guarded, then wrinkled his brow. "I'm embarrassed to admit that I haven't really dated anyone since my wife passed six years ago. I certainly haven't brought any women home to meet Pheobe," he said, waiting for my reaction.

A part of me wanted to squeal with joy. *Cameron was all mine.* But a larger part ached for their loss. "I'm so sorry. I had no idea." *What else do you say to that?* "Poor Pheobe. She would've been so young."

Cameron nodded. "Her mother died in a car accident when she was just a baby. Pheobe was in the car when it happened and I was told she was lucky to have survived. I was the lucky one," he admitted, being dragged back into the grief.

I nodded, but that was not the expression I had hoped to see on his face tonight. He must have really loved his wife. It pained me to see him like that and yet another part of me just wanted to kiss all his troubles away.

After a calm silence, I took his hand in mine and squeezed it. "Okay, so why me?"

He lightly brushed my hair away from my eyes, and I wondered if he was trying to figure that out for himself. After a brief silence he let out a big sigh. "I don't want to scare you off."

I grasped his shoulder firmly and locked my eyes onto his. "I don't scare very easily."

He moved closer, hovered over me, and wrinkled his forehead. "What we have right here is really something special. I need you to know that."

A breath caught in my throat. I was speechless. But I felt it too.

He slouched in the bed, bringing his lips closer to mine. "If you feel like you're getting in too deep and need to walk, I would understand.   Just please spare us both the heartache and tell me now."

When he paused, his voice was near a whisper, but I couldn't respond because I was too busy swooning. He slowly inched closer, giving me time to stop him. My eyes fluttered shut as he pressed his parted lips gently against mine. My heart flooded with a wash of emotions.

He pulled back after a few seconds and waited for my lids to flutter open. I gazed back into his mystical eyes and smiled.   Then he kissed me again, softly, parting his lips wider for a deeper connection. When he lowered himself on top of me, I felt his hard, lean body mould into my soft curves. I yearned for his touch and, when his tongue dipped inside my mouth, it only spiked my temptation.

Cameron drew my t-shirt up and caressed my slim waist beneath the soft white fabric. He captured my healthy thighs and wrapped them around him one at a time. Careful and attentive, he brushed his lips along my collarbone, his breath tickling my soft, aroused flesh.

His skilful fingers trimmed along my silky panties, tantalizing my sensitive body, while his fierce erection strained against me. I shuddered in response to all of the sensations flooding my brain at once, as his lips returned to my mouth with a new hungry aggression.

He pressed his hard, sleek body against me in all the right places. I felt hypnotized; like I was feeling an intense out-of-body experience. As I gasped for air, I wanted to moan in pleasure, but restrained myself so he wouldn't stop. I never wanted him to stop.

I clutched at his back, sinking my nails into him, as he nearly brought me to climax through our underwear. "We can't," I breathed, with a raspy breath. I was ready to cry. Cry out in pleasure, and then frustration.

"I know," he said, with a sigh. He lightened the pressure

from my lower region, but he continued to throb against me, my insides clenching with need.

"It's not because I don't want to," I whispered, closing my eyes to ward off the tears. I tried to collect my bearings, but they were scattered all over the bed ready for his consumption.

"I know," he replied again, then pressed a slow sexless kiss on my forehead.

He rolled off of me, leaned over the side of the bed and turned off the lamp. I rotated onto my side, facing away from him, feeling so overwhelmed with pent up desire that I either needed to sob with shame or plead for release.

Cameron slid up behind me, without saying another word. He nuzzled his nose in my hair and cuddled his smooth, bare chest against my back.

'Just a warm body to lie next to.'

I tried to force away my depraved thoughts to ease my craving for Cameron, but it was difficult with his hard, steely body pressed against my back. Though I wanted to feel his tender lips on my skin and his hands on my anything, I felt entirely secure and loved in his embrace. He had a way of making me feel special, just being in the same room with him.

My head was spinning and I wasn't sure whether it was from the drinking or from the sudden throng of emotions flowing through me. I knew Cameron passed out because he was already breathing deeply behind me, mere minutes after our heated encounter.

His warm breath tickled my neck and a little rumble slipped from his throat. He was already out and I laid there very much awake. Staring at the pale blue walls, I wished I could go to sleep and worry about things in the morning. If I had to worry, I wished I could think about minor, insignificant things, like the imminent hangover I was going to regret when I woke up.

I began to wonder if I would ever fall asleep. The most significant issue weighing heavily on my heart, even more than the dead weight of Cameron's arm, was regret. Not mine, but his.

Had liquid courage fed his adorations? Maybe. And the competition with Edwin was just the cherry on top. I would have to face this man at work on Monday morning, and every day after that. I was afraid that we could never go back to the way it was, after this night. I was even more afraid to admit that I didn't want it to.

CHAPTER ELEVEN

A door slammed shut, startling me awake. My emerald eyes watered from the stunning brightness of the room, as I stared at the dark chocolate ceiling, my mind slowly easing into reality.

I was in Cameron Clarke's bedroom.

Sunshine poured in through the blinds and tree branches cascaded soothing shadows on the tastefully decorated pale blue walls.

My mind was hazy, but my desire was strong, despite the empty bed. I listened for some indication that there was life in the house, but I couldn't hear anything over the constant ringing in my ears. I urgently clambered to my feet and wavered unsteadily. My head pounded, as a dizzy spell overcame me. I decidedly sat down before I fell down.

When I thought it was safe to try again, I slowly rose to my feet and tip-toed to the window. The pain in my side faded into a dull ache, as I fought off the early onset of the anxiety attack that loomed over me like a noose. I rustled through my purse and pulled out a small bottle of pills. I popped one under my tongue and snapped the bottle shut, as it began to melt my worries away.

I peered out the window and took a few deep breaths. The beautiful morning made it easier for me to pull myself together. The sun was shining brightly, the birds singing a lovely song, and I saw two squirrels running up a tree wearing leaves of all colours.

"Hey, sunshine," I heard from the door.

I spun around, startling my balance, and grabbed onto the window sill for stability.

Cameron looked as good as ever, in a pair of dark wash jeans and a dark grey button-up shirt. His sleeves were rolled up to his elbows, as though he had been working on something important. All I could do was smile at him, as I stood there in nothing but his clingy white t-shirt.

"Did you sleep well?"

"Mmm, hmm," I replied softly. *Surprisingly well, under the circumstances.*

"I was thinking you could probably use some greasy food to settle your stomach after last night. I know I could definitely use that right about now," he said, as though I wasn't standing there half naked.

I probably looked a mess. I didn't even have a chance to check my makeup, which I hadn't removed from last night. *I'm sure I look real fan-fucking-tastic right about now.* "What do you have in mind?" I asked.

"There's this small diner I like to take my daughter to. I thought maybe you'd like it there."

So thoughtful. He makes me smile. "It sounds great. But I think I'd better hit home first for a change of clothes. Actually a quick shower would do me a lot of good too, if you don't mind."

There was no way I would be seen in public wearing my cocktail dress from the night before. It was bad enough I would have to wear it home for Edwin's criticism.

"I've already considered that and it's taken care of," Cam said, as he left the room and quickly returned with a garment bag.

I stood there stunned, when I realized what he had done.

"My sister had to pick up Pheobe anyway, to take her to skating lessons this morning, so I asked if she could pick up a little something for you on the way."

"You didn't have to do that, Cam. It's too much."

"It's the least I could do. I just hope you like it." He hooked the bag on the back of the bathroom door and returned a moment later. "I already put a bath towel out and there's a fresh washcloth on the shelf next to the shower. Help yourself to anything else you need."

He disappeared out the door before I could even say thanks. On one hand I was feeling pretty glad that I didn't have to do the walk of shame in front of Edwin, but I was also worried that Ashley would try to sabotage me with a ridiculous outfit.

My curiosity had me rushing over to the bag of anonymous clothes. I slowly pulled the zipper down exposing Ashley's finds. I was impressed. She really did good; maybe a little too good.

There were two outfits to choose from. I pulled out the stylish boot cut jeans and the black v-neck shirt. Nothing too elaborate, but clearly designer quality and they still had the tags on them. When I saw a small lingerie bag, I figured Ashley had thought of everything. I opened it anxiously, but there were no lacy garments inside. Only a less than friendly note, folded into a small square.

I deftly unfolded the note and read it.

You'd better not be playing my brother. If you're not serious about him, leave now. I mean it. I want to see him happy, but if you hurt him you're dead.
    Your friend, Ash

My friend? In what world? Nothing like a little death threat after your first date to keep the relationship alive.

I knew her threats were empty. If anything, the note only indicated how close his family ties were. *So she's a little over-protective of her big bro. I can handle that.*

After a quick shower, I scrunched some gel into my hair, since I couldn't locate a hairdryer. I scurried back into his room, found my purse on the floor next to the bed and scrambled to make myself decent with the few items I had packed into the small clutch.

I busted out of his bedroom, with my dress over my arm, and wandered around his house to find him. I peeked inside his office door, where I found him reclined in a chair at his desk. Music blared from his ear buds and his eyes were closed. He mumbled something unintelligible and turned his head away from me.

"Cameron!" I said rather forcefully, shaking his shoulder gently to wake him.

He nearly jumped two feet out of his chair. "I'm awake!" he shouted, as he pulled the buds from his ears.

"Well, you are now," I said with a giggle. "Sorry for taking so long."

Once he became alert he gave me a once over. "Wow, look at that. I see the clothes worked out then." He rubbed my thigh lightly, sending a refreshed sexual awareness pulsing through my veins. If he only knew I wasn't wearing any panties.

"Thank you, again. I really appreciate it. I'll pay you for the clothes."

"Forget about it. Ready to go? You must be starving." His hand brushed across my cheek, but he made no attempt to kiss me.

I nodded and smiled, eager to get some fresh air in my lungs and slick food in my belly.

As we put on our shoes, I wondered what he might expect in exchange for the gifts he showered me with. I hardly doubted that last night was enough for full repayment. I could think of a few things I could do for him that might even the playing field. A smirk teased my lips.

Cameron opened his holly red door and waited for me to walk through. I glanced down the driveway, curious to see how I was getting home, and quite surprised to find Cameron's sleek black car sparkling in the driveway.

"How did you get your car back here?" I wondered, aloud.

"Ashley drove it home from the party. It was here in the driveway when we got home last night. Don't you remember?"

"My memory's a little fuzzy from last night," I admitted, hoping he wouldn't take offence.

He opened the passenger door for me and I shot him an appreciative smile. "Thanks."

He returned a warm smile and a nod before he swiftly walked around the sophisticated car and entered the other side. A twinge of desire stalked me as I remembered his warm lips all over my trembling bare skin.

The diner was exactly how he described it, friendly and cozy. We sat at a table for four and each of us ordered a greasy breakfast skillet even though it was nearly noon. The conversation was casual, covering nothing but random, insignificant things, including work gossip and the weather.

Just as Cameron finished with his platter, his cell phone started buzzing. He looked at the screen and apprehension immediately transformed his contentment. "I have to take this. Please excuse me," he said, standing from the table. He hurried out the door before answering the call.

I watched out the window until Cameron came back into my view. He didn't look too happy. He may have even been raising his voice. Suddenly, catching my eye, he spun away so I couldn't scrutinize him. I was a little worried and even more jealous. *Who was he talking to?*

While the seconds faded into minutes, I finished my meal alone. I remembered the intimacy we had shared the night before. I was extremely disappointed by the turn of events, now that we had our sobriety intact.

Since waking in his bed, Cameron had not once kissed me. Disappointment set in when I realized he had not shared a single intimate word or private detail with me all morning. In fact, today, everything seemed chummy. Maybe a little too chummy.

When Cameron finally returned to the table I must have been wearing my emotions on my sleeve. He seemed to decipher them instantly.

"Sorry about that," he said. He stood behind his chair, but didn't take a seat, his hands gripping the back of it irritably.

"Everything okay," I pried, hoping he'd tell me what that was all about.

He didn't.

"Ready to go?" he asked, acknowledging that the plates were cleared from the table.

Suddenly the waitress appeared, returning his credit card to him. *When did he do that?*

I nodded and forced an unauthentic smile on my face. I

was suddenly uncomfortable with the whole situation. "Thank you for dinner," I said, as we walked back to his car separate and apart.

"You're welcome," he replied, then set off for his door.

I let myself in the passenger side and studied his face as he snapped in his seat belt. Something had changed. Something was bothering him. *Me?*

I cringed, as he drove toward my house in silence. I wondered how our relationship had so quickly taken a turn for the worse. Overall, our brunch seemed more like a friendly meeting than a second date. My stomach twisted into a treacherous knot.

When he pulled up to my house, I thanked him again. Testing the waters with a goodbye kiss, I rested my hand on his chest and leaned into him. At first he hesitated, making my heart clench painfully in my chest. Then he delivered an emotionless peck on my lips, acting as though nothing was amiss.

Stunned, I picked up my clutch from his floor and yanked my dress from the back seat. "Call me," I said, almost teasingly, as I got out of his car. I was feeling extremely confused and rather angry.

He looked so grim when I shut the door, so very distant, that I decided I would just leave it alone. I felt his eyes on me as I stalked up to my front door, but I didn't look back to confirm it. I jammed my key into the slot, whipped the door shut behind me and sunk into the back of it. Slumped there, I was seriously bent out of shape, just waiting for the tears to come.

What went so terribly wrong? Wetness started to well in my eyes. He must have regretted taking me home to meet his daughter. That could be the only explanation.

I needed my pillow. I needed to spill my tears, before I emptied my upset stomach onto the floor. But before I could concentrate on that problem, down walked another. Compared to seeing this person at this very moment, Edwin would have been a sight for sore eyes.

CHAPTER TWELVE

It was as though the sky opened up, swallowed the sun and cast me off on my own. Darkness reigned. *As if my morning could get any worse. Oh, but it just did.*

Seeing Jessica Sanders prancing down my hall, wearing nothing but a lacy purple bra and thong, was the last thing I wanted to deal with after being crushed by Cameron's sudden change of heart.

"Oh, hey Abby. I didn't hear you come in. I'm just grabbing a bottle of water. You want one?" Jessica asked. Her smile said it all.

I shook my head no, as the vomit rose up my throat. I swallowed it back.

Jessica sashayed to the kitchen, suddenly proud and self-assured, as though she weren't walking around my house with her ass hanging out. If she was trying to make me jealous, she had succeeded. I tried to remain unaffected by it all, but my emotions were already on standby for an explosion and I couldn't fathom the thought of Edwin spending the night with her.

I booked it up the stairs, so I wouldn't have to face her again, and slammed right into Edwin. My hands were bunched into fists and landed right on his shirtless chest. He was fresh out of the shower, with a pair of faded jeans hanging from his hips, but he hadn't bothered to do up the top button. *Damn him.*

He didn't move, so I glared at him. We didn't exchange words. He could see I was hurting. He knew me well enough to read the pain in my eyes, but his smug, insensitive expression only twisted the dagger in deeper.

I pushed by him, rushed inside my bedroom and slammed the door out of anger and sadness. I was confused. So very confused.

What the hell am I doing here? Does nobody want me, for me?

Cameron was everything I was looking for in a man. He was sexy as hell, with a good future and a loving family. Besides that, he was just an overall great guy that any woman would be lucky to date. *I blew that. How? Who knows; but it's clearly over between us.*

Edwin, on the other hand, had laid it all out on the table. Me, I bitch flipped that table onto his lap. *Someday* just wasn't soon enough for me, but how did I expect him to treat me now? I had yanked his heart from his chest and crushed it before him. Now I actually expect him to respect *my* heart?

I sighed, pinching my eyes shut with my index finger and thumb. A tear slipped down my face, while I struggled to find the right response to what I had just witnessed. Could Edwin truly like Jessica like that? She was a prime target for an easy lay, considering her long-time crush on him, but that thought didn't make me feel any better.

The more I fretted, the more I realized it wasn't doing me any good. I needed Aliah to tell me how big of a dumbass Cameron was being and what a jerk Edwin was. *Yes. I need her now.*

I plucked my cordless phone from the charger and started to dial, but it didn't ring when I was finished.

"Hello," a man said, on the other end.

What the hell? "Who is this?" I snapped.

"Caleb. Who's this?"

"Abby. Who do you think?"

"I'm on the phone, Abs," Edwin finally intercepted.

"Oh. I'm sorry," I said sarcastically, "I thought you had a guest to tend to."

"What, I'm not allowed to have guests now?"

"No, it's fine with me, but I'd prefer that they not trot around my house bare-assed."

"Don't get your panties in a bunch," Edwin replied with a chuckle, ticking me off even more.

"That's it. I'm on my way over!" Caleb shouted, then his

line went dead.

Edwin didn't hang up the phone. Then I heard him sigh. "She didn't know you were home," he insisted, as if he cared.

"Oh, please. You're telling me she suddenly needed a drink when she heard me pull up out front? More like she was watching out the window, waiting for me to get home." *Ugh. Why did I have to share my paranoia with him?*

"Does this even have anything to do with her?" Edwin asked.

"No." I wished that were true. "This has everything to do with *you* letting your slutty guests strut around my house half naked. You need to learn to keep 'em on a leash," I hollered.

"Who's that?" Jessica asked suddenly, on the other side of the phone.

"It's no one," Edwin told her.

"Whatever. Get the hell off the phone. I need it," I ordered.

"Glad to hear you enjoyed yourself last night. Love you too, mom. We'll talk later." Edwin made smooching noises into the phone and hung it up before I could scold him some more.

What an asshole. Lucky for him I had shit to do. I needed to discuss my new man troubles with Aliah. After turning the phone back on, I quickly redialed her number. It rang only twice before Aliah picked up.

"Hello," she answered.

"Ally. Thank God you're home. We need to talk."

"My company's just walking out the front door now. I'll be right over."

"Wait! Aliah, no!"

She had hung up the phone and I knew that she was likely already barreling out her door to come see me. Aliah had always been a good friend of mine. She wasn't afraid to speak the truth and if something needed said, then you'd better be ready to hear it. *Was I ready to hear what she had to say?*

The next fifteen minutes passed slowly as I waited in my bedroom for the doorbell to ring. When it finally did, I ran downstairs and swung the door open before Edwin could get in on my business.

"Oh. Caleb. I thought you were Aliah," I said, unimpressed.

"You make me feel so welcome," he mocked, stepping past me.

"Come in," I said sarcastically, while he kicked off his shoes.

I spun around, placed my hands on my hips and hollered up the stairs. "Edwin! Caleb's here!" I didn't dare go near his room while he had a guest.

Suddenly, there was another quick knock and in walked Aliah.

I spun around and wrapped my arms around her neck. "It's you!" I gave her a long, overly friendly hug, feeling in need of a little love.

"Why didn't I get that kind of reception?" Caleb moaned, with a boyish pout.

"What is it, boy trouble?" Aliah asked, ignoring Caleb entirely.

"Let's go to my room to talk. Eddie has a guest." I narrowed my eyes at Caleb, but I wasn't referring to him.

"He picked up some slut last night, did he?" she asked, as we started up the stairs.

Just then, Jessica curled around the barrister at the top. "Nice to see you too," she answered.

At least now she had clothes on. Edwin wasn't far behind her. He too was fully clothed now.

"You don't have to go to your room. I'm leaving," Edwin said.

"Whatever. Let's go," I said to Aliah. "Just lock the door when you leave."

"Got it," Edwin replied, as I shut my bedroom door.

"What the hell was that?" Aliah asked, stunned by the exchange.

I scurried over to my bed and crashed onto it, burying

my head into my pillow. "I was wondering the same thing," I pouted, my voice being muffled by the fabric.

"Is that why you called me over? You still crushing on my brother, Eddie?"

I lifted my head and glared at her. "No! There's other stuff I really need to talk to you about." I pouted for a second, then softened a bit. "Why don't you go first? I could use some good news." I hugged my pillow and stared at Aliah.

"Do you want a play-by-play or a summary?" She shared a wicked smirk and it made me smile.

"That depends on how raunchy it is."

"Well, first we went to his place. We barely made it in the house before I ripped all of his clothes off. Damn, he has a fine bod! He's well hung too!"

"Okay." I laughed. "Maybe a few less details."

"Let's just say I put it on him right. He won't even think about any other ladies now that he knows where it's at," she said, pointing two thumbs at herself.

"I'm sure." I laughed, mostly because Aliah wasn't even joking.

"Now you!" Aliah insisted. "How was Cam and when did you get those jeans? I like 'em."

I flung my head backwards, not ready to get into the jean thing. "Cam was great. *Was* being the operative word. And no we didn't do it. It wasn't like that."

"If it wasn't like *that*, then how was it?" Aliah probed.

"I don't know. That's where it gets complicated. I'm so confused right now."

"I saw you two at the bar. He was all over you. Then when we were leaving there were definitely stars in his eyes. So, what's the problem?"

"It's a long story," I said.

Aliah answered with a smile. "I have all day."

CHAPTER THIRTEEN

The office had been a vortex of gossip ever since Owen's party. Among the rumours about Cameron and I, there was talk about Edwin's hot rebound girl. One whole week had passed and Cameron hadn't said more than two words to me. I hardly thought that *'Good Morning'* or *'See Ya'* even counted as a conversation.

It was a cool, cloudy Saturday afternoon and I was sitting at home alone in my quiet house. The fact that I hadn't made any plans to go out for the evening not only saddened me, but left me incredibly depressed. I tried to focus on scrubbing my floors and ironing my laundry, but my scattered thoughts kept rushing back to the forefront of my mind.

After my talk with Aliah, we had agreed that Cameron had three days to get his shit together and make his move or we were finished. The deadline long overdue, it became crystal clear that if it wasn't for work, I would have never seen or spoken to Cameron Clarke ever again. Boy did that realization suck.

Being realistic, there was only one thing I could do and that was to move on with my life. I really wanted to ask him what the deal-breaker was, but one sort-of-date hardly made Cameron responsible to me for an explanation.

After finishing my housework and the cold left-overs in the fridge, I curled up on the couch with a blanket and turned on the boob tube. The way Edwin shuffled around the house, I figured it meant he'd be going out with his friends shortly. At least then I could wallow in my misery in peace.

After half an hour passed, with Edwin still roaming the house, I decided I was getting into my pj's. I left the TV on and headed to my room to change into my comfy clothes. I stripped down, exchanging my jeans and blouse for comfy plaid pants that hugged my curves and a hot pink v-neck shirt.

I knew I should probably leave my bra on, in case Edwin's friends decided to visit before they took off, but decided I really didn't care. It was my house too, and if Edwin could have ladies walking around in their thongs, then I could certainly walk around without wearing a bra.

As I tied my hair up into a high pony, someone knocked at my bedroom door. "Yup," I called.

Edwin let himself in. "Are you getting ready to go out?"

I let his eyes do the answering first. "No. I could use some down time."

"Are you expecting company?"

"No. Why? Is someone here?" I asked, hopeful.

"No. I was just wondering."

I nodded, hesitating near the door, waiting for Edwin to leave. His eyes trailed down to my chest and it lit my body on fire. My nipples defied me and became razor sharp under the intensity of his stare.

When he didn't move or speak, I brushed past him, walked down the hall and continued down the stairs. "I already called the TV, so you'll have to go to your buddies if you want to watch a show with them," I hollered back.

"The guys aren't coming over," Edwin said. He swiftly caught up with me at the bottom of the stairs.

"Good," I snapped. When I took my seat, I folded my arms over my unsupported breasts.

Edwin rounded the couch and held a cold eye on me. "Are you avoiding me again?"

"Really? I'm just watching TV. What more do you want from me?" I was ready to burst into tears.

"Nothing, I guess," he replied, though I could tell there was something on his mind.

I sighed, turned off the TV and twisted sideways to give him my undivided attention. I could use the company. "What is it?"

"Can I sit?" he asked.

I rolled my eyes. "You know you can."

"Don't be like that. This is me we're talking."

"Sorry," I said. "But forgive me if I've been a little on edge lately."

"Hey, you're not alone," Edwin insisted. "I hear my name flying around out there too. They're going to talk. There's no two ways about it."

"Why do you think I'm staying home?"

"You really think that's safe? I'm sure they'll concoct something out of it, what with me staying home all night too."

Huh? "I thought you were going out."

"I never said that. I planned to just hang around the house tonight. But I don't want to bother you. If you'd rather I leave you alone, I will."

I sighed, a little relieved. "No. I don't mind," I said softly.

Edwin settled back and seemed a lot more relaxed, as he searched for the right words to say. "I'm sorry," he finally admitted.

"For what?"

"Everything."

"You're going to have to elaborate. I have no idea what you're talking about," I admitted.

"If it wasn't for me acting out that night, everything would have worked out just fine. You and Cam would be together and I wouldn't have Jessica harassing me."

"Thank you for saying that, but you can't take all the blame. Sure, you pissed me off, but you really had nothing to do with the whole Cam thing."

"I pissed you off?" he said, smirking.

I slapped him playfully. "Eddie. You don't need to jeopardize everything you worked so hard for. That's all I'm saying."

"You're avoiding the question. Admit it."

"I admit that men drive me crazy; especially you. As for Cam, he's a mature adult, he can make his own decisions. He just made the wrong one."

Edwin laughed, a devious glimmer twinkling in his aqua

blue eyes. "So, you're saying I'm more of a man than him."

"Edwin!"

"It's okay, you don't have to agree with me, I know it's true."

I got up from the couch and shoved him as I passed. I retrieved a bottle of water from the fridge and returned to the living room, relieved that I didn't have to be totally miserable all night *alone*. That's when I found Edwin sitting in my spot. He knew how picky I was about *my spot*.

"Excuse me," I scolded.

"What?" he asked smugly.

"Don't act like you don't know. Get out of my seat!"

"Make me!" he taunted.

"I'll make you alright." I put down my water bottle and yanked on his thick-muscled arms. He didn't budge an inch. "Edwin," I whined. "My spot was warm. Please!" I pleaded.

He sat with his feet planted firmly on the floor and his godly arms folded over his chest. I yanked and yanked, but he didn't move. His smiled curved even higher

"You asked for it. Now I'm gonna have to lay the smack down on you," I announced.

"Oh, I'm scared now."

Having too much fun to stop, I walked behind the couch, wrapped my arms around his neck and flung myself over the top of the sofa. He willingly submitted to the attack and, though I may have knocked him out of my spot, I unintentionally flattened myself beneath him.

"I see you got your place back," he growled softly.

I inadvertently smiled, but secretly wished it didn't feel so good to be wanted by him.

"I'm gonna kiss you now," he warned, as he closed his eyes. He eased closer, then fastened my lips to his, with a soft and sensual caress that could only come from Edwin's mouth. His large hands drew up my sides and cupped my bare breasts, as though he were worshiping them.

That's when I pushed him off of me. "Eddie! What do you think you're doing?"

"Mmm," he moaned, as I awkwardly scrambled to get out

from under him. He couldn't wipe the wide grin from his face.

"Fine! You can have my spot!" I snapped.

He laughed, low and rough, and slid aside. "You can have it. I already got what I wanted."

With my arms folded over my chest, in an attempt to hide my arousal, I took back my spot and acted like that kiss hadn't just shattered my world. My eyes flashed forward at the blank TV screen.

Edwin stayed on the cushion right next to me, his eyes locked on my face. "You can't help it. I'm just that damn irresistible," he said, arrogantly.

I flashed him a sassy scowl. "Don't bother getting your horny hopes up."

"If I asked for it, you'd be all about it."

"No, you must be thinking of Jessica."

He acknowledged the jab. "Burn."

So he had slept with her then. A sharp pain stabbed at my side. I refused to admit it, but man was I jealous. I wrapped my fingers around my side. *At least someone got laid that night.*

"I didn't sleep with her, if that's what you're thinking," Edwin said, reading my mind. "She claimed that her parents had company last weekend and she didn't want to go home. What else could I do?"

"Yeah, I buy that. I saw you leave the party with her. You had cruel intentions."

"My intentions may have been bad, but I couldn't go through with it. The second I hit the fresh air, I regretted dragging her into it. I knew it was a mistake."

"Admit it. You were trying to get to me."

"Maybe," he replied. "Did it work?"

"Maybe."

"It wasn't a total waste then. Now I just have to deal with Jessica. She tried to put the moves on me that night, but I resisted." His large hand swiped over his eyes, then he dug his fingers into his temple. "Calling me persistently all week is hardly helping her situation."

"It's better than my situation."

"I hate to ask, but I figure he must have really messed up big time. I've heard the rumours, but you guys looked just fine when I left."

"Then you'll be surprised to hear that I'm the one who messed up."

"I find that hard to believe. The way he was looking at you that night, there's no way it was you."

"Well it was."

"What could you have possibly done that was so terrible?"

"That's the thing: I don't know what I did. He never said and I'm not about to ask. It could be that his sister has had it out for me since day one, or maybe he didn't like that I put his little girl to bed without his permission. I don't know."

"Yeah, that sounds rotten of you. Did you iron his underwear while you were at it?"

"Quit it," I said, scowling. My eyes glazed over as I tried to find other reasons. There were none.

"Did you put out?"

"Is that any of your business?" I snapped, being slammed back into reality.

"Just sayin'."

"No I didn't put out and he didn't try. His daughter was in the room next to us, if you must know."

"He's gay."

"He's not gay!"

"What straight man wouldn't at least try to have sex with you?"

"A man with morals. What about you and Jessica?" I pressed, to prove a point.

"That's different. He actually wanted you. I doubt morals would be enough to stop a man from trying once he's got you in his bed. It's in our nature. He's a pillow biter."

I gave it some real thought while Edwin shook his head yes. I closed my eyes to rehash over that night in Cameron's bedroom. Though it was fuzzy now, the way his lips tickled my body wasn't something I was going to forget anytime soon. "No. It had to be something I did."

Frustrated, I stood up next to the couch but was unsure where I was heading. I couldn't get away from myself.

Edwin chuckled and got to his feet. "That's not the tale I've heard going around the office. Sounds like you had quite the scandalous weekend."

I spun around and snapped at him. "Cut it out!"

Using my twisting motion against me, Edwin scooped me into his arms and pinned my elbow behind me, leaving nothing between us, but the thin fabric of our shirts. I was sure he could feel me razor sharp against him, but he stayed completely serious.

"I don't care what happens between the two of you, as long as we can always be like this."

I sighed, feeling defeated, and relaxed in his arms. "Agreed."

Edwin tugged me into the corner of the couch and pulled me close, so I would rest my cheek on his chest. I closed my eyes and accepted his offer for comfort. It was too cozy, as his hand brushed up and down the length of my arm and his heart beat beneath my ear.

Minutes passed before I felt the sudden urge to confess to Edwin. "If Cameron wanted me that night, I was his for the having," I blurted. *What is wrong with me?*

"You don't have to tell me that," Edwin answered.

"Yes I do. I just want you to know that it's okay with me if you want a relationship with Jessica, or any other girl for that matter. You don't have to act like you don't like her if you do."

"Trust me, I don't." Edwin's phone rang, saving me from having to press the awkward topic.

I stared at his cell, propped on the ottoman. "Are you going to get it or what?"

Edwin shrugged a heavy shoulder, acting like he didn't plan on it.

I dove off the couch and answered it on the next ring.

"Hello?"

"Is Edwin there?" the woman asked, clearly surprised.

I held the phone against my chest. "Speak of the devil," I whispered, then brought the phone back to my ear with a wink. "May I ask who's calling?" I knew exactly who it was.

"Oh, hey Jessica!" I replied.

"I'm not here," Edwin mouthed dramatically, waving his hands in a large X.

"Yup, Edwin's right here. I'll get him for you." I reached out the phone to him and he shot me some evil looks before he ripped the phone from my hand. "It's Jessica," I said.

"Hey. What's up?" he answered. And then he said, "Actually, I just wanted to take it easy tonight, but I'll be here all night if you want to stop by."

My eyes bugged out of my head as I shook my head no, but he was already off the phone. "What the hell?"

"She said she might stop by later."

"So we have like twenty minutes of peace and quiet before all hell breaks loose? I think I'm going to move it to the bedroom."

"Oh, come on. You don't have to go," Edwin urged, stealing my hand. "Stay. I can only handle the girl in small doses."

"Why the hell did you invite her over then? To lead her on? That's just cruel."

"Not exactly. I have other plans."

"Leave me out of 'em," I ordered. "I'm sure I'm the last person she wants to see right now."

"Come on, Abs. I need you for this plan to work. Just go with it."

Why is it so difficult for me to say no to this man?
"I don't like the sounds of this," I said, as headlights flashed into my front room less than a half-hour later.

Edwin peeked out the blinds. "It's her."

"Okay, catch you later then." I hopped up from the couch

and hurried toward the stairs to go to my room.

"No, remember? You said you'd help," he said, his glorious aqua eyes pleading with me. He pulled me into his arms, knowing I wouldn't fight him anymore, then he guided me in front of the frosted glass sidelight. "You just have to stand here. Trust me. This will hurt me as much at it hurts you," he teased, leaning down. For a kiss?

I pushed him off before his lips reached mine. "Whoa, wait!" I screeched, inches from the front door.

"Please, just do this for me," he begged. "It's the only way to get rid of her."

"Or you could just tell her you're not interested; you know, like a normal human being."

"Trust me, Abs. When it comes to me and you, she'll know it's a losing battle. Come on," he begged. "For me?"

I mulled it over in my mind, knowing he was probably right, but also knowing it was a really dumb idea. Edwin gripped around my waist tighter, holding me against his rigid abs. My heart already ached and I *was* desperate for love. His love? All I knew was, it wouldn't hurt to get a little revenge on Jessica after the prancing panty incident.

"Fine, but don't press your luck with me," I said, not believing the words that came out of my mouth.

Edwin grinned and wasted no time fixing his lips on mine. I doubted that tongue was necessary in the circumstances, but Edwin tasted good and I'd never half-ass anything. He spun us around, and stepped backwards, until he was planted firmly between me and the wall.

His eager lips were impatient and I sadly enjoyed every second of it. He slid one of his hands from my hip to my ass and squeezed gently.

I broke my lips from his and gasped. "Really?"

He nipped at my ear. "Yes. It has to be believable," he growled.

With my head tilted sideways, Edwin devoured the soft flesh of my neck. I closed my eyes as a sharp sigh escaped my lips. When I swallowed, Edwin's lips returned to my ear.

"Don't worry. I'll be gentle." His lips captured mine and he was careful to caress away any worry that might have slipped into my mind from his intriguing promise.

I only wished that I had one.

Without pause, he clutched my thighs in both his hands and hiked me up onto his hips.

Too turned on to say no, I decided to let it slide. I tugged at his shirt and pulled it over his head. *He wasn't the only one allowed to enjoy this.*

"Mmm. I like how you think," he growled, as he yanked off my top spilling my naked breasts.

"Eddie, no!" I covered my breasts with one hand.

"Ooh. What do we have here?" He cupped my ass and walked across the foyer, with my long legs wrapped around him. He lowered my bottom onto the foyer table and continued with his passionate assault on my mouth.

There was still no sign of Jessica. *What was taking her?*

"Oh, Abby," Edwin moaned, a little too loud.

Faker. If Jessica were at the door, I doubted she would've fallen for it either. Taking things into my own hands, I ran my fingers through his hair and pressed hot wet kisses to his mouth. A shadow on the wall finally told me that we had company.

Edwin spread my legs wider and firmly pressed against me, testing my willpower. The length and hardness of his erection told me he was enjoying this a little too much. When his warm, rough finger brushed over my perky, exposed nipple, I shuddered around breathless gasps for air.

Something that felt this right couldn't possibly be wrong.

"Ahh," I moaned, fulfilling my role, but the response was real. Edwin knew how to push my buttons and he was pushing all of them. The fact that we had a spectator only amped up the excitement.

After exchanging another scorching kiss, Edwin drew his warm soft, lips across my neck. I flashed a sideways glance at the door to see what was taking Jessica so long. There was a shadowed silhouette planted right in front of the door, but she wasn't doing anything.

"We have company," I whispered.

"Do you like that?" he growled. His tongue drew a circle on my neck, then his mouth closed over it.

"Mmm," I moaned, for dramatic effect. "Don't stop." Voicing it was hot, but my conscience was sneaking up on me. "What is she waiting for?" I whispered. I couldn't imagine that she was waiting for us to finish.

Edwin took my hand and rubbed it between us, flattening his tented jeans with my palm. "Mmm, I like it when you touch me like that," he said, rather convincingly. His bedroom eyes only urged me to continue touching him after he retrieved his hand.

"Like this?" I taunted. I clutched him through his pants, in hopes of threatening him, but my intentions backfired.

Edwin's eyes opened wide with excitement. "Yes!"

I had to put a stop to all of this madness. "Shhh!" I said, as loud as my lips would allow. It sounded so real. "I think someone's here."

Suddenly there was a ring of the doorbell, followed by three short, but persistent, knocks.

"I wonder who it could be," Edwin teased.

I pushed Edwin aside so our guest wouldn't see him. "Go hide," I told him theatrically, covering my breasts with an arm.

"Just a second!" I called out, as I frantically picked up my shirt from the floor and intentionally put it on backwards. Why did I feel so nervous all of a sudden? Shaking it off, I opened the door a crack and peeked my head out. "Oh, hey Jessica. What's going on?"

"I'm actually here to see Edwin."

"Well, Edwin's not here right now."

"That's funny because his truck's parked in the driveway. Who was that you were just talking to?"

"Oh, uh, you must have heard the television. I think he went for a walk. I'll let him know that you stopped by."

I started to shut the door and Jessica stuck her foot in the way. She must have grew a pair while living in Toronto, because never would she have done something so bold before.

"Maybe I'll just wait for him to come home then. You don't mind if I wait inside, do you?" She pushed on the door and let herself in.

"Actually, I uh..." I moved out of the way and her eyes immediately zeroed in on my reversed shirt. I folded my arms over my chest, suddenly self-conscious about my free breasts.

Just then, I realized that Edwin hadn't hid like I had ordered. Instead, he stood there behind me, his hair a sexy mess, his shirt on the floor at his feet. He picked it up and pulled it on, covering his twitching muscles.

Man, had this ever turned awkward. Suddenly, I felt like I was actually caught screwing around with Edwin. *Wait! I was.*

"Gone for a walk, eh?" she asked, her eyes fixed on Edwin's. "I should have known better. I could tell that it wasn't over between you two; what with Abigail throwing herself at that blonde guy and you playing the jealous ex who's clearly not ready to move on."

"Jessica. I'm really sorry," Edwin said, sounding very convincing.

"Whatever," she stammered. "It's your loss."

Jessica spun around and stomped over the threshold, but paused briefly to let me have it. "By the way, your shirt's on backwards," she snapped. She grabbed the door and rudely slammed it in my face.

I reopened the door and yelled out to her ignorantly. "Good to see you too!" I forced the door shut, without giving her a chance to respond.

CHAPTER FOURTEEN

I showered Edwin with a blank stare. His wicked grin told me he was ecstatic. We both broke out in gut-wrenching laughter. I tucked my arms into my shirt and spun it around the right way.

"That was quite the performance." He chuckled.

"Jessica certainly believed it."

"Love the shirt thing. That was a nice touch."

I sighed. "Yeah, but I'm sure we'll pay for that," I said, as I headed back to the living room.

"Oh well. Hopefully it pisses Cameron off. I'll enjoy that," Edwin admitted, following me to the sofa.

I smiled to myself and took my seat. I hoped it would make Cameron jealous too, but for that he would have to care. "You owe me big!"

"Anything you want."

I smirked. "I think I'll hold on to the IOU for another time."

Edwin took a seat next to me. I swung my legs over him and rested them on his lap. He adjusted himself in his pants. It looked like he was still flagging down a plane.

"I could pay you in mindless sex," he said, drawing his hand up my inner thigh.

I swatted his hand off of me. "Mindless sex. Really?"

"Okay, mind-blowing then?"

"Why would I waste an IOU on that when I could get it from you anytime for free?"

Edwin's smile slanted into a smirk. "Good point."

"Just be happy that I helped you get Jessica off your back. I hope you learned your lesson."

"What lesson?"

"You ignorant ass! Quit picking up chicks to piss me off, unless you plan on making it work!"

Edwin smirked again. "Okay, okay. I get it."

Monday morning came surprisingly fast and, for a change, I was feeling calm and refreshed. Tuesday came even faster and, despite the stormy weather, I was still in good spirits.

By five to eight I was ready for my office conference with Owen, to prepare for an upcoming trial, but he was nowhere to be found. Add to that the fact that Taylor was off sick and things were starting to take a turn for the worse.

At the stroke of nine, just as I opened a new file, my phone began to ring.

"Good morning. Abby speaking," I answered.

"Abby, it's Owen. I am so sorry to do this to you, but do you think you could review the Badman file with Cam? The Assignment Court list is longer than expected and I'm not going to have time for it when I get back."

He knew how tense my relationship with Cameron had become, so he must have been desperate to ask me to work with him.

"I can do that," I answered.

After hanging up the phone, I took a deep breath to try to regain my calm, but it felt like fireworks were going off in my brain. There was no way around it, so I picked up the heavy file, walked straight over to Cameron's office and knocked on his open door.

Cameron hadn't even pulled the blinds for the morning and, while he had done a good job of ignoring me lately, he'd have a hard time doing that now. When he looked up at me, silence hung between us and his fathomless eyes blazed with emotion.

My stomach did a flip-flop, as I swallowed my nerve. "Do you have a minute? Owen asked me to review the Badman file with you." My feet firmly planted in place, I waited for his invitation.

He nodded and gestured for me to take a seat. "Come in." He stood from his chair and rounded his desk. "Here. Let me get that for you." He took the heavy file from my hands, his fingers brushing over mine, our eyes meeting very briefly.

My breath caught in my throat, as I jerked my gaze away and stood there awkwardly, internally scolding myself for getting too close. Cameron settled the file on the corner of his desk and turned back in my direction.

"Have a seat," he insisted, gesturing again to the empty wooden chair.

I did, quickly, before my legs dropped me, and then pressed my thighs tightly together, suddenly relieved that I was wearing black slacks. My pen jiggled in my trembling hand, as Cameron paced around his desk. I clipped my pen onto my notebook, rested it on my thighs, and clutched the thick arms of the chair for support.

I closed my eyes and, out of nowhere, the memory of Cameron's penetrating gaze and passionate kiss flooded my senses. Thanks to my vivid photographic memory, all of our intimate interactions reeled through my mind like an HD movie.

I had spent so many hours thinking about that kiss, dreaming about Cameron's touch, and wondering what I had done wrong. Sure, playing around with Edwin was fun, but it wasn't the same. Despite our short time together, Cameron's rejection had truly scorched me. I had been branded, marked for life.

"Abigail. Are you even listening to me?" Cameron asked from behind his desk, dragging me out of my reverie.

"Uh huh," I lied.

"What did I say just now?" he tested, as he got up from his chair and stalked back toward me.

I parted my lips but, with no inspiration, I pressed them shut. My heart hammered in my chest as he drew closer yet. "I'm listening now," I finally said.

Navy clouds rolled and crashed in the nearby sky, rapidly wrapping around our building, threatening a vicious attack. Thundered boomed and shook the room, concealing my twitchy limbs and the rumble of my heartbeat.

Cameron pulled up another wooden chair, took a seat in it and dragged it closer to me until our knees were just touching. He nudged my notebook aside, leaned forward intimately and rested his hand on my lap. "I can understand if you don't want to work with me anymore. I know I've been less than friendly lately and I think I owe you an explanation."

That's an understatement! And yet I was already squirming in my seat, just from the friendly touch of his hand. Now, sitting this close to him, I was wound up like a toy. After all this time, I had never once told him how I felt about his rejection. And yet now I couldn't let him speak until he heard me out.

"Honestly, Cam, I'm going to come out with it. I can't stop thinking about the night of Owen's party. Our kiss...," I paused, slightly embarrassed, and glanced to the open doorway to ensure that it was empty.

After another breath I regained my composure. "I had a good time that night. But the morning after, when you left the breakfast table..." I paused again and sighed, exposing my utter disappointment.

I saw him wrinkle his adorable forehead. His eyes were marked with serious regret and his lips were downturned into an apologetic frown. And then the hydro flashed out, leaving the room heavily draped in shadows and my mind flaming colourful images of his dramatic expression.

Cameron's haunting eyes never left mine as the office fell eerily silent, except for the random curse of staff trying to wrap up their work before the battery backup shut down. The hydro didn't flash back on; not even a flicker.

I tried to focus on the man before me, until I realized his dark silhouette was drawing closer. I closed my eyes and gulped, not knowing what to expect next, as his face hovered so close I could feel his warm breath teasing over my lips.

I heard when his breath hitched and I felt when he

cautiously captured my upper lip between his. His mouth made a soft smooching sound that jump started my heart.

That single soft kiss was so electrically charged that I wondered if the whole office had felt it. There was no doubt in my mind that the sparks flying between us could have serviced the entire building. I was lucky to have been grounded, my knuckles turning white from the firm grip my fingers had on the wooden chair.

My feelings for him came rushing back like a tsunami, as his mouth touched mine again. I was overwhelmed with emotions: confusion, excitement and relief. He was careful and controlled, yet I could taste his urgency; his tongue savouring every lick. Then his mouth covered mine, hot and urgent and sensational.

When he stopped, I slowly lifted my lids and watched him sit back in his chair, cool and collected. I was startled by the fact that the hydro had already kicked back on. I straightened my shirt, to keep my trembling hands busy and my notepad fell to the floor.

I leaned forward to pick it up and dared to flash a look at his face. He was still slouched comfortably in his chair, only now his face was covered in a manly grin. I sat back myself and tried to assess his mood, but searching his eyes only turned me on more.

"I would say I hope I didn't offend you, but you didn't seem to put up much of a fight," Cameron said, after a moment of silence. His soft smirk tugged at my heart strings.

"Ah, funny guy. Real professional, by the way," I teased. All of my anger had diminished and my curiosity was getting the better of me. "Please tell me what you're doing here. Is this some sort of game to you?" I asked, very serious.

His face turned more serious than mine. "This is no game, Abigail; believe you me. These past few weeks have been difficult to say the least. I've been struggling with myself. I just can't stay away. I can't do it anymore. You win," he admitted, with defeat evident in his tone.

"I win? What do you mean exactly when you say I win? I thought this wasn't a game."

There was a knock at his door and we both glared at it. The hired help stood there stunned and fidgeting. "Your ten o'clock is here. They're early. I tried your phone, but it's on do-not-disturb." She abruptly turned back toward reception and scampered off.

Cameron looked at me, more concerned than before, but didn't say a word. After a few seconds of silence, I couldn't take it anymore. It shouldn't have been that difficult.

"You should go," I snapped, sarcastically. "You don't want to leave them waiting."

Though I was worried that we would never get back to this place emotionally, I had to protect my heart. I clutched my notepad to my chest and dashed for the door, my sadness flooding my thoughts.

"I owe you a better explanation," he called after me.

I paused in his doorway, waiting to hear what he had to say.

"We'll talk again very soon. I promise."

I drifted into the hall, without turning to face him, and slowly returned to my desk without responding. I felt as though my demonstration sent my feelings home with him. I wasn't waiting around anymore, and I certainly wasn't going to keep my hopes up. Now, if I could only get my heart to follow suit.

I sat at my desk and scanned over my notes, but glimmers of our kiss, each time better and more passionate than the last, enveloped my thoughts. It was devastating to be stuck reliving a past that may never replay again in reality.

The colour drained from my face, as a depressive panic set in. My stomach started to mimic the vicious clouds that were still storming around the City just waiting to strike again. I found myself short of breath, but refused to answer to the pills in my purse that were calling my name.

My mind was now on one track. I could've sat staring at my screen for the next hour, rehashing over all of the lost possibilities, or I could go home and let it out in private. It was imminent. It was only a matter of when.

The prospect of having a nervous breakdown or a crying fit in front of all of my coworkers was enough to give me the courage to ask. So when Owen tapped on my wall to say hello, only half an hour later, I took that as my opportunity to leave.

"Hey Owen, do you mind if I go home for a while? I'm not feeling all that well," I mumbled, with a real scratchy voice, no acting necessary. I took an unrewarding gulp.

"You don't look all that well. Did you and Cam have a chance to review the Badman file?" he asked. "We're on the trial list for the next sittings."

"My memo's clipped on the front of the file. I left it with him," I said. "I can come in early tomorrow morning to show you what I've done."

"No, no. I've been working you really hard lately. It's no wonder you're sick. I'll talk to Cameron about it. He can finalize the brief himself."

"Are you sure?"

"You take the day off and get better. You need only call if you need tomorrow too. Seriously Abby, we've got everything covered here."

I considered saying no, but having the day off could do me a lot of good. I could sort my tangled thoughts and Cam would have time to get his shit together.

"Thank you so much, Owen. I'll make up the time."

"Don't worry about the time, just get better," he insisted.

I nodded, feeling less than pleasant, as my breakfast burned up my wind pipe. I leapt from my chair, pushed Owen out of the way, and ran for the bathroom. I dashed into the first stall and it was like a badly aimed projectile that never quite made it to the toilet.

Moments later, as I was wiped up the last of the orange chunks off of the white porcelain tiles, Aliah snuck into the room with her fingers pinching her nose. "Everything alright in here?" she asked, pausing just inside the door.

"I don't know what's going on, but I'm not well at all," I

moaned.

"When Owen said you were sick, I didn't realize he meant you were actually blowing chunks. Nasty."

"I'm alright now," I insisted.

"Uh, let's not take any chances. It could be the stomach flu. You should go. Seriously, ew!"

I didn't want to be in the office when Cameron got out of his appointment, so I took Aliah's advice and hurriedly collected my things before racing off to my car.

Though it was still morning, it was so dark outside from the mixture of black and grey storm clouds. After I dropped into my car, I glanced in the front window of the office building. The boardroom was lit up like a stage and I could see through the reflective glass perfectly. I caught Cameron's expression, a mix of concern and curiosity, as he stared after my car pulling away from the parking lot.

I had already settled into a funk and couldn't have cared less about what he was feeling at the moment. Owen was right. I was not well. The burning sensation returned to my throat, warning me to pull over.

The right lane was packed, so I swerved into the left turning lane and slammed on my brakes. I yanked open my door and spilled my guts into the busy street. The traffic light turned red, granting me another moment, but a dry heave was all I had left. I slammed my door shut and pulled a napkin from the glove box to wipe my mouth.

Maybe I did have the flu; or food poisoning. I shivered, as unfriendly goose bumps scattered across my body. Somehow I couldn't find a way to lay the blame on Cameron. But I really wanted to.

Later that night, I was awakened by a knock on my bedroom door. It was dark and I could only see a large gray mass standing in the doorway. The hallway was illuminated behind him.

"Abby. You okay?"

"Mmm," I moaned. My head still felt like a ball of fire, but my body trembled from the cold.

"Owen told me you came home sick. I wanted to make

sure you weren't dead in here," Edwin said.

I cleared my dry throat. "Mmm, hmm," I replied, my voice still scratchy.

"I figured you would want me to wait until a stench was coming from your room before I checked up on you, but I just can't do it."

I couldn't even bring myself to laugh, though I knew he was trying to make me feel better. "What time is it anyway?" I croaked, as I squinted at the alarm clock. I squeezed my eyes shut. They still stung from the endless tears that I had shed before finally falling asleep. I rolled away from the light, so Edwin wouldn't notice.

He walked farther into the room and placed a glass of water on top of a book I had resting on my nightstand. "It's almost six thirty. I brought you a drink. Can I get you anything else?" Edwin pressed his palm to my forehead and brushed my hair aside.

"No. I'm going to try and sleep it off, okay?" Sure, I could sleep off the illness, but the heartache would be a little more tricky.

When I woke up the next morning the sun shone between two fluffy clouds, breaking through the thick morning fog. I slowly sat up in my bed, feeling a bit dizzy from the length of time I had been horizontal, but I quickly adjusted.

My stomach clenched with hunger pains and I was glad to see that it was already past eight thirty. I couldn't believe that I had slept through Edwin's morning routine. On the other hand, I was relieved that I could have some privacy in the house for the day.

I moped to the kitchen and took a seat at the table, feeling less than inspired for breakfast. I noticed a folded piece of paper there, but ignored it to rest my elbows on the tabletop and drop my hot forehead into my palms. After rummaging up the courage to open it, I unfolded the note.

Abs,
I was a little worried about you, so I made you breakfast.
You have to eat something. I hope it's still good when you get
your butt out of bed. It's in the fridge.
~ Eddie

P.S. Cameron called. He's worried too, BUT I'M WORRIED
MORE. Hope you're feeling better.

I laughed inside and it brought a sore smile to my face. I
didn't want to think about Cameron just now, it hurt my
brain, so I focused on Edwin and his sweetness. He had
made me chocolate chip pancakes, with extra chocolate
chips, just how I liked them. Unfortunately, after two
mouthfuls, my belly reminded me to take it easy, so I tossed
the rest in the garbage and settled for dry toast.

I enjoyed a drama-free day alone, took a long nap and
then prepared a nice meal for Edwin, even though my
stomach really couldn't handle eating much of it.

"I'm just glad you're feeling better," Edwin said, as he
loaded a pile of potatoes onto his plate and drowned them
in gravy.

I smiled and enjoyed his company, while he enjoyed his
beer.

"It's amazing how quickly you forget about what this
stuff can do to you, eh?" He laughed as he took a drink from
his bottle. "It's a vicious cycle."

My eyes had glazed over, my heart lost in the tangled
depths of my mind. "Isn't it though?" I said, referring
secretly to the mistakes I continued to make with men.

CHAPTER FIFTEEN

I managed to suffer through a long, gruelling day at work, after my two day absence. Owen was still in court, so I knew there was no urgent need for me to stay long past five o'clock. I was looking forward to cuddling up on the couch with a movie and calling it an early night.

As I lifted the heavy stack of files off my desk, I wondered if Cam was ever going to grow the balls to initiate that talk with me. I rushed to the vault, pushed that thought aside, and piled the files on the small desk against the wall. I shuffled through the shelves and returned each file to its home. One file left and I was out of there.

It was when I reached back for the last file that I realized I wasn't alone. The small, stuffy, cave-like room suddenly felt like a dungeon. A cold hand rested on top of mine and startled me, tipping my nerves to a ridiculous state of anxiety. My sharp squeal didn't quite escape the back of my throat.

My eyes flashed up, through long dark lashes, to see the man standing over me. "Cam." I pulled my hand away from his with an agitated snap.

He slowly retrieved his hand, seeming hurt by my sudden withdrawal. "I'm sorry. I didn't mean to startle you."

Ignoring that, I lifted the last file from the table. "If you'll excuse me," I said, and awkwardly scuffled past him. "After I put this file back, I'll be out of your way." I whirled away and frantically searched for the file's place, wanting desperately to escape from that suffocating room.

"Please don't run off." He took a step closer to me, and then another. He was much too close now. "How are you feeling?"

"Fine," I said, only referring to my gut. My heart was

sobbing as we spoke. "You?" I asked without turning to look at him.

"Not very well," he said smoothly, without elaborating.

I ordered myself not to believe for one second that it was because of me. "Sorry to hear that."

When I found where the file went, I slipped it into place, just as one of our new coworkers appeared in the doorway. "Mr. Clarke. I'm sorry to interrupt, but there's an Ashley Clarke on line two."

Cameron turned his head toward her, his body unmoved. "Thank you. Can you please tell her I'm busy?" he said, in a firm authoritative voice. His eyes returned to mine. "What are you up to tonight?"

"I, uh, uh...," I stuttered, scouring my brain for a decent lie. "I guess nothing much."

A smile returned to his eyes, though his low brows still heavily shadowed them in the poorly lit room. I glanced over his shoulder to see that we still had company. I pressed my lips together and covered my mouth with one hand, my other resting on my elbow as I glanced toward the floor.

Cameron spun around and gave the girl a deep shadowed stare. "Yes?"

"I do apologize sir, but she thought you might say that and insisted that it was quite urgent. She really wouldn't take no for an answer," she explained, with a blush.

He closed his eyes and sighed. The girl remained in the door, frozen in place, waiting for his instructions.

"You'd better go," I said, then ignorantly brushed past him. "We wouldn't want to piss Ashley off."

He eloquently grabbed my elbow with his well-groomed fingers. I cranked my head around to glare at him, my shiny brown hair dramatically fanning from my head. He had effectively stopped me in my tracks and held me in place with his arresting eyes.

Without releasing me from his haunting stare, he raised his voice so the girl knew he was talking to her. "If you will be so kind, please tell Ms. Clarke that I'm busy and will be sure to call her when I'm free."

"Yes sir," she replied, and immediately scurried away.

I smiled inwardly, imagining Ashley's fury when the poor temp girl delivered her the message, until Cameron's eyes burrowed into mine.

"Dinner. My place. Meet me there at six thirty and I won't take no for an answer."

His orders left me with an aching desire that both intrigued and disgusted me. My inflamed heart was beating wildly from my chest and I only hoped he couldn't hear it, being so close to me. Air was forcing in and out of my swollen wind pipe, as a heightened awareness honed through the length of my body.

Could we really be back on, just like that? I could've sworn I saw it in his eyes.

His hand released my arm and his skillful fingers briefly brushed my cheek, before he stormed away, leaving me standing there in total shock.

Long after Cameron was out of sight, he was still on my mind. Consumed by a mixture of anxiety and exhilaration, I hurried home to get ready for my date. I picked out my cutest outfit and applied a darker coat of makeup. I dabbed my lips with a fruity red gloss, brushed my cheeks with a rosy shimmer and heavily shadowed my eyes with a rainbow of darkness.

My mood followed suit, fueling a sassy attitude that was sure to show him what he had been missing out on.

When I arrived on his doorstep, fashionably late, I lightly tapped on his ravenous red door. I heard him shuffling around inside, then it became silent for a few seconds. I wondered if he had suddenly changed his mind. I shivered from a cool, unexpected breeze, but it fired up my intrigue. I even considered kicking down the door with my spiked heel, if necessary. I was going in.

Just then the door swung open and Cameron stood before me, looking drop dead gorgeous, a charming sweetness spilling from his face. His sleeves were folded back to his elbows and he had a dish towel thrown over his shoulder, which I found incredibly sexy.

"Hey," I said. No matter how hard I tried to be a selfish bitch, I couldn't deny my attraction to him and his charm made it difficult to be so callous.

"Come in," he replied.

I flashed him a smile and a lash-full glance, as I brushed past him.

He closed the door behind me and then froze in place, as I bent over to remove my shoes. "You look amazing," he said, softly.

While I had planned on confronting him immediately and demanding an explanation, he warmed my cold heart, making it difficult for me to be rude. Since he didn't make any move toward the kitchen, I boldly took his hand, pulled him past the elephant in the room and led him there myself. "What's for dinner? I'm starving."

A grin curled onto his lips, the beginning of a very handsome smile. Once we reached the kitchen, I stopped in the entry, stunned to see that the table was empty. I glanced at him confused. He pulled the towel from his shoulder and tossed it onto the countertop. His smiling eyes led me to another doorway I hadn't noticed before.

"Come," he said, his hand still in mine as he led me to the small, but cozy, dining room.

My eyes immediately zoned in on the candles of all sizes, thoughtfully decorated as the table centerpiece. More candles were sprinkled around the room, the dim glow sensually setting the mood. I absently gasped at the stunning romantic gesture, my sparkly cheeks flushed with a warm glow of disbelief.

Cameron watched me, smiled, and let go of my hand to pull out my chair.

As I took my seat, it became obvious that dinner was ready and I was late. I nibbled on my glossy lower lip, suddenly feeling a bit impolite for being tardy. "It looks lovely," I admitted, as I admired the two place settings.

"I'm glad you like it." He rounded the table and the flames all seemed to magnetize to him.

"Where's Pheobe?" I asked, curious to know.

Cameron took his seat and poured me a glass of wine from the chilled bottle. "I wanted you for myself tonight."

That statement delivered a chilling intrigue that set me right back in the office, in the darkness, with that kiss. With a deep inhale, I appreciated the aroma of the expensive wine and the tantalizing words coming from the sexy man who poured it. I took a sip as he filled his glass, then he lifted the lid from the pasta dish.

"Help yourself," he said.

I did, and it was delicious. The pasta was covered in a rose blush sauce and had slices of blackened chicken breast on top. It smelled divine. I took another bite and I closed my eyes to fully appreciate the flavour. It was even tastier than it looked. "Mmm, this is really good Cam. I'm impressed." My tongue darted out over my lower lip and when I opened my eyes, I realized Cameron was studying me.

"You're not the only one," he said, in a low, velvety voice. His eyes sparkled in the dim candlelight.

The combination of the fruity wine and his attention, sent good vibrations spiralling through me. Without losing contact with those eyes, I took another sip from my glass.

The rest of our dinner was rather quiet, as I tried to tamp down the desire exploding through my insides. Despite my efforts, a restless charge arched through the room and unnerved my body.

"I didn't know you were such a romantic," I said, as I slid out of my chair to help clean up.

Cam smiled at me from across the table and it fired up those feelings again full force. "There's a first time for everything," he replied, leaving me immersed in a special place.

I headed to the sink with my hands full of dirty dishes and a smile on my face. Cam rushed up behind me and took them from my hands. "I can get the rest of the dishes later," he insisted. One of his hands lingered on mine as he put the dishes in the sink with his other hand.

Before he could woo me further, and avoid the subject of *what the hell happened the morning after Owen's party*, I spoke up. "There's something we need to talk about." I paused, wondering how to say it nicely. "You never did tell me why you've been avoiding me. I have to tell you it wasn't a very good feeling to be shunned like that."

There. I said it. The elephant has been exposed. Now what?

My heart took to a gallop as I waited for his response.

He slowly slid his hand off of mine and hesitated even longer before he answered. "I guess I owe you that much," he said. "I just hate to throw her under the bus like that."

My stare told him he'd better damn well tell me right now, but I remained tight lipped.

He took my hand back into both of his and gazed at me, his eyes growing as dark and deep as a well. "Ash really does mean well," he said with pause. "She just felt that I would be better off without a woman in my life right now. Without you. She thought I should establish myself at the firm first."

A breath left my lungs and it felt as though I might never breathe again. I wanted to cry, one tear welling in my left eye. *He's not looking for a relationship. Then what the hell is this?*

His eyes swirled with darkness when he looked deeper into mine. "She was wrong."

The light instantly touched my lungs with a breath of fresh air. *Sure, life isn't a game but: Yay, I win! Score one for me beotch!*

Cameron pressed a soft kiss to my cheek, with a promise of more. I needed so much more than that. His parted lips slowly trailed across my skin, until he had a taste of my mouth. I melted into him, willing to take everything and anything that he had to offer.

He left me hanging, hot and bothered, as he swiftly glided to the fridge and pulled out another bottle of wine. He tucked it under his arm, reached into his cabinet for another pair of wine glasses and stretched his free hand out to me.

I took it, feeling a little weak in the knees, as he nudged a pair of his leather loafers toward me. I slipped them on then let him pull me through the screened gazebo, out past the patio and deeper into his backyard.

We walked down the long flagstone pathway in silence. Solar lights lit up the path like a meandering landing strip. The trail crept through the landscape, rounding big old trees and cutting through the thick blue lawn.

I noticed a clearing up ahead and, after passing through an ivy covered arbour, I could see the entire flagstone space stretching out the entire width of the yard. It was like our own little garden getaway and I had him all to myself.

A heady excitement sharpened my senses, as a cool breeze rushed past me. I watched Cameron flip some switches until flames began to flicker from the built-in fire pit. Large flat-topped rocks flanked the fire and acted as permanent seating. I went to take a seat, but he stopped me, quickly retrieving a soft, neutral cushion from a cute wooden garden shed.

When he returned to my side, he filled his empty wine glass rather full and placed it on an exquisite table nearby, then snatched up my glass and filled it to the brim.

When I finally sat down, I was giddy from all his efforts at romanticizing me, and was fighting hard to hide it. "You don't have to do that, you know," I said, unintentionally fluttering my eyelashes.

He offered me my wine glass. "Do what?"

I took a sip of the tasty wine. "Mmm. The wine. Don't get me wrong. It's delicious. But I like you just fine when I'm sober."

He sat beside me, just as he had at the office, our knees touching. A quick reminder of our scorching kiss flashed through my memory and warmed my blood. The wicked smile that played on his lips did things to my heart and another region due south.

His eyebrows hung low over his eyes, shadowing his charming stare. "I'll do anything if it'll up the odds of keeping you here longer," he said, drawing me into his mesmeric gaze.

I took another sip of the warming liquid and sighed. I didn't want to feel so damn content. I stared into the flames for a long while, until an uncomfortable silence fell between us. I chewed on my bottom lip and Cameron seemed to notice the distress that began to settle in my posture.

"Everything alright?" he asked.

"Actually, I hate to say this but, we still need to talk."

"Uh oh. Am I in trouble?"

I sighed, a bit flustered by his mischievous behaviour. I doubted the onset of intoxication was helping my situation. "I'm serious. This is serious."

He straightened himself and his face fell blank. He reached for my hand and gently caressed it with his thumb. "I'm sorry. Go on."

My skin moulded into little bumps and his hand massaged up my arm chasing the chill. "I know you gave me an explanation, and I'm happy to hear that you'll be making your own decisions from now on, but..."

My voice began to tremble, like my nerves. I tried to pull myself together, but my hesitation only made things worse. "I thought everything was going good after Owen's party, and even over brunch," I said. "Then you got that call." I paused again, choking on my words.

He sat there all attentive and concerned, looking so god-damned gorgeous, waiting patiently for me to finish. His seductive fingers continued to caress erotically over my skin like a strip of silk.

"It was like we were done. Your goodbye kiss was cold. You never called. I don't know that I'm ready to go through that again," I admitted, as I pulled my hand free of his. I hated that I was boo-hooing after such a short relationship, but I had already let him get to me.

When Cameron tipped my chin up, I was toast. A tear slipped from my eye. I hated that. He took in a deep breath and exhaled out loud, his face now wrought with tension, as he carefully considered his words.

"Honestly, I invited you here tonight so I could explain." The fire flickered higher, licking the night sky, casting shadows across his face. Cameron's voice shook with trepidation, when he usually thrived under pressure. He took another careful breath and shook his head, confused by his own reaction. "I'm sorry," he said. "I'm just a little nervous." He took a healthy swallow of his wine.

The damn liquor was testing me, pulling out emotions that I thought were bottled up for good. I wanted to wrap my arms around him and shout it to the world how amazing he made me feel. I felt like such a goof, fighting to stifle those evil innards from exposing my weakness.

"It was Ashley, Abigail. It was her on the phone that morning at the diner. She told me that Pheobe was sick and needed me. I panicked."

"And was she?"

"She had an upset stomach. She was crying for me. Nothing Ash couldn't have dealt with, but I felt incredibly guilty. She suggested I obviously don't have time in my life for family, work *and* you..."

"Particularly me," I interrupted, the liquor controlling my big mouth.

He swallowed and nodded reluctantly. "I thought I was being selfish, taking time away from Pheobe to spend it with you. Ashley had me convinced that I wasn't being fair to her. It's bad enough she has to grow up without her mother, but for me not to be there for her when she needed me. It was too much."

"And now?" Another tear dripped down my cheek and Cameron quickly smeared it away. I hugged his arm and pressed my lips into his warm shirted shoulder, absorbing his heat as his hand stroked gently over my hair.

"I know that you're not going to take me away from Pheobe," he said softly, next to my ear. "I'll never leave her. She's my blood; the most important little person to me in the whole world."

I tilted my head to gaze into Cameron's sad, sad eyes. "I would never try to separate you from your daughter. I know that you two are a package deal."

When Cameron smiled, I nearly fell backwards, but it only made him clutch onto me tighter.

He weaved his fingers into my hair. "That's just it. Ash doesn't get it. Pheobe may have a large piece of my heart, but there's a certain vacancy there that can't be filled by my little girl."

Reflecting on his words, I focused on his dark brooding eyes. "Do you have another girl in mind?" I asked, softly.

When he smirked this time, his forehead wrinkled. "Well, actually, there is this one girl," he said. Then, slow and careful, he leaned down to kiss me.

His warm, soft lips set my body ablaze. "Mmm, I can't get enough of her," he growled. "Her skin's so smooth." His fingers whispered over my arm. "Her lips are so soft." He brushed his mouth softly across mine. "She's really quite a looker; intelligent too. You wouldn't know her," he teased.

I giggled at his playfulness. *Oh, I like this side of him.* He dipped in for another devastating kiss.

Cameron cupped my cheek and his gaze turned serious. "You don't have to worry about Ashley anymore. I'm done with the blank stares at work and being a zombie at home. I refuse to punish the people I love like this. It's not fair to Pheobe and it's not fair to you."

I sat there dumbfounded, but didn't take my eyes from his.

Did he just say love?

No. I must have misunderstood.

But no woman in her right mind could be angry at a man who was only doing what he thought was best for his child. For me though, I had to know for sure.

"Are you positive you're ready to move on?"

A gust of wind passed between us and I shivered, little goose bumps returning to my arms. Though the wine was keeping my cheeks warm, and the constant flicker from the fire kept my feet toasty, my body was frigid, an icy realization hounding my thoughts.

All nightmares and run-ins with my monstrous late sister

had all but vanished ever since the day I met Cameron. Peculiar.

I should have felt relieved, but instead I felt harassed with worry. Cameron wrapped his arm around my shoulder, his body heat instantly warming my mass and my heart. When he squeezed me close, it was difficult for me to think about anything but him in that moment.

"Without a doubt, I'm ready for you," he whispered.

My heart fluttered as he leaned closer. My eyes dropped closed to kiss him. His sensitivity overwhelmed me and, as our lips caressed, a few more tears slipped from my eyes. His tenderness moved me and made me want to show him how much I cared.

The words *'I love you'* rang in my ears like wedding bells. *I bet that's the last thing he wants to hear about now.* But those feelings ran strong and stabbed at my heart like it was meant to be.

Cameron lifted me onto his lap and caressed the length of my thigh. "I mean it, Abby. I'm not letting go this time."

CHAPTER SIXTEEN

Edwin downed another shot, but nothing seemed to take the edge off tonight. He had every intention of getting wasted beyond recognition and was well on his way already. His boys said they'd be meeting him at the club tonight, but he decided to get a head start by himself. He'd be lucky if he could even stand by the time they got there.

He knew it was as good as fact now: Abigail was good as gone. Cameron Clarke had swooped in, stole her heart and left Edwin to clean up the irreparable damage; the destruction to his heart from a lifetime of love lost.

Tonight had solidified his worries. When he saw Abigail leave the house, it hardened his fears and amped up his anxiety. She had stepped up her game and was determined to make Cameron hers. She was good at getting what she wanted; especially in the man department.

Edwin had tried to seduce Abby, time and time again, but she just wasn't having it anymore. She wasn't opening herself to his provocation and so he was left high and dry. Helpless. Hopeless. He had been putting up a good front, but he was sinking; sinking into a deep, dark depression.

Edwin felt lost. Then his thoughts started to get foggy. The shadows started to close in on him. His vision was blurred and his head was all wishy-washy. He downed another shot and rested his forehead against the cold, hard bar. He closed his eyes and gave in to the darkness dragging him under.

Jenny Jenkins hugged the shadows and followed Edwin to the club unnoticed. She was satisfied that Abby was in good hands for the night, so she could finally focus her attention on Edwin. He had taken a cab all on his own, which was different from his usual routine. *It's about time.* She had been working that angle for so many months and it was finally happening.

He was all hers.

Jenny had a thing for Edwin ever since they met all those years earlier. She was only a small girl, but it was love at first sight; at least for her it was. As Edwin grew up, he only filled out and became more of the man that she wanted, but could never have. Tonight that would all change.

Jenny didn't leave anything to chance tonight. She had been planning this encounter for years. Six years to be exact. Ever since Cameron's nightmare of a child decided she had a fighting chance in her, Jenny had made it her full time job to make sure Pheobe didn't upset her progress.

It irked her that Pheobe was her only real human contact in eighteen long years and she hated to admit that she started to take a liking to her. *For that, Pheobe can live another day.*

Jenny was ready to put her plan into action. Everything was going perfectly. Edwin was desperate and she was looking fly in her super short, plaid skirt and ruffled white blouse; a school girl from every man's wildest fantasy.

She had gone all out tonight too, having made a stop at a lingerie store to purchase a sexy white lace push-up bra. It was doing its job, thrusting her supple breasts out the top of her unbuttoned blouse and drawing every man's attention to her. If they only knew that the thigh high white stockings had a silky garter belt fastened to them.

The club was packed and her duplication of Abigail's ID had worked like a charm. Even with her hair in braided pig-tails, her lips draped in a glossy dark purple and her eyes covered with black framed glasses, Jenny could still pass for her identical twin sister.

Now, she only wished that she had looked into those contacts sooner. Who knew that the same coloured contacts that could turn a human into a monster could cover her red eyes and give her another chance to roam about undetected. She had gone for the dark violet colour and now her eyes were as striking as every other asset she had on display.

It was so exciting for her to be out in society mingling with the living. She hadn't dared try her luck sooner, in case her experiment failed. She had saved herself, for Edwin.

It wouldn't be long now. Edwin had tried to pass out at the bar, but the bartender had shoved him awake only a moment later, and it didn't take long for a horde of girls to attack him. Sitting at a small table in the upper balcony that framed the entire club, Jenny watched Edwin stumble onto the dance floor.

Edwin was good and drunk and none of his friends were anywhere to be found. She doubted they'd be there anytime soon too, since she had taken care of their cars. A couple of slashed tires and a disconnected battery never hurt anyone.

Jenny sipped her drink, as a waitress stopped and dropped another on her table. She was curious to know where it had come from. The waitress pointed at a handsome young man, who was staring at her with eager, hungry eyes. He had nothing on Edwin.

"Thanks," Jenny said, accepting the drink. She raised it up to the handsome young man in acknowledgement, but he was too mesmerized with her beauty to grow the balls to approach her. She was glad. She had more important things to worry about tonight.

Her nerves were starting to get to her, but for this she had to be sober. After a couple of sips of her friendly drink, she winked at the purchaser and slunk through the shadows toward the stairs. The main floor was crowded and she warmed to the idea of feeling Edwin under her nails. She would remember this night for the rest of her death.

Walking down the stairs, every man's head turned to watch her. Her smile was sexy and her target was fixed. She didn't take her eyes off the prize.

That girl better get her hands off of him before she suffers from some unforeseen injury. She giggled wickedly. *This would be fun.*

Edwin hunched over the petite girl in front of him and swayed drunkenly to the music. It felt good to just let go. No worries. No responsibilities. He squinted at the girl whose hands kept stroking his ass and her words his ego. He wished she'd just shut the fuck up already.

So when she started limping, as though she somehow twisted her ankle, he was happy that her lady friends took care of her. *Klutz.*

Moments later, he focused his heavy, squinted eyes on a stunning beauty who danced provocatively on the other end of the dance floor. It was like she was dancing for him; mesmerizing him with her hips, her hands gliding up and down her long slim body.

He wanted to do that.

When she bounced, so did her breasts, and her skirt floated a little too high, exposing naked thigh above her sexy white stockings. He gulped back his desire as he adjusted his boner. This girl was gorgeous, straight out of his dreams, and he wanted her.

He hadn't wanted anyone like this since Abigail but, as the girl moved closer to him, he ached with a need to touch. She twirled around and slipped into his arms, as though she belonged there. She took his hands and drew them up her slim waist , then dropped them to her wide hips.

He was so fucking hard.

She danced in front of him like a seductive sea nymph, resting her head back on his chest and drawing his body against her. He needed more. It was like she could read his mind. She rocked against him until he was ready to blow, then spun around and pressed her full perky breasts against him.

He had only caught a glimpse of her violet eyes. They

were a melancholic oddity, but to him they were as glorious as her body. She pressed her cheek against his partially exposed chest and dug her nails into his back, like she never wanted to let him go.

He felt the sudden urge to stroke her; to tell her that everything would be okay. He smoothed his hand over her braid and drew his other hand up her back. Then, unable to stop himself, he wrapped his hand around that braid and pulled her head back, willing her to give him another look at her stunning eyes.

When she fluttered her lashes open and glanced up at him through those gorgeous, violet eyes, he wanted nothing more than to kiss her. He cupped her cheek and smoothed his thumb over her baby soft flesh. She seemed so familiar, but the need he was suffering from was something else entirely.

She looked scared; but why? He wanted to make it okay. He needed to make it good. Releasing her pony tail, he slowly inched closer to those luscious, purple lips and had a taste. She was hesitant and breathless, and he hoped that was a good thing. Her fingers tightened on his shirt, telling him it was.

He pressed another kiss to her soft glossy pout and she barely parted her lips for him. He wanted more; needed more. He deepened the kiss, his tongue, soft and wet and demanding. He felt the moment when she softened beneath him and welcomed his expert tongue at last.

Jenny stole a glimpse of Edwin's swimming, blue eyes in between a bout of passionate kisses. She hadn't expected there to be such a rush when he looked into her soul. It was more intense than she could have ever imagined. His hands smoothed over her body and gripped onto her thighs, twisting her insides into knots, as he held her possessively and fed from her mouth.

Everything was better than she could have ever thought

possible. The feel of his solid chest under her fingers. His skin under her nails. His strong arms wrapped snugly around her. Even the pain in his swimming, aqua eyes couldn't compare to the intensity of his erection pushing against her hip. Just the scent of Edwin; living, breathing, Edwin. She was desperate for more.

But she knew her time was running short, as TJ stormed into the building. "Yeah, baby," he hollered, when he saw the crowd of dancers.

A couple of TJ's buddies strolled up next to him and Caleb followed suit, with a girl already hooked onto his waist.

"Drinks," Caleb hollered, as they all stormed the bar. Not a one saw Edwin locking lips heatedly with Abigail's evil twin.

As Jenny came up for air, her intuition forced her to note her surroundings.

Dammit! How did they get here so soon?

Edwin's friends were more resourceful than she gave them credit for.

Edwin saw her heated stare toward his approaching friends and when he turned to see what she was looking at, she disappeared into the shadows.

"Hey, bro!" TJ shouted, fist pumping to the music.

Edwin turned around to loop his arm back around his mysterious, fantasy girl, but she was already gone. He spun around again, searching for her desperately, but she had vanished. She had disappeared right from underneath his nose; gone out of his life before he could even ask her name.

But they had shared something special. It wasn't just carnal desire, though there was plenty of that. It was something more. He had to find her. She had to be here somewhere.

"Yo, TJ! Did you see that girl who was with me like two seconds ago?" Edwin slurred.

TJ narrowed his eyes like a stoned criminal.

"Tall, brunette, long legs, pig-tails, glasses. Did you see her?"

TJ patted him on his shoulder, a huge smile cracking onto his face. "Right, Bro. I saw her alright. In my dreams."

Edwin shook his head, confusion fogging his brain as TJ laughed at him. He hadn't dreamt her up; had he? She was real. She had to be real. He could still feel her soft skin on his fingers, taste her purple lips on his tongue.

"What's that on your face?" TJ asked, staring at him like he had something atrocious growing from his mouth.

Edwin wiped his mouth onto his hand and a streak of coloured gloss smeared across it. Edwin smiled and licked his bottom lip. He knew it. She was real.

CHAPTER SEVENTEEN

The emotions I felt, I refused to call love for fear of jinxing it. Back in Cameron's house, there was definitely an air of romance about it. It was intimate. Me and him and no one else.

A smoky mist poured from the dining room, as Cameron blew out the last of the candles. When he appeared in the doorway an incredibly sexy storm swirled behind him, drawing me to him. Cameron tucked me into his arms and stunned me with his dark, dreamy eyes.

"I hope you realize I won't be shy with you at the office anymore," I said softly, drawing my fingers through his short, spiky hair.

"You're my girl, Abby, and I want everyone to know it. I mean, you are my girl, *right*?"

I smiled and batted my eyelashes at him and any uncertainty that had shown in his expression was wiped away in an instant. "While I'm happy to hear you say those words, I think maybe you should tell Ashley before you start hollering it from the rooftops." I pulled free from his arms and headed toward his front door.

"I have nothing to hide," he insisted, dragging his feet behind me.

"You should also know that random office romances never work out." I peered over my shoulder and smirked.

He bundled me back in his arms and not a breath of air could squeeze between us. "This is hardly random. But if you mean you want to be the first to tell Edwin, before we start flaunting each other in public, I can be patient. But not too patient."

His smile did wicked things to my insides, and the fact that he could read my mind just blew me away. "Thank you for understanding," I whispered.

"Don't keep me waiting too long though. I feel like I've already waited long enough. I say they should brace themselves because it's time for everyone to know that you're mine, yeah?"

I nodded my head, yes, mesmerized by his possessive infatuation.

Cameron smiled again and his hands grasped onto me so tight, like he thought I might run away if he let go. He stole a slow, soft nibble of my upper lip and I was like putty in his hands. "Stay with me tonight."

I wanted to. "I shouldn't. I mean, I can't."

"Well, which one is it?" he said, smirking.

"I can't. I'm sorry, Cam. I know Ashley'll be back soon and you have some convincing to do. I don't think she'll be very pleasant if I'm still here when she returns."

"It's not up to Ashley. I'll deal with her. I don't need permission. I need you."

His words sprinkled over me like warm, summer sunshine, causing me to uncontrolledly attack him, like a misty, raging waterfall. I kissed him with all that I had, passion pouring from every inch of me. Cameron took it all in, the intensity of his response arousing every fiber of my being.

Quickly seeing where things were heading, I broke away from the kiss and gasped for a breath. As the rise and fall of my chest steadied, my heart continued to gallop like it was winning a race. I pressed my lips together and closed my eyes, not super excited to say what I was thinking.

"Good night, Cameron," I said softly, leaning down to slip on my shoes.

He took my hand and trailed his other one down my side, hesitating at his door, hoping his pleading eyes could convince me to stay. I fought the internal battle, ready to lose, until he suddenly opened the door.

"I don't want you to go, but I won't make you stay either."

He wasn't happy with me, but I had to go. In an attempt to strut my sexy ass down the three stairs to my car, I stumbled forward. In my heels, there was no way around the awkward twist of my ankle, as I nearly fell on my face. I caught myself before I face-planted, but not before satisfactorily bruising my self-confidence.

Cameron could tell I was fine, except for my utter embarrassment, and just stared at me from his perch on the deck. "I think you've had a little too much to drink. You'd better come back inside." That wicked smile returned, making flutters ripple through my insides.

"Oh, and I wonder who's responsible for that one," I said, propping my hands on my hips. "I don't think so."

"I'll drive you home," he insisted, not leaving me any other option. He grabbed his keys from a hook next to the door, locked the knob and raced down the steps.

"No, I can call a cab." I didn't want to put him out and he had drank just as much as me.

He stood next to me, brooding, staring me down with a frown; but I held my chin high, as stubborn as always.

"If you insist," he said with a sigh. "I'll call you a cab. But I really wish you would just stay." His fingers trickled over my cheek.

Holding on tight to my purse, as though it was my resolve, I carefully walked back up the stairs and had a seat on the top step. The cement was cold, but I acted like it wasn't uncomfortable. For once I felt like I was actually proceeding with caution.

While waiting for the cab, Cam continued to plead with me and showered me with kisses, until the car pulled into his driveway. *Who knew begging could be so damn sexy?*

After walking me to the bright blue car, he stopped me and brushed my hair from my eyes, his touch so light but his eyes shadowed and intense. He dipped for another kiss.

I expected it to be soft and short, but it was long and hard, and full of passion. When his lips left mine, I thought I might fall over, stunned by his hot-blooded seduction.

"I'll call you tomorrow." He smiled, then delivered another delicious kiss.

"You'd better."

My eyes flashed open at nine a.m. sharp, but I was still out of it; in a deep drugged-like state. The phone had been ringing and ringing and ringing. Finally, after the fifth annoying chime, I groaned.

Where the hell was Edwin?

My eyes were so sleepy, I didn't bother to check the call display. "Hello?" I answered, my voice a grouchy growl.

"Rise and shine."

"Cameron?"

"What? Were you planning on sleeping the whole day away? Pheobe and I want you to come out and play."

I felt like I had been hit over the head with a brick. Wine always had a way of doing that to me and, so far, so did Cameron. Regardless, he had my attention and awoke me from my drunken slumber with a wide smile on my face. "What are you doing, Cam?"

"I'm calling you. I told you I'd call. Are you going to come out with us or what?"

"Whose idea was it to invite me?" I asked, as I sat up and folded my legs together.

"Pheobe's actually."

"Right," I said, sarcastically.

"I may have put a bug in her ear," he admitted.

Pheobe screamed in the background. "Ewww! No, Daddy."

"I didn't actually put a bug in your ear honey. It's just a saying." Talking to his daughter, he sounded incredibly sweet. "So, are you with me? It's a beautiful autumn day."

A smile was now plastered on my face. "I would love to, but I don't want to hold you up. You have no idea how long it takes me to get ready."

Cameron chuckled. "We'll give you as much time as you need. Pheobe will be really disappointed if you say no and I may be a little upset too," he teased.

"No Daddy, don't be sad," Pheobe said, her mouth right

next to the phone.

"I'm getting up," I said, unable to resist the adorable pair. "I'll be ready in an hour."

After hanging up the phone, I leapt from my bed with a surprising spring in my step. I pranced to the bathroom and jumped into the shower to wash away my exhaustion.

Cameron showed up at my house two minutes after ten, not leaving me an extra second to get ready.

"Just a minute," I hollered, as I ran down the hall and scaled the stairs. I pounced on the door and opened it wide.

Pheobe skipped past her handsome father and hugged my leg. "Hi, Abby. Are you ready to go?" she exclaimed, clearly excited about our play date.

"Just another minute. Come on in," I said to Cam, as Pheobe began to investigate my home.

She pulled a framed picture from the decorative table. "Who's that boy in the picture with you?" she asked.

Embarrassed, I pulled the picture from her hand and returned it to the table, leaving it flat on the surface. "That's my roommate. He lives here too."

"Oh," she said, then skipped off into the other room.

"Kids," Cam said to me. "Pheobe; get back here."

"It's fine," I said. "She won't hurt anything."

"You're sure?" he asked hesitantly, not sharing my confidence.

"Absolutely. We're the only ones here." I jogged up a couple of stairs. "Coming? I can give you the grand tour later."

Cameron glanced back, until he caught Pheobe nosing around the living room and bouncing her butt on the cushy sofa. "We're going upstairs, honey," Cameron called.

"Okay, Daddy," Pheobe hollered back, staying behind.

Cameron followed me up the stairs and stopped at my bedroom door, waiting for an invitation.

"You can come in," I insisted, with a smirk.

He checked over his shoulder again and then followed me into my room, studying it as I tossed my phone in my purse. I walked to my closet and stood there, thoughtfully deciding what jacket to wear. I was pleasantly surprised when Cameron embraced me from behind.

"I missed you," he growled, dropping kisses behind my ear.

"Seriously?" A smile curled onto my lips. "It's only been a few hours since I left you and for most of them you were sleeping."

He nipped at my ear. "Let me correct you. Most of them *you* were sleeping; me not so much. I couldn't stop thinking about you. You should've stayed."

He twirled me around and kissed me passionately, his lips devouring mine; his tongue tasting my fresh mouthwash. His hands explored every curve of my body, as we kissed and touched, hot and unguardedly.

Out of the blue, I had an attack of the parental police. "Wait! What about your rule?" I stammered, still clutched in his arms near ready to scream in release.

"What rule?" he asked, curiously amused. He tugged my lip with his teeth and my insides twisted into a tight, delicious knot. He ran his hand down my arm and slipped my hand into his.

"Pheobe's in the house," I whispered. "What if she saw you touching me like that?"

"That rule has to do with my house," he said, and then he laughed.

"Daddy?" Pheobe called sweetly, as she peeked in the door.

She playfully trotted into the room and checked everything out. I was worried to see her reaction to her father being wrapped around me, but she didn't seem to notice.

"Hey, babe. We're all ready to go now," he told her, without letting me go. "Right, Abby?"

I pulled away from Cameron, feeling a little self-conscious in front of Pheobe, but he refused to let go of my hand and jerked me back toward him.

I pulled my favourite jacket from a hook in my closet. "I know I'm ready," I said, flashing a smile at Pheobe. I inspected her reaction again, to see what she thought of her daddy holding my hand, but it didn't seem to garner her attention.

I was stunned.

"Let's go then!" she shouted, with a giggle. She enthusiastically rushed to her father and tugged on his free hand.

When Pheobe pulled her father away, I took the opportunity to pull on my jacket and sling my purse over my shoulder. I followed close behind them and, if possible, Cameron just got more amazing. Seeing him with Pheobe truly stopped my heart. He was so soft and sweet with her and yet deliciously dangerous with me. How did he do that?

After quickly pulling on his shoes, Cameron took my hand and kissed me briefly. "I'm glad you decided to join us," he said softly, his words whispering across my heart.

"Look, Daddy, I got my shoes on already," Pheobe chimed, as she slapped the second velcro-strap over her miniature shoe. She showered her dad with a genuine smile, then absently grabbed onto my hand.

Cameron's eyes popped open, then darted to mine, to catch my reaction. Of course, I was smiling. He grabbed onto her other hand and unleashed his warm smile on me.

"Very good, sweetheart," he said, his praise and smile lighting up both of our lives.

It was all rainbows and sunshine, until Cameron reached for the front door. The knob turned before he grabbed a hold of it, so he quickly stepped back, guarding Pheobe from the threatening swing of the door.

Edwin stepped inside the house, instantly shattering the warm, fuzzy feeling that had enveloped us. "What do we have here?" Edwin asked, selfish sarcasm dripping from every blunt word.

"Hey, Edwin," Cam said, with a friendly nod. "I don't believe you've met my daughter before. This is Pheobe."

Pheobe smiled. "That's the boy from the picture," she said, staring up at the monstrous man.

Edwin didn't respond. He only nodded and it made me

mad. He loved kids. What was his problem?

I watched him quickly put the pieces together, when he saw our hands all linked together. Sure, I hadn't given him any heads up about me and Cameron being back on, but was it really necessary for me to notify him of everything?

"Let's go, Pheobe. We'll wait for Abigail in the car," Cameron said, pulling her hand from mine.

"Maybe that's a good idea." I spoke only to repel the awkward silence that had immersed into the suddenly frigid room.

Edwin still didn't respond, continuously studying me with menacing eyes.

Pheobe skipped off to the car and Cameron reluctantly followed her. "I'll be right outside if you need me," he said.

Edwin scowled at him like a wild dog, but beneath his anger I could see tired, troubled eyes.

"I'll be right out," I said, then closed the door for some privacy.

Edwin looked at me like his agitation was gnawing at his insides. "What are you waiting for? Don't let me spoil your little party," he snapped, then stormed off.

I stood there contemplating his sassy behaviour, complete with him slamming his bedroom door shut. I winced at the sudden bang, but knew I couldn't let that ruin my day. I sighed with indecision and a yucky feeling settled in my chest. *No. I can't let his hissy fit affect my lovely mood.*

With a deep breath, I escaped the house and headed for Cameron's car. He stood watch behind his open door, until I flashed him a golden smile.

"Everything good?" he asked.

"It is now." I winked at him and let myself into the passenger door. Just smiling made me feel good. Just being in Cameron's presence made it that much better. I was going to have a good time today, because I said so and I'm the boss of myself.

Edwin would have to get used to Cam and Pheobe being around, because they were an important part of my life now. They made me happy and there was nothing wrong with surrounding yourself with others who can share in the happiness.

I sunk into the comfy leather seat and admired the sparkling clean car as Cameron sped off, away from life as I knew it. I flashed a glance in the side mirror at Pheobe and was amazed by how simply watching this little girl discover the world could elevate your mood and lighten your heart.

There were a lot of smiles and laughs all day. After a morning cruise and a surprise ferry ride, we found a quiet spot in a downtown park for a snack. We lounged on a picnic table and appreciated the fresh open air, as Pheobe pointed at butterflies and chased after squirrels giggling.

Pheobe found a large round fountain, spraying water from its center, and insisted that we all toss in a coin and make a wish. I closed my eyes and tossed it over my shoulder. Pheobe giggled excitedly. When she tried it, she missed the fountain entirely and the nickel went rolling off. Pheobe chased after it.

"What did *you* wish for?" Cam asked me, as he tossed his coin in the water.

I smiled back at him, my lips unable to uncurl from my grandiose smile. "I'm not telling."

Cam hooked his arm around my waist and pulled me up close to him. "I wished for you," he said, "and here you are."

Swoon!

Pheobe instantly yanked on her dad's jeans, startling us both. "Daddy, you're not supposed to tell, cuz then it won't come true!" She stomped her little feet to make her point.

I smiled with wide eyes acknowledging Cam's mistake. "It's your turn now," I said, reminding Pheobe about her own wish.

Cameron picked her up and whispered privately in her ear. They both smiled at me, Cameron's smirk more devious, while Pheobe seemed just happy to have all the attention.

"That's a good one, Daddy," she whispered aloud. Pheobe wiggled out of his arms, until he lowered her feet to the ground. Then she threw the coin into the pool with all her might. We all watched as it settled to the bottom with the rest.

After grabbing a bite to eat, we drove to a walking trail for a bit of solitude in the city. We walked down the paved trail that traced along the windy riverbank. Pheobe skipped ahead of us, happily humming a little tune that I had never heard before.

"Thank you for including me today," I gushed, as we walked hand in hand.

"It wouldn't have been the same without you," he vowed.

That tore my eyes from the trail. *My gawd, he's gorgeous.* I just wanted to sink into those glimmering baby blues.

A nagging itch caused me to steal a glimpse at Pheobe, my motherly instincts kicking in. I had always loved kids and Pheobe's safety was my primary concern, even with this amazing man staring me down. Noticing she hadn't made it very far ahead of us, I allowed my eyes to explore the rest of the park, while I took in the fresh, autumn atmosphere.

Cameron watched me carefully, squeezed my hand and drew me back to him. He continued to stare, motionless but meaningful; wordless but filled with promise.

"Seeing the city from this perspective isn't something I plan to forget any time soon," he admitted.

"I won't ever forget it," I whispered.

When he gently brushed my cheek with his knuckles, I closed my eyes to relish the tingle of my skin. But when he dipped closer for a kiss, an anxious little girl hindered his progress, by squeezing in between us and thrusting us apart.

"Oh! Pheobe!" I said, startled.

She yanked on my pants, until I looked down at her. "Abby, come! I want to keep going," she said, her eyes as wide as her smile.

Cameron and I had a little laugh, before Pheobe finally pulled on each of our hands to drag us both along. Despite her energetic intentions, the afternoon was starting to fade and so was she.

"I'd say it's about time we go home," Cam said.

"No, Daddy! Can we please stay? I don't want Abby to go."

"Pheobe," he warned, nudging her toward the car.

"Fine. But can Abby come over and watch a movie with me?"

I giggled softly, but covered my mouth with my hand in an attempt to hide my encouragement.

"Maybe, if you ask her nicely, Abby will come over for supper and help put you to bed," Cam suggested, hopeful.

"Will you? Pretty please! I want you to read me a story about princesses. Daddy doesn't really like those ones, but I do!" Pheobe said, her sweet little eyes begging for my approval.

How could I say no to that? "Of course I can, sweetie. I love stories about princesses; especially the ones where they live happily ever after."

"Abby," she advised dramatically, "they always live happily ever after."

"Oh! Maybe that's why I like them so much."

Pheobe had let Cameron's hand go and he had roamed ahead of us. She was lagging on our way back to the car, but had a grip on my hand like a death lock. I scooped her into my arms and rested her on my hip. She let me carry her the rest of the way, showing just how tired she was. Then she rested her head on my shoulder. Her hair smelled like strawberries and sweetness.

Cameron had left her door open for me, so I eased her into her booster seat. I reached for the seat belt, and snapped it in, then proceeded to take my own seat in the front.

"*You* never help me with my seat belt, *Dad*," Pheobe jabbed, half asleep.

"That's because you're a big girl now. You know how to do it yourself."

Oops, my bad. "Sorry. Should I not have helped her? I didn't know I wasn't supposed to."

"But I still like help, *Dad!*" Pheobe informed him,

ignoring my awkward apology.

"No, it's okay," he said to me, then teased Pheobe in the rear-view mirror. "As long as she doesn't get too used to it."

Pheobe started to giggle. That sweet little laugh would make any dull day bright.

As we headed for home I glanced out the window in wonder that we didn't even have to leave the city to find such a wealth of outdoor fun. As he pulled up to his house, I found my car sitting right where I had left it the night before.

"You're coming in, right?" Cam asked, his eyes turning dangerously dark, exposing his ulterior motives.

"Of course. I promised Pheobe I'd tuck her in, remember. But I should probably go after that. It is a work night, you know," I informed him, teasing.

He smiled at me and looked at Pheobe again, who still hadn't nodded off.

"It's okay, Abby. You're a big girl," Pheobe insisted. "You're allowed to stay up late if you want to."

Cameron smiled. "Yeah. What she said."

Before I knew it, dinner was done. Time went by too fast when I was with Cam, but I was happy. After playing around all day, Pheobe was starting to get whiny and it was officially past her bed time.

"Okay, Pheebs, let's go brush your teeth. Then it's pj time," Cam said.

"Aww. Can't Abby help me?"

"I don't think Abby wants to brush your teeth. Now let's go."

She pouted all the way to the bathroom and, after a few minutes, came running back to me for a hug. With her pj's on, she was ready for bed, and even had picked out her favourite book. Of course, it was about princesses. Rapunzel to be exact.

"Can you read it to me?" she begged.

"Absolutely! I love this one."

"Then you can come back over to watch Tangled with me tomorrow. Dad bought it for me a long time ago and I've only watched it two times," she stated, like it was a crime.

"Pheobe. It's time for bed," Cameron said, more sternly. "You don't have to worry, you'll see Abby again."

After a brief silence and no movement from Pheobe, I decided to give it a try. "Why don't we get you in bed and I'll read you that story, hmm?"

"Okaaayyy," Pheobe whined.

"Go give your dad a hug."

I caught Cameron smiling at me from afar and watched as Pheobe ran to him and jumped into his outstretched arms. She flung her little arms around his neck and squeezed so tight, with her cheek smushed against his.

"Love you, Daddy."

"Love you too, sweets."

Pheobe didn't give another fuss as she led the way to her bedroom and flipped on her nightlight. She slid under her sheets and asked for her favourite stuffy. I tucked her snugly in her blankets, handed her the soft little monkey and started into the book. Two pages in and I noticed her eyes getting heavy.

"Close your eyes honey. You can still listen," I whispered.

She let out a big yawn and then her eyes fell shut. I was almost certain she had fallen right to sleep, but I read the rest of the story just in case. When the story was over, I wished her sweet dreams and turned out the bedside lamp.

When I joined Cameron in the living room moments later, he looked stunned. "That's it? She's in bed?" he asked.

"Yep."

"Amazing. You are something else." He shook his head with astonishment. "I would've had to fight with her for at least an hour."

I shrugged a shoulder. "I guess I just have the magic touch."

Cameron took that a little too literal and stood up to get close to me. "You definitely have the touch," he whispered, brushing his nose along my jaw.

I closed my eyes as he pressed his lips softly against my neck and inhaled deeply. I was consumed with emotion and recognized the greedy sensations starting to cloud my reality. "I should probably get going, before I get you in trouble," I said.

"Do you have to go?" He held me tightly so I couldn't move from my place and stuck out his juicy bottom lip in a pout.

I hooked my lips onto that juicy offering and nearly squealed with excitement. "You know I do," I whispered, kissing him again.

Ignoring conversation altogether, Cameron gently seduced me with his mouth. His kisses were quickly becoming more devouring and laced with desire. "Could I persuade you to stay?" He ran his hand along my side, his lips still very close to mine.

"You have rules, Daddy," I reminded him softly.

His forehead wrinkled and a smile curled onto the side of his mouth. "Is that all you're worried about? I'd say that rule's done with now. Pheobe and you are good." He kissed me. "We're good." Another kiss. "And if we're as serious as I hope we are, then..."

When his lips came for another taste, I gently pushed him back. "You're bad," I said, then gripped his shirt to pull him back to me. "Do you always bend the rules like that?"

A mischievous smile took over his mouth. "Only for beautiful women," he teased.

"Well this woman has had a long day and needs her beauty sleep." I started toward the door and Cameron reluctantly let me go.

He walked with me to the door and silently watched me put on my shoes. He sighed. "Thanks for coming with us today. You don't know what it meant to Pheobe... to me."

I pulled on my last shoe, and then wrapped my arms around his waist. "Thank you. I had a great time."

He smiled and kissed me, too slow and sweet, making it extremely difficult to leave his arms.

"Bye," I whispered, then ran my hand down his chest and left his warm embrace.

On my way to my car, I took in a deep breath of air. I felt so good, like I was being swept off of my feet by the wind. It was dark and yet everything was so clear for a change.

Two minutes down the road and it already felt as though I was leaving paradise. It felt like I was slowly creeping back into a dark, foggy abyss, the closer I got to my house. I pulled to the side of the road to thoughtfully consider my options.

I had to follow my heart.

CHAPTER EIGHTEEN

I stepped on the gas and spun my car around, urgently racing back to Cameron. I stood outside the front of his house and lightly tapped on the door. If he didn't answer, and I mean quick, I was going to turn back and make a run for it. My heart leapt from my chest as I heard him unlock the dead bolt. Then the door opened.

"Hi," I said, softly.

"Hi," he replied, and his face gave no indication of what he was thinking.

"Can I come in?" I asked, anxiously. The night had started to chill me to my bones.

He opened the door further and I stepped inside. Silence wrapped around the room like a noose. The fact that he was robed, told me he had probably already went to bed. I silently criticised myself for returning, as humiliation crept into the back of my thoughts.

"Should I go?" I asked, feeling terribly awkward.

"That depends," he answered, looking thoughtful. "Am I the one you want?"

Whoa! The conversation had just turned very real, very fast.

Breathlessness choked my words. "Yes," I said with a whisper. And I realized, just then, that I had never wanted something quite so bad.

He stared at me for a long time, assessing my answer, as I held back the urge to throw myself in his arms and tell him how much I loved him.

"You *are* the one, Cameron. Please don't give up on me," I said softly, pleading for his forgiveness.

He turned his eyes to the floor and let out a breathy sigh. "You're in my heart now, you can't get out that easily," he said, as if it were a curse. Then a smile crept onto his mouth.

His smile eased my mind, but I still stuttered. "I-I-I mean, if you don't want to do this n-n-now..."

Cameron brought his finger to my lips and fixed his mesmeric eyes on mine. "We have all the time in the world; starting right now."

He took my hand and quietly led me to his bedroom. My heart began to race, as I considered whether he wanted me as badly as I wanted him.

This was a natural progression for our relationship, but the pieces were coming together so intimately. My legs were trembling as bad as my lips and my heart skittered against my ribs. When we walked in his room, he closed the door behind us, and suddenly I could hear nothing but the beat of my heart galloping in my ears.

A lamp in the corner left a soft glow on an open book resting on his arm chair. Music flowed melodiously from a hidden speaker in the room. I took a seat on the end of his bed and turned to watch him, but he didn't move. He had already lost the robe and, with his hands on his hips, his chest muscles did magnificent things.

He smiled at me and took a few steps closer. I urgently wanted to be in those sculpted arms, with his warm chiseled abs pressed against my cool skin, but it looked as if he were waiting for me to inspire his next move.

I gulped the anxious lump from the back of my throat, stood from the bed and slowly drew closer to him. When I came within his reach, a captivating smile spread across his lips.

"Hi," he said.

"Hi," I replied. Slow and deliberate, I edged our bodies closer, until our lips were only inches apart. Our bodies were so close that mine electrically demanded that we be connected.

"We can take it slow, if that's what you want," he whispered.

My insides clenched with need. That's not what I wanted. I wanted to be all over him, to show him how I felt.

And I would.

My eyes turned down to his hips, as I ran my fingers over those rippling muscles, each of them tightening beneath my fingers. I slid my hands up to his chest and then hooked my arms under his, until our bodies were pressed tight together. He closed his eyes and shivered from my closeness, as I drew my nails sensually down his back. He felt so good.

He was the epitome of athletic perfection. Every inch of him called out to me, including the bulge in his boxers. I rested my head against his smooth, bare chest, as I continued to run my hands over his sleek muscled body, groping every rigid muscle. His mind may have been cautious, and his hands were securely fastened to my hips, but his body urged me to continue.

I glanced up into Cameron's eyes and wondered if he could see how much I wanted him. It was apparent that he was struggling to resist me. He reached my arms over his shoulders, pressing me flat against him, and let out a groan, that only half explained the dilemma stabbing from his shorts.

I enjoyed every second of his hands on me. His breath was warm and steady on my lips, sending an assortment of tingling sensations running through me. We stared, all-consumed, into each other's eyes; wrought with anticipation. Emotion poured from my heart because, though my body so badly wanted him in bed, my heart decided it was time to verbalize how I really felt for him.

I tucked my head on his shoulder, suddenly feeling too shy to profess my love for him to his face. *I could only hope he feels the same way, but I couldn't bear to learn that he doesn't.* "I have something to say," I whispered, too anxious to spit out the actual words.

His hands latched onto my arms pulling my head from his chest. "What is it?" He looked concerned.

Staring him right in the eyes, I said it. "Just that I love you."

A smile slowly crept across his face. "Oh, was that it?"

My cheeks warmed as hot as his sexy smile. "Yeah."

"Then I guess you'll be happy to hear that I love you too."

My smile faded slightly. "You don't have to say that just because I did. It's okay if you're not feeling it."

Cameron looked deep into my eyes and pierced my soul. "Abigail, I've loved you since the day I first set eyes on you." His eyes were so dark and intense that I thought I might sink into them and drown.

Instead, happiness burst from my lips and a warm, fuzzy feeling immersed my body. My mouth quivered in anticipation of his luscious lips and I tilted my head to meet him half way. His soft, juicy lower lip lingered in my mouth, as his passionate kiss scorched my senses. He slowly pulled away and the magnetism forced our lips back together.

Cameron carefully removed my clothes with his strong, magnificent hands, piece by agonizing piece. My body ached to feel his bare skin against mine.

As he let my clothes fall from his fingers to the floor, I flattened my hands over his sleek muscles, then pressed my breasts against him. His body felt amazing under my fingertips, but feeling him pressed against my naked core was even better. Now he was in the flesh and all mine.

I leaned backward and stumbled toward the bed. Cameron caught me in his arms before lowering me down onto the soft dark-suede comforter. He skillfully removed my panties and tossed them aside, leaving me completely naked and pooling with wetness.

He kissed and caressed my smooth thighs, before pulling them over his hips. I locked my legs around him and he lifted me up, so I was hanging over the bed from his lean muscled body. He crawled up the bed, effortlessly sliding my bare skin across the silky sheets, and then lowered me onto the soft pillows.

We continued to kiss, as Cameron rested his weight on top of me. I tousled his short, sexy hair in my fingers, holding him close. His attraction was evident in the hardness of his body. He rocked naughtily against me and it felt amazing, but I craved a closer connection. He did too.

When he gently snuck his hand between us, I nearly blurted out a profanity, but bit my lip instead. He stroked me sensually, using desirous circles to wind me up before sinking his fingers inside. One. Two. My need deepened with every stroke, as he touched me like he had never touched me before.

I whimpered softly as my desire mounted at a ridiculous rate. And I felt each and every spasm, as my insides squeezed around his fingers lodged deep inside me. When he retrieved his hand, he gently sucked on his fingers, expressing his appreciation with closed eyes. It should have been erotic, but it felt undeniably intimate, with his heart beating as loud as my own.

His lips trailed along my jaw, as harsh breaths whispered over my skin. This time, when he pressed himself against me, I curved my back to accept all of his pressure. The way his deliciously hard body pushed against me left me trembling with need.

"Are you okay?" he whispered affectionately.

"Yes," I breathed.

Wanting to touch him, I teased my fingers down his delightfully soft, blonde treasure trail. Nothing could have prepared me for the unyielding size of him, now throbbing in my hand. I squeezed him gently between my fingers and stroked his smooth length, revelling in his hardness. He groaned in approval and thrust his hips forward. I wanted that thrust for myself.

Our eyes met, a new hunger burning in them, as Cameron stole another kiss and then urgently reached inside his nightstand. He ripped open the small silver packet, making quick work of it, crawled back on top of me and boxed his arms around my head.

When he dropped down for another passionate kiss, I took him in my hand. With one long stroke, I guided him right to where I needed him. His lips softly caressed mine as he eased inside of me and I immediately let out a gasp of pleasure. I squeezed my eyes shut, stunned by the almost unbearable tightness as he withdrew himself and took me again.

I arched my back and he dipped inside, filling me so deeply that I had to bite his shoulder to muffle my voice. He continued, unhurriedly, easing in and out. With each motion, I could feel every inch of him, making me want to cry out to the heavens.

He revelled in my painless agony, with slow steady strokes. I dug my feet into his back and panted in harmony with his unexpectedly shallow motions, demanding that he drive himself faster and deeper.

Our bodies were in sync, our natural chemistry working magically. I tightened my legs around him and clung to his agile form. He dipped his tongue inside my willing mouth as he surged deeper inside me yet. My legs trembled as I felt a sweet release building again.

When he almost withdrew from me completely, my body demanded that the void be filled. He complied, pushing the full length of himself inside me. I moaned loud with approval, unable to contain my arousal with each driving thrust.

Cameron's pace had quickened and my exhilaration followed suit. My heart galloped wildly, as loud as the banging headboard. I latched my mouth on his and it muffled my moans, as delicious tremors rocked through my body again and again. Needing more support, I dug my fingers into the silky bed sheets for stability. It wasn't enough.

The pleasure was too overwhelming to hold on any longer, so I released my muscles giving Cameron full reign. My body craved more, so I tightened again selfishly, a stronger climax flooding every sense in my body. "Yes, Cameron. Yes!" I shouted.

My clenching muscles sent Cameron into a frenzy of pleasure as he plunged into me with one final thrust. When his mouth gaped open on a sexy grunt, I knew he had joined me in my happy place. Pleasant emotions swirled around us, as he rested on top of me, fully satisfied; heart and soul.

After a blissful calm, Cameron kissed the corner of my

mouth and rolled to my side. Once my breathing finally regulated, I heard a door shut softly outside the room. My eyes popped open, as I was rocked back into reality.

"Did you lock the door?" I whispered.

He chuckled. "No." Then naked, he quickly dashed to the bedroom door to lock it.

I checked out his perfect, toned ass before he turned the lock on the handle. I quickly yanked the sheets over myself and tucked them under my arms, covering my vulnerable body, suddenly feeling self-conscious after admiring his male perfection.

"We must have been too loud. What if Pheobe's awake?" I whispered, incredibly worried.

"Don't worry. It was just the bathroom door. Pheobe's not used to having someone else in the house." Cameron knelt on the bed next to me and smiled.

"She knows I'm here?" I asked, horrified.

He cupped my cheek with his hand. "It's been just the two of us for a long time. The house sounds different when you're here. I'm sure she knows." His thumb brushed over my sensitive skin, but a rush of anxiety chased away the tingles.

Great. His daughter heard us doing it. How embarrassing. I would have to remember to be more discreet in the future.

After returning from his ensuite bathroom, Cameron rejoined me on the bed. He gave me a smooch and I stared into his starry eyes in wonder. Everything had fallen into place so naturally. Everything seemed to be right with the world. It was all happening so fast, but I knew it wasn't smart to mark love with a stopwatch. Turning back was the right decision.

Cameron rolled onto his back, stretched out his hands and then clasped them behind his head, putting his muscular arms out on display. I curled up beside him and ran my hand along his excellent abdominals. *What a beautiful man.* It was unbelievable that he managed to stay single for this long.

I traced his abs with a finger, studying every rigid

muscle. I was surprised to find a scar on his side that I hadn't noticed before. I ran my finger back and forth along the faded white line. "What's this from?

He smiled at me for being so observant and moved my hand to rest it on his chest. He sighed, as he thoughtfully prepared to tell me the story. "You know how I said Pheobe was lucky to be alive after the car accident?"

"Right."

"Well, that didn't mean she got away without major complications. The trauma was so severe that eventually both of her kidneys had to be removed. She was too young to be a transplant candidate and so she relied on dialysis for years."

"I had no idea." My fingers returned to the scar, as Cameron's memories stirred.

"I got tested right after the accident and learned that I was a compatible match as her donor. Shortly after she turned three we went ahead with the procedure. Everyone was concerned with me going under the knife, after everything the family had been through, but she was all I had."

Cameron stopped to clear the emotion from his voice. "It was a miracle. She wasn't supposed to live." His eyes grew wet, but they didn't produce any tears. "She's come so far this past year, but she still has a long way to go. She'll have to be monitored by a specialist for the rest of her life."

I lightly caressed the scar and smiled softly. "You've been through so much. I don't know how you've done it." I rested my cheek against his chest, clinging to him, hoping he knew that he wasn't alone anymore.

"She's the one that got me through it. Her little life has been far from easy, but she's a fighter. I spent all of my waking hours either working or visiting her at the hospital. She practically lived there after the accident. It made it difficult for her to make friends, and me too I guess. That's why I was so surprised to see how easily she's taken to you."

"What about your wife?"

Cameron raised a brow in surprise. "You mean my ex-wife. Pheobe's been so hesitant around other women ever since her mother died. To this day, my mom and Ashley are the only ones she's comfortable with. But you..." He smiled, with a sharp breath, emotion hitching his words.

"Enough about me," I said, softly. "Tell me about your life before your wife died."

I hoped I hadn't crossed the line, but I had to know how he had felt about her then, and how he still feels about her now.

"Do you really want to know? My life was far from perfect, I'll tell you that," he said, with a soft humourless chuckle. "Pheobe came from an unplanned pregnancy. At least *I* thought so. I later found out that Tessa had it planned out all along. The night she died, she was running away from me and she was taking Pheobe with her."

"Do you mean she wanted a divorce?"

"Yeah, there's that, but she knew she wasn't taking my baby without a fight."

"That's horrible. You must have been so worried." My hand absently stroked his chest, as I paid very close attention to his facial expressions.

"I hate to admit it, but I was mostly angry. Even more so when I got the divorce papers from her lawyer the day before her funeral. She had already signed them."

"Wow."

We laid there quietly and I didn't have it in me to press for any more information. I wondered if he felt like he had already divulged too much information, but he soon blasted my theory out of the water.

"While we're on the topic, I might as well just tell you everything," he said. "I'd like you to know the whole story."

"Okay," I said softly, unsure how much more I wanted to hear.

He nodded, and it was like he was relieving his guilt brick by brick. "We met at one of my sister's parties when I was in university. We had only been dating for a few weeks when she got pregnant. She told me she was on birth control. I should've known better." He closed his eyes and pinched the bridge of his nose.

I watched his toned body rise and fall, as jealousy ate away at my heart. Now that he was openly talking about his ex-wife, I wondered how much more I could handle.

"It was my fault," he said. "We were miserable. But I asked her to marry me when she was five months pregnant. We weren't in love, but I refused to let Pheobe be born into this world without a family. We went to a justice of the peace at the courthouse and Ashley watched me sign my life away. She was Tessa's best friend."

I nodded, in acknowledgement. *That would explain her blatant hatred toward me.*

"After Pheobe was born, it only got worse. I wanted her to nurse our baby, but she refused to try. Tessa kept making decisions on her own and acted like I didn't exist. I believe to this day that she actually wanted to be a single parent. Of course she accepted my money, but she made it clear on a number of occasions that she wished I had never stepped up to the plate."

I couldn't take much more of it, but curiosity gnawed at my insides. "What happened that night to set her off?" I asked, soft and anxious.

"The night of her accident, we argued about I can't remember what. She took off in a fit of emotions, like she always did, but this time she said she wasn't coming back. Little did I know she had her bags pre-packed in the car."

"I'm so sorry." I brushed my hand down his arm and clasped onto his hand.

"So am I. I'm sorry that Pheobe never had a chance to know her mother. But that woman, Tessa, she was stealing my baby girl from me. She nearly did." His grip tightened on my hand.

I cupped his cheek and pressed a kiss to his lips. I wanted to soothe away all his troubles. "You're both okay now though, right?"

He sighed, with me still hovering in front of him. "I don't know. I've made Pheobe switch schools again. She's already so shy. I wish she could just enjoy her childhood, instead of having to grow up so damn fast."

"Aww, Daddy," I swooned, still softly cupping his face. I leaned down and again kissed his soft, downturned lips.

His eyes pierced mine. "Thank you for listening."

My breath hitched until I parted my lips to smile. "I'm glad you told me. But I have to say, Tessa's lucky she's not here right now. Because if she was, I would totally have to kick her ass."

He smirked at my jealous sarcasm and then wet his lips for a more sensuous kiss. "But you are here. So you're going to join us next weekend, right? I was thinking we could go hiking at Rouge National Park. Pheobe wants to go on the guided nature walk. They told her all about it at her school and now that's all she ever talks about."

I smiled, imagining another fun day with them. "I'm in. I mean, if Pheobe's okay with it."

"I don't need to ask. She likes having you around."

I laid back down and snuggled up against Cameron. He wrapped himself around me and nuzzled his nose in my hair. Being physically and mentally exhausted, I welcomed his warm embrace.

"I love you, Abby," he whispered, close to my ear.

"I love you too, Cam."

CHAPTER NINETEEN

After a really late night, an early morning rise and a day chock full of scowling from Edwin at work, I decided what better time than now to confront him head on. It was already past dark by the time I finished dinner with Aliah, and I was in good spirits knowing that tonight was the night Cameron was going to inform Ashley about our relationship.

When I drove home from the restaurant and saw Edwin's truck in the driveway, it took all that I had to pull in beside him. The house was quiet, but it wasn't like Edwin to be asleep already. Regardless, it was time to set things straight.

Maybe it was wrong for me to invade his privacy, but I refused to make excuses for putting this off any longer. I tip-toed to his bedroom and knocked three times before letting myself in. Edwin seemed startled when I caught him texting on his phone, as though he was doing something wrong.

"I suppose you'd like an explanation," I said, and he knew exactly what I was talking about.

"You know what, Abs? I've done a lot of thinking these past few days. You don't owe me anything." He tucked his cell under his thigh. He was definitely hiding something.

I took a couple of steps into his room. "I was going to tell you two nights ago, but you weren't home. We never crossed paths yesterday. Then I didn't want to say anything at work."

He continued to stare at his wall, his body a blank silhouette. "I told you: I don't care. I've got my own stuff going on. Now, if you don't mind..." he insisted, ushering me out with his words.

I would go, but not until I said my part; and the fact that

he was acting all weird was tripping me up. "We're clear then. Cam and I are together for real. You'll stay out of our way?"

"You got it," he answered, undoubtedly. It almost hurt how little he cared. It was like he had done a one eighty since the other day.

I scowled at him and spun away, but that only drove him to speak up.

"I'm actually surprised you fell for him. I would've thought you learned a lesson or two from Spencer about schemers. He's only looking to bed you, so I can't, and I can't believe that you're falling for it. You need work."

What the fuck is he talking about?

"I need work? Are you fucking kidding me? Trying to maintain this fucking relationship is work! I'll take Cam and Pheobe over that any day." I was so angry I thought I might explode.

"Well, don't you have yourself a cute little insta-family," Edwin snapped.

"Fuck you." Suddenly feeling very sick, my stomach rolled around like dark, vicious twister. "Who are you to judge? You have no idea what they've been through. I love that little girl and I love..."

"You love who?" Edwin asked rhetorically, glaring at me with beady, black eyes.

I quickly corrected myself, uncomfortable with the notion of explaining it to Edwin. "I love the way I feel when I'm with them."

"Yeah. I'm sure that's exactly what you were going to say."

I rolled my eyes and spun away for the door. "I think we're done here."

"While we're sharing, maybe I should let you in on a little something. I'm seeing someone too. I expect you'll respect that," Edwin snapped, as I stormed off and slammed his door shut.

Luckily I had left the room so quickly because my breath was cut off from the sudden news. Though I had just admitted to Edwin that I had fallen in love with Cameron, I still couldn't help but feel jealous of this other woman. *What is wrong with me?*

If this woman existed, which was still undetermined, I was sure it would only be a matter of time before her identity was brought to the surface.

"Jessica Saunders? You have got to be kidding me," I said, clutching the phone to my shoulder as I grabbed a water bottle from the fridge.

"No lie. It's true," Aliah said, on the other end of the phone.

Edwin joined me in the kitchen and he looked like he was ready for a night on the town. It didn't take long for him to change into his sex-god self. His shirt clung to every heavy muscle, sure to tempt every woman within a twenty foot radius of him. Unfortunately, I was the only one present at the moment.

"Aliah, I have to let you go. I'll talk to you later, kay?"

"Don't let me keep you," Edwin said, smugly. "I'll be out of here in no time."

I ended the call and dropped the phone on the kitchen table. "Whatever. I don't want to fight."

"Don't you have plans with your lover boy?" Edwin mocked, testing my nerve.

"Screw you."

"Fine, forget I asked," he said, his face expressing a smug arrogance.

"I wouldn't want to keep you from Jessica," I snapped, as I walked past him and rushed toward the stairs.

"Wait. How do you know I'm seeing Jess?"

I spun around, my eyes so narrow that I could barely see out of the angry slits. "Do I look that stupid to you? It's written all over your face."

"Ugh. I told Caleb to keep his mouth shut," Edwin growled.

"It wasn't Caleb," I snapped.

"What do you care anyway? It looks like Cameron's taking care of you just fine."

"Did I say I cared?"

"Good then, because she wants you two to be friends again; like before."

"Like before? Is this some kind of joke? You know we were never very good friends. She was a backstabbing bitch then and I doubt anything's changed now."

"She has changed. You just have to give her a chance. For me?" The only thing missing was a pouty lip.

"Seriously, Eddie? I don't want to talk about this right now. Actually, I don't want to talk about it ever. You do what you want. She's your problem, not mine."

"Are you saying you don't want me to hang out with her?"

"Do I like her? Not a great deal right about now. But I just told you to do what you want. You will anyway." I started up the stairs and Edwin called up after me.

"I know you can't see it now, but she'll grow on you."

"Doubt it," I hollered back, then pushed my bedroom door shut.

I plopped on my bed and stared at the ceiling for what seemed like an hour. Even after spending the better part of the night gossiping with Aliah, the stabbing cramps from Edwin's insistence that I befriend his new lover only intensified while I focused on my preoccupied loneliness.

When I finally managed to rest my heavy eyes, I came to realize that whenever I'm with Cameron, all things seemed to turn right with the world. The sun was a little brighter; my heart a little lighter. Cameron was the answer; the solution to all of my problems. With that new resolve, I knew things were about to change for me in a big way.

The grey skies were unable to dampenk my new sense of purpose. Normally it would have diminished my enthusiasm for the day, but not today. I had a different outlook on life.

I lingered in bed longer than necessary, until the hunger

pains were close to unbearable. If Jessica was there at the house, I was ready for her. If Edwin wanted me to befriend her, then I would fake it. What did I care?

I pulled on a silky house coat, fully anticipating some company, and proceeded to the kitchen for breakfast. I popped some bread in the toaster and rummaged around the fridge.

"Good morning," Jessica said to me, cheerily, as she entered the kitchen after me.

Friendly. Think friendly. "Morning. Did you want some toast?" I asked.

"Sure. But I can get it," she insisted.

"No, I don't mind."

"Okay. Thanks," she said, slipping into a vacant seat at the table. An awkward silence sliced across the room. "Edwin was saying you were acting a little off last night. I hope it's nothing I did."

I was taken by surprise by the actual care glowing in her words. *What did Edwin tell her?* There's no way he could've known the pain I was suffering. "It was nothing. I'm feeling much better already."

"That's good." She rested her elbows on the table and dropped her chin into her hands.

After a much less awkward silence, I knew what I had to do. "Jess?"

"Yeah?" she answered, straightening up.

"I want to apologize. I haven't been very nice to you since you've come back to town and you've never really done anything for me to treat you that way. I really am sorry."

"I appreciate that," she said, smiling warmly. She reached out and accepted a plate from me.

I poured some orange juice into two large glasses. "Are you up for a mimosa?" I asked, looking forward to the tasty treat.

"Absolutely."

I poured the sparkling wine into the glasses, slid a cup in front of her and took a sip of my own. As I took a seat across from her, I was feeling much better about everything.

"Did you guys have a good date night?" I asked.

"It was fun. A whole bunch of us went out actually. You should've come."

I smiled, but was certain that my sarcasm blasted away any chance of her believing my words. "Yeah, maybe next time."

Edwin came into the kitchen as I took a nibble out of my toast. "Where's mine?"

"You snooze, you lose," I mumbled, covering my full mouth with my hand. I continued to munch on my toast and appreciated my smooth drink as Edwin got out some cereal.

"Mmm, this is excellent," Jessica said, clearly enjoying her drink. "Cheers." She raised her glass and I clinked mine off of it before taking another drink.

Edwin narrowed his eyes, seemingly pissed about our newfound friendship. "Lushes," he mumbled, under his breath.

Jessica polished off her drink and then excused herself from the room.

A moment later, Edwin smiled. "Thank you."

"For what?"

"You know what. You didn't have to do that, but you did. Thank you."

"You know me, little miss nicety nice-girl." My teasing sparked his smile and he let out a gentle laugh. It was good to see him smiling again.

"I like you just like this," Edwin said, hitching my heart in my chest.

After guzzling every last drop of my drink, I hurried to the sink and then dashed out of the room before Jessica returned. I knew I should give them their space. So, back upstairs, I claimed the bathroom and took a nice long soak in the steaming hot tub, thinking of nothing and no one but Cameron.

After shaving my legs and covering my entire body in a fragrant black cherry lotion, I dried my hair, styled it into loose curls and perfected my makeup. I had hoped Cameron would have shown up by now. He was planning to check in on me sometime today and I was anxious for him to come by already.

With nothing left to do, I returned downstairs and joined Edwin and Jessica in the living room. Their chatter about last night's events and other random gossip from the club wasn't enough to occupy my mind, but I tried to act like I cared. Edwin could see that it was a front, but Jessica just ate it up. I was scoring points with him big time, on a friendly scale, and so I just went with it.

"Do you think you could give me a ride home?" Jessica finally asked him.

"Yeah, no problem," Edwin replied. He got up from the couch and headed straight for the front door.

I wondered what his hurry was and so did Jessica as she followed after him.

She looked back to me inquisitively. "I guess were going now," she said, surprised but cheery. "Thanks for breakfast."

"Kay. See you, Jess."

When the door clicked open, I heard some garbled conversation and I knew instantly that we had company. A smile splashed onto my face straightaway. There was an incredibly sexy, brilliant, amazingly hot man standing there and I wasn't talking about Edwin.

"Come on in. She's in the living room," Edwin said, nodding toward me.

Cameron took off his shoes and gave Jessica a quick nod, as she exited the house. I stood from the couch to wrap my arms around my man, then he pecked my cheek and did a pain-stakingly slow perusal of my body.

"I thought you'd still be in bed." The way his voice growled made me wish that I was. "You look great," he added.

"Thanks. I'm actually feeling pretty awesome today."

He took my hand in his and smoothed his thumb over my soft, sensitive skin. "Do you want to do something then?

Pheobe's with the babysitter for the next hour or so."

"I have something in mind," I replied, my desirous stare delivering my naughty message. I hooked my arm around his neck and kissed him, passion dripping from my lips as I attached my body to his.

"Mmm. Maybe we should take this upstairs," he said, his growl doing wondrous things to my insides.

"I like the way you think, Mr. Clarke," I breathed seductively, before clamping onto his hand and tearing up the stairs to my room for the most intensely hot sixty minute ride of my life.

One hour later, we were both fully dressed and running out my front door with ridiculously large smiles painted on our faces.

Cameron drove straight to his house and Pheobe came running to the car as soon as we pulled up. She hopped into the backseat with her headphones blaring and, with her I-pad on her lap, she left us to our own. Cameron was busy watching traffic, giving me the opportunity to gawk at him uninterrupted.

This man was so dreamy, with deep set eyes that sparkled baby blue from their bottomless depths. His short clean-cut blonde hair was a little messy after our romp in the bedroom, but it only made him look that much sexier. He didn't even notice how entranced I was, which only added to his appeal.

"It really is amazing having a wilderness area like this so close to the city, don't you think?" He finally looked over at me and caught me staring. He delivered a huge grin and then lifted his eyebrows at me in question.

If it weren't for his daughter being in the back seat, I would've been all over him right there. Instead, I nodded and calmly redirected my attention out the window to appreciate the scene and tamp down my desire. "It really is something else," I said.

We passed a historic farm with century-old trees and a peaceful meadow. A handful of kids ran around a large front yard, chasing each other in a game of tag. It suddenly reminded me how much I wanted to start a family myself.

"Are we there yet?" Pheobe hollered, much louder than necessary.

"Phoebe, take off your headphones," Cameron answered.

"Sorry," Pheobe whispered loudly, without removing the plugs. "Are we there yet?" Her voice was still about two notches too high. I couldn't help but giggle.

"We're almost there," Cameron said.

"What?" Pheobe hollered.

A pointed glance from Cameron was all it took for Pheobe to pull off the head phones.

"Abby. Did my dad tell you that there's going to be a nature walk through the trails? There's a tour guide and everything."

"Yes, he did. It sounds pretty cool."

Just then, Cameron pulled into the park entrance. "This is it."

Pheobe got even more excited as she inspected the area. "This is going to be the best day ever!"

"Are you ladies ready for this? I hope you brought your hiking shoes," he told Pheobe.

"I did, Dad! Remember?"

He laughed at Pheobe's enthusiasm and then we all got out of the car.

"Hold my hand, Pheebs. I don't want you to get run over in the parking lot."

"Okay, Daddy," Pheobe replied, clasping onto his hand.

"What about me?" I teased.

"Lucky for you, I have two hands." He reached his hand out to me and I took it.

As we walked toward the registration cabin Pheobe got more and more excited.

"Abby, guess what I learned at school the other day? That we should try to fill other people's buckets whenever we can."

"What buckets?" I asked, not having a clue what she was talking about.

Pheobe giggled at me and went on with her story.

"When you fill someone else's bucket, then you fill your own too!"

"Okay, so how do you fill a bucket?" I asked, with Cam smiling at me.

"Well, like if you say nice things to someone or if you help them out, that fills their bucket. Life isn't always rainbows and roses, but you don't have to be a bucket dipper."

I laughed so hard. She was so darn cute. When I realized how serious she was, I straightened up my face, pressed my lips together to thin out my smile and let her continue.

"That means you steal out of someone's bucket when you're mean to them or hurt their feelings," she advised me, with confidence.

"Oh, I see."

"I like what you're wearing," Pheobe said, smiling adorably at me.

"Thanks! You're really good at that bucket filling thing; such a sweetheart."

Pheobe giggled out of control, bouncing up and down with excitement. "Abby filled my bucket when she said I was a sweetheart!"

Cameron crouched down to talk to his daughter on her level. "Abby filled my bucket when she said she'd come with us today."

Pheobe giggled delightedly and smiled at her father, but it couldn't compare to what I was feeling right at that moment.

"Now all of our buckets are full!" Pheobe cheered.

Eventually she broke free from Cameron's loving grip and ran through the open grass toward the cabin. When she wasn't paying attention, Cameron stopped me briefly to steal a kiss, his soft lips moving over mine with a lovers caress. I enjoyed it thoroughly. It definitely filled my bucket.

After registering for the tour in the cabin, Cameron pulled a folded paper from his pocket and handed it to Pheobe. "I have a surprise for you."

I watched Pheobe's wide eyes as her eager fingers unfolded the paper the rest of the way.

The paper read: *If you go out to the Park today, you may meet some of our friends!*

"What is it, Daddy?"

"It's a checklist. You have to record your wildlife sightings. See the picture? You have to try and find that bird."

Cameron handed Pheobe a small pencil, the perfect size for her delicate, little hand. "What do you say?" he asked.

A smile lit up her face. "I'm going to find everything on the list!"

"What are you looking for? Maybe I can help," I suggested.

"Thanks, Abby, but I'm a big girl. I can find them myself."

She immediately crouched in the grass and started exploring for the list of creatures. "Look!" she cheered, less than a minute later. Down on one knee, she pointed at a small blade of grass that had a lady bug crawling on it. "Check!" she said excitedly, as she marked it off her list. "Only four more to go."

All of a sudden, a bubbly, middle-aged woman with short, red hair and full bangs came out of the cabin. She was wearing a vest with matching khaki pants, a tilly hat and a name tag. She reminded me of an overly enthusiastic summer camp counsellor and there was no doubt in my mind that she was our tour guide.

The lady spoke with a deep, projective voice. "Welcome to Rosella Park. Hi everyone, I'm Linda. I'll be your tour guide for today. If you're registered for the nature walk, please show me your registration card and we'll be on our way."

There were twelve in our group and we all followed the guide as she told us about the history of our surroundings. We strolled down the leafy, brown trails. Boughs of pine trees formed a cool covering overhead, as we plunged further into the wilderness. Pheobe skipped ahead of Cameron and me and, as the tour went on, we casually faded to the back of the crowd.

Cameron turned to me and smiled. "Did you know that Rouge River got its name from riverbank clay causing the stream to look red, or 'Rouge' in French," Cameron explained.

"I did not know that, Mr. Encyclopedia. But I like when you talk to me in French," I said, wearing a naughty smirk.

Cameron acted like he wanted to beat me up for being smart, so I ran away from him, heading for Pheobe and the rest of the group. He chased behind me and I couldn't help but let out a squeal like a little girl. When he caught up with me he wrapped his arms around my waist and lifted me up. I had caught Phoebe's attention and she seemed to be amused by her father's playfulness.

"Oh, look Pheobe!" I said mid-flight. I pointed out the two beautiful orange butterflies that were swirling around each other in the cool, autumn air.

The tour guide stopped in her tracks when she heard Pheobe's excited response. Linda approached Pheobe, who was chasing the fluttery pair. "You're pretty lucky to check these butterflies off your list today, young lady. These two must be stragglers. I'd bet the rest of their family has already migrated for the season."

Pheobe listened with wonder in her eyes and happily checked the monarch butterfly off her list. When everyone's attention was focused on Pheobe, again Cameron took my lips in a passionate kiss. This time we carried on a little too long and our love didn't go unnoticed. Thankfully, Linda only flashed us a smile and continued on with the tour.

Cameron was content to stay behind, but I grabbed his hand and pulled him on, trying to keep up with the group. Pheobe was right up at the front, hanging on every word Linda uttered.

"There are over two hundred and twenty five different kinds of birds that live here in Rosella Park. Oh, look here," she pointed. "Do you see it, Pheobe?"

"I do! I do!" It was the small bird on Pheobe's wildlife

checklist.

"That's the black-capped chickadee or the Poecile atricapilla, as they call it," Linda explained.

Cameron whispered in my ear. "Its French name is *Mésange à tête noire*." He waggled his eye brows at me seductively and I couldn't help but bite my lip when I smiled back at him.

He sounded so sexy when he spoke French. "How do you know that?"

Cameron smirked. "I read it in the brochure when we came in."

"Do you speak French fluently?" I asked, terribly turned on by the notion.

"I do my best. I'm not comfortable giving legal advice like that, but my French clients respect that I try."

"You're so darn cute," I said, wrapping my arms around him.

"I'm not cute," he said, bluntly.

"Yes, you are."

"I'll show you cute," he said, as he kissed me sweetly and then grabbed my ass in both of his hands. We had some onlookers watching us, but he didn't care to stop the entertainment.

As the day went on, we continued our hike through the woodlands and Cameron carried on playfully kissing and touching me whenever Pheobe wasn't looking. Hand-in-hand we walked down the trails, captivated by each other.

"Daddy, I have to go pee," Pheobe hollered anxiously, interrupting the guide.

"There's a pit stop in about twenty minutes," Linda advised. "Then another ten will take you back to the front gate."

"Can you hold it?" Cam asked, crouching down to meet Pheobe on eye level.

Pheobe was already bouncing around, doing the potty dance. "No, Dad. I have to go really bad," she whined.

"You'll have to go in the bush then," he suggested.

"No, I won't. I need a potty," she pouted.

"There is a short cut," Linda said, while the others in the group waited for her impatiently. "Here. I'll show you." She pulled out her map and ran her finger along the trail that would take us to the nearest public washroom.

"Thanks. I appreciate it," Cameron said. "What do you ladies say? Are we ready to go it alone?"

"I think that sounds like a plan," I said, watching Pheobe prance around in front of us. "Thank you for the tour, Linda."

"My pleasure. Thanks for joining us today," Linda said, then turned and headed back to the front of the pack.

"Come on," Cam said, scooping Pheobe off her feet.

It was a good ten minute trek before we finally located the washroom. I was starting to worry that Pheobe might not make it. When Cameron lowered her onto her feet, she took off in an all-out race for the potty.

I strode quickly after her. "I can go in with you, if you want," I hollered.

"I don't need any help. I'm a big girl," Pheobe hollered back, disappearing inside the building.

After taking a peek at the facilities, that were surprisingly clean and modern for an outdoor washroom, I rejoined Cameron outside.

"I offered to stay with her, but she insisted that she doesn't need my help," I told Cam, shrugging my shoulders. Feeling the effects from the long hike, I leaned against the brick building and pressed my foot against the wall with one bent knee. "Ahh, that's better."

Cameron came toward me with a purpose and put his fisted hands against the wall on either side of my head. "Did you notice there's no one around here?" His voice was low, dark and devious.

"Your daughter is right inside there and she'll be back out any minute."

He bent his arms and rested them against the wall, his face now only inches from mine. He closed the gap between our bodies and kissed me tenderly. I couldn't resist him. He tasted so good.

His arms protected me from the crisp breeze and his kisses sent me into a lust-filled frenzy for more. Our lips caressed more aggressively now and Cameron couldn't seem to restrain himself. Demonstrating the intensity of his enthrallment, he pressed the rock hard bulge in his pants flat against me.

"Mmm," I groaned, as the hand dryer clicked on. Knowing it was time to wrap things up, I forced myself to dash under Cameron's arm and out of the hold he had on me.

He turned toward me swiftly and locked his arms around me, leaning me slightly back against him, controlling my weight. "You're not getting away from me that easily," he said, as he smoothly massaged my breast.

I spun around and kissed him and he lowered both of his hands until they cradled my ass. My nerves were gnawing at me something fierce. I broke away from the kiss. "You should really cut it out, Cam. Pheobe..."

"Eww, Daddy!" Pheobe screeched.

Cam's hands immediately released me and I stepped away giggling. "Yeah, Daddy. Eww!"

He smiled at his daughter, as he clearly struggled with his urge to pull me back into his arms. Pheobe on the other hand had a rather pouty face on and it was pretty comical.

"I'm going to get you next," he teased, as he chased Pheobe away with pinching fingers.

He came back carrying her effortlessly over his shoulder. She was giggling uncontrolledly in his arms. When he reached my side, he returned Pheobe to her feet and it took a second for her to steady herself. He crouched down to make sure she was okay.

I watched him with his daughter. He was such a good father. He was also charming, witty and devastatingly handsome. My gosh. Every ounce of this man appealed to me.

Oh, how I love this man.

CHAPTER TWENTY

The day was growing late when we decided to go exploring. On our way back toward the park entrance, we hiked down an unbeaten trail into the wilderness and discovered a hidden stream. There was a couple canoeing together and it looked incredibly peaceful and utterly romantic.

"Can we try that?" Pheobe asked.

"I don't think there's enough time in the day to do all the things you want to do," Cam answered, smirking. He rustled her hair and scooped up her hand.

The leaves were whirling in the wind and covering the ground with a carpet of colour. I was surrounded by large, old trees and wrapped in the sounds of nature with the man I love and his sweet, little girl. I inhaled a deep breath of fresh air. *Life can't get much better than this.*

Pheobe released Cameron's hand and scurried down the trail ahead of us toward the sound of rushing water. Cam didn't let her get more than a few steps away, before looping his arm around her and plopping her on his broad shoulder. It was nice to be together, just the three of us, to enjoy the simple pleasures in life.

Cam stopped when the untraveled trail branched into two directions. One led us back to the cabin; the other to the river.

"Can we go that way?" Pheobe begged, pointing toward the raging river.

Cameron lifted her off his shoulder like she weighed not more than a feather. "Okay, but stay close please."

"I will, Daddy," she insisted, carefully trotting ahead of us.

We approached the steep riverbank and kept our distance from the loose edge. Cameron took Pheobe's hand as we proceeded onto the less stable shoulder. We glanced out at the rushing water that was a good drop from where we were standing. Pheobe wanted to get closer, to see the fish that were swimming by.

"Careful sweetie, not too close," Cameron said protectively, as she pulled his arm to full extension.

She crouched down, near the edge of the bend in the river, causing Cameron to hunch at her side as she pointed excitedly into the water. "Look at the fish, Dad!"

"Those are rainbow trout," he explained.

Pheobe's proximity to the edge made me very nervous. I hadn't lifeguarded since I was a teenager, but I could still remember the torment in the children's eyes when they scooted out a little too far at the beach and realized that they couldn't make it back on their own.

"Maybe you should come away from the edge, Pheobe. That's not very safe there for a little girl."

"She's okay. I've got her," Cam said, as he glanced in my direction to smile.

Without warning, Pheobe stood up swiftly and tugged her hand from her Dad.

"No!" I hollered, frozen with panic.

She spun towards me on impulse and I saw her feet fail her as her shoes lost grip on the loose ground. Her eyes popped open wide with fear as her arms wagged backwards. Cameron reached for her desperately, but her jacket slipped from his fingers and she plummeted backward; drifting through the air, a terrifying screech ringing in my ears until she splashed into the pool of icy water.

I couldn't move, all life-saving training gone out with the wind, until Pheobe resurfaced from her vertical drop. She let out another blood curdling scream. Coming to my senses, I rushed to Cameron's side, just in time to watch her submerge beneath the depths of the frosty river again.

The water was much too deep for her to touch bottom and I doubted she would last long in the frigid, fast water. She had already started travelling downstream, much too small to fight the strong current.

"Does she know how to swim?" I shouted feverishly, as I watched on fearful for her life. I cringed, as her head bobbed up and down in the water.

"She's just learning. She's not very strong," Cam belted out. "I'm going in."

I saw her clawing at the surface, unable to fight the undertow. From the look on Cameron's face, I was certain he wasn't a very confident swimmer. When he hesitated to pull off his jacket, it solidified my fears. He didn't have any lifesaving skills at all.

"Call for help!" I cried, then leapt from the steep bank.

I attempted a compact jump and, even though I did it to the textbook, when I hit the water it felt like I had broken through a brick wall. My feet curled upwards and water ushered up my nose. When I finally broke the surface, I choked on the intake of water and my breath stung as I inhaled the brisk air.

My body felt heavy, weighed down by my saturated layers of clothes, and torn by the tug of the current. I frantically scoured the water for my target, as the undertow dragged me under against my will. I knew what I had to do. According to our tour guide, the water couldn't have been much deeper than ten feet. Giving in to the towing force, I plunged to the bottom until I connected with land.

Thrusting myself upward I broke the surface again, gasping for air and kicking as hard as I could to stay up. My lungs burned as I desperately searched for Pheobe. There she was, clawing hopelessly at a slippery rock. I swam with the current, stroking head up in her direction.

I knew if I outright grabbed her she would sink us both. But when I saw her little face submerge again, even longer than the last time, I couldn't fight my heart; even if I was fighting to keep my own head above water. I was going to grab onto her and hold on at all costs.

"I'm going to help you, Pheobe," I screeched. "Keep kicking!"

I could see the terror in her eyes, just like I had seen so

many times before, as she gasped for a breath like it might be her last and choked back a mouthful of water. The only thing keeping me from falling to pieces was the fact that she was still coughing.

When I was only a few feet from her, she submerged again and I couldn't take the chance of her not resurfacing. I forced myself under the treacherous water to swim after her.

I plunged under the water foot first and noticed the river was shallower now. When my fingers latched onto Pheobe's jacket, I pulled her to my hip and pushed off the bottom to force her head up for air.

After a few seconds, I found I was in dire need for air myself, so I kicked with all that I had, to keep us both above the whipping water. I managed a sharp breath and held our position, but I was struggling.

"Abby," Pheobe choked out, with a whimper. "I'm scared."

"It's okay, Pheobe. I'm scared too," I rasped. "But we're together now. I've got you."

She wept constantly, but tried to stay still. For that I was glad because I could feel my muscles tightening with each whip of my legs.

"I won't let you go. I promise," I reassured her, though my confidence was waning.

The rocks were too slippery and the banks too steep to climb. The sharp rocks were starting to rip my clothes and scratch my exposed skin. I tried to protect Pheobe as we struggled against the current and looked for a safe place to rest.

"Do you see a big rock or branch?" I asked desperately, as I used all of my energy to keep us afloat.

Exhaustion was starting to set in and my muscles were ceasing up from the cold, but I couldn't give up. Both of our lives depended on it. On me. With sheer determination, I held Pheobe up as long as I could until we both submerged in the rapids.

We rolled through the water, as I squeezed onto her with

my last ounce of energy, her little fingers clung to my heavy jacket for dear life. Clawing at the water I managed to break through one more time. After choking on another intake of river water, a muffled sound caught my attention.

"Abigail!" Cameron hollered again, deep and damaged.

Lying on my back to float as best I could, I glanced up at the river bank. Cameron's eyes were locked on us like a hawk. I felt a false sense of relief, knowing that Cameron was there, then I realized that he was motioning farther down the river.

"Grab onto that boulder!" he hollered. "Help is on its way!"

I tiredly looked to where he was pointing, searching for safety. I saw the large rock jutting out of the water exposed to the cold, November air. We floated toward it as the current pulled us in its direction.

"Okay, Pheobe, I know you can do this. When we get to that big rock, I need you to grab onto it and hold on as tight as you can, okay?"

"Okay," she cried, her lips blue and trembling.

"Whatever you do, don't let go," I ordered, as I guided her to the boulder.

Without any further direction, Pheobe stretched out bravely to grab on. I feared that if this plan didn't work, neither of us would make it out alive. I pushed her out of the rushing water and secured her safely on top of the rock. I tried to reach for it myself, but my numb fingers refused to grab on and there wasn't enough room on top for the two of us.

"Don't let go!" I ordered, as I uncontrolledly slipped under the water, unable to fight the rapids that were suddenly far more challenging than before.

"Abby!" she screamed, wailing like a helpless baby.

Powerless, I drifted out of control, crashing between sharp rocks as the current swept me farther downriver. I swallowed more of the cool, fast flowing water as I forced my mouth to the sky. I could feel something brushing on my badly bruised body and I grabbed on as tight as my tense fingers would allow.

Tree roots. They were jutting through a rock. I pulled myself closer to the edge and groaned as I lifted my upper body onto a fallen branch. Fatigue overwhelmed me and I rolled in and out of consciousness, as I laid there utterly spent.

My body experienced violent tremors and suddenly red glowing eyes were upon me. Watching. Glaring. Judging. Vicious shivers rocked through my limbs as my sister's scream rang in my ear drums. My lungs, my eyes, my toes burned, and the screaming continued to haunt me. Tears stung my cheeks, as I tried to force the unforgettable horror from my head. *This must be death.*

The trembling started to fade and I was certain that it meant my life was slipping away. The rescuers weren't fast enough and there was absolutely nothing left that I could do.

"Unbelievable. You're giving up?" my sister screeched. My dead sister. And she had two red globes strobing from her otherwise flawless face. "And after all I've done for you," Jenny snapped.

The tears continued to burn in my eyes, like a raging winter fire, blurring my vision and burning my heart. The glowing eyes slowly faded away, until they were replaced with an orange blob upstream.

A rescue boat!

I wanted to scream for help, but my throat wouldn't allow it. It was getting difficult to breathe. I closed my eyes and my consciousness threatened to leave me entirely.

"Stay with me, Abigail," Cameron hollered.

I forced my eyes open, but the burning was unbearable. To hear that voice one last time, was worth the pain, even if it was muffled by the sound of the nearby falls. My lips were cracked and dry and my legs began to cramp. My grip was nonexistent, my fingers useless, my voice a raspy whisper.

Feeling terribly lightheaded, the tree roots slipped free from my frozen hands and my heavy clothes began to drag me from the narrow branch to my death. When I slid beneath the surface, I squeezed my eyes shut. Tired. So tired, as the cold dragged me into oblivion.

The rescuers had retrieved Pheobe from the water successfully, and she was now safe on a bright orange boat. A female team member wrapped her in a blanket and embraced her as she tried to calm her overactive nerves.

Cameron never lost sight of Abigail, as he pleaded with the rescue crew to help her. "She can't hold on much longer. Somebody's got to do something!" he yelled, his hands helplessly plastered to his head.

"We need a plan," the team leader snapped. "The banks are too steep, we'll need to haul her out," he advised his crew.

The first rescuer looked out to the victim anxiously, as her position began to fail. "There's no time!" he hollered, as Abigail dropped beneath the surface. Against his leader's orders, he pulled on his gear, plunged into the frigid water and performed a submerged victim rescue.

He plugged her nose and pointed her head to the river floor, then swiftly re-emerged. He turned her head up, pointing it toward the grey sky, effectively opening her wind pipe and exposing her sensitive flesh to the cold, dry air.

He held the victim's head skyward as his big, strong legs thrust them toward the riverbank at exemplary speed. "Damn it, Abigail," he barked.

Another rescuer dropped into the water to assist him.

"We have to get her out of here, now!" the first responder ordered. His shiny, black wetsuit was no comfort in waters of this temperature, but his adrenaline was pumping and his blood was boiling to point where he was breaking a sweat.

"They can't do it," the second rescuer hollered, as he forced a pfd around the victim's neck. "The falls are too close. It would put our entire team in danger. It's too risky."

The first rescuer growled with frustration. "Stay with me, Abigail. We're going to get you out of here," he reassured her.

"This will all be over real soon, Abigail. I promise," the man said.

That voice; it sounded so familiar. I gasped for a breath. Water swished in my belly and spewed from my mouth. The violent shivers returned to me, as the man snapped me into a lift seat.

"I should go up with her. She's too weak," the familiar voice insisted. "The strap, it's not enough support. She's not stable enough to go it alone."

"No. You'll be too heavy together. She'll be fine," the other assured him, as he reluctantly tightened the single strap between her thighs.

"Hold on tight, Abigail. Cameron needs you."

I wanted to tell him I couldn't, but my lips were not mine to control. Then I was in the air, swiftly swinging higher. As I neared the landing, it was blurry, but I couldn't miss the panic in Cameron's stance. Someone forced him away as another man extended his arms out to me.

Seeing Cameron like that was too much. My eyes rolled up as a dizzy spell took me. The weight of my unconscious frame tilted the lift forward until my body spilled out of the overturned seat and sent me plummeting back into the icy depths of the raging river below.

When I hit the slab of water, it stunned me back awake, but I didn't know which way was up. My human helplessness forced me to breathe in a large gulp of water before my life vest returned me to reality.

It was only a matter of seconds before I was back in my rescuers heated arms. I could hear him hollering angrily, but I couldn't make out the words over my raspy, irregular breaths. Finally the words rang in my ears, loud and clear.

"I told you she needed me! We do this my way," he snapped at his partner. "Can you hear me, Abigail? It's Hunter. I'm not going to let anything happen to you. You hear me?"

I wanted to believe him, but I recalled saying very similar words to Pheobe in an attempt to give her the illusion of safety. He pulled me to the lift and strapped us together.

"Go!" he ordered.

I could hear the rope creaking above us, tugging on every fiber, as the crew lifted our dangling bodies to freedom.

"Stay with me, Abby. We're almost there," he reassured me

It was the first time I had felt an ounce of safety, with his strong arms clutching me against his burning hot skin. I closed my eyes, unable to control the trembling, as the wind whipped us like a violent lover. I begged, whimpered for my voice but found myself unable to conjure it up.

I felt my body being exchanged between hands and when I reopened my eyes, Cameron was kneeling over me.

"Abigail? Please wake up," he said softly, squeezing my limp hand in his.

I stared at him, through the slits that were my tear-filled eyes, wondering if this man was for real. Even in his state of panic, his glimmering gaze filled with worry, he was completely beautiful. Hunter stood next to him, peeling his upper body from his wetsuit, while a couple of paramedics assessed my condition.

"I think she's going to be okay," Hunter told Cameron, nodding at one of the paramedics.

Cameron worriedly lifted my body into his arms and squeezed me, soggy clothes and all, with his burning hot embrace.

"Cam," I managed to rasp, tears swimming in my eyes.

"Shhh. Save your voice," he urged.

"Let's get her to the hospital," Hunter barked, his voice a solid command.

Cameron helped me sit up and looped his arm around my body. Hunter grabbed my other side, but Cameron carried the majority of my weight when he scooped me into his arms and lowered me onto the gurney.

"We need to get her out of these wet clothes," Hunter ordered.

Cameron hurriedly unzipped my jacket and pulled it off of me, while a paramedic methodically removed the rest of my soaking wet clothes. After being locked in securely, layers of blankets pinned me to the make-shift bed.

I was still unable to spill words from my frozen lips. "Pheobe?" I sputtered.

"Pheobe's fine. It's you I'm worried about," Cameron said.

Tears flowed out of my eyes and a sob escaped my mouth, as they carted me down the narrow dirt trail. I was physically and emotionally exhausted, as they lifted me onto the motorized vehicle and raced for the park entrance.

I squeezed my eyes shut, but the tears still dripped down my cheeks and Cameron kissed them repeatedly. Each time it sent extremely hot, throbbing sensations to the surface of my skin, which was an agonizing reminder of my sister's painful death, but I couldn't bring him to stop.

"It's okay. Everything's going to be okay," Cam said. And it was the last words I remembered before falling into a deep, terror-filled sleep.

I awoke staring at a white ceiling. Tears were still wet in my eyes. I was feeling very confused, my head fuzzy, because I had no recollection of where I was or how I got there. After a few blinks, I realized I was wearing a powder blue hospital gown and I knew I had no part in dressing in it. My aching body throbbed in pain.

"Hey there," Cameron said, smiling. Pheobe was wrapped in his arms and her hand was grasped tightly onto mine.

"I'm not letting go this time," she said to me, in her soft little voice.

I didn't have the heart to tell her that she was making my

hand feel like it was on fire. I was just happy she was okay.

Cameron lifted Pheobe to her feet and called for a nurse. After a quick check of my vitals, she insisted that I take it easy. The drugs were working, but apparently they could only do so much. I still felt like hell, hot lava in my lungs and desert chapping my lips.

My bladder felt full as the cold fluid steadily flowed through my veins. "Can I walk?" I asked the nurse, desperate to use the facilities.

"I don't know, can you?" she asked.

Cameron nodded his head and the nurse helped me to my feet. She unplugged the machine I was connected to from the wall and towed it behind me.

When I returned to my bed, Pheobe was gone, crushing my positivity. "Pheobe?"

"My mom has her. She's getting something to eat."

I nodded, slight relief returning to me as I adjusted my bruised body in the firm bed.

"I'm so sorry, Abby. This is all my fault." Cam dropped his forehead into his hand. "If I would have listened to you, none of this would have happened."

"No. If I hadn't startled Pheobe, she wouldn't have fallen backwards."

"It's not your fault. You did great," Cameron said, kissing my frosty cheek. He smoothed one hand over my face and cupped my cheek, then kissed my parched lips.

His warm hands wrapped around me and he pulled me into his arms. "I owe you my life," he whispered softly, pressing a hot kiss to my temple.

Sad thoughts spilled into my mind and a big swoosh of emotions overcame me. I was lucky. Pheobe was lucky. Jenny wasn't so fortunate. I closed my eyes, hoping to find more rest, but I couldn't fight the memories that had haunted me day and night for the better part of my childhood.

Cameron stroked my hair and sprinkled kisses over my cheeks and eyes and forehead. He was amazing and I was a blubbering fool.

After he swiped away the endless tears, I noticed the nurse had been replaced with a handsome doctor. He was standing over me with his soft, black hair and skin as milky white as his coat. He was thoughtfully reviewing my chart with striking, steel grey eyes.

The doctor looked up at me and then down at my chart, and then at me again. "Abigail. Nice of you to join us," he said.

"You know her?" the nurse asked, gawking over his shoulder to see what she had missed on the chart.

"Yeah, this is my buddy's girlfriend. Uh, I mean, ex-girlfriend," he corrected, without taking notice of Cameron's distress as he slunk back into the chair next to the bed.

Dr. Dexter Allbright looked as amazing as ever, while I laid there shrivelled like a prune, bruised and emotionally ruined.

"I got the page that we had a submerged victim coming in, but no one told me it was you," he said. "I hear the rescue team ran into some trouble, but I see their persistence paid off. Your condition is improving already."

I smiled softly, not knowing what to say to that. My head was pounding and shivers continued to jolt my body. Even though I was covered in blankets, I just couldn't stop the shaking.

Dr. Dex came to my side, glanced at my monitor and then flipped open my chart. "Your blood pressure is a little low. It's a pretty common symptom of shock though. I'm not surprised to see these results after hearing the traumatic incident you encountered."

He scribbled on the paper and then turned his head to the nurse. She was eagerly awaiting her instructions from the handsome doctor. He told her softly to up my meds, in some medical mumbo jumbo, and she hurried off to obey his gentle command. He glanced back at me and smiled acknowledging her obvious infatuation with him.

"Other than the disorientation, you seem to be suffering only minor cuts and bruises. It's actually quite amazing. I would have expected much worse. I always knew you were a tough girl. That's why I always thought you were the perfect match for Spencer."

Cameron slipped out of his chair and returned to my side. "Actually, this one's mine," he stated, taking my hand in his and squeezing it gently. "You can tell your friend - Spencer is it?- that he's out of luck."

"Oh, I apologize." Dr. Dex looked at me curiously. "I didn't realize you were in a relationship."

"Dexter, this is my boyfriend, Cameron Clarke."

"Dr. Dexter Allbright. Pleased to meet you," he said, smooth and professional, as he extended his hand to Cameron.

"I'm sure you are," Cam replied, giving his hand a firm shake.

Dexter was no fool. He gathered Cameron's sarcasm. "I'll leave you two alone. Please excuse me. A nurse will be in soon to help you with the pain. I'll come check on you later."

"Okay," I rasped.

"Take good care of this one," Dr. Dex said, with a pointed glance at Cameron.

"Thank you, Doctor. I will," Cameron replied.

Dr. Dex disappeared out of the small room, but Cameron couldn't manage to hide his tension-filled brow. "It sounds like they plan on keeping you here for a while."

"I'll be fine. Just a little sore. They want to keep me for observation tonight, but I could go home as soon as tomorrow."

"I'm staying with you," Cameron stated.

"No. Pheobe needs you."

"Phoebe's fine. She's already been cleared and my mother's taking her home. I'm staying. You just concentrate on getting better," Cameron ordered.

I felt a soft smile playing on my lips, though my entire body hurt with every uncomfortable breath.

Cameron crouched in close to the bed and delivered a heartfelt kiss. "I love you, Abby."

I smiled at that, and Cam resealed his soft lips to mine,

just as a nurse entered my room. Before long, the pain started to subside, but the cold stream that flowed through my limbs caused the shivers to return full force.

"Will you be staying the night, sir?" the nurse asked Cameron.

"Yes, ma'am."

She nodded. "I'll see what I can do about a bed."

"That won't be necessary. A chair will suffice; as long as Abigail's comfortable."

"Cameron," I moaned with disappointment.

The nurse looked at me and then back to Cameron. "Just let me know if you change your mind. I know she's a friend of Dr. Allbright, so I want you all to be comfortable."

"We appreciate it," he replied, as she excused herself from the room.

Cameron came back to my side and pulled the chair up close to my bed. "If you don't want to talk about it now, I understand; but I wonder about your ex-boyfriend," Cameron asked, jealousy leaking from him like an old faucet.

"Who, Spencer?"

"Right. Who is he and why did the good doctor call him your boyfriend?"

CHAPTER TWENTY ONE

After my transfer to a private room, I had a steady stream of visitors lasting late into the night. After suffering through my parent's visit, which was their first time meeting Cameron, I was looking forward to getting some rest.

Cameron had taken the news about Spencer relatively well. I gave him a very brief summary of our relationship together and told him about our latest meeting over dinner and drinks. I admitted that Spencer was just a torn up page in my book of life that I would never turn back to. Cam seemed satisfied that it was over between us. That's because it was.

Though my mind was numb from all of the day's events and my entire body ached, the recent dose of pain medication seemed to do the trick, dulling the realization that Edwin never cared to see that I was still alive.

When I woke up with the sun, I couldn't help but admire Cameron, his sleeping frame slumped in the arm chair at my side. *What a sweetheart, staying with me and sleeping in a chair no less.* I had to admit, if I have any luck at all it had to be in the man department.

Moments after waking, his gorgeous sleepy eyes opened slowly, but they were on me in an instant. Cameron sat up quickly and glanced anxiously around the room. "Is everything okay?"

"I think so," I answered, softly.

He stretched his arms over his head and let out a loud groan as he twisted his tense body. "I guess sleeping on a chair wasn't the best idea I ever had," he said, rubbing his lower back. After another little stretch, he hunched over the bed and delivered a heartfelt kiss on my lips. "Do you need anything?"

"No. I'm alright. I'm stuck on this IV until the nurse makes her rounds. If you're hungry, you can go ahead."

"I can wait. Let me see if I can get a nurse in here." He squeezed my hand gently and gave me a quick smooch before he walked to the door and disappeared into the hall. Within a few minutes, he returned with a nurse and a wink.

"Good morning, Ms. Jenkins. How are you feeling?" the nurse asked.

"Better than before," I admitted. The shivers had finally stopped. "I was just wondering when I can go home."

She smiled softly. "I've been given the okay to take you off the IV, but I'm not able to grant your release. Doctor's orders."

Cameron cleared his throat, with his fisted hand covering his mouth, and turned his head away to hide his smirk from me.

"When is Dr. Allbright expected?" I asked, my voice finding its depth.

"Unfortunately, he's not expected for another half hour. I'll let him know you're asking for him as soon as he arrives."

After tucking in my pouty lip, I blew out an exasperated sigh. Cameron only chuckled.

"In the meantime, let's get these tubes off of you and see how you handle some solid food," the nurse suggested.

"I'm not really hungry," I insisted.

"You need to keep up with the fluids or you'll be back in here in no time. You should try some food this morning too, whether you're hungry or not. I don't think you realize the severity of your condition."

"Don't you worry," Cameron said. "I'm going to be her manservant. She'll be eating and drinking all day and night. I'll spoon feed her if I have to," he insisted playfully, delighting the nurse.

She smiled pleasantly at him and patted me on the shoulder gently, then walked out of the room.

I glanced playfully stern at Cameron, but was swooning inside. "Manservant? Do you forget you have to work tomorrow?"

His lips curled into a smile and he took a seat on my bed. He brushed the hair from my face and paused long enough to send butterflies on flight in my tummy. "Actually, after you fell asleep last night I called Owen. He gave us both the day off. I told him I didn't know how long you needed, but he insisted we take it one day at a time."

"You always think of everything."

He smiled. "Now, what do you say we hit the cafeteria? That is if you are up to it."

"You know I am. I'll do whatever it takes to get out of here." I swung my legs over the side of the bed and groaned from the all-over ache.

"Don't push yourself. I'll take you in the wheelchair." Cameron hurried toward the door and before I could demand that he stop, Aliah peeked her head in the room.

"Did I hear someone say wheelchair? What, are your legs broken?" Aliah asked, sarcastically.

"No! As I was just telling Cameron, I'm fine."

Cameron slipped past her and disappeared into the hall. I shook my head, feeling irritated.

Aliah took a few awkward steps into the room, her eyes dark with makeup. She anxiously stood in the stark white space in her tallest pair of stilettos.

"What the hell are you doing here at this hour?" I asked.

"I was just heading home for the night," she said.

"The night? That explains why you look like a tramp, but you could have just called."

Aliah snorted. "And here I felt guilty for not coming sooner. I just found out. Give me a break."

"I take it you talked to Hunter."

Aliah folded her arms under her chest. "No. He's been working twelve hour shifts lately. I wasn't about to sit at home alone all weekend. I haven't seen him since yesterday."

"If Hunter didn't tell you, then how did you hear about the accident?"

"I ran into Spencer, or rather he ran into me on my way

home. I might have been speeding and he might have pulled me over. He told me you were hurt."

In hopes of avoiding that subject, I ignored it entirely. "You really haven't talked to Hunter?"

"Nope, not since yesterday afternoon when he got called in for an emergency. Why the sudden interest in Hunter?"

"The man saved my life," I stated, with emotions ready to burst.

"My man?"

I nodded. "Hunter's the one that pulled me out of the water. Twice."

"What, he didn't do a good enough job the first time?"

I sighed and closed my tired eyes. "Long story and I really don't want to get into it. I'm sure Hunter will tell you later anyways."

"Man, what a downer," Aliah moaned.

"Tell me about it," Cameron said grumpily, as he pushed the wheelchair through the door and past her.

"What's your problem?" she asked.

"Woke up on the wrong side of the chair," he growled.

Aliah laughed. "At least you haven't lost your sense of humour, fun guy. And what about this one," she said, nodding toward me. "You look fine."

"She may seem fine to you, but she seriously could've lost her life yesterday. If it wasn't for her, so could have Pheobe," Cam admitted, emotion evident in his tone.

A tear rolled down my cheek when I remembered poor, little Pheobe left all alone on that rock. "If I let her die, I wouldn't be able to live with myself."

"Whoa, whoa, calm down," Aliah ordered. "I don't need you two getting all emotional on me. It looks like you're doing great now, so that's a bonus. Why don't you just give me the rundown?"

I flashed a reluctant glance at Cameron and he nodded. Despite my lack of enthusiasm, I would tell the story one last time.

"Alright. The short of it is, we were out hiking at Rosella Park and Pheobe fell in the river. You know the banks are super steep, right? Well she couldn't fight the rapids so I had to go in after her."

"Of course you did, little Miss Trouble. Why didn't you just tell her to climb up on the bank and wait for help?"

"Yeah, you really have no idea. The banks along that portion of the river were vertical drops and the current had already pulled her downstream before she even resurfaced."

"Sorry. I didn't know."

"You do realize she's only six years old. She can barely tread water in a pool let alone hold her head up in the rapids. She was petrified."

I closed my eyes to block the hurt that was settling back in from remembering the life threatening episode. I felt like bawling, but I knew Aliah wasn't the type of friend to lend her shoulder for that sort of thing.

"Hey, wait a minute. You're not going to cry on me, are you?"

I giggled at her snappy words and the smile temporarily ushered away the bad memories.

"Good, a smile. It's a start. I don't suppose telling you Spencer says *'hi'* will keep that smile on your face."

Dr. Dexter appeared in my doorway, cleared his throat and again reviewed my chart. "About that. I do apologize. I shouldn't have called him. But I did before I knew you were otherwise engaged."

"Ugh," I moaned, burying my head in my arms, not wanting to hear that man's name again today.

"Don't worry about it," Dexter said. "I told him not to come. You just concentrate on getting better."

Cameron massaged his hands over my shoulders, while Aliah flashed Dexter a trampy glance.

"Dr. Allbright," she expressed provocatively, selfishly trying to get the doctor's attention.

He gave Aliah a quick nod and smiled warmly at me, avoiding Aliah's death gaze from all but ignoring her. "What's this about you threatening the nurses?" he asked me, teasing.

"Is that what they told you? I just want out of here already."

"Hey, I'm just looking out. I want to be sure it's safe for you to leave before you go. There are a lot of people who care about you."

"Yeah, like Spencer," Aliah huffed, under her breath.

Dr. Dex squinted unhappily at Aliah for acting so immature. "Do you think I could get a minute here?" he asked her.

"Yes, sir," Aliah snapped, smirking. "My lips are sealed." After raising her brow, she motioned the locking of her lips and threw away the key.

The doctor monitored my heart rate and nodded with approval. "It sounds good. And your blood pressure seems to be back within normal range."

I smiled. "Does that mean I can get out of this joint or what?"

"Not so fast. I want to wait until we get your blood work back to confirm everything's in order. You don't want to get home and have to turn around and come back for more tests."

I sighed deeply and flashed a weak glance at Cameron.

"It's okay, babe. I'm here for you. Let's get you something to eat. I'm sure the tests won't take that long, will they doctor?" Cameron looked to Dr. Dex with concern in his eyes and hope that he hadn't just told a lie.

"You're right. I expect to get the results by noon. In fact, they could be on my desk right now."

"Then what are you waiting for? Get over there and check it out," I ordered.

He chuckled and stepped away from my bedside. "You take it easy for a while. Go get yourself something to eat and drink and we'll see what your body thinks about that. If you don't run into any troubles, I'll send you on your way after lunch."

"Fine. It's not like Cam will let me out of his sight anyway," I grumbled.

Dr. Dex smiled at me and ignored my half-hearted

compliance. "Good. So, how are you doing for pain?"

"No thanks, I've got plenty of that," I replied.

He chuckled briefly, though Cameron didn't seem to think it was quite so funny. "Would you like something for it?" Dex offered.

"Why, can you hook me up with some drugs?"

"I can get that machine back in here. Then I can guarantee you'll be stuck here for another day."

"Tylenol should do the trick," I said.

He smiled at me and nodded. "That's what I thought. I'll have some sent in." With a nod at Cameron and a smile for Aliah, he briskly walked to the door. "Aliah, always a pleasure," he said, then escaped into the hall.

"See ya, Doc," Aliah said, then turned her smoldering eyes back on me. "He's stuck up when he's working, eh?"

"He seemed fine to me," I said, smirking. "I think you're just cranky cuz you're tired and hung over."

"At least I came to see you. I could've gone home to bed and totally blew you off." *Like Edwin.*

"Thanks, Aliah; it really shows that you care," I teased.

She came to my side and gave me a bear hug. "Well, get better soon, so we can be hung over together," she said, as I winced in pain from the squeeze. "Oh sorry!"

I tried to act like it didn't hurt, forcing a smile on my face. "Thanks for coming."

"You know I love ya," she replied, then shuffled her petite body to the door in her ski-scraper heels. "Catcha later. I've gotsta get my beauty sleep," she chimed, as she made her exit.

Cameron pushed the wheelchair up beside my bed. "Quite the friends you have," he teased.

"Hey, she came, didn't she?"

He acknowledged that with a smile and reached for my hand to guide me to the wheelchair. "Here, let me help you."

I slapped away his hand. "Seriously, Cam, I'm not paralyzed. If you got this chair any closer, it'd be in the bed."

"Take my hand. You don't have to play the tough girl with me."

I huffed, but I took his hand to let him help me to my feet. I immediately felt a cold breeze on my backside. "Uhhh?" I said, with my eyes bugging out of my head.

Cam's smile was priceless. "Yeah, let me get you your robe. Will you be okay?" he asked, before letting my hand go.

"Please!" I exclaimed, as I bunched the gown together behind me.

He let out a chuckle as he hustled over to grab my robe. He quickly returned to me, wrapped me up and tied it snugly around my waist.

"Seriously? I'm not disabled."

"Get used to it. I'm going to be helping you with a lot of things you're used to doing yourself," he insisted. "Remember? Manservant."

"Does that mean you'll be taking orders from me?" *I could have fun with that.*

After batting my tired eyelashes at him, he eased back and smirked. "What are my orders, madam?"

"Kiss me." I tried to lower myself into the chair for more stability, but I had been cooped up for so long that my muscles forgot how to work and quickly dropped me into the seat.

Cameron narrowed his eyes, his intensity warning me to take his advice, but he still dipped down for a kiss.

"Okay, now get pushing," I snapped, after stealing another kiss.

"As you wish," he said, with a handsome smile. He walked slowly down to the cafeteria. When he slid into the chair next to me, his food wafted my way.

"That smells so good. *You would* try to tempt me like that."

"You eat your dry toast and like it," he snapped. "I never said I was going to be a good manservant." His smile was gorgeous.

"Yes, you did."

"Then I promise to be a better one after I'm done eating my bacon." After swallowing the bacon in two bites, he lifted a large portion of the pancake he had drenched in syrup and held it my way. "Do you want a bite?" It was limping from the fork, but it smelled amazing.

"I'd better pass. I have to be on my best behaviour if I want to get out of here," I said, nibbling on my flavourless jello.

"So she does listen," Cameron teased.

After we were done eating, Cameron cleared our table and started to push my chair toward the hall. "Where to, my love?"

When I didn't respond, his immediate worry caused him to crouch in front of me. "Are you okay?"

I couldn't help but smile. "I'd love to go for a little walk." I slowly lifted myself from the seat and stood next to him, clinging to his broad shoulders. "See? I'm fine."

"Please be careful," he urged, standing to loop his arms around me.

With Cameron's help, I inched down the narrow hall. A short trip was the best I could do and still every muscle in my body ached. When we returned to the wheelchair, Cameron stood in front of me and I playfully nudged him, so he took the seat himself.

"Oops," I teased, as I dropped onto his lap. I was exhausted, but starting to feel quite a bit better already, finally having some solid food in my empty belly. I smiled into his eyes and they sparkled back at me. I had to have another kiss.

"Okay, you've got my attention; now what do you want?" he asked.

I smiled and continued to gaze at him. "I want you."

I was in such a lovable mood that it surprised me when I heard clapping from a few feet away. It had felt as though we were the only two people in the hospital, but as Spencer brought to my attention, that was definitely not the case.

"Bravo. You've put on quite the performance," Spencer said.

"Spencer? What are you doing here?"

He took my hand and pulled me up from Cameron's lap. Cameron helped with both his hands on my hips.

Spencer dragged me a few steps away from him, as Cameron remained seated, cautiously observing my reaction. "Excuse us a moment," Spencer said, with his stunning English accent.

When Cameron saw the anger in my eyes, he willingly let me go. "Be my guest."

"I'll never be your guest," Spencer rebuked, as he pulled my arm gently to move us farther down the hall.

Cameron chuckled, as if he didn't despise the interruption, and turned his gaze out the window.

"That's far enough," I growled. I tried to yank my arm from his hand, but he was strong.

"What did I do?" He looked at me through disappointed eyes.

"What do you want?" I snapped.

"I came straightaway once my shift ended. How are you doing?"

Not wanting to answer him, I huffed. "How did you know I was here?"

A smirk curled onto his gorgeous lips. "I asked a lovely nurse at the front desk and she told me this is where I'd find you."

"Good to know they value confidentiality around here," I said, scowling. "Maybe I should have a talk with Dexter about that."

"I may have dropped a few names and flashed my badge for the info," he said, with his alluring charm.

I shook my head and couldn't help but smile at his efforts.

"I knew you had one of those in there for me," he said, motioning at my smile with a nod.

I immediately wiped it off my face, knowing Cameron was likely watching. I couldn't bring myself to check and see if he was. "Why are you really here?"

"What? I can't come and check on my girl?" A sexy smile

slanted across his face, as if he needed anything more than that accent to catch my attention.

"Spencer, you know I'm not your girl. What are you doing here?"

"Are you telling me what just transpired wasn't an act? You really want him?" Spencer asked, not entirely believing it.

"Yes," I answered, without hesitating. "More than you'll ever know."

"I don't mean to upset you," he insisted, but I was already upset.

What was he even doing here?

"Oh, really? How did you think this was going to go exactly?"

"I don't know," he drawled.

"You can't just go dragging me around wherever you please." I spun around, too quickly, and Spencer had to grab onto my arm to give me support.

I ignored the all-over pain, to chastise him. "Why don't you pull yourself together so I can properly introduce you?" I lifted my eyes to Cameron, who was now standing behind the wheelchair, his eyes fixed on Spencer with a ferocious stare.

He could see I was a little unsteady on my feet and so he quickly pushed the chair up to me and helped me ease down into it. "Are we done here?" he asked me, glaring at Spencer, who was still in full uniform.

Spencer shot an evil look toward us. Though it was clearly intended for Cameron, I took extreme offence to it.

"Okay, that's enough!" I scowled at Spencer to get his reaction and he flashed me a mischievous smile, his icy eyes sparkling in the sunlight.

"I'll behave," Spencer drawled.

I didn't believe him. "Whatever. You need to accept that Cam's in my life now and if you want to ever see me again then you'll treat him fair."

"I can be fair," Spencer replied.

"Cam, as I'm sure you've already figured out, this is

Spencer Caldwell. Spencer this is my boyfriend, Cameron Clarke. He's a lawyer at my firm."

Spencer reached his hand out to Cameron to officially greet him. "It's *Detective* Caldwell, but I see Abigail failed to tell you that," he said, peeved and dramatic.

"I've heard a lot about you, but that wasn't part of it," Cameron sniped.

"That's funny because I haven't heard anything about you," Spencer jabbed.

I ignored their petty argument. "Since when were you a detective?"

"I was promoted months ago. If you would have returned my calls, maybe I could've told you."

"I guess I had other things on my mind," I said, smiling at my man.

Disbelief marked Spencer's face. "You've been dating this loser that long?"

Cameron puffed up his chest and hiked his sleeves, preparing to knock Spencer out, his lip protruding like a rabid animal.

"Cameron! Please." I put my arm out to stop him and looked back to Spencer to set him straight. "I met him shortly after that night we had dinner. I guess we started dating a while after that."

"You guess? What girl guesses when she starts dating a guy? I see you're really taking this relationship seriously. Call me when it doesn't work out."

Luckily Cameron backed off, focusing on taking steady breaths and twitching muscles, so I could fight my own battle.

"Not gonna happen," I stated. "In fact, if I ever make a list of the dumbest things I've ever done, you'll be right on top."

"I honestly doubt that," Spencer said, very confident in himself.

I anxiously held his icy stare as he walked closer to me. When he was standing at my feet, only steps away from Cameron, he took my hand and kissed my cheek.

"Keep out of trouble. Let's hope I don't run in to you when I'm working," he said.

"You won't."

"Oh, I'm sure that'll be next. Ever since you left me, you've gotten into nothing but trouble," he drawled.

"Back off, Spencer," Cameron warned. "I'll take care of her." Cameron wrapped his arms around me and drew me close, standing his ground and staring Spencer down.

I cupped Cameron's cheek and shared a soft peck with him, before taking my seat in the wheelchair. "Let's go," I said.

Spencer ignored Cameron's impressive gesture and looked me right in the eyes as we passed him. "Call me," he drawled. But his icy eyes and handsome accent had no effect on me while I could still taste Cameron's love on my lips.

CHAPTER TWENTY TWO

A few weeks had passed since our river incident and, though the bruises had faded and I had made a full recovery, Cameron was still being particularly careful with Pheobe. I had finally convinced him that we needed some alone time and he finally agreed to let Ashley take Pheobe off his hands for a few hours.

"Pheobe, what do you think? Do you want to come shopping with me?" Ashley asked.

"Yeah, yeah!" Pheobe cheered.

"Go get your coat then. It's pretty chilly out today."

Pheobe ran to the closet to pull out her jacket. "Can Abby come with us?"

"Um, no. I think your dad might get too lonely if we all leave," Ashley suggested, gritting her teeth.

I was happy to be sitting in the next room over because I couldn't help but smirk.

"Why don't you grab your mittens too," Cam suggested, as he went to help her find some.

Before he even reached her, Pheobe dove into the closet and reappeared with a pair of mittens and a big, cheesy grin.

"Are you ready to go?" Ashley asked her.

"Yup," Pheobe cheered, as she waved her mitted hands in the air.

"Have fun," Cam said, planting a kiss on Pheobe's cheek before she skipped out the door. "Stay out of trouble," he called after her.

"We'll probably be a couple of hours. I have a few stops to make," Ashley explained, as she exited the house.

"Thanks, Ash." When Cam closed the door behind them, it suddenly got really quiet.

In no time at all, Cam parked himself next to me on the

sofa and draped his arm over my shoulder. "Looks like we've got this place all to ourselves," he pointed out.

I smiled, as he leaned in for a soft kiss. Being a little devious, I took his lower lip between mine and tugged on it with my teeth.

"Mmm," he growled, with approval. "I wonder what we can do while they're gone." His eyebrows hung low over his eyelids casting a mysterious shadow over his sparkling eyes.

I only hoped that batting my long, dark lashes at him innocently, would get him to pull me off to his bedroom.

A torturously handsome smile curled onto his lips as he leaned in to taste my neck. "You're suddenly very quiet, Miss Jenkins. Have you no ideas?" he charmed, as he deliciously trailed wet kisses along my jaw.

His mouth closed around my chin, his warmth caressing my face, as I sensed his heightened arousal swirling around me. His lack of urgency somehow ignited my excitement, when his hot mouth covered mine at last.

I can't believe we just did that.

I smiled down at Cameron, our warm bodies fused together. After a few more fantastic seconds, a chill overcame my bare back as my mind returned to reality and a stab of pain knifed into my side.

I glanced at the door, suddenly worried that someone might appear there and find us latched together, totally naked and spent on the living room floor.

"Don't worry; I locked the door," he assured me.

"But Ashley has a key," I reminded him, as I observed our clothing littered all over the living room floor.

Just then the doorbell rang and stole Cameron's attention, while another jabbing pain caused me to hunch into a twisted heap on the floor. I grasped at the side stich with both my hands and gasped for a breath, frozen in place, waiting to see what would happen next. The pain quickly subsided, so I got onto my knees. I was ready to bolt.

There was no sound of a key in the hole or Ashley's big mouth.

"The front blinds are open," Cam whispered. "We should probably get out of here, in case our visitor decides to take a peek."

Following Cameron, I quietly crawled behind the couch and then dashed to the dining room, giggling, wearing nothing but my embarrassment. I couldn't help but notice that every exposed muscle on his body was held tight and tense. *How did he manage to scam his underwear on the way?*

There was pounding at the door. This person was not giving up. I pouted up my lips, as Cameron flashed me a wicked smile and pulled on his shorts.

"It's not Ashley. She wouldn't have knocked," Cam whispered.

"She would if she knew what we were up to."

Cameron wrapped his arms around me and pressed his lips to mine. The doorbell rang again and we both snickered.

"Who do you think it is?" I asked.

"No one important. It's probably just a salesman."

We crouched together at the floor, waiting for our guest to leave. The person rang the bell yet again and banged on the door some more.

"They're awfully persistent. Maybe you should get it," I suggested.

"I'm sure they'll leave soon."

We waited an entire minute of total silence before peeking around the corner. Cameron crept to the front door and heard a car pulling away from the driveway, but wasn't able to catch a glimpse of it before it disappeared behind the neighbours bushes.

"We're clear," he said.

"Oh, thank God." I scurried into the living room, collected up my clothes and frantically redressed.

Ashley and Pheobe had finished at their first stop and headed straight for the huge superstore to get some groceries. Ashley pulled out a shopping cart and helped Pheobe hop into it. "I don't know. You're getting pretty big to ride in the cart," Ashley said, teasing.

"Dad lets me do this all the time," Pheobe explained.

"If you say so," Ashley replied, giving her a wink.

They approached the apples and Pheobe helped Ashley pick out the most perfect, shiniest apples of the bunch. After filling her cart with fruits and veggies, Ashley pushed the cart toward the meat counter. Before she made her request, she noticed Pheobe rocking back and forth.

"Is there something you'd like to tell me?" Ashley asked.

Pheobe nodded her head urgently.

"You're sure you can't hold it for a few more minutes? We just got here," Ashley whined.

"Auntie Ashleeyyy, I really have to goooo!"

It came as no surprise to Ashley, because this had happened every single time she brought Pheobe shopping without fail. For whatever reason, Pheobe found it necessary to try out the store's facilities with each and every visit.

"Alright. Let's go," Ashley said. She quickly pushed the cart to a vacant space at the bottom of the stairs, grabbed onto Pheobe's outstretched hand and helped her jump out of the cart.

They raced up the stairs toward the washrooms on the second floor. Pheobe especially enjoyed this store because the second level overlooked the entire massive main floor. As Ashley walked down the long, wide-open hallway toward the facilities, Pheobe released her hand and rushed away from her.

"Auntie Ashley, can I sit on that bench?" she hollered, as she pointed to a park bench located right outside the door of the ladies washroom.

"I thought you had to go potty really bad."

"I do."

"Well then get in there, silly!"

Unable to hold it another minute, Pheobe skipped the complaining and blasted into the ladies room. Not wanting to have to take another trip later, Ashley decided to give it a go too.

As Ashley locked up her door, Pheobe's swung open.

"You're done already?" Ashley asked.

"Yup!" Pheobe replied happily, heading for the sinks.

"Okay, well, wash your hands and then wait there for me please."

The water rushed for mere seconds. "I want to go sit on the bench," Pheobe said, while the hand dryer blasted super loud.

"Pheobe. Wait for me, please. I don't want a stranger to take you."

Ashley's warning fell on deaf ears, Pheobe having already raced out to the bench that was backed against the balcony railing. After a moment of silence, Ashley had a feeling she was alone.

"Pheobe? Pheobe?" She huffed disappointedly and hurried to zip up her pants, all the while Pheobe was enjoying the view.

Pheobe knelt on the park bench, holding onto the back of it and gazed excitedly over the railing, amazed at the expanse of the colourful store. She noticed the recently hung Christmas decorations and looked down to see the new ones on the wall below her. She leaned over the edge to get a good look and giggled at the hurried shoppers below.

An adorable toddler, who was sitting in a cart down below, caught Pheobe's eye. Pheobe leaned over the ledge a little farther and pointed at the smiling girl, who was happy to give Pheobe her undivided attention.

Pheobe eagerly leaned a little harder against the back of the bench, to see what she could see, and it unsteadily tipped backward.

"Clank!" It slammed against the wobbly railing, which began to quiver and shake under the weight of the tipped bench. The toddler's mother curiously gazed up to see what the commotion was all about and gasped in horror as the bench forced the barrier to break loose.

"Nooo!" she screeched, as Pheobe went sailing over the edge, along with the bench.

Pheobe's little hand clasped onto the railing, but as it broke loose, the jolt sent Pheobe flying toward the floor. The shrill sound reverberating from Pheobe's throat as she plummeted toward the ground was not something the woman was going to forget any time soon. She watched the bench break into tiny little pieces only milliseconds before the little girl followed it.

Ashley had just finished washing her hands and was wiping them on her pants as she hurried out to scorn Pheobe. That's when she heard the shrieks of terror echoing from the main floor. She ran out into the hallway, instantly noticing the missing bench and broken railing. There was no Pheobe either. She was too late.

"No. No. No!" she howled.

Gasps and screams filled the area, as Ashley stood there in horror staring out over the open balcony.

"Nooooo!" Ashley screamed hysterically, frozen in place. She fell to her knees when she saw Pheobe laying still and silent down a floor below.

A worried bystander ran to Ashley, pulled her away from the ledge and tried to help her toward the elevator. The woman found Ashley in complete shock, unable to speak, her body limp.

"Someone call 911!" a concerned shopper screeched, from the main floor.

By the time Ashley made it to Pheobe, there were staff tending to the disaster. Pheobe was unconscious, motionless, sprawled out over the crushed display. She was seriously injured from the fall and blood continued to spill from her tiny body, covering the pile of tumbled watermelons in a splash of bright red.

The manager had his fingers pressed against her neck. "There's a pulse," he hollered. He had a large towel pressed against her delicate body, in an attempt to stop the bleeding, but it was entirely blood soaked and a bone was protruding from her leg.

"Why don't you do something?" a woman cried.

"We have to wait for the paramedics. She may have suffered a spinal injury from the fall."

A police officer arrived moments before the ambulance and directed the staff to get the patrons to back away and carry on. When he reached the body, he checked for vitals. "She's not breathing," he announced.

Ashley choked on her panic and began to cry hysterically. The paramedics arrived and carefully lifted Pheobe's mangled body onto a spinal board and immediately began to breathe for her.

"She fell quite a distance," one staff told the police officer.

"She's lucky she didn't hit the floor or she would've died on impact for sure," a distraught bystander added.

Ashley shuddered, then ran for the door, until her knees gave out. A police officer rushed after her and lifted her from the floor. Boneless, she collapsed into his arms.

"Ma'am; I presume you're the girl's mother," he said, lifting her up and grasping her elbow.

"No," Ashley cried. "Her mother's dead. I'm her aunt."

One of the paramedics called out to them. "Is she coming with us? We have to go now!"

"You go," the officer insisted. "She'll do you no good. I'll drive her over to the hospital."

The paramedic nodded and raced into the driver seat. The lights flashed and they let out a siren to get the nosy shoppers to move out of their way.

The officer pointed toward his car. "Please come with me," he said, flapping his notepad shut. "We can do this at the hospital."

Ashley walked alongside him, a blank stare on her ghostly white face.

The police officer opened the backseat of the police cruiser and helped Ashley in. "Is there someone you need to call?" he asked. "Or maybe we could send an officer over to notify her guardian of the accident."

Ashley fumbled with her words. "My brother. Cameron. He's her father. 400 Humber Street West."

The officer nodded and typed the information into his Blackberry. Less than a minute later he pulled out of the parking lot, with his lights flashing, and headed straight for the hospital. "We have a uniformed officer attending your brother's house as we speak."

Ashley put her face in her hands and shook her head sobbing. She knew how Cameron was going to react. She hated herself too.

A short time later, the officer pulled into the hospital parking lot. He put his car in park and flashed a glance at his phone. "No one's home. Can we reach the father by phone?"

"Yeah, I can call his cell," she replied, fumbling through her purse for her phone. She shakily punched the numbers and it rang for what seemed like a lifetime before it went to voicemail.

"Dammit, Cameron!" Ashley hollered at the phone. She ended the call and dialed Cameron's home number urgently.

I rested on the sofa, filled with relief that we didn't get caught in the act. Cameron took a trip to the bathroom, when the phone began to ring. Knowing he wouldn't make it to the phone in time, I picked it up off the receiver.

"Hello?"

"Abby. There's been a terrible accident. It's Pheobe," Ashley cried.

"Okay, calm down," I said, trying to comfort her. "Tell me what happened."

"She fell. She fell from the balcony. She's hurt. She's

hurt real bad. Oh my God, Abby. Cam's never going to forgive me."

I gasped and held my breath, trying to remain calm. "Okay, where are you?"

"She got away from me for one second and then..." She cried again, not finishing her sentence.

I walked to the front door and whispered into the phone. "How bad is it?"

"She wasn't breathing when the ambulance took her to the Regional. I'm really worried. It's bad. They need Cameron at the hospital now."

"Okay. I'll take care of it," I assured her. I ended the call and scanned through Cam's caller-id to find his parents number. I knew Ashley was going to need some support and Cameron wasn't going to be the one to give it. I dialed the number and glanced over my shoulder to make sure Cameron wasn't coming.

"Mrs. Clarke? It's Abigail."

"Oh, hi sweetheart. Please call me Sadie. How are things?"

"Not good, I'm afraid. I'm calling because there's been an emergency and I think you're needed at the hospital. Ashley's there now."

"Oh no! Is she okay?"

"She will be. It's Pheobe," I said, my voice breaking up. "Can you meet us there?"

"Of course, dear. You take care of Cameron and I'll be there as quick as I can."

A tear streamed down my cheek.

"Who was that?" Cam asked, wrapping his arms around me from behind.

I wiped the tear from my face and cleared my throat. He kissed my cheek and nuzzled up against my neck, his warm breath spilling over my skin, but not warming my icy, cold blood.

"There's been an accident," I said, with a harsh whisper. "We need to go to the hospital right away. I'll explain on the way; but please, let's just go."

He got in the car and moments later we were speeding down the road for the hospital. I didn't say a word.

"Are you going to tell me what happened?"

"Just give me a minute," I said, letting another tear sneak from my eye. I wiped it quickly away, but Cameron caught me from the corner of his eye.

"Are you going to tell me now, or do I have to pull over?" he threatened.

"Please don't," I begged.

"Is it Edwin?" he asked, agitated.

"No," I squealed, scowling, wishing selfishly at that moment that it was.

"Then who?"

"Cam; it's Pheobe."

He responded by pressing the gas pedal to the floor and ran through a hard yellow light. "No," he said sternly, unwilling to believe me.

"Yes. Ashley said...,"

"I'll deal with Ashley later," Cam snapped, cutting me off. "Just tell me; how bad is it?"

I cried, with a sigh of frustration, the tears streaming heavily down my wet cheeks. "It's serious. Pheobe had a fall."

His eyes glared out the wet windshield, as rain began to pour from the sky. "She should have been there," he said, under his breath.

Cameron pulled right up to the emergency doors and practically leapt out of the car. I slid over into the driver seat and hurriedly parked the car. I punched the lock, slammed the door shut and flipped my collar up to keep the rain off my face. The wind had picked up and was whipping my hair into a tangled mess.

It was freezing cold outside and the large raindrops sliced through the air, wetting my light jacket. My fingers were going numb from the cold, even through my black leather gloves. As I walked through the cold, deep emergency parking lot, it only reminded me of my own terrible accident.

Shaking off the chill, I rushed through the hospital's emergency entrance and quickly located Sadie. She was rubbing Ashley's shoulders in an attempt to console her. Before I could announce my arrival, I heard Ashley say my name, stopping me in my tracks.

"If it weren't for her, this would have never happened," Ashley accused.

Sadie slowly flashed a glance at the nearby police officer, then turned her weary eyes on me. "Abigail," she said, with an emotional gasp.

I rushed over to Sadie as soon as she saw me and she drew me into her arms. "How is she?" I cried.

"Cameron needs you. Pheobe's still unconscious." Her voice was steady and controlled, but I could see the sadness in her honest eyes.

Ashley stuck her nose in the air, ignoring me altogether.

"I don't know, maybe I should give him some space," I suggested, unsure how to cope.

"I think he'd want you there, honey. You're a part of our family now," Sadie said. "You should go."

"I don't know," I replied, scared as hell. I had been through more emotions in the past few months than I had in the past ten years. Just imagining sweet, little Pheobe laid up in a hospital bed left my heart lurching in my chest.

Ashley finally chimed in, agitated by my very presence. "You're right, Mom. Maybe she should go. Away!" Her voice rose, until she was shouting hysterically. "If Cameron would spend less time with you, he'd have more time for his daughter and this would have never happened."

Alarmed by her ridiculous accusations, the police officer stepped in between us and turned to Ashley. "I think maybe it's time we had that talk. I need to take your statement now," he insisted.

"Whatever," Ashley replied, rudely.

"Ashley please. This is serious," her mother scolded. "If you or Cameron decide to take any action against the store, your statement could be crucial to the case."

"Fine," Ashley said, pointing an angry glance at me. "But

I'm only doing this for Cam."

Unable to deal with any more of her slander, I had to get away. "Let me know if you hear anything," I said to Sadie, then walked a good distance down the hall to cool off.

Taking a seat in the far corner of the emergency waiting room, I stared blankly in space, worrying myself to death about Pheobe and Cam. After what felt like forever, I glanced up at an opening door, to find Dr. Dex waving for me to come see him. I rushed to his side, anxious to hear what he had to say.

Ashley cautiously watched me as I entered the triage area with the doctor.

"I suppose you've heard already," I said.

"I did. Cameron's been asking for you. Why don't you come back with me?"

I followed him through the emergency department to the bed where Pheobe was lying, hooked to multiple machines, her body looking pale and fragile. Cameron was slumped at her bedside with his head down and his eyes closed.

"I'll give you two some time," Dr. Dex said, then quietly took his leave.

"Oh, Cam," I cried, rushing to him.

Cameron's tired eyes looked up at me in despair. He stood to his feet weakly and I crashed into his arms, overwhelmed from seeing Pheobe's motionless frame and hearing the depressing silence.

He pressed his forehead against mine and held on tight. "What took you so long?" he asked.

"I didn't know if you'd want me in here. Ashley thought it was a bad idea."

"Don't ever question yourself, Abby. I want you here. Pheobe would want you here. We will always want you."

I buried my face in his chest, my emotions crowding my head and swelling my overworked heart.

"I'm sick of Ashley's bullshit," he said, hushed. He dropped a kiss on my hair. "I think I need to set her straight right now."

He stormed away and I knew he was in no frame of mind

to be talking to Ashley just yet. I hated to leave Pheobe alone, but she had a full staff of doctors, nurses and machines looking out for her, and Ashley had no one but Sadie.

As soon as Cameron was in ear shot of Ashley he shouted her name. Sadie was nowhere to be found.

"What's your deal anyway? Abby's my girl now and she's not going anywhere. If you've got a problem with that, you'll have to take it up with me."

Ashley reared her head around and scowled ferociously at me, then turned those wicked eyes on Cameron. "You know exactly what *my deal* is. Everything was just fine until she came along," she raged, pointing at me. "Now that you have Cam all messed up, he can't seem to keep his priorities straight!"

"You know what, Ash? I think I need a break. From you. I know exactly what my priorities are and that's just too damn bad if you don't like it."

"Cam, you know that's not what I meant," Ashley cried.

"I know exactly what you meant. You've been causing Abby all kinds of trouble, and for what? And now Pheobe? I'm finding it hard just to look at you right now."

Ashley put her head down in defeat but, to my surprise, when she looked up again, revenge flared in her soft brown eyes. "Do you have any idea what I'm going through right now?"

Cameron didn't care. "Not now. For once let's not make this about you."

I noticed Dr. Dex waiting anxiously at the desk for our attention. "Cam. The doctor," I breathed.

Cam ran to the desk. "What is it, Doctor?"

"Pheobe's scans just came back. She needs surgery. I need your approval."

"Anything," he said, reaching his hand out to me.

I hurried to his side, slipping my fingers into his hand. The nurse pointed to the door and Cameron dashed through it, pulling me along with him.

Minutes passed like hours and we didn't exchange any

words. When Pheobe was moved into a recovery room, Cam insisted that they let us in to see her. She was still out cold, even longer than they had expected. Cameron thought the worst.

After discussing the results of the the operation with the surgeon privately, Cameron had pulled me into his lap and held me tight in his arms.

Unable to live with the painful silence, I asked, "Were there any complications?"

He pressed out a long, tired breath. "Apparently everything went well." But Cam's uncertainty was painted all over his face. "Now we just have to wait for her to wake up."

I cupped his cheek and pressed a kiss to his lips. "Pheobe will be okay. She's a strong little girl," I said softly.

"I know."

"You haven't eaten in hours. You need your energy for when she wakes up. Why don't you take a walk and get something to eat?" I suggested. "I'll stay here in case anything changes."

He sighed loudly, staring at his delicate, little girl. "Huuhhh," he sighed, emotionally exhausted. "Maybe you're right."

I slipped off his lap and he stood next to me, delivering a chaste kiss. "I'll just grab something quick from the vending machine," he said, not wanting to stray too far.

Cameron walked out the door and I inched back to Phoebe's bedside. I took her precious little hand and caressed it gently, enveloped in the depressing silence for too many minutes. I couldn't take it anymore.

"Pheobe; I don't know if you can hear me, but it's Abby. I need you to come back to us now. Your daddy and I miss you very much."

A tear formed in my eye and I took in a deep breath fighting back my emotions. Suddenly, the heart rate monitor started to fluctuate and my worry escalated, until Pheobe's beautiful black lashes began to flutter.

"Cameron," I shrieked, but he was gone.

I leaned over and held Pheobe's hand, waiting in anticipation to see if she'd open her big, blue eyes. "That's it sweetheart. Abby's here," I cried, unable to hold back the tears.

Just then, Cameron strolled back into the room, dropped his food to the floor and raced to his baby girl's side.

The tears blurred my vision and I hiccupped on a breath. "She just fluttered her eye lashes," I said.

He stared at me for a long time and then at Pheobe. Nothing. "I believe you," he said, pulling me into his arms. "What were you doing when it happened?"

I sniffled. "I guess, I was talking to her; telling her that it's time to wake up." The heart rate monitor kicked up again and my heart began to match the irregular pace.

"Keep talking," Cam suggested, his eyes never leaving his little girl. He kissed her hand and held it to his face with hope.

We both hovered over her anxiously and I stroked her soft, brown hair. "Pheobe. Your dad's here now. You've given everyone quite a scare today. If you could just wake up, we would be so happy."

Cam and I stared in amazement as her big, dark lashes fluttered again. This time Pheobe squinted through soft, tired eyes.

"Pheobe! You're awake," I cried.

"Hi, baby," Cameron said, with relief.

Her eyes scattered around the small, bare room. "Abby? Daddy? Where am I?" she asked, in her sweet, little voice.

Cameron kissed her hand again, while I ran to the door to call a nurse. "You're in the hospital, honey. Don't try to move. It's okay. You'll be back to normal before you know it."

"Daddy, it hurts," Pheobe cried.

"I know, honey," Cam said, squeezing her hand to comfort her.

A nurse hurried into the room and carefully inspected Pheobe. Before long, a doctor arrived to give her a full exam. Cameron and I hugged, rocking back and forth in each other's arms. After a full report from the doctor, Cameron sat right next to Pheobe on the bed.

"Don't you do that to me again, pretty princess," he said, dropping a big kiss on her forehead.

Pheobe lifted her chin and thrust her pouty lip out extra far. "Daddy, I didn't mean to. I was just looking at the Santa decorations."

"It's okay, baby. Everything's okay now."

It was clear that Cameron would be okay now too.

Days later, I finally convinced Cameron he could leave Pheobe's bedside long enough to take a shower. He even agreed that I could go with him, as long as his mother stayed at the hospital with Pheobe. I thought we were taking a step in the right direction but, as he unlocked his front door, he ignored me entirely and headed straight for the tub.

Frustrated, I plunked down on the couch and twiddled my thumbs, impatiently waiting for him to get ready. Boredom caused me to stir and I had to move to keep it together. I paced the room a couple of times before I noticed the flashing red light on his answering machine.

"Cam! You have some messages on your phone," I hollered, peering at the display.

It sounded like he was shaving, when he hollered back. "Can you get them for me?"

I searched around for paper and ended up in his office. He had another phone on his desk and so I took a seat and opened up the pad of paper before I hit the keypad to answer the calls.

It was Edwin. Of all the people it could have been, why him? The thought turned my stomach and plucked at my brain. After getting through the small talk, Edwin got down to business.

"The actual reason for my call is because I heard about your daughter's accident. I'm really sorry to hear it by the

way. And I know you probably aren't in the best frame of mind to look at it from a litigation standpoint right now, but I've already summarized the issues in your case. I figured I could give you an objective opinion, since you have other things on your mind."

When Edwin paused, I had to catch my breath. *What a sweet, sweet man.*

"Anyways, I did a little digging and, well, let's just say I found some interesting dirt on the owner of that store. I think you've got yourself a good case for a negligence claim and depending on how quickly she recovers, you may want to consider a claim for personal injury. I'm sure you don't want to think about that right away, so just give me a call when you're ready to talk about it. Later, brother."

My heart flitted in my chest, a stunned expression painted on my face. Why was I so impressed with Edwin's offer to help? I had heard that he and Jessica had recently broken things off, though I had been too consumed with my own life to worry about his girl troubles.

I scribbled down the gist of it and deleted his message, before collecting my bearings to catch the next one. Go figure, it was from Cam's sister and there was no need to write anything down.

"You can't ignore me forever, Cam. I'm your sister. I'm not going to stop ringing you until you return my calls. It was an accident. These things happen. Abby should know that with all the shit she's caused."

If only I could ring Ashley's neck through the phone. I imagined doing just that and it gave me mild pleasure. She continued to whine and complain, until her time ran out and her message was cut off mid-sentence.

One more message and I could only hazard a guess at who it might be. Again. Ashley. Picking up right where she left off.

I deleted the message and stared blankly at the wall.

CHAPTER TWENTY THREE

One month later.

I was looking forward to the office Christmas party, being in desperate need of some holiday cheer. The closer it got to the date, the more excited I became.

It was late on a Friday afternoon, when I walked past the copier room and caught a glimpse of Maddie fumbling with a paper jam. I stopped in the doorway, to admire her adorable baby bump, but she seemed to be getting more frustrated by the second.

"Troubles," I asked, smirking.

"Ugh! This stupid thing does it to me every time," she snapped. "Only because I'm on a deadline."

I slipped in between her and the machine and quickly cleared the jam. After slamming the front door on the copier shut, it hummed back to life.

"Thanks, Abby. You have no idea how much that was stressing me out," she said.

I only smiled, staring at her glorious figure. "Look at you. I can't believe it," I announced, smiling uncontrolledly at her belly.

"Are you calling me fat? Ugghh! I really don't need this today." She was actually upset and balancing on the brink of tears

"Calm down or you're going to spook your baby right out of there," I teased. "You're not fat. I was just admiring your cute, little baby bump. I thought new mothers were supposed to be proud of it."

"Do I look like the average mother to you?" she growled.

"Absolutely not. You look fabulous."

Her eyes flashed to the floor. "Thanks. Even though I don't believe you."

"Well, you do," I insisted. "How's the baby?"

"The baby's fine. Thank, God. Hunter, not so much. I thought he was going to be my date for the Christmas party and everything was going great, until Aliah just opened her fat mouth a minute ago."

"What's the problem?" I asked, hesitantly.

"Hunter is going with Aliah."

"Well, they are dating." I cowered under her glare. The woman was five months pregnant, but still her eyes warned me not to mess with her. "I can see why that'd piss you off," I added, hoping not to spoil the friendly chat.

"I know, right? Now who the hell am I supposed to bring? Seriously, what am I supposed to do? *Hey, I know it's only like one day's notice, and I'm fucking knocked up, but do you want to be my date for tomorrow?* Yeah, that'll go over well," she complained.

I giggled at the thought of it, though Maddie was totally serious. I couldn't think of anyone in particular who would be up for that challenge and Cam really didn't have a whole lot of friends in the City. I had to think of something. Maddie's sanity wavered in the balance.

"You know what? Don't worry. I've got your back," I said, coming up with a brilliant plan. I stole away and headed for Edwin's office, determined to strike a deal with him.

I flashed a glance in Edwin's door and immediately caught his eye. He saluted me, thinking I was passing by, and I couldn't stop the smile that came with little effort when he realized I was stopping in for a visit.

"Hey, Brother. Are you going to help a girl out or what?" I asked.

A glimmer flashed in Edwin's aqua eyes that heated my blood and scared the living daylights out of me. "If you're insinuating what I hope you are, then I'm totally up for that," he said, with a devastating, wolfish grin.

"Ugh, Edwin. What I meant was, are you going to help a poor, desperate, pregnant lady find a date?"

"Ha, ha, ha," he chuckled. "Not likely."

"I'm not joking. Maddie's on the verge of a breakdown

and do you want to be the one responsible for her premature delivery? Didn't think so. Her date bailed and now she feels like a failure and that's beside her obvious hormonal issues."

"Can't she just take TJ?" he asked.

"Seriously, Edwin, are you kidding me? She already feels like a loser. Nothing like taking your brother along to spell it out for everyone. She needs a real date and you need to make it happen."

"And who do you have in mind exactly?" he asked, a curious smirk lurking on his masculine face.

I anxiously chewed on my bottom lip. "I figured you must have a buddy who owes you a favour or something. Can't you rummage someone up for tomorrow night?" My lashes started fluttering. *What the hell was I doing?*

"Nothing like giving me some time to work my magic." Edwin looked thoughtful for a short second and nodded his head at me. "Actually, I know someone who just moved into the City and he's probably looking to make some social contacts. It'll take a little coercion to get him past the pregnancy bit, but I bet I can convince him."

I propped my hands onto my generous hips. "Good then. Just make it happen and fast."

"What do I get out of this?" Edwin asked, raising a dark, devious brow.

My lips parted to compensate for the extra breath I had to take to slow my pattering heart. "Nice try. You get a pat on your back for being a good guy and you're saved from having to hear Maddie mope in misery all night."

"That's not going to cut it, Abs. You owe me big for this. And I'm keeping that IOU in my back pocket."

I rolled my eyes. "Fine. I owe you. Just do it already."

He nodded and smiled, satisfied that I was submitting to him. I shook my head and scowled, to avoid his direct stare, then pointed a doubting finger at him. "Make it happen."

It made him smirk and that was enough for me to take my leave. I strolled over to Maddie's desk, where I found her fretting over her printer.

"You've got to take it easy, girl. I told you I've got your back, didn't I? You'd better pull yourself together because you've got a blind date."

"Great, just what I need, more stress," Maddie sulked, dropping her face into her hands.

"Don't look at it that way then. Look at it as an opportunity to make a new friend, who might even be a nice guy."

"Is there even such a thing?" she snapped, staring at me wide-eyed.

"I have Cameron, don't I?" I realized how corny I sounded, but the words were already out there for her to pass judgment.

"Not everyone is as lucky as you," Maddie scolded, a hint of true jealousy shimmering in her voice. "Now I just have to find something to wear," she moaned. "I'm growing out of all of my pants and I'm terrified of going into a maternity store alone."

"Oh, no you don't," I said. "I've done my part. I'm sure Hunter will take you."

"Screw Hunter. He had his chance. Now I'm going to show him what he's missing out on."

I gave her a wink and headed back for my desk. I strode quickly past Cameron's door, catching a glimpse of him deep in thought. He wore thick rimmed glasses, which made him look even sexier than normal. Knowing that there was only one more hour until he'd be all mine, a balloon of excitement constricted in my chest. I really was a lucky girl.

While searching through my closet for inspiration, my heart pounded with excitement. The party was supposed to be casual, so I figured I could pull something together without a major shopping trip. I held up my cute, lacy, white camisole and laid it on top of my stylish grey blazer. It was sophisticated, but far from stuffy.

After pulling my look together, I drew a long white scarf around my neck and secured it off to the side. Glancing at myself in the long angled mirror, I liked what I saw. My dark fitted jeans, with fading on the legs and butt, fit me like a glove. The rouching on the ankles looked totally hot and would draw everyone's eyes to my strappy peep toe pumps.

It had been a while since Cameron and I had gone out together as a couple, though our relationship had grown stronger than ever. With Pheobe's injury, he found it difficult to leave her. I had been looking forward to this night, so I was glad when Cam agreed to keep our room reservation.

I had just finished polishing my look when I heard the doorbell ring. I picked up my glittery purse and rushed to the door to greet my handsome visitor. When I pulled open the door, my jaw nearly dropped to the floor.

Cameron was wearing his black leather jacket, with a grey shirt that clung to his incredibly fit body, displaying him as one delicious package. He hadn't shaved in a couple of days and his dirty blonde stubble had my mouth stripped dry and sent a tingling sensation spilling lower by the second.

The hair on his head had grown longer than his usual clean-cut crop and was dishelved in a wayward fashion that was sexy as hell. Not sharing any words as I noted how hot his ass looked in those jeans, I clicked the door shut and he turned to face me.

He pulled me into his arms and tilted his head down for a kiss. I couldn't breathe, suddenly ready to throw out the whole idea of going out, so I could take him to my room for some stay-in fun instead.

After releasing my lips from another slow, drugging kiss, a sexy smile crept onto his mouth. "Merry Christmas," he drawled.

Too aroused to respond, I pulled on my long, winter jacket before I resolved to tear all of his clothes off of him. After doing up a few buttons, Cameron had me back in his arms, pulling me in for another devastating kiss. He paid close attention to me and I enjoyed every lap of his tongue and touch of his lips.

"I've missed this," I breathed, my hands clung on the collar of his jacket.

An earth-shattering smile slanted on his lips. "There's lots more where that came from," he said, tugging me closer and slipping his tongue between my parted lips. "And tonight, I'm all yours."

"I like that," I said, nibbling my swollen bottom lip.

"I like you," he said, kissing me harder.

Edwin hustled down the stairs, walked up to the closet behind us and pulled out his jacket. "Okay, people, get a room," he said.

I could note the disgust in his voice and it gave me a sharp stab in my gut. After Cam released me from his mesmeric gaze, I drew my eyes away and looked to Edwin. Cam kept his arms firmly wrapped around my waist.

"Did you end up finding Maddie a date?" I asked, worried but hopeful.

"I told you I would," he replied.

I was surprised how quickly his mood had changed. "Thanks. You have no idea what this will mean to her," I said, as Cameron leaned me back and planted a wet kiss on my neck.

"Uh, yes I do," he answered, his eyes burning holes through mine. "Ever since you told her I'd find her a man, she's been bugging me steady," Edwin said, narrowing his eyes.

I was experiencing seriously twisted emotions, being spoiled by Cam's devouring lips while talking with Edwin, who looked crushed by the act. Guilt was eating away at my heart. I pulled away from Cam, suddenly uncomfortable with sharing our love publicly.

But Cam was persistent. He locked his arms back around my waist and nibbled at the skin behind my ear. When Edwin turned away to find a tuque, I closed my eyes, unable to resist Cam's steady attack.

"Nice," Edwin said, sarcastically, unable to hide his bitterness.

I rested my head back against Cam and shared a soft smile. "Haven't you heard about filling someone's bucket?" I asked, playfully mocking Edwin.

"I'll fill your bucket," he snapped, his sexual inference urging Cam to stop with his sensual assault.

Cam wrapped his arm across my chest, clinging to me like I was a valuable possession. "I'll be the only one filling this bucket," he retorted.

I smiled at him over my shoulder and he drew my lips into his. Edwin left the room and retrieved his cell phone from the kitchen counter. When he returned, Cameron had loosened up his hold on me.

"I'm out of here," Edwin said. "I have to pick up Maddie's date."

"What did you say that guy's name is again?" I asked, wondering if Cam would know him. "Didn't you say he's a lawyer?"

"Yup. Wesley Carver."

"Did you say Carver?" Cam asked, his eyes turning dangerously intense.

"That's what I said. Why, do you know him?" Edwin asked.

"If it's the same guy. I worked with a Wes Carver in Toronto. It was a huge firm. We were both in the litigation department, but we rarely crossed paths. I guess you could say we had an unspoken rivalry."

"Yeah, it sounds like the same guy. He just moved to the area for a job at the courthouse in the prosecutor's department. He's gone out with the boys a few times now. He seems cool."

"Why haven't I heard about this guy before?" I asked.

"You'll see. I'm not stupid. Any guy in his right mind wouldn't bring his girl around him. You'd better hold on tight, Cam," Edwin said, smirking.

I could feel the warmth rushing over my cheeks, as Edwin chuckled and Cameron retightened his grip defensively.

I knew if I didn't intervene soon, they would break into an all-out fist fight. Heading for the door, I whipped it open and garnered both of their undivided attention.

"Out," I said. I stepped outside and to my surprise Cam smoothly proceeded to the door and Edwin followed suit, locking up behind us.

"Maddie's going to have her hands full tonight, if you know what I mean." Cam chuckled as he moseyed to his car, the epitome of masculine grace.

"I definitely do," Edwin said, with a laugh, as he lifted his heavily muscled body into his truck.

I didn't get it. Had they just shared an insiders' joke? Baby steps.

Snowflakes sparkled in the night sky as they floated delicately in the air, occasionally blowing away when a gust of wind would pass. I watched out the window in silence, as we drove to the hotel on the waterway, the only sound coming from the dull whisper of music turned much too low to enjoy.

The wind chilled me to the bone as we hustled into the brown, brick building. Then we headed into the private hall where the party was already in full swing. The other guests seemed more concerned with the holiday décor and themselves to even notice that we had joined them.

Hunter was chatting with Aliah at a candle-lit table, while Aliah checked her makeup in the reflection of her wine glass. Taylor and a temp girl were sitting together, sipping on festive drinks, as their guests hung back behind them uncomfortably. Not even Miller or Bailey noticed that we had entered the room. I guess we were old news.

I checked out my incredibly handsome date at my side, who I just noticed was eyeing me naughtily. I squeezed his arm tighter and drifted off into his oceanic eyes, vowing to absorb every ounce of his undivided attention tonight.

Taking advantage of our moment of privacy, I kissed my man, and Cameron didn't hold anything back from the public. When I opened my eyes, his smile was wicked. He already noticed that everyone's attention had turned on us. My tongue darted out over my lips, as I stared at the floor in embarrassment.

"I dare you to do that again," Cam said, his voice a smooth growl.

What was with him tonight? Whatever it was, it was hot!

"Merry Christmas, everyone!" Cameron boomed, lifting both of his arms in a welcoming gesture. Not releasing any of the gawkers, he turned back to me and brushed his hand over my rosy cheek. "You have nothing to be embarrassed about, Abby. I love you and I'm secure enough to share that with our friends and colleagues."

He took my mouth again, until I was weak in the knees and light in the heart.

Within half an hour, all of the guests had arrived. I was happy to see that there was no sign of Ashley and it became rather obvious why the men in my life were so insistent that I avoid Wesley Carver. The man was drop dead gorgeous, the slant of his smile mysteriously attracting every woman's eye. Maddie was sure pleased.

After a cheerful dinner and a couple of toasts and well wishes, everyone seemed to be getting along just fine. Edwin had ignored his date for the better part of dinner and had spent a lot of time at the bar. That likely had something to do with the slutty bartender, with glittery cleavage, who kept hitting on him.

Maddie was absolutely glowing and seemed to be taking a liking to her date. Thanks to Wesley Carver, Aliah got Hunter all to herself.

"Hello. Abby. Are you in there?" Cam asked, flashing me a sweet smile. "I wish I knew what was going on in that pretty, little head of yours."

"I was just thinking I need a drink," I said, turning all of my attention on him.

"Okay. I'll pretend I believe that," he said, dropping his chin and smiling. Then I watched him glare across the room at Wesley Carver. "Oh, yeah. I could definitely use a drink," Cam said.

Stealing Cam's attention back, I tugged on his soft, leather jacket to bring him closer to me and then stole a soft, wet kiss.

"Come," he said. He took my hand and pulled me to the small bar. He ordered from the busty babe and didn't give her a second glance.

I flashed him another smile, admiring his loyalty. Three drinks later and I was totally buzzing. I didn't even notice when Cameron took off, though he said he'd be right back. Another drink slid my way and I thought for sure it was from him. Being in a rather frisky mood, I reached behind him and gave his butt a good squeeze.

"Whoa, nice to meet you too!" the man gloated, and then squeezed my butt in response.

"Oh. My. Gosh. I am so... sorry." My face flushed a deep red when I realized that the firm ass I had just squeezed was indeed that of another man. Not just any man, but Wesley Carver. I put one hand over my eyes hoping that the handsome fellow would just go away.

"It's all good," he replied, completely confident.

When I peeked through my fingers, hoping he had already vanished, it was blatantly clear that he wasn't going to go away that easily.

I anxiously looked over each of my shoulders, but I couldn't see Cameron anywhere. Carver continued to smile at me, the damn slant of his mouth lazily drawing my eyes to it. I'd be damned if I let him get kicks out of my mortification, but he sure seemed to be doing a good job of it.

"He said he'd be right back," he explained.

I nodded, mortified. "I'm really sorry about that. I thought you were Cam. I didn't mean to... you know."

"No worries," he said, with a smirk. Then he leaned in to whisper. "I didn't mind it."

A gush of relief rushed me when he finally backed away.

Carver extended his hand, suddenly trying to pull the friend card. "I'm Wes by the way."

"Abby." I shook his hand briskly, hoping to finish the

introduction before Cam returned.

"I'll have to hang around you more often, Abby," he said, swiping his tongue over his full lower lip, then subconsciously tugging it with his teeth.

I gazed into his dark, blue eyes and silently pleaded with him to let it go. But from the look on his face, I now knew that Cameron was standing behind me.

"If you could see the look in Cam's eyes right now." He paused to smile. "I don't think he likes me very much."

"Carver," Cam said.

I spun around and Cameron's riled eyes locked on my mine. A painful jab in my chest restricted the air from getting to my limbs.

"Well, that's my cue to get out of here," Carver drawled. "Enjoy the drink. It's on me." He swiftly glided across the floor returning to Maddie who was impatiently awaiting his return.

Cam's eyes were now glued on Carver. "What did he want?" he snapped.

"Dunno. I think he was just getting a drink." I worried my bottom lip between my teeth, wondering how I was going to tell him the news about my latest friendly greeting.

"You should stay away from him. I don't trust him."

"About that," I paused, as Cam ordered another drink for himself.

He looked at me with serious concern shielding his eyes.

"I may have grabbed his ass a minute ago." I moaned with disappointment, waiting for the barrage of questions.

"You may have?" Cam looked at the bartender and the girl started to giggle, as she poured his drink.

"Well, I did it, but I thought he was you. It happened by total accident," I explained, waiting for his anger to slap me upside the head.

It took me by total surprise when he burst out laughing. The bartender started laughing with him, so hard in fact that tears began to stream from her eyes and she continued on that like that until no sound could escape her mouth anymore. Apparently she had caught the whole thing and thought it was just hilarious.

"That's what you have to do to get a free drink around here?" Cam teased, when he could finally get a word out.

I put on a pouty lip and picked up my drink, but was happy to see Cam smiling. I cautiously glanced around the room and noticed Wes across the way. It was hard to miss him with his dark blonde curls and protruding lower lip. I was startled to find him staring at me, raising his glass in salute. I raised mine to him before downing it, pissed that I was being made a fool.

Maddie noticed the little exchange and pulled his arm so he was facing her, tearing his eyes from me.

"Honestly though, nothing that happens around that man is an accident," Cam said in my ear, also noting the exchange.

After finishing my drink, with one last gulp, I reached past Cameron and exaggeratedly slammed my empty cup on the bar. I carefully brushed extra close to him, my eyes locked on his, as I slowly retrieved my extended arm. He was the only object of my desire and he needed to know that.

Cameron leaned against the bar, with one hand in his pocket and one foot resting on a bar stool looking incredibly sexy. He responded to my distraction and swiftly pulled me against him. He wrapped my arms around his waist, his eyes full of yearning.

The music seemed to grow louder now, Christmas in nature, but the song was slow and charming. It suddenly felt like we were the only two people in the room.

Cam brushed my cheek with his hand, sending tingles bubbling in my blood. His lips met the corner of my mouth then he backed up to gaze into my eyes. "We dance."

The song 'Merry Christmas', sang by a swoon-worthy pop-star, flowed melodiously from every corner of the room.

"Just let me get another drink first?" I said, asking for permission.

"I need you now, Abby," he pleaded, then walked away

from me.

Drawn in by his urgency, I willingly followed him out to the dance floor. He extended his arms out to me and, when I reached for his hand, he tugged me in close and wrapped his arms around me, moulding his long, lean body to mine.

Cameron took my other hand and gave it a soft kiss before he wrapped it tightly around his neck, linking our bodies together like a chain. His arms hugged my waist, as he stared into my gracious eyes with the most appreciative smile.

I was overcome with emotion, revelling in the festive mood. Although we didn't say a single word as we swayed slowly in each other's arms, our chemistry was magnetic and no one dared interrupt us. It felt like we were surrounded by a sensual bubble that no one could burst, even if they wanted to.

His loving eyes drew me into a dream-like trance, his body guiding my motion. I couldn't even tell if my feet were moving anymore because he had certainly swept me off of them.

As the song neared the end, he broke our piercing gaze to look toward the door. I forcefully turned his chin so he was looking back into my eyes. When he lifted his eyes to explain himself, I recognized the desire burning in them.

His mouth covered mine, sending my emotions raging. Our lips fused together and his warm, soft tongue gently stroked along my teeth. He delivered another soft, passionate kiss that lasted only a few short seconds, but left me aching for so much more.

I didn't open my eyes, my body pleading with him to continue, and I smiled as his smooth lips brushed along mine again. He parted his mouth and our lips interlaced, again and again. I was under his control, putty in his hands, silk beneath his touch.

His hand cupped my chin and with one final kiss, gentle and romantic, he pulled away from me. It took me a moment to revive myself from the heart-stopping trance I was under, until I understood his apprehension. The once preoccupied bunch was now a truly captivated audience. Everyone had witnessed our exchange of love and Cameron didn't seem startled in the slightest.

My eyes darted over the growing crowd, and I found Edwin glaring at me from across the room.

I turned back to the hunk before me, still mesmerized by his romancing, and slowly stepped back into his embrace. I rested my head on his shoulder, my breath on his neck, my arms hooked around him. With a deep sigh, I closed my eyes and reveled in the moment.

"I'm glad you made that decision," Cam whispered. He squeezed me tight against him and we continued to dance, slow, even though the song was much more merry than that.

At that very moment, I realized how very serious things had gotten between us.

CHAPTER TWENTY FOUR

The overwhelming attraction I felt for Cameron in that moment, made me want to climb his leg and lick his face.

"Get a room!" Hunter hollered.

That was the second time tonight someone had made that recommendation and I thought it was about time to make that happen. Cameron's eyes indicated to me that he felt the same.

My eyes shot for the door. "Do you think we could make a dash for it, without anybody noticing?" I asked.

"No," he said, smiling.

"To hell with it." I yanked him urgently toward the door. "Goodnight," I called out to everyone. "Merry Christmas."

Cameron was amused and waved a hand at the other guests, as I tugged him to the exit.

After we slipped into the stairwell, Cameron pressed me against the wall, unable to contain his own arousal. He pinned me hard against the cold cement wall and brushed my hair out of my face, but it fell right back into my eyes. He kissed me with such urgency, while feeling every inch of my thighs. I felt every touch like he was electrocuting me.

Tipsy, and a little legless, I let Cameron draw me back into his arms. I smoothed my hands over his chest, reveling in the feel of the smooth fabric clinging to his muscles and the cool leather of his jacket.

When his hand scooped inside my shirt and his thumb swiped over my aroused nipple, I moaned into his mouth. We both knew it was time to take it upstairs. With a smile, he stole my hand and dragged me up to the next floor. I let out a giggle as we hunted down our room. Finding it rather quickly, Cameron opened it up. After he delivered me inside, he slung the do not disturb sign on the door.

I glanced in the mirror at my muddled appearance. Cameron hadn't said a word when I left the bed after our heated encounter but I looked a mess. My hair was a total wreck and my mascara had run off, but I was content. Cameron had made me feel like a goddess, again and again with every life-affirming climax. I didn't think I would ever get enough of him.

I decided a quick shower might be in order. I opened the door a crack before I cranked on the water, hoping Cameron would accept the silent invitation. A moment after slipping into the steamy hot shower, water rushing over my overexerted body, I felt a cool gust of air breezing behind me. *Cam had taken the bait.*

Peeking in the curtain at me, staring at my naked behind, he smiled. He looked very pleased. "Mind if I join you?" He opened the curtain a little more, just enough for me to see that he was still beautifully naked.

"Absolutely," I answered. I pulled him into the tub and spun around so he was under the spray of water with me.

My touch was like a whisper, as I slid my soapy body all over his. My breasts slipped across his smooth chest and my nipples teased his warm, wet flesh. I thought Cam had entirely exhausted my desire, from taking me quick and wild against the wall, then slow and sensual in the massive bed, but my arousal returned with a vengeance when I saw him standing at attention yet again.

His body screamed with sex appeal, his spiky, wet hair a hot mess, his amazing muscled body even more defined than usual after our vigorous workout between the sheets. He kissed me with desperation, his mouth hot with need, his soft, sexy stubble gently teasing my aroused flesh.

My hands slipped over his wet, sleek muscles and the water poured over me, stimulating every sense in my body. Cameron spread my feet with his own, his erection hard on my hip. He lifted me up and pressed me into the shower wall, giving in to his guttural urges. He held my thighs, rough and possessive, as he hiked me higher only to lower me on top of him.

When I instinctively wrapped my legs around him, it tightened our connection with a delicious clench. Cameron's mouth covered mine again, and he deepened our tongue-filled kiss. We quickly found a hypnotic escape, wet and hot and fervent. We were linked together like a puzzle, challenging and complete.

Cameron propped me against the wall and drove into me with long, steady strokes. Water slipped between us, as I leaned back and held the shower bar with both my hands for support. He continued on determinedly, until I was screaming out in release, with my heels dug into his back.

Then I felt him come undone inside me and I squealed again with the knowledge that the man I loved had just shared with me his everything.

The morning after, I found the room still dark, the blinds shut tight. I squinted at the alarm clock, it read one minute to nine. A smile crept onto my face to know that my man was still lying next to me, not that he could have escaped with my one thigh hiked over his clean, satiated body.

Curled up in the rumpled, white sheets together, we laid silent and replete. I cuddled him with closed eyes and a hand on his firm chest. With only a thin sheet draped over us, I relied on his body for warmth and it was like heaven.

Cameron sighed with contentment and kissed me on my temple. "I love you."

I could get used to waking up to that.

"Love you too," I replied, in a daze of sleepiness and dedication. I tried to open my eyes, to take another look at his remarkably fit body, but they fluttered shut from exhaustion. I fell fast asleep in his warm, strong embrace, with my smile still intact.

When Cameron drove me home from the hotel, I stared

out my window wondering how I would function without him. A glimmer of disappointment twinged in my gut. I didn't even want to imagine not having him around, but sadness rushed me like a football player.

Cameron watched me with idle curiosity, but he didn't say anything. Feeling his warm stare, I finally fluttered my lashes to connect with him and we shared a soft smile. Selfish and needy, I pulled Cameron's hand over to my side of the car and linked our fingers together.

When we reached my house, Cameron carried my bag and walked me to the front door. The wind whipped, nasty and cold, but we kissed on my front porch like it was the middle of summer.

Despite my zeal, discouraging thoughts ate away at my heart. The way his lips tasted mine, with such intensity, it felt like we were never going to share a kiss again. My stomach plummeted at the thought.

"I love you," I whispered, near tears.

"I love you too," he said, then pressed a kiss to my temple. His hands rubbed up and down my arms, then slid up to my shoulders to hold me in place as his eyes searched mine. "I don't know what has you so worried, but I guarantee there's nothing that will stop us from being together," he said, with such certainty.

I wanted to believe him. "I know, but..."

"But nothing," he interrupted. "I love you and I think you love me too. That's enough for me. Nothing and no one else matters. Except for Pheobe of course," he added, with a dangerously sexy smirk.

I nodded, a soft smile pressed on my lips, surprised to find any form of relief.

Cam cupped his hand over my cheek and dropped to kiss me, long and deep. "I'll call you later?"

"Kay," I replied, tugging on his leather jacket, wishing he didn't have to go.

"God, I hate leaving you like this." He pulled me back in his arms for a tight squeeze, his arms wrapping right around me, holding me like a love he never wanted to let go.

"Now get in there before you catch a cold."

My mouth turned up into a real smile, as I let myself inside. Tugging aside the curtain in the front room, I peered out the window and watched my man walk back to his car, cool and swift. I breathed a sigh of happiness as it sunk in just how good I had it. *That man was mine.*

CHAPTER TWENTY FIVE

With only a couple of days before Christmas, I was getting a little anxious, since Cam and I really hadn't settled our plans for the holidays just yet. We had been inseparable since the night of the Christmas party. I was addicted to the high of being with Cameron and all of the love that came with that.

It was seriously getting to the point where I couldn't bear to leave him at night. It was past the point where I'd spend most of my nights in his bed. Nights spent at my place had become few and far between.

Cameron had a late appointment that night, so I headed home from work down snow filled roads. I trudged through the fresh pile of snow on my front porch and kicked a good heap of it aside with my tall boots, before heading inside.

Before I could even put down my keys, the phone started ringing. My heart dropped as fast as my coat. Ever since Pheobe's accident, panic struck me with every ring of the phone.

"Hello," I answered, breathless.

"Hey, it's me," Cam said. He sounded fine.

"Miss me already?" I teased, a swift smile reaching my lips.

"Yeah. Do you have a problem with that?"

My smile grew three sizes. "Yeah. Maybe you should come over and do something about it."

Cameron's voice turned serious, startling me from my playful attitude. "Actually, I'm calling for another reason."

My body froze and a clump formed in the back of my throat, nearly suffocating me. I could tell it was important. I swallowed the dryness from my throat and tried to lighten the mood back up. "And here I thought you were making a booty call."

As the words left my lips, the door clicked shut and Edwin knocked his boots together. His jaw was slack, his eyes wide, and that's when I knew he had heard me. Feeling uneasy, I turned away, but he wasn't going to let me ignore him.

"Hey, Abs," Edwin whispered.

I flashed him an uninterested look and took in the gorgeous smile plastered on his face. His thumb was pointing eagerly to his chest. "You owe me!" he whispered.

I shook my head vigorously to say 'no way in hell' and scowled at him before moving to the kitchen for a little bit of privacy.

Edwin's feisty chuckle haunted my path.

"I've actually been meaning to talk to you about this," Cam said. "I figure now is as good as ever."

Terrified, slowly, I said, "Okay." My anxiety trembled in my voice.

"Stop worrying, it's nothing bad. At least I hope you don't think so," Cam said, with a touch of sunshine in his words.

"Phew. Don't do that to me." The knot in my stomach loosened ever so slightly.

"You know how we both have two weeks off for holidays, since the firm's shut down between Christmas and New Year's, right?"

"Right."

Cam cleared his throat. "Pheobe and I were wondering if you would like to spend the holidays with us."

"Umm, no," I replied, without a second of thought.

"What?" Cam sounded incredibly confused. It hurt me to know that he took me so seriously.

"I would *love* to Cam. I was only teasing. Of course I will," I said. "Anything to spend more time with you."

Cam was silent on the other end. Had he already hung up on me?

"Cam?"

Edwin was having a laughing fit behind me, having listened in on my conversation.

I waved an angry hand at him and scowled. He was being so annoying. "Screw off," I snapped, then rushed up the stairs to my room.

"Are you talking to me?" Cam asked, stunned.

"No. Edwin's being a tool. He's gone now. Did you hear me?"

"Yeah, it just took me a second to restart my heart there," he admitted.

"I'm sorry. I couldn't help myself. But I love you and I'd like nothing more."

His sigh of relief was like a breath of fresh air. "Pack your bags then. I'll pick you up tomorrow morning. How does eleven o'clock work for you?"

"I can't wait," I replied, softly. "I'll be thinking about you."

"Me too," he said.

When I hung up the phone, I was so giddy I danced around my room with a squeal, absolutely overjoyed, until it hit me. *How was I going to tell Edwin the news?* I paced in circles and then sat on the floor in a pile, worry slamming me. We had always spent the Christmas holidays together regardless of our relationship status. He would be beyond pissed.

When the front door slammed shut, I snapped out of my trance. When my eyes focused from my blank stare, I found a heaping pile of laundry staring back at me. I welcomed the task to avoid my troubles.

I dutifully separated my clothes, tossed them into the washer and set out to tidy up the house. I swiped the dust away, but I couldn't seem to get Edwin out of my brain. I wiped a little faster and scrubbed a little harder, but he was still there. Worrying about Edwin was certainly helping me catch up on my house work, but the dread alone was killing my mood.

Why couldn't he just get home already?

The house was dusted, carpets vacuumed, toilet scrubbed, and kitchen spic and span. By the time I was done dancing with the mop to Christmas carols, the house looked great, but Edwin was still gone.

Exhausted, I finished folding my laundry and packed most of it into my bag. That's when I heard the front door quietly click shut. *Finally!*

When a woman's voice called from the front foyer, my eyes popped open. *Shit!* I ran to my stereo, turned the music way down and leaned against my dresser for stability. My chest heaved and my hands trembled. *What was wrong with me?*

"Edwin's not home," I choked. "I'll be right down."

I struggled to zip up my heaping bag and then lugged it downstairs to greet our guest. It was Edwin's mother. Her long, dark hair was as glossy as ever, her full, wide-mouthed smile waiting for me.

"Abigail! So nice to see you." She reached her arms out for a hug. "It's been too long." She planted a kiss on each of my cheeks.

That family and their loving. Every one of them huggers. I gave her a quick squeeze. "It certainly has. Great to see you too, Vera. Please come in." I took her jacket and swiftly retrieved a hanger from the closet. "Where's Jason?" I asked curiously, wondering why Edwin's father wasn't with her.

"Oh, Jason's with the boys." She flashed me a look of concern. "The whole clan is coming down this year. Didn't Edwin tell you?"

I tried to hide my annoyance, but the expression on my face said it all. "No."

Vera pressed her lips together in apology. "Jason's driving up with the others. I have all the luggage in my car. But we'll let the men take care of that," she said, trying to cheer me up.

"That must have been a quiet ride for you, for a change," I said, smiling through my guilt.

"And what a nice change it was. We switched up cars at the last stop and I decided to go ahead alone. Payton was talking my ear off." She flashed me a sweet smile.

"Smart woman," I said. Edwin's older brother, Payton,

did like to hear himself talk, but he was a total sweetheart. "Are they here now?" I asked. *Please say no. I needed a few minutes to collect my sanity. I was not prepared for this; thanks to Edwin.*

"They shouldn't be too far behind. They must have made another pit stop. Those boys are always eating. They're just like their father."

"That must be where Edwin gets it from," I said, making Vera smirk. "Please make yourself at home. The guest room is all yours. If you'll excuse me for a minute, I was just finishing up some laundry."

"Oh, of course. Don't let me keep you," she said.

Vera disappeared down the hall. I took the stairs, two at a time, relieved to wind up the holiday rush. *What was she doing here anyway? Edwin didn't say he invited his family over. I guess he didn't plan to include me in the festivities this year.* It was only a tradition we had kept every year for the past six. So was it bad that I was sort of happy I didn't have to entertain them this year?

Just the thought of having to face the rest of his brothers, the whole handsome lot of them, made my stomach roil. *I've got to bolt. Now.*

I lifted my second suitcase, carried it downstairs and dropped it right next to the door. I hurried to the closet to retrieve my jacket, when the front door started to open. *No!*

It was only Edwin. *Oh, no! I'd been worrying about this part all night.* Vera returned to the foyer.

"Hey, Mom. You made it! Wow, the house looks good," he said, flashing me an appreciative glance.

Edwin put down the bags of groceries, gave his mother a huge bear hug and then picked up my luggage. "Here. Let me help you with your bags."

I chewed on my bottom lip. "Actually, Eddie, those bags are mine."

"You're leaving?" he asked, looking hurt and confused.

I nodded. "If you have a minute, I'd like to talk to you about it."

"Take all the time you need," Vera said, and then took the

groceries to the kitchen.

"Forget it. I don't care," Edwin said. He spun around and hustled up the stairs.

I chased after him. "I'm not leaving until you talk to me."

He stopped outside my room and flashed me a teasing look. "Now I'm not talking to you for sure then."

I made a pouty face and folded my arms over my chest. "I really need to talk to you." I peered down the stairs. "Privately."

When I stepped inside my room, Edwin followed behind me and gave the door a good push, but it didn't quite latch. He didn't move any closer to me either. He seemed so cold and distant all of a sudden.

I glanced out my window, at the sparkling fresh snow, then turned to face him. "Cam has asked me to spend the holidays with him. I told him yes."

"You're what?" he snapped.

"It's only for a couple of weeks. It sounds like you're going to have a houseful anyway. You won't even notice I'm gone."

"The next couple of weeks? You didn't think to tell me this sooner?" he said, his eyes accusatory and hard.

"You mean, like you told me your whole family's coming down?" I scowled at first, but softened when I saw the disappointment in his eyes.

He folded his arms across his buff chest and gave me a cool stare. "Do I get a say in this?"

"Seriously? It's not your place. Did you really think we were going to hang out like one big, happy family all week?"

He worked his jaw with his hand. "You can't just stay here for Christmas and then go to his place after that?" Now he was begging.

I didn't want to hurt him, but he had to understand. "I've already made my decision."

"I can't believe you're pulling this stunt on me," he growled.

With a brief knock and a swift push, the door swung open nearly hitting Edwin in the ass. My heart raced, my mouth grew dry, and even though I tried to fight it, a grin curled onto my lips.

There was Cameron, unsmiling, his eyes fixated on mine. "Sorry to intrude, but I could hear everything out there anyway." He glanced at Edwin as he passed by him. "It didn't sound like your conversation was going anywhere at any rate." He gave me a soft kiss hello, as though he were claiming me, with that sexy stubble still framing his chiseled jaw.

His hand rested on my shoulder and the rest of my body was totally aware of that. The weight that had been bearing down on me only moments earlier had started to subside. Standing slightly behind me, protective, Cam waited patiently for us to finish the conversation.

"Please don't make this difficult, Eddie. I don't want to fight with you," I pleaded. "It's Christmas time."

"Cam, could you please excuse us?" Edwin said, very serious and very stern. "I'd like to speak to Abigail. Alone."

The way he said it, dark and dangerous, made me nervous, though I knew he'd never cause me any harm.

"I don't think it'll get you anywhere," Cam said. He searched my eyes and I don't know what he found but he was suddenly content to leave the room. "Okay?"

I gave him an anxious nod.

Cameron kissed my right cheek. "Alright. I'll be downstairs if you need me."

I put my hand on my tingling cheek, touching where Cam's lips had just left. He was so gentle.

Yet, when he passed Edwin, his glare was hot and locked. "Keep your hands to yourself," he warned.

Edwin stood still, silent, brooding. Then the door clicked shut.

Just the thought of Cameron sitting in the living room with Edwin's mother reminded me how quick this needed to be settled. She was probably already poking into my business and I hadn't even opened my mouth yet.

"I don't want you to go," Edwin started, being blunt and honest. "Are you sure this is what you want?"

I dropped my hand and pressed my lips together in a hard line. "This is what I want, Eddie. I love Cameron and I want to spend time with him."

He shuddered when I said the L word. "And his daughter? Did you think about that? You shouldn't be playing with her emotions like this, Abs. Are you sure you're that serious about him?" His voice broke. Edwin's voice never broke. "You can really see yourself raising someone else's daughter?" His eyes grew sad as he grasped at straws.

It pained me to watch him. "I've already thought about it. Pheobe didn't choose to lose her mother. She's a very sweet girl and deserves to have a mother-like figure in her life. I'm not trying to replace anyone, but if I'm going to be in Cam's life, then she's going to be a major part of it."

He took a step closer to me, but remained cautious and brittle. Then he took another step. "And what about me?"

I gasped for a breath and swallowed back the lump that was expanding, like a balloon, in my throat. "What about you?" I replied, with a whisper.

He spun away from me and flailed a heavily muscled arm. "At least I know where I stand." He tried to be angry, but I could sense his upset. He couldn't even look at me.

Feeling terribly guilty, my breath unsteady, I inched toward him and slowly reached for his hand. He pulled away from me, his warm, strong hand slipping from my cool fingers. I took his hand against his will and squeezed onto it, but he still wouldn't look at me.

I walked around in front of him and placed his hand over my heart, my hand covering his. "You will always have a place in my heart, Eddie. That will never change," I said, my eyes closing on a tear.

His eyes lifted to mine. They were even more sad and confused than before.

I plummeted into the depths of that aqua sea. "Love you," I whispered, confusing him even more. *Hell, I confused myself.*

He said nothing. And thank God for that. Unfortunately,

he didn't need to; his eyes told me the entire story. *Shit!*

My heart kicked up and I laid my head on his firm chest, to tear my eyes from his longing gaze. Eyes sealed shut, trying to steady my heart, I suddenly wished I hadn't gotten so close to him. Chin tucked tight, terrified yet stirred, Edwin's arms closed around me. He enfolded me in his arms, but it was hollow.

I took a sharp breath and it cut through the icy silence. "I know raising another woman's child isn't an ideal situation, but I've accepted it. You should too."

Edwin pulled me off of him, still holding me in his grip, his eyes unwilling to release me. Then he hit me with a cool, sarcastic gaze. "Go on then. Run along with your little man-made family."

My heart twisted into an ugly black knot. I tugged out of his sadistic grasp. "Why are you being like this?"

He raised an arched brow, but didn't say another word. Then he turned and left the room.

I stared out the wide open door long after he had vanished, frozen in place, the only thing breaking my trance being Cameron coming to the rescue.

"Everything okay?" He approached me slow and careful.

I forced a smile, but it wasn't until he wrapped his strong arms around me that the warmth returned to it. "Everything's good, now that you're here."

He rewarded me with a long, deep kiss. "Are you ready to go then?"

"How did you know?"

"Is that not your leather suitcase at the door? I assume you're all packed. I might as well bring your bags with me tonight." He smiled, warm and handsome. "While I'm at it, I might as well take you home with me too."

I gave Cameron a big smooch and quickly gathered a few things, stuffing them into another small bag that was already full to the brim.

Cameron laughed. "It's not like you live in a different country," he teased. "If you need something, we can always come and get it." His smile was intoxicating.

"Too much?" I asked.

"It looks like you've packed enough to move in permanently," he said, smiling ear to ear. He lifted his hand, palm to me. "Hey, I'm not saying you can't."

My breath hitched in my windpipe. *Did he just proposition me?* I scanned his eyes to see whether he was joking. It wasn't all fun and games.

"I'm a woman and I need my things," I said, avoiding his test. "Besides, I think Pheobe will like having a lady in the house."

He smiled, big and happy. "She will *love* having you around, Abby. It's getting you to stay that's the trouble."

He was playing treacherous games with my heart. Was he was toying with me? He pulled me into his arms and kissed me with love; then he took my bag from my hand and briskly headed for the door.

"I'll wait for you in the car," he said, abruptly leaving the room.

It would have been easier if he had stayed. I hurried down the stairs as the front door clicked shut behind him.

"Edwin? Vera?" I called, as I barreled down the stairs. "I'm heading out now."

To my surprise, they both came to say goodbye.

"Merry Christmas, Vera," I said, kissing both her cheeks.

"Edwin told me the news. I wish you could stay. It just won't be the same without you," she said.

"Another time. I promise," I said. *A part of me wished I didn't mean it.*

To my surprise, Edwin reached his arms out to me for a hug and I couldn't bear to leave him hanging. When he swooped his heavy arms around me this time, he held on tight and extra-long. "If you change your mind, I'll be here," he whispered, his warm breath tickling my ear.

With a kiss to my right cheek, I closed my eyes, fighting back the tears. When he went to kiss my other cheek, his lips brushed softly past mine, then kissed the side of my mouth, firm and tender.

We had just shared the most adulterous kiss and it

wasn't even wet.

Vera's eyes widened, silently scolding Edwin, but none-the-less she walked away to leave us to our own.

Stunned and upset, I pulled away and glowered at him. I could see it in his eyes. He was being smug, but he was hurting. *I guess I could overlook his foolish behaviour. This time.*

"Happy holidays?" I said.

He pressed out a frown. "Yeah. Happy. I'll see you in two weeks."

I ignored his sarcasm and looked to his mother in the other room, trying to quietly mind her own business. "Please tell Jason and the others I said hello and that I'm sorry I missed them."

"Absolutely. Merry Christmas, Abby," she replied.

Another glance at Edwin and that was a mistake. *God, my heart hurt. Why did he have to look at me like that?* Not actually wanting to meet up with the rest of his family, I hurried out the door without another word.

Cameron didn't say anything as he pulled out of my driveway. *What a relief. I was ready to fall to pieces.* And as Cam drove away, I saw Jason's vehicle driving up the road. Though our windows were darkly tinted, I waved out the front windshield at them, and one of Edwin's brothers gave me a cool nod and wave back.

I sighed aloud, then settled back in my seat, relieved to have avoided that mix up.

Cameron raised a brow and peeked at me. "Who was that?"

I cringed at the thought of Vera alone with Cameron. "I'm surprised Vera didn't tell you."

"Actually, she spent most of the time interrogating me. She seems nice," he said, smiling. "Are you going to tell me who that was?"

"Edwin's family," I said. *Yes, they're all as tall, dark and handsome as Edwin, and yes,* "Apparently they're staying at my place for Christmas."

Cameron looked at me through curious eyes. "What, you

don't want to hang out with the family?" His smirk showed he wanted me to ease up already.

"Hah! Don't get me wrong, they're super nice people, but I couldn't be happier that I'm staying with you." I gnawed on my bottom lip like it was a chew toy.

"You'll be happy to know that Mrs. Santora had nothing but nice things to say about you," he said, which would have been fine except for that devious smile playing on his lips.

"Vera? What did she tell you?" I demanded.

"I promised her I wouldn't say," he said with a wink. "You're better off if I keep my word."

I huffed, wishing he'd spill the beans, but he was probably right. It wouldn't change a thing.

My holiday favourite was on TV and Pheobe was watching it intently. Cameron was in the kitchen rinsing our snack bowls, while I stood just outside the room waiting for him to rejoin me. I was totally lost in my own warm world of happiness on the night before Christmas.

Out of the blue, Pheobe started to giggle and it made me smile. I glared at her, trying to find out what was so funny. The way she peered over the back of the sofa at me, with a huge smile on her face, it was obvious she and Cameron were up to something sneaky. I teased her with narrowed eyes and it only made her giggle more.

Cameron's arms now around my waist, I leaned back against him to cuddle. "What are all those giggles about?" he asked Pheobe, smirking. His chin rested on my shoulder and I saw him giving her googly eyes, like she was giving up their secret.

I pouted my lips, hoping she would give it up to me. "What is it?" I asked.

Pheobe didn't answer, but Cameron sneakily peeked up above our heads. Then he pointed a finger at the mistletoe hanging from the archway directly above us.

I looked back at Pheobe. "You little stinker. You did this,

didn't you?"

"Daddy helped," she said, giggling. "Now you have to kiss!"

Cameron twirled me in his arms, until our smiles nearly touched. Closing my eyes, I leaned in and pressed my lips against his. Our kiss was long, soft and tender, but electricity still seemed to arch between us.

Pheobe watched and clapped excitedly. "It worked!" She cheered and flopped back on the couch, covering her giggling mouth with her hand, her little foot excitedly kicking in the air. It was amazing how one little girl could bring so much happiness to everything we did.

It was officially Pheobe's bedtime, just as the movie ended. I was looking forward to a little alone time with Cam, but there was something I had to do for Pheobe first.

"Pheobe. Let's go to your room," I said. "There's something I'd like to show you. I used to do it every Christmas eve with my mom when I was a kid and I think you'll like it too."

Without question, her smile crept wider, and she took a leap into my arms.

"Ump! You're almost too big to carry," I teased, then carried her to her room. With her skinny little legs, it was hardly laborious, even with one still hidden beneath a cast.

Cameron followed us to Pheobe's room, content and curious to know what I was doing. I drew the blinds open and peered out at the dark night. There were few stars to be seen in the otherwise black sky. Luckily, it was only a healthy imagination needed for this exercise to work.

"When I was a little girl, I would sit in my bedroom window with my mom and my sisters on the night before Christmas and watch the sky. Do you know what we were looking for?" I asked.

"Santa!" she squealed, awed and excited. She squeezed her arms around my neck and my heart seemed to grow two sizes. When she let go, I hiked her higher on my hip, so she didn't slip down.

"Definitely, Santa. And if you look super carefully, you

might even see Rudolph's nose shining when he passes by."

When I pointed out the window, her wide, blue eyes scoured the night sky. She stared wondrously, waiting. It was so funny watching her. She was trying so hard not to blink.

I looked back at Cameron, his arms were folded across his chest, his lean body supported by the door frame. He watched me with an appreciative smile.

"Hoh! Abby. I just saw something!" Phoebe squealed.

I looked her in her honest, little eyes and gave her a quick squeeze. "Wow, you're extra lucky then. In all my years, I only saw the sleigh a couple of times."

Pheobe wiggled out of my arms to the floor and tottered to her dad. "Daddy, I saw him. I really did!"

He gave her a great big hug. "Well, you'd better get to bed then. He doesn't leave presents unless you're asleep."

She pushed out of Cameron's hug and dove into her bed. I crouched down next to her and gave her a goodnight kiss on the cheek.

Cameron lifted the covers on top of her and gave her a juicy smooch on the lips. "Good night, baby girl. I love you," he said, as he tucked the covers under her chin.

"Love you, Daddy. Love you, Abby."

And there it was. The most amazing Christmas gift a girl could ever ask for. "Night, night, sweetheart," I whispered, then planted another kiss on her forehead.

She closed her eyes and tried extra hard to go to sleep.

Cameron took my hand and led me out of her room. The living room was only lit by the gentle glow from the Christmas tree and the flickering fireplace. Holding Cameron's hand, I felt so safe and loved. Complete. A warm, serene feeling wrapped around me, as Cameron sat down next to me on the love seat and pulled me close.

He lifted my hand to his mouth and pressed a kiss into my palm. I was never so aware of such a gentle touch.

"You always manage to amaze me," he said, his gorgeous stare fixed on me.

I smiled, and bashfully glanced down at the floor,

reacting to the butterflies dancing in my tummy.

He lifted my chin to redirect my eyes back to his. "Thank you for staying with us." His lips melted into mine, then his warm tongue gently explored my mouth.

I gasped for air, taken by his sensuality. "I love you," I whispered. And I meant it in every sense of the word.

His mouth covered mine again, as he slowly pressed me down into the soft cushion. We kissed for a long while, until my mouth was tired and my heart content.

When Cameron released me from his mouth, it left my face feeling naked and chilled. "May I escort you to your room, Mrs. Clause?" he asked, a sexy smile perching on his lips.

A new heat zapped right through my limbs and stung my heart. *Mrs. Clause.* Every time he made a reference to marriage, it made my heart race and my head sing.

I stood up from my seat and Cam ushered me to his room. We crept down the hall, careful not to bother Pheobe.

Cam closed the door behind us, then wrapped his arms around my waist and touched his forehead to mine. "I can't wait to get you out of these clothes," he growled.

I smirked, then flashed him a naughty glance. "I think that can be arranged. What time does Santa come by here usually?"

"Not for a few hours, at least," he replied, with that wicked smile gracing his delicious lips.

With a kiss to the corner of his mouth, I tugged away to search for my suitcase. "How would you like an early Christmas present?" I pulled out some racy, red lingerie from my bag.

When I held it up against my pale skin, Cam's eyebrows shot up and he had it in his hands before I could form a word to describe how incredibly hot he looked in that moment. His fingers manipulated the soft, delicate fabric, then he teased it over my cheek and dropped the skimpy lace to the floor. His hands skimmed inside the bottom of my loose shirt, tickling my sensitized skin.

He held my soft, slim waist in both of his hands. "Please don't take offence, but maybe we can save that for another night," he said, with a groan. "I'd hate for you to get all dressed up, just for me to rip it right off of you." Humourless and greedy, his hands swallowed me whole and the way he touched me I thought Santa was going to be naughty. And he was. But it was nice.

My heart thundered in my chest as he took my mouth, hard and possessive. Cam's hands skimmed up and down my flesh, my excitement growing with every hard press of his mouth and every gentle touch of his hands. His lips devoured mine, as he lowered me to the bed and I whimpered in anticipation of what he was going to do to me.

When I pulled away from his mouth, his growl urged me to obey him. "So, no to the lingerie?"

He gazed at me through deep, fathomless eyes. "For Christmas, all I need is you."

CHAPTER TWENTY SIX

After being at Cameron's mercy for hours, I closed my eyes and rested in his arms, sweaty and spent. Still naked, I fell into a deep and restful sleep, until my eyes fluttered back open.

"Cameron," I whispered, harshly. "We must have fallen asleep." I yanked on his arm anxiously. "Wake up," I demanded. I squinted at the alarm clock. It was barely five in the morning.

"Don't worry. I've taken care of it," he mumbled.

I sat up to collect myself, my heart still pounding out of my chest. I was so worried that Pheobe might awaken and there would be no presents under the tree. "But, Santa," I said.

"I told you. Relax. It's in the bag."

When I realized that I had slept through it all, I was feeling a little childish. "Are you saying I blew my first chance at being Mrs. Clause?"

He rolled over and admired the panic in my eyes, slightly amused by it. "I don't know, Santa's pretty satisfied. I think you've done a pretty good job," he said, dropping a soft kiss on my swollen lips.

"I can't believe I missed the best part," I moped.

Cam chuckled. "Don't worry, babe, there'll be many more years for that."

I plunked my head back down on the pillow and exhaled loudly, sinking back into the comfy bed.

"You might want to get dressed though. I'm sure Pheobe will be getting up soon and I guarantee this bed will be her first stop."

I immediately got up and fumbled around the room to collect my clothes from the floor. They were cold and wrinkled, so I quickly tossed them all in his hamper. "I hope you don't mind," I said softly, as I pulled on some cozy pajamas.

He smiled. "What's mine is yours."

I slipped back into bed, curling up close behind him to steal his warmth. When he rolled onto his back, I couldn't help but kiss him before I rested my head on his buff chest. He wrapped his arm around my body, his hand running up and down me, warming me right up.

"I know now's probably not the best time, but I have a question to ask," Cam said, startling me.

I teased my fingers over his smooth chest. "Okay."

"When you were with Pheobe in the window last night, you told her the tradition you used to do when you were a child. When were you going to tell me about your other sister?"

My heart tightened and my throat swelled shut.

His hand stopped moving and he focused on my reaction. "I'm sorry. Have I overstepped? I just want to know everything about you."

After a deep breath, I found the words. "It's not that. I *had* another sister."

"Oh, Abby, I'm sorry. I had no idea." He pulled me into an all-consuming embrace, but didn't make another sound.

After a couple of minutes, I swallowed back my nerve and told him about my twin sister, Jenny. The horrifying accident. The terrifying nightmares. I left out some of the more recent hallucinations, but was relieved to realize how few they'd been since I'd been with Cameron.

"When did you say that accident was?" Cam asked, his eyes growing anxious.

"It was on my sixth birthday. A day I'll never forget. It was March twenty first. Trust me, not fun sharing that day with the annual reminder of your sister's horrendous death."

Cam was holding his breath. "You're not going to believe this," he said, his eyes filled with pain. He raked a hand through his messy hair. "Pheobe's accident, the day Tessa died, was March twenty first."

My heart squeezed in my chest and I wondered if it had rung out every last drop of my blood. My limbs numbed and my core stung like a son of a bitch. It still hurt to hear him say her name.

He scratched his head and tilted it sideways. "That's really peculiar. Wouldn't you say?"

Too uncanny, but I refused to rehash over all of my ridiculous conspiracy theories. My therapist told me it was a bad habit and very unhealthy. "So much tragedy. It can be a cruel world," I said, still unable to completely catch my breath.

His hand started to rub my arm anxiously. "It can be, but there is some good. You survived, and so did Pheobe."

Had I? He certainly made me feel like I had.

Not taking my gaze from his, I cupped my hand against his soft facial hair and pressed a loving kiss to his lips. He squeezed me tight, ushering away the black thoughts, holding me in his layer of comfort. In his arms, gripped tightly against him, I slowly, unexpectedly, found sleep.

"Daddy! Daddy! He came! Abby, come quick!" Pheobe hollered.

It was impossible to ignore the alarming sweetness emanating from Pheobe as she hobbled into the room squealing with joy. She had a spring in her step, despite the awkward cast she still had to wear from her accident, and she was simply radiating happiness. I checked the clock for the time and Cam was right. It wasn't a minute passed six thirty.

"Come on!" she ordered, cheery but impatient. She grasped onto Cameron's limp arm and started to yank.

"Okay, okay," Cameron finally said, slowly pulling back the covers.

Pheobe disappeared out of the room as quickly as she had appeared.

Cameron waited for me to wrap up in my robe. "You'll want to see this," he said, holding out his hand to me.

Surprised to feel so rested after our late night of love making and the early morning conversation, I clasped onto his hand and headed for the Christmas tree. Pheobe was already planted next to the presents and was picking them all up and reading the labels. She was super excited, truly ecstatic. Cam took a seat on the chair next to the fully-lit tree and I sat on the floor next to Pheobe.

"Are you going to open them, or what?" Cam asked, smirking.

"Which one should I open first?" she squealed.

I crawled closer to the tree and reached for a large pink gift with a big silver bow on it. "I think I would want to open this one first," I said.

She grabbed it from me, happy that I joined her under the tree. "Okay," she replied giddily, ripping open the paper. "This is just what I wanted!" she shouted with joy, showing it to her dad. She tossed it beside her quickly and started in on the next ones.

Sitting amongst the flying pieces of paper, I realized just how badly I wanted a kid of my own. It was still fun, watching Pheobe toss the gifts around, seemingly more concerned with the unwrapping than the actual gifts themselves. But to have a child born from my own love, that would be a dream come true.

Pheobe made quick work of it, until there were but two gifts left under the tree.

"Abigail, these ones are for you," Pheobe said. "The small one says it's from Daddy and the big one is from Santa. How did Santa know you were spending Christmas with us? That's crazy!" She giggled uncontrolledly, as she cleared some paper out of the way with her foot and laid the gifts in front of me.

I picked up the small one first and looked to Cameron for a hint. It was obviously jewellery, and it had my stomach flipping with an excitement only a woman could fully understand.

"You should open the other one first," he said, with a wrinkle of his forehead.

Pheobe hopped in front of me and dropped down onto my lap, with the large gift from Santa in her hands. "Open this one!" she cheered.

"Alright," I said, smiling. I tore off a slice of paper and with Pheobe's help, the gift was free in mere seconds. It was a gorgeous designer handbag and I absolutely loved it. "Wow, Santa has some good taste!"

"You should check to see if he put anything inside it," Cam suggested, inconspicuously.

I smiled and opened it up, only to find a few smaller gifts wrapped up inside. Awestruck with Santa's charity, I winked at him, while Pheobe ripped the wrapping off the rest of the presents hiding inside.

Pheobe delivered the contents to me. I held out the rouched, red jersey dress before me and draped it over my body. Again, it was designer, strapless with a sweetheart neckline.

"Ooh, that's beautiful," Pheobe said.

"It is. But I don't know where I'm going to wear it."

Cameron smirked at me. "That dress will be perfect for the party on New Year's Eve. You'll look stunning in it."

Party? "What party?"

"You know that ski trip your friends are going on next week?"

"Yeah, they're leaving in a couple of days."

He nodded. "You'd better repack your bags."

I covered my mouth, overcome with excitement, but silenced. Setting Pheobe aside, I jumped up and flung my arms around his neck, kissing that smile right off his face.

"Well then. If you liked that, then you're going to love this." Cam presented the small jewellery box to me and I nearly squealed with anticipation.

Pheobe leaned forward, curiously awaiting the reveal. "I wonder what it is," she said, her eyes brimmed with excitement.

Sitting on Cam's lap, I popped the top off the box and pulled out the small velvet one. When I cracked it open, I found two stunning diamonds sparkling back at me. The clarity was impeccable and they had to be at least one carat each. I covered my mouth again, on a gasp, speechless.

Cameron waited, expectantly. "Do you like them?"

"Oh my gosh. That's an understatement" I flashed a glance up at my man. "Cam; it's too much." I couldn't even hazard a guess at how many dollars were lying in that tiny velvet box.

A smile crept onto his lips and his eyes sparkled as glorious as the diamonds. "That's just the beginning."

We felt like a family. We looked like a family. But by the way Ashley greeted me when we entered the Clarke residence later that day, I was reminded that I was not a welcome part of her family. Shaun and Sadie Clarke had gone out of their way to decorate their house with Christmas cheer, but Ashley had a way of dampening the most delightful of moods.

"Doesn't your family hold Christmas for *you*?" Ashley snapped.

"Merry Christmas to you too," I replied, as nicely as possible.

"Abby's parents go down south for the holidays, so her family doesn't celebrate Christmas together," Cam explained.

"Aubrey's celebrating with a friend this year, so it all worked out," I said, smiling at Cam.

"Aubrey already told me her plans. I still can't believe she went away for the holidays without me."

I shrugged my shoulders indifferently. "Aubrey seemed pretty excited about it."

Ashley scowled.

"Grandma!" Pheobe squealed, when she saw Sadie walk into the room.

"Oh, hello Pheobe. Don't you look beautiful!"

"Abby did my hair for me!" she said excitedly, showing her sparkly bow with pride.

"You have to come see my Christmas tree," Sadie told Pheobe. "I think Santa might have accidentally dropped off some of your presents here."

Pheobe shuffled to the living room to see all the gifts. "Whoa!"

"I don't know," I said, smiling at Sadie. "I thought Santa did a pretty good job of spoiling her at home."

She smiled back, delighted, and squeezed her son's shoulder. "Of course he did."

We followed Pheobe to the living room and I curled up in Cam's arms on a loveseat, while Pheobe eyed up the presents. Sadie passed right through to the kitchen to continue her preparations for the holiday feast.

"Ashley, could you please get Abigail a glass of wine?" she asked, as she entered the kitchen.

"Ugh. Yes, mother." I could hear Ashley's annoyance from the other room. Nevertheless, she appeared in the door only moments later, with a beautiful glass of red just for me.

As she handed me my drink, she spoke softly. "I gave you a charm so you'd know which glass is yours."

How thoughtful. "Thank you."

She spoke to me softer yet. "It's a four leaf clover. Because you're going to need all the luck in the world if you think my brother's going to stay with you," she hissed. She turned away swiftly and stomped back to the fiery depths of the earth; I mean the kitchen.

Forgetting about the bitch was easy, once she left the room. Inspecting the perfectly lit tree, immediately brought me back into the Christmas spirit. The gifts were neatly stacked beneath the tree and had been packaged so perfectly with matching sparkling paper and bows. Resting against Cameron's warm masculine physique felt amazing and only added to my Christmas cheer.

Before long, Pheobe peeked into the living room. "Auntie Ashley said supper's almost ready!" she cheered. "Come on Abby."

I slipped away from Cameron and made my way to the kitchen, but the men didn't follow. Pheobe clutched onto my hand and dragged me inside the kitchen, where Ashley was emptying the gravy into an elaborate boat and Sadie was seasoning the mashed potatoes.

"Is there anything I can do to help?" I offered, as Pheobe left the room to go get her father.

"Yeah, you can leave," Ashley snapped.

"Ashley! I won't have it in my home," her mother scorned.

"Fine, my lips are sealed." But no one could have stopped the daggers pointing from those evil eyes.

"You don't have to seal them," Sadie warned, "just choose your words more carefully. There's a little girl in the house and she looks up to you. She clearly loves having Abigail around, so you'd better learn to like her."

For a moment it felt like I wasn't in the room, then Sadie turned her disappointed eyes up and her glance softened. "I'm sorry, honey. I would be glad to accept your help."

I scooped up the beautiful dishes of potatoes, carrots and cranberries, and carried them one at a time to the dining room. The table was tastefully decorated, in harmony with the tree and gifts.

"Wow, Sadie, this looks fabulous," I said, as I re-entered the kitchen.

Ashley flashed me a look, and I thought she was going to let me have it for buttering up her mother, but she didn't. "Mom always overdoes it at Christmas. If you think that's fabulous, just wait until you see the gifts."

Sadie smiled. "Thank you, Ashley. That's much better," she said, merrily.

Dinner was as good as it smelled and everyone was cordial at the dinner table. After filling my plate more than once, I indulged in the most delicious piece of cherry cheesecake.

"Is it time to open presents yet?" Pheobe whined. It was only the fifth time she had asked in the past five minutes.

Cameron smiled at me from across the room, as Ashley placed the dishes into the dishwasher. Sadie was smudging the ice cream off of Pheobe's face, as Shaun piled another piece of cheesecake onto his plate. For once, it felt like I was a part of the family.

After a day chock full of excitement from Pheobe, insolence from Ashley and questions from Cam, I was secretly ecstatic when he hinted that we call it a night.

Pheobe had passed out on the drive back to their house, so after stacking all of the gifts in a pile, I headed to the kitchen and brewed up a night cap. While I waited for Cam, my brain had a little time to think. Thinking about life was always a bad thing for me.

Earlier, I had felt like I was in this little bubble of holiday happiness and nothing could touch me. But standing there, mind reeling, in the cold stainless kitchen, reality broke my little bubble. I was a firm believer that things were always best when they didn't get *too good*.

News flash: life is pretty damn good right about now. Anxiety crept into the front of my mind and I feared that there was nowhere to go but *down*.

"Do you know anything about the resort we're going to?" Cam asked me, materializing out of nowhere and breaking me out of the onset of my anxiety attack.

"Not really. Why don't you enlighten me?" I said, trying my best to scare off my wicked thoughts.

"Alright. The place is called Pine Stone. It's a ski resort in the Halliburton Highlands area. It's about a two hour drive. I got us our own private suite with a hot tub and fireplace. I don't really know too much more about it, I guess, but it should be excellent. Private. Quiet."

I nodded my head and sipped my latte from my piping hot mug. "You do realize I'm not much of a downhill skier. The last time I tried, I did more falling than skiing."

"There's always snowmobiling, if you're not up for the slopes," Cam suggested. "Or we can take it slow and maybe take a lesson."

I squeezed his forearm, realizing how lucky I truly was to have such a kind, considerate man who cared about me. "That sounds like it could be fun."

Cam smiled. "I guess I should tell you my other surprise then."

"Please, no more surprises," I begged. "You've already done so much."

"One more thing," he insisted.

I closed my eyes and sighed.

"So, you know Pheobe's going to need a babysitter while we're gone. She's going to stay with her grandparents in Windsor."

"Oh. I thought your parents had plans," I replied, confused.

"Not my parents; Tessa's."

A sharp stake jabbed at my chest. "Oh," I managed to say. *Of course they're still involved in Pheobe's life. What was I thinking?*

"I thought since we have to drive her down there anyway, maybe we could stay at the Casino for a night. It's right on the Detroit River and quite a spectacular place. It sure beats the long drive back home."

I huffed a breath, still collecting my thoughts. "I don't know, Cam. This is getting to be one expensive holiday." *At this rate, I would break him. And with all this talk of Tessa, he would break me.*

He rested his hand on mine and brushed his thumb over my knuckles. "Money is of no importance to me. I've spent way too many years doing nothing but work. I've saved up a lot and now that I have someone to enjoy it with, I want to play a little. I don't think that's too unreasonable; is it?"

Darn it. Why does he have to be so damn smooth? "Well... when you put it that way..."

"Good! Then it's settled. We leave tomorrow."

CHAPTER TWENTY SEVEN

"It's a long drive. You aren't going to fall asleep are you?" Cam teased.

We were only halfway to Windsor, but Pheobe couldn't keep her little eyes open another minute. When her eyes fluttered shut, a part of me wished she was still awake. I loved that sweet, little girl. She was a piece of Cameron, only more youthful and animated, and she helped to keep my mind comforted and free.

Now, with her fast asleep, my mind turned to darker thoughts. I knew I would have to meet Pheobe's grandparents. Tessa's parents. Would they talk about her; about Cam's life before she died? Overwhelmed with worry, my head began to ache, and it only grew worse the closer we got.

Cameron's hand found mine, shaking and cold. "Are you okay?"

I forced a smile. "Mmm, hmm."

He answered my unspoken questions, as if he could read my mind. "They don't get to see Pheobe very often. I thought it would be a nice gesture to bring her down. Pheobe's their only grandchild. Tessa's sister is infertile, so Pheobe will be their only one."

I stared out the window trying to hide how upset I was. He was talking about her again. Every time he spoke of his deceased wife, I became breathless. I turned my gaze out the window and focused on the land. It was so flat and unappealing. The trees held no leaves and the dirt fields were barely coated in snow.

Cameron took the next exit off the highway, but couldn't seem to ignore the emotions I continued to wear on my sleeve. He squeezed my hand and searched my pain-filled eyes. "You're upset." He didn't understand.

"It's selfish, I know. But hearing you talk about Tessa - her family - I don't know." *I was incredibly self-conscious.* I barely managed to keep the tears at bay.

He pulled my hand to his lips and pressed a kiss against my palm, igniting a fire that seemed to have died. "You're everything I need. Everything I ever wanted. Even though life can take a twist and turn, know that I will always want to be right here. With you."

Pheobe shuffled in the backseat, bringing our conversation to an abrupt halt, as we searched for a restaurant to eat a late lunch in Chatham.

Through sleepy eyes, Pheobe stared out the window. "Look Daddy, the stinky castle!" Pheobe pointed at the stacks on the ethanol plant.

"It's funny the things kids remember," Cam said, shaking his head with wonder.

Even that squeezed my heart. So many memories.

Darkness was closing in around us and all of the street lights flickered on as day turned to night. I watched out the window anxiously as Cameron slowed the car. I knew we must have been close now.

While years had passed since Pheobe had lost her mother, I didn't know how her grandparents would handle seeing Cam and Pheobe with another woman. As we pulled into their driveway, I was suddenly feeling very sick.

"Maybe I should wait in the car," I suggested, with my stomach twisted in knots.

"Seriously, Abby. It's fine. I've already told them about you."

Really? I wonder what he said. "Okay."

After the long drive, I was desperate to stretch my legs anyway, and so I nervously got out of the car. Cam pulled out the bags, while I opened the back door to find that Pheobe had fallen back asleep. I unclicked the sleeping beauty's seatbelt and picked her up, careful not to bump her injured leg, then I wrapped her over my shoulder like a warm security blanket.

I followed Cameron to the door and waited for someone to answer. Pheobe continued to sleep sweetly on my shoulder, blissfully unaware of my anxiety. Looking at the sweet, little girl in my arms made me ache for the bond I would share with my own baby someday.

"We should wake her up," Cam suggested. "She'll be upset if I don't say goodbye."

I nodded, as Cam gently tugged at her arm. "Pheobe, we're at Grandma and Grandpa's."

Since no one was answering the door, Cameron gave it a good knock. The pounding seemed to startle Pheobe.

She started to open her big, sleepy, blue eyes and her long black lashes fluttered open. "Are we there yet?" she asked.

Cam and I both chuckled at Pheobe as she rubbed her tired eyes.

"We're here, honey," I said. She rested back down on my shoulder, but kept her eyes open, and the front door opened at last.

"I'm sorry. I didn't hear the doorbell. I hope you weren't standing here long. Please, come in," said the woman, who could only be Tessa's mother. She had big, blue eyes and long, straight, brown hair, strikingly similar to Pheobe's, but she was much older than I expected and a little weathered.

"Hi, Greta. How have you been?" Cam asked.

"Oh, same old I guess. I was so surprised when you called, and what a lovely surprise." Greta stared at her beautiful grandchild. "I'm so happy to have Pheobe for the week. We're going to have so much fun! Oh, and look at her, she's grown so much."

"I'm six and a half now, Grandma," Pheobe advised Greta.

"Wow, six years old. Come here and let me see you."

I put Pheobe down and she hesitated before going into her grandmother's open arms.

"Look how tall you are. I see you get your height from your mother," Greta said, giving Pheobe a hug.

My heart stuttered in my chest. Tessa was tall like me, with long, brown hair. I noticed the photos plastered all over the walls. But there was one photo that stung the worst. It could only have been a photo of Tessa, holding Pheobe as a newborn. I should have stopped staring, but the image had already burned into my memory anyway. Tessa was beautiful. *Of course she was.*

I felt like running outside in tears to put out the fire in my chest. What better time for introductions?

"Greta, I'd like you to meet my girlfriend, Abigail."

"Nice to meet you," she said, extending her hand for a shake. As I shook her wrinkled hand her smile seemed sincere, but I could sense in her honest eyes that she was judging me.

"It's nice meeting you as well," I replied.

Cam held out a piece of paper to Greta, as his other hand caught onto mine. "Here's a list of phone numbers where you can reach me at any time. Oh, and Pheobe's health card. Let's hope you don't need it." His voice caught and his fingers gripped mine with a tension-filled squeeze.

"Oh, don't worry about Pheobe. You know she'll be safe with us."

Pheobe hobbled over to her father, her leg cast still intact, and gave him a big squeeze around the legs. It tugged at my heart strings, even more when she whimpered. "Love you, Daddy. I'll miss you."

"Love you too, sweets. Be extra safe for Daddy." He dropped to his knees and planted a kiss right smack on her lips.

Pheobe smiled sweetly. "I will."

Greta whispered next to my ear. "Take good care of him. He's a good man." She gave me a serious eye.

I nodded and turned to the adorable, little girl, who was clinging to her father. "Bye, Pheobe. Don't have too much fun without us," I teased.

Pheobe released her father and latched onto my leg. "Love you, Abby."

I could see the horror in Greta's eyes, but I ignored it for

Pheobe's sake. I crouched down to give her a hug. "Love you too, sweetie," I said softly, locking her in my arms.

"We'll be in town until tomorrow around noon," Cam explained. "I'm only a call away if you need anything. I mean it, Greta; anything." Cam's voice had turned serious and stern, as though he was trying to program it into her brain.

Greta forced a smile for Cam. "We'll be fine, Cameron." I could sense the subtle displeasure in her tone as she forced herself to be friendly. "You go enjoy yourselves."

We travelled along the Detroit River and I watched out the window as the bridge came into focus. Moments later, I gawked at the magnificent fountain and noticed a rainbow of lights flashing around the front of the Windsor Casino.

I could sense Cameron's grin, so I turned to look at him. "What are you smiling at?" I inquired, wickedly.

"You, of course." He turned in front of the casino and pulled his car up a steep ramp.

"What are you doing?"

"It's called valet," Cam said, chuckling.

"My legs aren't broken. We could've walked."

"With all those bags you packed? I couldn't have."

I laughed at his sarcasm. It was true though, I had packed two bags for one night. Nearly everything I had brought to his house was in my bags. He wouldn't tell me what we were doing, so I had to come prepared for anything.

A man opened my door and I got out quickly. "Thank you."

Cameron popped his truck and gave one man his keys, while another helped him place our bags on a wheeled cart. I admired him from a few feet away while he registered for our room and unintentionally charmed the receptionist. We were out of there in a matter of minutes.

"Look at you," I said, as we stood in the elevator face to

face.

He tugged to closer. "What?" he asked, with a sexy smile. "You're in your zone tonight."

"What do you expect? I have a beautiful girlfriend, who I've got all to myself, in this incredible hotel and this crazy City."

I bit my lip, then squeezed up nice and close to him, momentarily forgetting that we were not alone in the elevator. Sensing the bell boy's discomfort, I gave Cam a quick kiss and then backed down, but naughty thoughts continued to stir in my mind.

When we reached our floor, Cam led the way and the bellboy followed close behind with our luggage. Cam opened the door to our suite and I was awestruck by the immediate view through the open blinds.

"This is great," I said, as I walked further into the room. With a huge grin, I flopped back carelessly on the king sized bed, my hair splayed out above me. I hadn't realized that the bellboy had followed us into the room, until I saw him unloading our bags next to me. His gaze didn't stray from my chest for more than two seconds at a time.

"Thanks a lot, buddy," Cam told the young fellow, handing him his tip and following him to the door. "A word of advice," he added quietly, not thinking I could hear him. "You'll keep your eyes to yourself, if you know what's good for you."

While I probably should have taken his possessiveness to be a terribly bad quality, it kind of turned me on. The door shut quietly on a flurry of apologies and when Cam walked back into my view I couldn't remove the giddiness from my face.

"What?" Cam asked, as if he didn't know.

I pulled my arm over my face to hide my huge smile. "Oh, nothing."

He sat on the bed next to me. "Don't get too cozy then. We have reservations." He rested his hand on my belly and his touch surged heat through my entire body.

"We don't have time to try out the bed first?" I asked

naughtily, as I pulled him on top of me.

He accepted my heated kiss, but resisted my tongue. He pressed a finger over my lips, so I parted them and gave him a lick.

"We'll have all night for that. Now we have to go to dinner," he said. "Don't make me feel guilty for saying no."

"Don't say no then," I purred, provocative and selfish.

"Abby," he begged, his control waning. He lifted himself up from the bed and pulled me up with him.

"Fine," I moaned, melodramatically. "Is it a nice restaurant?"

"Yes," he admitted. "But please hurry." He was growing impatient.

"Two minutes is all I need," I insisted, knowing full well that I needed at least ten.

Fifteen minutes later I walked out of the bathroom and grabbed my hand bag.

"You can't go like that. You'll freeze." Cam stood up and grabbed his jacket.

"A winter jacket does not go with this look." I pulled on a soft cardigan that still left my neck entirely exposed.

Cam shook his head, because he knew he wouldn't win. He reached his elbow out to me, and as soon as I finished slipping on my sexy high-heeled peep-toe booties, I grabbed on. He froze in place staring at my feet.

"You might want to rethink those shoes," he warned again.

"These booties are hot. I'm wearing them."

"Don't get me wrong, you look beyond amazing, but we'll be doing a little walking and maybe dancing. Are you sure those will hold up for the night?"

I'm going to make them work. "They'll work."

After an amazing candle lit dinner, at a fabulous Italian restaurant, we headed back to the Casino.

It didn't take long for him to lose a good chunk of change

at the black jack tables and, as I sunk his last coin into the slot machine, I looked to him. "Kiss for good luck?"

His tongue found mine, knocking my socks off -even though I wasn't wearing any- and I considered dropping the machine and dragging him back to our room. He pulled his sexy lips away from me.

"This is it!" I pulled on the lever and stared at the screen. "Come on baby!"

Cameron laughed as a bar rolled into place next to the cherries. "Nothing!"

I cast a scornful gaze on him. "You're the only one I know who laughs about losing that kind of money."

He raised his brows and pulled me into his arms. "Did you have fun?"

"Yes," I admitted, unable to stop smiling.

He tipped my chin with his index finger. "Then it was worth it."

His kiss was passionate, leaving me wanting more. He kissed me again, his lips soft and sweet when I wanted him to be hard and swift. I was ready for him to take me back to our room.

"I want to take you out dancing," he said, in my ear. The machines chimed loudly around us. "Are you ready for a night on the town with Cameron Clarke?"

I was definitely ready to flash around my man candy. "You know it."

Cameron didn't argue when I suggested we take a cab downtown. The cab driver dropped us off a few blocks from Wyandotte, so we could step out on foot to find a place to go. There was a number of hot spots lining the street and lines had already started to form outside the nightclubs.

It was extremely cold and my legs were exposed, so we dashed inside the first bar we approached that had decent music. It wasn't very large and, as we walked into the long narrow space, you could see the reason the bass was pounding so hard. The speakers were huge, as tall as the ceilings, and there were a lot of them.

As we walked toward the bar to get a drink, I realized

that the stools were filled with greasy-looking locals. There were young women, dressed incredibly slutty, dancing on the floor toward the back of the establishment. A collection of decently dressed young men framed the dance floor ogling the ladies.

We squeezed up to the bar and ordered some drinks, before we found a free bar height table to stand at.

"I don't think this is what I had in mind," I whispered to Cam.

"We'll finish these drinks, then we can go," he agreed.

I nodded my head and took a big gulp through my straw. After a few more sips, it was time to break the seal. "Okay, I really have to go to the washroom."

"Do you want me to come with you?" he teased, quirking an eyebrow.

"I'll survive," I said, but from the filth in the main room, I was scared to see what the washrooms looked like.

As I walked past the gawkers, they hooted and hollered at me like construction workers. I wasn't at all surprised, since I was looking fly in my fitted, black dress and because I had an air of sophistication that the other ladies were clearly lacking.

When I walked into the bathroom, my suspicions were confirmed. It was absolutely filthy. The first two stalls were not near clean enough for me to even consider using, so I looked into the last stall and hoped for the best. It wasn't much better, but it would have to do.

Inside the stall, hovering over the toilet, I heard two girls chatting about which guys they were going home with. *Classy.* I scrubbed my hands with soap, but I still felt dirty just being in the place.

When I flashed a look at my reflection, I was unexpectedly struck with red glowing eyes that choked the breath out of me and nearly knocked me on my ass. I blinked away the tears. "Jenny?"

One of the girls looked at me through the mirror like I was nuts. "No. Jackie. Whack job," she said, exiting the washroom, giggling with her friend.

There were no red eyes.

I vigorously dried my hands on a brown paper towel, but the eerie feeling was not going away. It was like the shadows were calling to me.

Great. Now I'm seeing things again.

Jenny Jenkins casually turned away from the bartender to sneak a glance at Cameron. He was alone at last. She watched Abigail disappear into the dingy depths of the club and knew this was the chance she had been waiting for. She had been following this man around for years. Six years to be exact. Now it was finally time to meet the stud.

Jenny was happy with her work. It took a lot longer than she could have ever expected, but the reward was no less sweet. Abigail couldn't have done a better job if she had searched a man out for herself. Cameron was prime meat. Jenny wouldn't have minded a taste for herself, if only to show Abigail how it felt.

After snaking between the tall bar tables, she slipped up behind Cameron and covered his eyes with her cool fingers. "Guess who, hot stuff," she purred, pressing her full, perky breasts against his back.

His smile was naughty and it was apparent he was turning to kiss her, until it hit him like a wall of bricks. "Whoa... what?"

She could see it in his eyes, as he traced their similarities. He was tracking the resemblances, right down to the scent of their skin. *Freaky, huh?*

Jenny cackled, recognizing the chaotic expression on Cameron's face. Oh, the thoughts that must have been racing through his mind at that very moment. Not only was she a spitting image of Abigail, but she sounded just like her too. *Only a lot more sexy. Maybe a little more wicked.*

"You look like you just saw a ghost. What, you don't want a little kiss?" she taunted. The tip of her tongue slipped over her lips in seduction. She bit on her bottom lip and gazed over the black rim of her glasses at him.

Up close and personal, Cameron was even better looking than she had realized. She had done good. Ever since the day she set eyes on Cameron, six long years ago, she knew he was the one. He was the one that would win Abigail's heart and finally leave Edwin free for the taking.

Jenny slid her hand over Cameron's chest, delivering her luscious skin to him on a silver platter.

He stumbled backwards awkwardly. "I don't know who you think I am, lady. But I'm not him. Now, if you'll excuse me," he said, turning away from her to search for Abigail.

"Wait," Jenny barked. "Abigail can wait."

He stopped in his place and peered over his shoulder, his concern showing in his features. "You know Abby?"

"You could say that." She laughed again, until a sharp pain sliced through her side. The warning signal, that had become all too frequent lately, gouged at her insides, stopping her from continuing with the verbal assault on Cameron.

She hunched over in pain, just like she had the time Abby fell into the river, and just like the time Abby had stabbed herself with the knife. She knew it could have only meant one thing: trouble for her other half.

Damn, that girl has issues.

Unable to spare another selfish second, Jenny lifted her finger and pointed. "Go!" she shouted. "She needs you now. Go!"

When I exited the bathroom, the other girls were standing there and quickly walked away from me, like I had an infectious disease. Between the three of us, we managed to get what seemed like every man's attention in the place. I hoped that if I walked back to Cam fast enough, I could avoid the onslaught of lame pickup lines. *No such luck.*

One of the more handsome young men stepped in front of me and demanded my attention. I didn't feel like chatting and, from the look on my face, I was sure he knew it.

"What's your name, sweetheart?"

"Amy. Not that it's any of your business," I snapped. I tried to push past him, but he blocked the way.

"You're a pretty girl, Amy. Sassy too. I like that. I haven't seen you around here before."

"I don't have time for small talk," I said, as I pushed him aside and took a few steps away.

The man grabbed me by the wrist and pulled me back to him. "What I have in mind won't take long at all." He was still acting playful, but when his buddies swarmed around me, I knew I wasn't going to like the game he was playing.

An eerie feeling crept up my spine. I could feel hands on me and I was getting ready to bust some balls if they didn't stop. "Back off!" I shouted, shoving the guy with my elbow.

"Leave the girl alone," one guy sounded, but his friends weren't listening. They gave me some space, but they didn't let me leave.

"What do you say, you and me?" the first guy asked.

"I'll get you out of here," another propositioned, licking his bottom lip.

Disgusting. "I don't think my boyfriend would like that very much. And if you don't let me go, I'm sure he'll kick your ass." I hated to put Cam on the spot like that, but I was desperate.

"I guess it's my lucky day then, cuz I don't see your boyfriend anywhere," the first guy asserted, glancing over his shoulders with a smirk.

"Look again, asshole." Cam appeared out of nowhere and punched the guy full swing in the face, knocking him onto the floor. "Come on. Let's go," Cam said. He took my hand and rushed me out of the place.

We hustled ass, until we were a good block away, and I finally felt like we had escaped trouble. Cam suddenly yanked me into a private entranceway of a storefront that was closed for the night. His hands devoured my body and his abs flexed against my belly.

"Are you okay?" he asked, hounding me like a caped

magician.

I smiled, but my eyes trailed away. "I'm not gonna lie. I was scared what might've happened if you didn't come."

He took my hand and kissed it and let out a huge sigh. "But I did, and now I'm not letting you out of my sight for the rest of the night. That is if you still want to go out."

I nodded. "I'm fine."

He didn't believe me. Hell, I didn't believe myself. My heart still raced from the adrenaline pumping through my veins. When my lips parted for a breath, he kissed me softly.

"How did you know I was in trouble?" I asked.

He slowly backed away from my lips and his eyes seemed to turn cold. "Do you have any relatives in Windsor; a cousin maybe?"

My stomach flip-flopped and I instantly feared the worst. "What colour were her eyes?" I asked with a gasp, afraid he might say red.

He gulped and stared back at me. "A striking violet colour actually. I've never seen anything like it. This woman looked a lot like you, Abby."

Relief rushed me, when I realized I had been overreacting. *Of course he didn't see Jenny. Jenny is dead.* "I used to think I saw Jenny, my sister, but thousands of dollars' worth of therapy has taught me that I didn't." I let out a nervous giggle.

Cam cupped my cheek and pressed his forehead against mine. "I'll do whatever it takes to keep that smile on your face," he said, dropping the entire subject. He captured my lips and it ushered away all of my fears.

"You're doing a good job so far," I whispered, with a smile.

He smirked against my lips and I shivered, as a gust of winter wind blasted by us. "Here, take my jacket," Cam said. He pulled off his coat and rested it over my shoulders, then squeezed me in his arms.

I absorbed his warmth and melted into him, as I inhaled the scent that wrapped around me like a toxic elixir.

Without taking his arm away, Cameron steered me down the sidewalk and back around a busy corner toward the Casino. A lineup of patrons wrapped right around the building, showing just how popular that nightclub was.

"That looks like it's the place to go tonight," Cam said. "What do you say?"

From the look of the people in line, there must have been a dress code. That was a plus, but it also looked like there'd be quite a long wait. "It'll be hours before we get in," I said, already shivering from the cold.

"Not if I have anything to do with it." Cam escorted me past the long lineup and drew me into the one marked VIP. After the couple ahead of us walked right in, Cam confronted the doorman.

"Can I see your passes?" the man asked.

Cam shook the guys hand and discreetly delivered him a cash incentive. "We're from out of town. But my girlfriend is freezing and we'd really appreciate if you could let us in now."

"Yeah, you and everyone else in line," he said, as he tucked the large bill in his pocket. "Let me see your ID," he said, nodding at me.

I opened my purse quickly and flashed him my licence. He plucked it from my fingers, glanced at it briefly and then unlocked the red rope, as two patrons left the club.

"You're a good man," Cam said to the bouncer, as he let us pass.

"Have a good time," he replied.

I smiled at Cam, proud of his clever tactics. He raised his eyebrows at me, as he placed his hand on my lower back and ushered me into the building. As soon as we got inside the door, we were met with a long flight of stairs heading straight underground. Music flooded from the dance floor and flashing lights reinforced the amazing energy in the place.

We checked our coats at the base of the stairs and headed inside the room with low ceilings and even lower lighting. The crowd stood shoulder to shoulder. There were contemporary sofas collected in a space for lounging, but they were full. There were bar height tables grouped together in another space, but again there didn't seem to be a single seat available in the house.

Hoards of dancers were strutting their stuff, split between the expansive dance floor and a series of narrow stages surrounding the perimeter and lining the centre floor. It was like everyone in the place was dancing and the vibe alone was intoxicating.

Cam brought his lips to my ear. "This is more like it, eh?"

Keeping me close at his side, our fingers interlocked and then he carved a trail through all of the sweaty, excitable people to the nearest bar.

I took a sip of my fruity cocktail, as soon as he handed it to me, and then another sip for good measure. "Woo!" I hollered, not at all out of line compared to the excitable crazies surrounding us.

I began to bounce to the devious beats flowing through the room. Cam stared at me with a mischievous smile playing on his lips. He was not going to take his eyes off of me and that was just fine by me.

"Come on," I hollered, dragging Cam over to a narrow stage filled with lovelies.

When a new song blended in I couldn't resist getting up there. Only two feet up, Cam lifted me onto the box like I was feather-light, making others have to push over to give me an inch of space.

Cameron's eyes lit up with a glimmer of seduction as he watched me. With arms over my head, I swayed my hips provocatively, seducing him with my curves. A naughty smile was plastered on his face, and it looked like his eyes could have drawn me to him with their mesmerizing force.

When I glanced over the crowd, I noticed that I wasn't the only one awestruck. Between the sweat glistening on Cam's partially exposed chest and the way his jeans hung on his narrow, masculine hips, he looked damn good. Edible even.

Jealousy taking me, I accepted a generous onlooker's

hand and jumped off the stage. Moments later, when Cam lifted me into his arms, I watched the hoard of giggling girls turn angry. *Sorry about your luck, ladies. But this one is mine.*

Cam wrapped me up in his arms. We danced. We kissed. We drank and danced some more, entertaining each other into the early morning hours. While time passed outside, it seemed to stand still for us. No windows meant no light. No light meant no intrusion. And thanks to that, we became utterly preoccupied with each other in such a magical way.

From all of my provocative dancing, Cam was like a walking boner. A man in his sexual prime, craving the body of his woman, uninhibited despite the steady flow of drinks he had been consuming. His hands slowly slid up my fitted dress, hiking it well above my knees, then skimmed over my bare thighs with a lovers caress.

I leaned forward and pressed back against him, finding him thick and stiff in his pants.

"You're bad," he growled, but I didn't stop teasing him. He spun me around and pulled me up hard against him and I liked it. "You're going to get yourself into trouble," he threatened, encouraging me even more.

I chewed on my lower lip. "From what; doing this?" I stroked the pulsing tent in his pants with my body, teasing myself to no end.

Cameron's kiss was aggressive, hard and controlled. His hands massaged all over my body, turning the tables and tantalizing my overexcited nerves. I was incredibly hot for him and we were both totally drunk. As he kissed my neck, we rocked to the music and I ran my fingers through his short sweaty hair. I was so hot in every way, to the point where I wanted him to have me right there and didn't care who watched. I needed him inside me.

His lips broke away from mine. "Abby?" he gasped, slipping back into consciousness.

"Yeah?" I breathed, between hot, devouring kisses.

"If you don't let me take you home now, I'm going to have to do you in the corner." From the dark crazed look in his eyes, he wasn't even joking.

I laughed and backed away from him, still holding both of his hands. His dark, heated stare devoured me.

"I'm getting you out of here. Now," he stated, instantly pulling me to the coat check.

He was on the phone with a cab company, before I even handed the tab to the coat check girl. He was obviously just as horny as I was. After waiting for his jacket, he slung it on leaving it open. I was plenty hot from our dancing.

We hurried up the stairs and I realized how badly my feet were aching. We walked out the door and onto the sidewalk. Fortunately, in that moment, a cab pulled up to the curb.

"Get in," Cam ordered.

With my dress hiked much too high, I crawled into the back seat, provoking him with a cheek of ass. He slapped that wiggling ass, before sliding in next to me. His mouth crashed into mine, the second his door shut.

"Casino," he mumbled to the driver, as he grabbed onto my ass and pulled me on top of him.

We continued to make out, hot and hungry, like we were unable to satisfy a craving. He couldn't take his hands off of me any more than I could keep my tongue out of his mouth. Cam slipped his fingers along my inner thigh and, when he cupped his hand at the juncture there, I nearly lost it.

A deep moan sounded my urgent need, as his fingers slipped beneath my panties. He was going to touch me right there.

"We're here," the driver notified us, interrupting my whimpers of pleasure.

I yanked on the door handle and tumbled onto the sidewalk. Cam tossed the driver some bills, collected me up and rushed me to our room where we indulged in every dirty fantasy that had been rushing through my thoughts all night.

Fast and hard, and fully clothed, Cam unbuttoned his pants, yanked aside my panties and screwed me to the door until I was squealing in release at the force of his need.

And he wasn't finished with me yet.

He took his time stripping me entirely naked. Then, slow and passionate, he began his sensual assault and continued with his tongue until I was clutching his head and crying to the world how much I loved this man.

After a night of fierce intoxication, spicy red-hot sex and an unbalanced sharing of bodily fluids, we slept like babies.

Knock. Knock. Knock. "Housekeeping!"

My eyes flung open. *Shit!* "Tell her we're still here," I whispered.

Cameron growled, half asleep. "We'll need a few more minutes," he shouted at the door.

We were wrapped up in each other's naked limbs, totally hung over. I covered our heads with a pillow, praying the lady wouldn't let herself in.

Cam pushed the pillow aside and glanced at the alarm clock. Then, with a sigh, he got up to check his wrist watch. "Abby, we have to go. We slept in, babe."

I moaned. "What time is it?"

"Let's just say, we were supposed to be out of here ten minutes ago."

"No!" I cried. "It must be wrong. The alarm hasn't gone off yet."

He looked at the clock again and clicked a few buttons. "I guess it would've helped if we set it for the a.m."

I moaned again and rolled myself out of the bed.

We both got ready in a groggy trance. I pulled on some clothes as quick as I could, adjusted my smeared makeup and brushed my teeth and hair. Cam had all of our bags packed and was waiting for me at the door.

I ran my hand along his sexy stubble and kissed him. A night like that and he still looked delicious. "I'm a total mess today and you're the one who has to look at me," I groaned.

He kissed me back. "You look beautiful; like you belong

to me."

I smirked. "Well then I definitely hit the jackpot. If you say that now, with the black rings under my eyes, then I can't go wrong with you."

He smiled and pressed his forehead against mine. "That's right. You can't," he growled.

I closed my eyes and tilted my head, ignoring our lateness. He squeezed me in his arms and we shared a tender, meaningful kiss.

Back at Cam's house I headed straight for his bed. He joined me minutes later. We snuggled together and went down for a late afternoon nap. The house was quiet, so utterly empty without Pheobe in it.

Cameron found sleep fast, but I laid there very awake, too many thoughts returning to me to find sleep. I remembered the reaction of Pheobe's grandmother when Pheobe confessed her love to me so naturally. It started to feel like we were becoming a little family of our own. Life seemed complete. Well, almost complete. The looming desire I had conveniently tucked away, had inched its way back into my life at full force. I couldn't deny that my priority in life was to have a family of my own.

While I loved Pheobe dearly, I still had a strong desire to add to that family. Though I knew, without a doubt, that giving Pheobe a little brother or sister would make her so very happy, I didn't know if her father would love the idea. In fact, I got the terrifying impression that it was going to be a tough sell with Cam.

With Ashley out of the bigger picture, I figured I had it in the bag and yet the worry overcame me with a sharp slice of reality. The air felt thin and I was having difficulty breathing. I felt Cam stir behind me and I worried that he would ask me what was wrong. I knew it was only a matter of time before I cracked and had that conversation with him.

I considered waking him, to lay it all out on the table, but I remembered what happened the last time I brought this talk to the surface. I couldn't survive that kind of loss again. Curled in a ball and silenced, I agonized over the small points and suffocated on my own anxieties.

"Abby? Are you up?"

I choked on a breath, then cleared my throat. "Mmm, hmm."

When Cam squeezed his arm around me it restarted my lungs. I took a gasp of air, relieved to regulate my shallow breaths. Cam could tell that something was wrong, but I tried to pass it off as a menacing hang over. I wanted to enjoy what was left of our holidays together and so I put that matter on the back burner and turned on a smiling face, like I was back to normal.

By day I was my usual sassy, loving, stubborn self. By night, I had the task of preparing myself for the journey. Not only were we going on a trip, but embarking on the next phase of our life together. It would be an exciting and terrifying experience with no end to the possible outcomes. Choices would have to be made and I hoped that the end result didn't involve me getting burned.

"Tomorrow's the big day," Cam said. "Are you all ready to go?"

"I think so. I mean, as ready as I'll ever be when it comes to skiing. What's the weather looking like?"

Cameron clicked the remote to the interactive weather channel and changed the location. "Snow, snow and more snow."

"What a surprise," I said. "It is winter and this *is* Canada."

Reacting to my snarky remark, he clicked off the TV and pinned me to the sofa. Holding himself up over me, his eyes smiling, he smirked. "Listen to you. You sound like a southerner. Next you'll be asking if I rented us an igloo for the weekend."

I smirked back. "Did you? Cuz that would be cool."

As he slowly leaned in closer, his warm breath tickled my lips. "I guess I have to kiss you now, so you'll stop talking."

I parted my lips on a smile and closed my eyes. When his mouth found my upper lip, I basked in the sweetness of his caress and closed my mouth around him. When his lips left mine, my eyes remained shut, waiting for him to come back to me. I had to peek out of one eye to see if he had planned on it. His glimmering baby blues posed a silent question.

"Yes?" I asked, recognizing that he had something to say.

"I like having you around," he said, softly.

I giggled and my eyes squinted from my massive smile. "I like you too," I said, playfully.

A smile slanted across his lips. "That's it. I think I'm going to have to keep you," he stated, his eyes flirting with danger.

But he was just teasing. *Right?*

I ran my fingers through his soft tousled hair and drew his sexy stubble closer to my lips. "You would've had a hard time getting rid of me."

ABOUT THE AUTHOR

Christa Simpson is a Canadian Romance Author and mother of two. She loves reading, writing, music, movies and dancing. She likes her men muscled, her music loud and her kids happy.

She lives in a small town in Southwestern Ontario with her husband and two beautiful little girls. She is a dreamer and has always believed that you can do anything you set your mind to.

You can visit her website:
http://christasimpson.com

Follow her blog:
http://christasimpson.wordpress.com

Or find her on Facebook:
www.facebook.com/authorchristasimpson

THE TWISTED TRILOGY
By Christa Simpson

Book 1: Twisted
Book 2: Twist & Turn
Book 3: A Twist of Fate

SUPPORT THIS INDIE AUTHOR!
LEAVE A REVIEW!

GOODREADS
www.goodreads.com/christasimpson

AMAZON
www.amazon.com/Christa-Simpson/e/B00BMTKM24

CHRISTA SIMPSON
Rules were made to be broken…

FINDING DESTINY

When Skylar is forced to invite Destiny back to his cabin, he can't ignore what is subtly unravelling between them. Skylar has rules. He has never strayed from those rules. And yet Destiny has him breaking every last one of them. But when tragedy strikes, torn from her arms at lightning speed, Skylar is left to wonder whether he would ever find his *destiny*.

For the full synopsis, please visit:
http://christasimpson.com

The Twisted Trilogy: Book 3

A Twist of Fate

If given the choice between the love of your life and the man of your dreams, who would you choose?

Excerpt:

Cameron didn't let me go and I couldn't help but smile in response to his seductive stare. I rustled my fingers through his short, messy hair and when he raised his eyebrows it made me laugh. He captured my smiling lips and tormented me with a soft brush of his mouth.

"Come on," he said, leading me back to our room. "Let's get you into your swimsuit before we have company."

Back in our room, I quickly stripped out of my clothes and pulled on the tiny bikini that I had chosen expecting only one man to see me in it.

"Would you like a glass of wine while we're waiting?" Cam asked, as I tucked my clothes away in my bag.

"That'll be my third one tonight."

Cam smirked, glancing at my glorious rear-end. "That sounds good to me."

I smirked right back and slung my arms over his shoulders. He pulled me against him, his hands groping my mostly exposed ass cheeks.

"If I didn't know any better, I would say that you're trying to get me drunk again."

"I would never," he teased, releasing one hand only to lift my wine glass to his mouth and take a sip. Then he kissed me, drizzling the fruity wine into my mouth.

I tasted it and I tasted him, and it was so hot. He handed me my glass, but wine was now the last thing on my mind, as the tip of his tongue licked across my teeth.

His hands drifted back down to my ass, barely covered by the small scrap of material I called my bikini bottoms. When he gave it a squeeze, he growled and it urged me to touch him back. I slipped my hand between us, to find him long and thick and hard, at the same moment that Aliah barged into our room ruining my fun.

"Woop," Aliah hollered, as she passed Cameron and headed for the electronics. She plugged in her I-pod and turned up the music, ignoring the state in which she found us.

Hunter picked up our half empty bottle of wine. "It looks like they got started without us."

Without releasing me, Cameron nodded toward the ice box. "Don't worry, there's more where that came from."

I took a big gulp from my glass and by the time the others had showed up, it was already going down real smooth. The wine was clearly having an effect on me. I was hyper and loud-mouthed and careless. Aliah loved it.

"Okay, enough of this! Let's test the water," I shouted over the music.

"I'll test the water for you," Cameron said to me. "I wouldn't make you do that."

As he went to lift his shirt over his head, Edwin stormed outside and removed the cover from the hot tub himself.

Cameron dropped his shirt back down and glanced at me in disbelief. "This should be a fun weekend."

Maddie walked up to the patio door in her one piece bathing suit, wrapped up in a giant bath towel. As Jessica ran outside, a freezing cold north wind gushed into the room and some flurries scattered across the floor.

"On second thought, I think I'll just hang out in here," Maddie said, then sealed the door shut. "I look like a cow anyways."

"Good, I don't want the baby getting sick," Hunter said, honestly concerned about it.

Aliah rolled her eyes and pulled Hunter outside with her.

"You look fabulous," I told Maddie. "Your baby bump is so adorable." I gulped down as much wine as I could, put my half emptied glass on the nightstand and reached for the patio door. "You're alright in here alone?"

Cameron peeled off his shirt and Maddie couldn't remove her gawking eyes from his toned flesh. He picked up my glass, smiled at Maddie's enthusiasm and returned to the other side of the room to top up my wine.

"Yup. I'm good. Definitely good," Maddie said.

Giggling, I tip-toed to the hot tub as fast as I could and sank into the bubbling water in the only empty spot available. Right next to Edwin. I looked up at him hesitantly.

"Oh, come on now, I won't bite," Edwin teased, then he whispered in my ear. "I know you only like that in the bedroom."

"Ugh, Eddie! Can you shut your fat mouth for like five minutes so I can enjoy myself?" I shoved his big shoulder, but he didn't budge.

He only laughed and it was hauntingly sexy. "I can probably do five, but I can't make any promises," he drawled, then leaned into me. "You'll probably be begging me to talk in like two though."

"Don't forget whose tub you're in." I backed away to scowl at him, just as Cameron put my glass on the edge of the tub.

When Cameron squeezed in next to me, he unintentionally squished me closer to Edwin again. There was no missing the press of Edwin's bulky arms and legs against my side. They were hot and large and thick.

Cameron reached his arm around me and gave me a slow, drugging kiss. It was nice, but I could tell it was more to piss Edwin off than to show me love. Not able to continue with the awkward attachment to Edwin's hulking arm, I curled into Cameron's and slid onto his lap. I strung my arms around his neck and gave him a healthy taste of my lips, to show everyone that there was no confusion as to who my man was.

Cameron smiled, in between kisses. "I see your glass is empty again."

"Good wine, eh?" Aliah chimed.

"Yeah, a little too good," I answered. "Cameron's been feeding it to me like water. I can hardly taste it anymore."

"Maybe I should go get you some more." Cameron kissed me again, dropped me into his spot and then leapt from the tub, every muscle tightening in the cold, winter air. Then he calmly walked to the door as if the cold didn't affect him.

"While you're in there why don't you get me one too?" Aliah hollered, as the door slid shut.

"I can get you one," Hunter decided. "I have to use the pisser anyway."

When Hunter left the tub, everyone shifted over and it felt like I could finally stretch out and relax. "Take your time," I teased, enjoying the space.

Aliah leaned over the edge of the tub and watched Hunter exchanging words with Maddie inside the toasty hotel room. I saw Cameron popping the cork to yet another bottle of wine, as Edwin reached his arm out and rested it on the tub behind me.

Edwin leaned down and whispered in my ear, the hurt evident in his tone. "What's this? You can't even stand to be around me anymore?"

"It's not like that and you know it," I answered, softly.

He locked his aqua eyes on me, holding my terrified gaze. "Oh? How is it then?"

I blew out a harsh breath. "Maybe if you weren't always trying to piss Cam off, then we could hang out more."

Not likely, though.

"I know I've been kind of an ass lately," he admitted, softening up.

"Kind of?"

"Fine. I've been a total jerk. But what do you expect? You chose him over me and that hurts."

My eyes were frozen on him, dread filling my sharp features, as I recognized the wounded look on his face. I wanted to hug him, to make him feel better, but I knew that would only escalate the problem. I kept my lips pressed tightly together.

"Now you're living with him and I've got the whole house to myself. It's really quiet when you're not around and not in a good way," Edwin told me.

"It's only temporary," I said. "Besides you had your family over for a few days. You weren't exactly alone the whole time."

"No, but it wasn't the same without you."

I flipped my long, dry hair behind me and the tips dipped into the bubbling water. "I'm sorry. I know it was kind of last minute, but you didn't exactly tell me your plans either." Reality began to cloud my buzz-induced smile. I dipped my chin and closed my eyes, suddenly feeling incredibly emotional.

Edwin lifted my chin with his index finger. My eyes grew wide in alarm. My heart pounded hard and fast, as I gasped for air, unable to steal my eyes from his. Then his hand dropped into the water, acknowledging my distress. Though his touch was gentle, it had zapped my senses.

Then he slid up next to me. Close. *Too close.*

"You know I just want you to be happy, right?"

My entire body trembled. "Okay." I should have pushed him away. *Why am I not pushing him away?*

He slowly gripped his hand on my thigh, sending my heart galloping. "If you can promise me one thing," he whispered, his breath tickling my ear, "I'll leave you two alone for the rest of the weekend."

Just the rest of the weekend? How about permanently?

"Don't go too overboard," I managed to blurt.

His hand squeezed on my thigh, then he loosened his grip but it remained where it didn't belong. "I'm being serious, Abs. All I ask is that you quit with the canoodling when you're around me. It just isn't right, having to see you like that." His pain-filled eyes begged me to stop tormenting him.

"Seeing me like what; happy?" I whispered, barely able to finish the sentence.

Edwin's hand began to casually caress my thigh. "Please, just promise me."

Aliah was watching us, chiding my indiscretion. Jessica was making a good effort to mind her own business. Cameron and Hunter were at the patio doors, not having a clue as to what was going on.

Did I even know what was going on?

Aliah flashed a look at Cameron, then scowled back at me. "Just promise the man already! You owe him that much." Her words stung me, even more than they should have.

"Please take your hand off my leg," I begged, suddenly envisioning the consequences.

Cameron approached us blissfully unaware.

"Promise!" Edwin demanded, holding his position.

Available now!